ROGUE STAR:
FROZEN EARTH
(1st Edition)

by Jasper T. Scott

JasperTscott.com
@JasperTscott

Cover Art by Tom Edwards
TomEdwardsDesign.com

CONTENT RATING: R

Intended Audience: 16+
Swearing: Moderate
Sex: Implicit only, but with adult references
Violence: Moderate

Author's Guarantee: If you find anything you consider inappropriate for this rating, please e-mail me at JasperTscott@gmail.com and I will either remove the content or change the rating accordingly.

ACKNOWLEDGEMENTS

A monumental effort went into writing and editing this book in just two months. As always, I have my wife to thank for her understanding. I worked lots of late nights and weekends to get done on time.

There's also a legion of people behind the scenes who helped to make this book happen in such a short time. My editors Aaron Sikes, Dave Cantrell, and William Schmidt made short work of big and small issues with plot, characters, and grammar, meanwhile, my proofreader, Ian F. Jedlica, and my advance readers helped me to find and fix more than a hundred typos. A big thanks goes out to these unpaid heroes of the literary world: B. Allen Thobois, Beverley Wilkinson, Claude Chavis, Harry Huyler, Ian Seccombe, Jacqueline Gartside, Jeff Belshaw, John Williams, Karol Ross, Lisa Garber, Mary Kastle, Mary Whitehead, Michael Madsen, Paul Burch, Raymond Burt, and Victor Biedrycki—you guys make my job a lot easier!

I'd also like to thank Tom Edwards for outdoing himself with a fantastic cover, and all of the authors who found time in their busy schedules to read and review an early copy of this book.

Then there's you, the reader. Without you, this

book wouldn't exist, and I'd be unemployed, so thank you for helping me put food on the table. You keep reading, and I'll keep writing.

Finally, many thanks to the muse.

To those who dare,
And to those who dream.
To everyone who's stronger than they seem.
—Jasper Scott

*"Believe in me / I know you've waited for so long /
Believe in me / Sometimes the weak become the strong."*
—STAIND, Believe

DRAMATIS PERSONAE

Main Characters
Logan Willis
Katherine Willis - "Kate"
Rachel Willis - "Rachie / Rachie Ray"
Alexander Sebastian Willis - "Alex"
Dr. Richard Greenhouse - "Rick / Richy"

Secondary Characters
Harry Hartford
Deborah Hartford
Celine Hartford

Bill Summers
Akron Massey
OneZero

Minor Characters
Duncan Mayfield
Ben Fields
Dr. Michael Haskins
Glenn Reese
Vera Lopez
Camila
Valeria
Deanna
CPL. West

Private Fields
Private Baker
Private Chong
CPL. Johnson
Wesley Parker

PART 1 - DISCOVERY

PROLOGUE

April 21st, 2021

"It has to be a mistake," Dr. Michael Haskins said as he leaned over his colleague's shoulder. Michael was the executive director for the Infrared Processing and Analysis Center (IPAC) at Caltech. His colleague, Dr. Richard Greenhouse, was an associate scientist whose job was to sift through infrared data from the James Webb Space Telescope (JWST).

"No mistake," Richard said. He pointed at the data on his screen with a shaking hand. All his sifting had just found gold.

"This is unbelievable! Tell me what you know so far."

Richard half turned his chair away from his computer. One of his knees began bouncing like a jackhammer. His expression was unreadable, cloaked by a thick brown beard, but his hazel eyes blazed with excitement. "We know that it's big, and it's close."

"Give me numbers, Rick," Michael said.

"At the time this data was collected, it was over two thousand AU from Earth."

"That's between the Oort Cloud and the Kupier Belt!"

"The size is around seventy Jovian masses."

Michael's jaw dropped. "That's too big to be a planet."

"It's a brown dwarf."

"You're telling me that we've found the infamous planet X, but it's actually a *star*? How the hell are we only finding this out now?"

"Because this mother is cold and dark—*really* cold and dark. The surface temperature is hovering somewhere between twenty-two and thirty-one degrees Kelvin. That's colder than Neptune. She burned out a long time ago in a galaxy far, far away. And while it's close for a star, it's still sixty times farther from the Sun than Neptune. Given all that, I'm not surprised that we've missed it—until now. The JWST is the most advanced tool we have to detect objects in the infrared spectrum, and that's exactly what we needed to pick this up. As for planet X... more like Nibiru."

"Nibiru? You're joking, right?"

"What little light this star is still giving off is all

blue-shifted. This thing is moving toward us at a relative velocity of five hundred and sixty two miles per second." Richard gestured vaguely to the data on his screen. Nibiru referred to the apocalypse conspiracy that a rogue planetary system crosses paths with Earth every 3600 years. This star hadn't crossed paths with Earth before, but it was certainly going to now.

"It's a *rogue* star? How close is it going to get?"

Dr. Greenhouse shook his head. "We'll need to crunch all the numbers and create an accurate simulation before I can tell you that. Chances are that it will pass harmlessly through the outskirts of the solar system."

Michael grinned and clapped a hand on Richard's shoulder. "This is incredible! I'm going to go tell the others the good news."

Richard frowned. "It's late. Almost everyone will be at home and in bed by now."

"If you were sitting at home while this discovery was being made, wouldn't you want me to call and tell you about it?"

Richard's frown turned to a wolfish grin, and he snorted. "Good point. All right, go rattle their cages, but Mike—" Michael regarded him curiously. "—when you tell them, make sure you mention that this is *Greenhouse's Star*."

Michael smiled. "Don't worry, no one's going to steal your discovery."

CHAPTER 1

—TEN YEARS LATER—
May 10th, 2031

I sat on a PATH train headed across the Hudson to Hoboken from Lower Manhattan. My briefcase sat in my lap, jumping with my knees. Tucked behind my legs was the Dreaded Box, stuffed with the entire contents of my big corner-office desk. Between my knees I could see the photo of me and Katy on our honeymoon peeking out. We were smiling as we sipped coconuts on a beach on the island of Kauai. Katy looked like a super model in that photo—her blue eyes a rival for the sky, her skin so smooth and perfect, ruby lips quirked into a grin. Even after two kids and twelve years of marriage my heart still fluttered at the sight of her—and not just because that picture was a time capsule from her youth. It was the same thing I felt every night when I came home from work and saw her again. I still couldn't believe that

I got to share a bed with this woman.

What had she ever seen in me? An English and business major from NYU with dreams of becoming an editor and maybe writing a book of my own. Not a bad career back then—the editor part, not the writer part, because how many people actually make a living from *that?*

Maybe Katy had been smart enough to see my potential, but I think she was just one of those blissfully ignorant souls who gets married for love and never thinks about how much love costs.

That's one of the things that attracted me to her the most. She was more interested in who I was as a person. Back then that had appealed to my artsy romantic nature, plus, I had no money, so I was definitely happy that she wasn't looking for it.

When our son, Alex, was born, Katy quit her job to look after him. At that point I had a world of financial pressure on my shoulders, but I did well. Five years later, I was *Logan Willis, Executive Editor* at Harper Collins. We moved out of the city and found that idealized neighborhood with the white picket fences, the good schools, and the cul-de-sac where Alex could play. Four years after that, Kate got pregnant again, and we had Rachel. Kate gave up thinking about a career and settled into her role as wife and mother, while I settled into mine as Mr.

Breadwinner. I know that's all very traditional, but it worked for us, and we were happy—past tense, thanks to the Dreaded Box, and the fact that I'm on a train headed home an hour after lunch. You do the math.

That math gets ugly fast. A hundred and sixty thousand a year before taxes equals one hundred and ten thousand take home salary. At forty-five years of age, I figured I'd only need to work for another fifteen to have retirement and the kids' college funds figured out. I did all that figuring in the back of my mind last week while sipping a five dollar microbrew and flipping burgers for my 45th birthday barbecue. Now I had to do that math in reverse. How long does forty-five thousand in savings last when you're spending more than six grand a month? The answer is a little more than half a year.

You might say I should pick myself up, dust myself off, and go get another job. Fifteen years ago, I'd have done just that, but that was before Kindles and e-Books hit the publishing scene. Traditional publishers are sinking ships. I should know, I was at the helm of one, bailing out water with a silver spoon. Sure, lots of people still buy paper books, but it's an ever-shrinking market, and when it comes to e-Books, we can't compete. We sell ours for $9.99 to cover costs while independent authors sell theirs for $4.99 or less. Long story short, big publishers have been consolidating and cutting costs for years. I was just another one of those costs. Even if I could find another job as an editor, it would never compare to the one I had.

I looked up from the Dreaded Box. The woman on the opposite side of the train was reading a copy of the Enquirer. The headline read: *Nasa Finds Nibiru and it's Headed for Earth!*

I had to stop myself in the middle of a smirk. That's probably what I had to look forward to now—a job editing fake news for the tabloids.

Swallowing a sigh, I laid my head back against the side of the train and let the sound and the gentle bumping down the tracks lull me into a quasi-conscious state. My mind was numb. I had no idea what I was going to say to Kate. *Hi, Honey, I'm home!* flickered through my mind with mocking clarity.

Where the hell are we going to go from here? I wondered, but the question was rhetorical. I already had a pretty good idea about our next step. *Goodbye picket fences.*

* * *

By the time I pulled into my driveway with the Dreaded Box, I was starting to question the wisdom of coming home. Katy's car was down at the end of the driveway, in front of our detached garage. Maybe I should have found a bar to drown my sorrows until I was actually *supposed to* come home—buy time, cushion the blow, yada yada... maybe I could get another job before I had to say anything.

I checked my watch: 3:05 PM. The kids wouldn't be home from school for another half hour. I took a deep breath and popped the car door open. Getting out, I deliberately left the Dreaded Box on the passenger's seat. I didn't want the very first look on my wife's face to be ashen dread. I was Mr. Breadwinner. I wasn't supposed to come home without the bread.

Shutting the door quietly behind me, I walked up the steps to the front door. My heart knocked against my sternum with ominous thumps. Fumbling for my keys on a faded Kauai key chain, I found the front door key and turned it in the lock. The door popped open, and I stepped into the foyer. A crystal chandelier hung from the ten foot ceiling. Hardwood floors gleamed in the golden light spilling from that chandelier. The stairs lay dead ahead, while three openings framed with maple wood led to different parts of the house— the formal dining room and kitchen on my right, divided by a wall, and the living room to my left. I glanced at the kitchen, then the other way to the living room. The ceilings were finished with ornate moldings and golden inlay. More crystal chandeliers hung over both rooms.

I cleared my throat. "Katy?"

No reply.

Maybe she was out running? But no, she liked to take morning runs, right after the bus took the kids to school. Thinking she might be watching TV in the sun room, I went left through the living room and opened the French door to the sun room. The couch was empty, the throw pillows undisturbed. Through the windows I caught a glimpse of our backyard and pool gleaming invitingly in the sun. We had a big house, and I was the big idiot who'd bought it and spent a fortune decorating, all the while thinking that my goose would only ever lay golden eggs. Now my goose was cooked.

I turned back around, my briefcase hanging from a limp arm and slumping shoulder, and walked slowly through the living room to the foyer and the stairs. I was in such a fraught state thinking about how I was going to break the news to my wife that I swear I didn't hear anything as I climbed the stairs. I just blundered right in and stood there in the bedroom doorway, blinking like a fool.

More like a sucker. My jaw hit the floor. I'd just become spectator to a live action porno film. On the life's-a-bitch flip side of that, I was also married to its star.

"Katy?" I croaked.

She was in mid-groan as I said that, but she had the decency to shut the fuck up and look over her shoulder at the sound of my voice.

CHAPTER 2

I turned and ran down the stairs, desperately trying to wipe that image from my head. I went straight to the bar in the living room and poured myself a glass of the first thing I could find. Vodka neat. It went down like acid. I grimaced and fumbled for a bottle of whiskey instead. That eased some of the burn.

Walking on shaking legs to the sun room, I opened the door to the back deck and went outside. My heart was racing and my brain buzzing. A part of me wanted to turn around and go kick some ass, but losing my job this morning had turned me into a pathetic puppy dog—one of those with the sad brown eyes and drooping face that looks like he just needs a hug. I sneered at that image and half-drained my glass to get some fire in my veins. Cold emptiness coursed through me instead. I took a seat on one of the swing benches facing the pool.

My mind was a blank as I stared out over the

shimmering water and sipped my drink. I heard the front door slam. A few minutes later, the back door clicked open, and Katy moved into my periphery. She was dressed now. I looked at her—speechless, my face as blank as my mind, but I'm pretty sure my eyes could have branded cattle.

Kate's composure cracked, her lips trembled, and she wiped an intrepid tear from one cheek before taking a seat in a wicker armchair beside me.

"I was going to tell you. We were going to end it," she said.

I took another sip of my whiskey and nodded as if that was all very reasonable.

"It wasn't love, Logan. I wasn't going to leave you for him. I just..." She looked away to stare out over the pool with me. "You work so much. You're never here, and even when you are it's like you're somewhere else. I was just trying to fill the hole that you left."

That drew a bitter smirk from my lips, and I regarded her with my eyebrows raised. "You were trying to fill a hole? Are you sure that's the defense you want to use?"

Katy flinched and her expression crumbled once more. She wiped away fresh tears. "What do you want me to say? I'm sorry, Logan. I know that's not enough, but you have to believe me. I love *you*. It wasn't like that with Ben."

I did a double-take and held up a hand for her to stop. "Hold on—*Ben? That's* who it was? Stay-at-home man-child, Ben Fields?" *Of course* it was him. He lived a block away from us. I knew that he and Katy liked to take their morning runs together, but apparently that wasn't the only kind of exercise they were into. Ben's wife was a magistrate, and he was the stay-at-home step-dad who spent all his time in the gym so that he could look like a bronze statue of a Greek god. Good thing I didn't go the ass-kicking route. I shook my head, speechless again.

"It wasn't just sex. We understood each other. He *listens* to me."

"Is that supposed to make me feel better?" I thundered and jumped to my feet. My legs were shaking again. I'd had enough of this. I gestured with my tumbler and half a finger of whiskey to the house. "Have you even stopped to wonder *why* I'm home?"

Katy's face was streaming with tears, her blue eyes red and puffy. She was locked in a private world of guilt and misery; oblivious, but she wasn't stupid. Realization clicked and hit pause on the waterworks. Her mouth formed a dramatic *O*.

"That's right. No need to worry about me working so much anymore. You're going to be seeing a lot more of me around here. The problem is, I'm not sure I want to see that much of *you*."

Katy didn't react to that barb. She slowly rose from her chair. "You got fired?"

"Ding ding ding—we have a winner!"

Katy blinked. "What are we going to do?"

I gave an elaborate shrug and drained the rest of my drink. "I'm not sure what *you're* going to do, but I'm going to go check into a hotel."

CHAPTER 3

I checked into the Ramada in East Orange, New Jersey. It was relatively close to our home in South Orange, and I had some experience with it since I'd had to bring Katy's brother here last year. He'd gotten drunk in front of our kids and started cursing and rambling about how we were all going to die if we didn't start preparing for the end of the world. I'd promptly driven him to this hotel and checked him in. I'd told him he could come back when he sobered up, but he left the next day without so much as an apology or a goodbye.

I smirked at the memory and washed a sleeping pill down with a mini bottle of Jim Beam from the bar fridge in my room. I tossed the empty bottle into the corner of the room. It hit the carpet with a dull *thunk*. Grabbing the next mini liquor bottle from the pile on the bed beside me, I cracked it open and downed it in one gulp. Whiskey followed by a Kahlua chaser. Yuck. I fumbled for another bottle, but this time I took a moment to study the label—Tanqueray Gin. Much better. I opened it and gulped it down. *Next!*

By the time I'd emptied eight bottles, the room was spinning pleasantly around my head. I felt warm and blissfully numb. Sleep beckoned, and I reached for the light switch to turn off the lamps beside the bed. Darkness fell with the switch. It was still light out, but I had the curtains drawn, so the only light getting in was a thin blue-white halo around the edges of the window. Between the alcohol and the sleeping pill I wouldn't be waking up anytime soon.

My eyes drifted shut and I floated off on a cloud. I dreamed that I was cheating *with* Kate on an associate editor from my work named Spencer. In my dreams he was the sucker who'd married her, not me. Kate and I lay in bed naked, wrapped in each other's arms, and laughing about how dumb Spencer was. Then suddenly I found myself standing in the door to our bedroom, watching us laugh, and I had the distinct impression that somehow I had just become Spencer.

A painful knot formed in my throat, and I tried to scream, but no sound came out.

In the next instant, I was walking down the street in my neighborhood in the middle of the night with a powerful urge to urinate. I unzipped and started peeing on Grumpy Old Man Taylor's lawn. He burst outside, the screen door banging behind him. He brandished a wireless phone at me like it was a gun. The phone was ringing.

"It's for you!" he yelled, suddenly inches from my face. Spittle gleamed on his lips as he held the phone to my ear.

"Hello?" I tried.

"I want a divorce," Kate said. "I don't love you anymore."

I gaped at that. Oddly enough, the phone was still ringing.

"Well?" Old Man Taylor demanded. "What have you got to say for yourself?"

What could I say? The phone just rang and rang. "Daddy?" Rachel's tiny voice asked. "When are you coming home?"

"Soon honey," I said in a broken voice.

My sobs woke me and I sat up in a hurry. The sheets fell away and I shivered as cold air made a cold sweat even colder. The room was dark. My bladder was bursting, my throat parched. My head felt like it was stuffed with cotton, and my stomach roiled with a confusing mixture of hunger and nausea. Police sirens wailed in the distance, and the phone was ringing. I reached for it and winced as the movement set off a stabbing headache behind my eyes.

"Hello?" I croaked.

"Logan!"

It was Kate. I blinked stupidly and stared in horror at the phone out of the corner of my eye. My dream was coming true. She must be calling to ask for a divorce.

"Where's your phone?" Kate demanded. "I've been trying to call you for hours!"

"My phone?"

"Your cell phone!"

I glanced at the bedside table. My phone sat there, dark and silent. I'd forgotten to bring my charger. "The battery's flat," I said, and held my free hand to the side of my head, trying to keep it from exploding.

"You need to come home *right now,*" she said.

"Look, Kate, I'm not ready to—"

"Have you seen the news?"

Some of the cotton in my head evaporated. "No, why?"

"Because everyone is going crazy, Logan, *that's* why! People are saying we've detected some kind of signal from space, and that it's headed straight for us!"

"The *signal* is headed straight for us? What kind of signal?"

"I don't know, radio or something. They're saying it has to be aliens. Logan, some kids were driving down the street earlier, throwing beer bottles at houses and shooting guns in the air. I tried to call 911, but the line was busy. We need you home."

My confusion vanished. "I'll be right there." I jumped out of bed with the phone still pressed to my ear, but tripped over the cord and fell on my hands and knees. The phone base fell on my hand, and I cursed as a sharp pain erupted there. The dial tone sang in my ear. I dropped the phone and got up on shaking legs. Police sirens were still wailing in the distance. I heard thumping footsteps as someone ran down the hall outside my door. Casting about for the TV remote, I found it on the bedside table beside my dead cell phone and flicked on the TV. CNN snapped into focus, the news anchor was in the middle of her announcement, but the volume was muted. My eyes read the news ticker at the bottom of the screen.

BREAKING NEWS

ALIEN SIGNALS DETECTED NEAR EARTH, SOURCE MOVING TOWARD US

CHAPTER 4

I raced down Sanford street on my way back from the Ramada. *Aliens?* That was the question that ran through my head over and over. I felt like I was trapped in some B movie remake. The news reports I'd seen before leaving my hotel room had said that the source of the radio signals was moving at more than five hundred miles per *second*, and it was already close to Earth. Best estimates gave us a year to prepare for their arrival. None of that connected to reality in my brain. It didn't seem possible. There had to be another explanation.

Streetlights blurred by me, each of them like a laser beam to my pounding head. I was hungover, and probably still way over the legal limit, but right now the police had more important things to do than hand out DUI's.

I turned right off Sanford onto South Orange Avenue. Not far now. I stopped for a red light at

Oakland Terrace, maybe half a dozen blocks from my house. Someone went screaming straight through the light in the left turn lane and narrowly missed getting hit by a truck. The blast of the truck's horn echoed in my ears.

Pop! A car had just backfired. *Pop!* That wasn't a car. My head whipped around, and I saw a dark blur running down the other side of the street with a duffel bag swinging from one shoulder. Someone burst out of the Belfort Convenience Store just behind the runner, screaming things that I couldn't hear from this distance.

I'd just witnessed an armed robbery a few blocks from my house. Visions of thugs breaking into my house and shooting my wife and kids for the money in our safe danced through my head. The light turned green, and I stomped on the gas.

I cruised through the next light. Storefronts disappeared, replaced by trees and old houses. This was the beginning of the Montrose Neighborhood. I drove past the gated end of my street with the no entry signs, reached the next light, and turned right up Centre Street. My tires squealed as I cornered too fast. I was close now. My heart raced as the trees closed in around me. Historic "character" homes with red brick walls lined both sides of the street, dimly illuminated by their porch lights and little else. Deep shadows pooled on the sidewalks in the long gaps between street lights. They weren't even proper street lights; they barely reached above the stop signs at the side streets. My mind populated the shadows with delinquents lying in wait for home owners to take out the trash or pull into their driveways. Knowing that this was an expensive neighborhood made those fears all the more pronounced.

A flashing yellow light presided over a four-way stop up ahead. There weren't any other cars waiting, so I did a rolling stop and turned right again onto Hamilton. The next right after that was mine—Kingman Road, a tranquil street with the other end blocked to simulate a proper cul-de-sac. My house was the second last to the right. The yellow brick walls were fuzzy and gray with the night, but every single window of my three story home was bright and glowing with light. Just past my neighbor's house I could see the wrought iron gate that barred the old T-junction onto South Orange Avenue. That gate would do nothing to stop pedestrians from getting in, however. My mind flashed back to the armed robber I'd seen running down South Orange just a few blocks away, and my heart rate kicked up another notch.

As I turned into our driveway, I watched my

headlights flash over the big tree and the pair of big flower bushes flanking the entrance. I couldn't see anyone lurking there, but there was no way to be sure. I cursed under my breath about the lack of proper streetlights in Montrose. When we'd first moved in that had seemed like a quaint bonus, but now I saw it for what it really was—a security risk.

I didn't bother pulling all the way up my driveway to the detached garage in the back, but instead stopped just as close as possible to the front door. I glanced over my shoulders for one last look around, but it was too dark to see anything without the car's headlights shining in that direction. By now my headache had become a full-blown migraine, but that was the least of my worries. Taking a quick breath, I popped the door open and sprinted up the walkway to the front steps. Hurrying up those steps, I fumbled in my pocket for my keys, and turned to watch the yard as I did so. Precious seconds slipped by. I struggled to see the keys in the dim yellow light radiating from the sconces to either side of the front doors. Suddenly I regretted not installing a third, overhead porch light, or one of those motion-activated spotlights. Police sirens wailed somewhere close by—investigating that convenience store robbery? My palms began to sweat. As soon as I found the key, I spun around and opened the door on the right with the handle. The other was blocked by a siding bolt in the floor. Seeing those doors as if for the first time, I realized that they were both made of aging wood with single panes of clear glass running down their centers. It would be easy to break that glass with a rock and flick the deadbolt aside. Plus I was pretty sure that a determined thief could just kick them open. A sticker in the window of the door on the right warned the house was monitored by a security company, but I'd stopped paying for their services long ago. I regretted that decision now.

Hurrying inside, I locked the door behind me. My thoughts went straight to the revolver I kept in the safe upstairs.

"Kate! I'm home!" I called.

I heard footsteps thumping around upstairs, followed by the sound of a door opening and then Kate's voice: "We're up here!"

I ran to the end of the foyer, stumbling with the sudden urge to vomit. I leaned heavily on the banister to compose myself, and then used it to haul myself up the stairs. Kate was waiting for me in the doorway to our bedroom. I hesitated before entering the room. Over Kate's shoulder I saw our kids huddled together under the covers. Flickering white and blue light from the TV flashed over their stricken faces, turning Rachel's blonde hair white, and making Alex's face look even paler than usual. Rachel's face glistened with tears. She was only five. I expected that from her. Alex was fifteen, so he wouldn't be caught dead crying, but I could see that he was scared.

Reporters droned on about the alien signals, looters, shootings, robberies, and drunken end-of-the-world parties. It was ironic that the media was partly responsible for sparking all of that chaos and now they got to report on it, too. *Someone's buttering their bread on both sides.*

"Logan?" Kate prompted.

I realized I was reluctant to go into the room. A lurid flashback hit me, along with an accompanying burst of anger that made it hard to think straight. Kate saw the look in my eyes and winced.

"Did you at least change the sheets?" I demanded in a low voice.

She nodded quickly. "Can we focus on what's going on right now?"

I nodded stiffly back and brushed by her.

"Daddy, what's happening?" Rachel asked as I walked past the foot of the bed.

"How did you get home so fast?" Alex put in.

— 34 —

"Your father missed his flight," Kate said.

Confusion swirled inside of me, and my brow furrowed. I glanced back at Kate. "My flight?"

"To Chicago, to sign that author for Harper," Kate said.

"Right..." I said, nodding slowly. That must have been the excuse she gave the kids when I didn't come home at the same time I usually did. Alex watched us suspiciously, but Rachel was oblivious.

Turning around, I opened the louvered doors of my closet and bent down to type in the combination to our safe.

"What are you doing?" Kate asked.

Locking bolts slid aside with a *thunk*. I opened the door and pulled out the black case at the bottom. Cracking it open, I pulled out my double-action revolver and checked the cylinder. It was already loaded, so I left the case of spare ammo inside the safe and shut the door. Turning from the closet, I saw my wife and kids watching me with big eyes.

"What's that for?" Alex asked.

"Just in case," I said as I pocketed the gun.

I went to sit on the edge of the bed beside Rachel. She wrapped an arm around me and leaned her head against my shoulder. Kate came and sat on the other side, next to Alex. Parents aren't supposed to have favorites, but kids do.

I rubbed Rachel's shoulder as I watched the news. The anchor woman on CNN said that President Fowler was holding an emergency press conference at the White House. I nodded along with that. Aliens invading Earth certainly qualified as an emergency, but that couldn't be what was happening here, could it?

CHAPTER 5

I watched the scene switch to a lectern flanked by the flag of the United States and the flag of the president, each hanging from a brass pole. The signature blue and white placard of the White House was on the wall behind the lectern. The camera panned to show President Alison Fowler walking in from the side to stand in front of the cameras.

"Good evening everyone," President Fowler began. "I want to begin by reassuring you that aliens are *not* coming to invade our planet." Nervous laughter from the press followed that statement, and she flashed a laughing smile for the cameras. That smile looked fake to me, but maybe she was just tired from a long day—like me. "I repeat, the mysterious radio signals we've detected are not alien in origin."

"Thank God," Kate breathed.

"Aww man," Alex said. "I knew it was too good to be true!"

The president went on: "...signals are being generated by a previously undetected, dark celestial body. It is widely known by the scientific community that planets and stars can emit radio waves as a part of natural processes. Until recently we were not able to detect the source of these emissions, but by cross referencing the radio wave data with infrared data from our James Webb Space Telescope, scientists have discovered a cold, dark star racing in from outside our solar system — a so-called *rogue*, named Greenhouse's Star after the scientist who discovered it."

My brow furrowed at that, and I glanced sharply at Kate. "Doesn't your brother work with NASA?" I asked. She nodded slowly but said nothing. Her maiden name was Greenhouse. Her brother worked with telescopes and all that space stuff down in California. Was that just a coincidence?

"We have been able to confirm that this star is moving at a high speed, but it does not represent any threat to us here on Earth. This is a remarkable scientific discovery, but nothing more, and certainly no reason for anyone to panic."

The president looked up from her lectern. "If you are listening to this broadcast now, please know that there is nothing to fear. As to the deplorable actions that some have taken while under the influence of their fears—rest assured, these people will be found and dealt with promptly by local authorities. Until then, it would be best to stay in your homes and wait for the commotion to settle down. Thank you, America, and good night."

The scene switched back to the talking heads. I reached for the remote on the bed at Rachel's feet and hit the mute button.

"Time to go to bed," I said. A flash of disappointment went through me at the abrupt return to normalcy, and I realized that some small part of me had been relieved for this crisis to take the attention off my own personal one.

I got up from the bed and dropped a kiss on Rachel's head. "You three should sleep in here tonight. I'll sleep on the couch downstairs and keep a lookout, just in case." For tonight, at least, I had a good excuse not to sleep in the bed that my wife had defiled.

Kate crawled out from under the covers. "Let's go brush our teeth and change into our pajamas. Come on." She ushered Alex out next.

I ran into him at the foot of the bed, gave him a hug and said goodnight. Rachel raced in from the other side, making sure that Alex wouldn't steal too much of my attention. "Night, Daddy," she said. I kissed her on the head again, and tightened our embrace. Kate caught my eye over our kids' shoulders. A broken smile trembled on her lips, and she wiped a tear from the corner of one eye.

"What's wrong, Mommy?" Rachel asked.

More tears broke loose, and Kate's smile shattered as she wiped them away with a shaking hand. "Nothing, sweetheart. I'm just relieved, that's all."

Another lie for the steaming pile. I left the room ahead of my family and headed downstairs while they filed through the bathroom that we all shared on the second level. This was a century-old home. En-suite's were a modern invention. Ironically, however, there was an en-suite on the third floor attached to the smallest bedroom of six. The logic of that had escaped me for the past ten years.

As I reached the foyer and saw the flimsy front doors—ancient wood painted blue with their fragile glass centers—my thoughts turned to more pressing concerns. How long would it take for all the real and wannabe criminals on the streets to get word of the president's address? Aliens might not be coming for us, but that didn't mean the danger had passed. I felt for the gun in my pocket. I wasn't worried about accidentally grazing the trigger and shooting my foot off. Triggers are surprisingly hard to pull. I'd figured that out when I was just ten years old and learning to shoot for the first time on my grandfather's farm. Back then I'd needed both hands to pull the trigger. Now I could do it with one, but certainly not by accident.

Walking up to the front doors, I peeked through the ruffled white curtains behind the panels of glass. The front yard was dark. The nearest street lamp was on the other side of the street and scarcely enough to illuminate the outline of the oak tree and flower bushes at the entrance of our driveway.

I gave up and went into the living room. Taking a seat on the couch beside the fireplace, I pressed the heels of my hands into my eyeballs, trying to drive away my still-stabbing headache.

Just then, the phone rang. I stared at it for a second before reaching over the side of the couch and snatching it off the charging base.

I pressed the green answer button. "Hello?"

"Logan," a deep male voice said.

I frowned. "Who is this?"

"It's Richard."

"Richard... Greenhouse?"

"Yeah."

— 41 —

After a year of no contact, Katy's brother was calling us out of the blue—I checked my watch. It was after nine at night, but it would be three hours earlier in California. "What's up?" I prompted.

"You've seen the news?" Richard asked.

"Who hasn't?" I asked.

"And the president's address?" he pressed.

My brow furrowed. "Yeah. We were just watching it. Were you the one who discovered that star?"

"Yes. Logan, listen to me. I'm calling from a pay phone, but I think I'm being followed, so I might not have long."

"Followed?" I echoed. "Have you been drinking again, Richard?"

"No, yes, but that's not the point! I'm not delusional."

I decided to humor him. "Okay..."

"Logan, you need to listen to me if you want your family to live. That star is going to mean the end of life as we know it."

Not this again. "Look, Rick, we went through all of this last year. This is why you haven't been allowed to visit again."

"I haven't *asked* to visit, have I?" Richard snapped. "But again—that's not the point. *This* is what I was talking about last year. The government has been covering up the existence of this rogue star for the past ten years. I was part of that cover-up. They paid me and everyone else at IPAC off, bugged our homes, and threatened us if we ever spoke about what we knew."

That surreal feeling was back. This didn't seem as unlikely as aliens, but it still felt pretty far-fetched. "So you've known about this for ten years?"

"Yes, now listen—when this star reaches us in a year's time, you don't want to be anywhere close to the coast, and you definitely don't want to be in the northern states. The star's passing will cause massive tidal waves, but that's nothing compared with what will follow. It's going to disrupt our orbit and plunge us into an ice age. That means temperatures are going to drop, snow is going to pile up, and eventually New York and New Jersey will be buried under a mountain of ice."

An amused smile tugged at my lips. There's no way the government was hiding all of that.

Richard went on, "I have a place down in San Antonio. It's all set up with enough supplies to last for a few years. It's on Calaveras Lake."

I absently scratched the side of my jaw, wondering what to say to that.

"Logan are you listening to me?" Richard

asked.

"Yeah, I'm listening."

"Just get down to San Antonio and I'll explain everything, okay? The address is 13241 Stuart Road, Calaveras Lake. I'm going there myself, but that means I'll be off the grid. There's no cell reception down there and I don't have a land line. It's better that way. We all need to bug out and lie low. Now that the news about the rogue is out, the president won't be able to keep this a secret any longer. More people are going to get access to the data, and then they're going to develop their own simulations. It's probably just a matter of weeks before everything goes to hell. If you thought the news about aliens coming was bad, just wait and see what happens when everyone finds out that they're either going to freeze or starve to death."

I shook my head quickly. "Rick, this is crazy. How do you expect me to believe you? The government wouldn't hide something like this. They'd make preparations."

A burst of static came through the phone as Richard sighed. "They have prepared, but quietly. You can't prepare for something when the whole country is tearing itself apart, hoarding food, and crowding into fifteen degrees of latitude along our southern border. Look, just do me a favor and tell

Kate about all of this. If she doesn't buy it either, then you'll have to wait to see the news break. When it does, get down to San Antonio as fast as you can, and remember where to find me—thirteen, two four one, Stuart Road, Calaveras Lake. You got that? Get a pen and write it down."

"Sure."

"I mean it, Logan."

"I'm making a note in my phone right now," I lied.

"Good. And Logan, whatever you do, *don't* take a Taxi from the airport, and don't tell anyone else where you're going. If people find out about my safe house, it won't be safe for long. Do you understand me?

I nodded slowly. "Perfectly."

"Good. Give my love to the kids."

The phone went dead, and a dial tone sang in my ear. I turned off the receiver and put it back on the base.

"Who was that?" Kate asked. I turned to see her standing in the threshold between the living room and the foyer, arms crossed defensively over her chest.

"Your brother," I said.

"Richard?"

I nodded. She only had one brother, so that

was a stupid question.

"What did he say?"

"A lot, but I'm not sure any of it's true. Sit down."

Kate sat at the far end of the L-shaped couch. I sat at the other end, beside the fireplace, and explained everything that Richard had told me.

"That doesn't make sense," Kate said, shaking her head. "Why would the president lie if the news is going to break in a few weeks, anyway?"

That was a good question. "She wouldn't," I decided. "He's gone off his head again."

We both nodded, and Kate gave a rueful smile before getting up and going back upstairs.

As she left, another explanation whispered through my thoughts: maybe the president had lied to buy time. A few weeks would be enough time to deploy the national guard and prepare for the chaos. It would also be enough time for the president and other high-ranking government officials to get to safety.

Still—an ice age? That didn't sound very likely. I dismissed the thought with a sigh, withdrew the gun from my pocket, and placed it on the table beside the couch. It was like the president had said, this was just a remarkable discovery, nothing more.

* * *

—THREE WEEKS LATER—
June 1st

I sat in my office on the third floor of my home, alternately checking job listing websites and preparing a new budget in Excel.

There'd be no vacations, no fancy food from the supermarket, no more dinner parties, or big birthday celebrations, and no more private schools, but we would live, and our savings would last eight months. That should be enough time for me to get another job.

I reached for a pencil on my desk and began chewing the end of it absently. A knock sounded on the door, and I looked up from my computer screen just as Kate popped her head in.

"Lunch is ready. Do you want to come down and eat with me?"

"Give me ten minutes."

"Okay," Kate said, and shut the door quietly.

I listened to the sound of her footsteps receding as she went back downstairs. We'd been sleeping apart ever since I'd spent that crazy night on the couch guarding the front door with my revolver. The third floor had become my sanctuary.

The guest bedroom with the en-suite next to my office was mine. Rachel was oblivious to our change in sleeping habits, but Alex understood perfectly: his parents were on the fast track to divorce.

I leaned back in my chair and steepled my hands in front of my lips. Is that what I wanted? A divorce?

But it was too soon to say, and I had too many other problems right now to be thinking about adding a new one. My stomach growled, and I got up with a sigh. By the time I reached the first floor, I heard the TV droning in the sun room.

"Kate?" Maybe she'd decided to start eating without me. I walked through the living room to the sun room. The door was open. Kate stood frozen in front of the TV, her food cooling on a tray beside the couch. Her blue eyes were wide with horror, and she'd clapped a hand over her mouth as if to stifle a gasp. Not tearing her eyes away from the screen, she slowly shook her head.

I glanced at the screen and read the news ticker just as I had done at the Ramada three weeks ago.

BREAKING NEWS

ARRIVAL OF GREENHOUSE'S STAR PREDICTED TO CAUSE EXTENSIVE COASTAL FLOODING AND A NEW ICE AGE ON EARTH

The news anchor was sharing the screen with a scientist, who was going into specifics.

"Global average temperatures will drop by almost twenty degrees within a year. When this winter comes and the snow starts to fall, it's never going to melt. The only habitable places left in the USA will be in Southern Florida and Southern Texas."

I looked back to Kate and she looked at me. "Richard was right," was all I could say. I couldn't believe it.

"The kids," Kate said. "You need to go pick them up from school right now, before everyone starts going crazy again."

My eyes flared as I remembered what had happened the last time news like this broke. I nodded quickly and ran for the door.

Kate ran after me. "I'm coming with you."

I was about to object, but the thought of leaving her here alone with people trying to break in and loot our house made me want to keep her close. Richard was right. This was going to be a lot worse than the last time.

CHAPTER 6

I roared down the driveway in my Mercedes 300C with Kate still rushing to put her seatbelt on. The tires squealed and the car jumped over a bump at the end of the driveway. Red brick houses and the summer green leaves of old trees blurred together on both sides of the street.

"This can't be real," Kate said.

I shook my head, speechless.

Kate raged on. "Richard knew about this for ten years and he never said anything? We have children!"

"I think he tried," I said. "Remember last year?" And that wasn't the first time he'd come to us preaching about the end of the world.

"But he didn't explain! He just ranted and raved like a lunatic!"

I nodded my agreement and turned left onto Hamilton Road. "He did explain three weeks ago. The problem is he spent so many years crying wolf that this time we didn't believe him."

"What are we going to do?"

I hit the flashing yellow light at the four-way-stop on Centre Street. There was a black SUV already cruising through the intersection. I slowed down just enough to glide smoothly in behind the SUV as I turned left down Centre Street. *What* are *we going to do?* I wondered.

"We can't sell the house now," I decided.

"Why not?" Kate demanded.

"Because *everyone* is going to be selling and no one is going to be buying, unless you've got property down south. You heard what that guy on the TV said. Southern Florida and Southern Texas are going to be the only places left in the USA that will be warm enough to live."

"But we have all of our money tied up in the house!" Kate thundered. "We can't move to Florida with forty-five thousand dollars."

The same concern was playing on repeat in my head. We hit the intersection on South Orange Ave. The light was red. I pulled into the turn lane beside the black SUV. There was a woman in the front seat, her hands clutching the steering wheel. I spied a car seat behind her. Leaning over the steering wheel, I looked for a break in traffic that would allow me to turn right. There were no breaks in sight. Giving up, I turned to Kate to address her concerns. "Your brother mentioned a place he bought down in San Antonio. He said we could join him there."

Kate looked at me, her eyes wide. "That's right! He knew, so he had time to prepare! Where in San Antonio? Do you have the address? Give me your cell phone; I'll call him."

"I left it at home. It doesn't matter, anyway. He said he doesn't have service down there, and there's no land line."

"Great! So how are we going to find him?"

The light turned green and the SUV ahead of me floored it, heading straight down Centre Street. I was just about to follow, but a silver sedan went screaming through the intersection on the other side, running the red light. Tires squealed and the cars hit with a thunderous *bang* and *crunch* of metal. Glass exploded in a glittering wave as the two vehicles danced around each other, their tires still squealing. Both cars skidded to a stop, leaving them badly crumpled, smoking, and slumping.

Kate blasphemed and gasped.

I remembered the car seat in the back of the SUV. "Shit!" Opening my door, I ran on shaking legs to check on the passengers of the two cars.

"Logan!" Kate called after me.

Broken glass glittered in the sun, crunching

under my feet as I darted through the intersection. The silver sedan had hit the SUV side-on, and at high speed. Neither vehicle looked to be in good shape, and no one had tried to get out of their vehicles yet.

When I reached the SUV I saw that the driver's side window was missing, and the driver was slumped against her airbag, her face buried in it. Blood streamed from a cut in the side of her head, but she wasn't moving.

"Ma'am?" I tried shaking her shoulder. She didn't stir. Then I glanced over her shoulder and saw the baby in the back. He was staring at me with wide blue eyes, and somehow not crying at all. He had to be about three years old. He was sitting in one of those upright, front-facing toddler seats rather than a baby seat. A side air bag had deployed beside him, pushing his seat away from the door. He looked fine, thank God. His mother was another story. The car had hit *her* door. "Hang on there, buddy," I said. "I'm going to try to get you out." I reached over his mother's shoulder and pulled the rear door open from the inside. The door groaned on its hinges, but I managed to open it halfway. Reaching in, I began to unbuckle the kid. He started to cry and fight me with his hands.

"Hey, take it easy," I said. "What's your

name?"

He just cried louder. "Mommy!" he said.

I grimaced and fought through his hands to pull him out of the vehicle. Cars were honking their horns now. A few of them came crawling through the intersection.

One driver leaned out of his window to get a better look. "Everything okay?" he asked as I carried a kicking and screaming three-year-old the two steps to the front of the car to check on his mother.

I grunted as the kid kicked me in the crotch, stealing the reply I'd been about to offer. The curious driver lost interest and wove around the crash.

I put the kid down, but held onto him by his wrist. With my free hand I shook his mother's shoulder again. This time she stirred and cried out in pain as she raised her head and turned to look at me. She clapped a bloody hand to the side of her head and stared dumbly at me. "Wha..."

"You've been in an accident," I explained. "I just got your son out, but he's not too happy about it. Do you think you can get out on the other side?" There was no way her door was going to open.

The woman blinked at me and glanced at the passenger's side door. "Maybe," she croaked. "Let me see."

She released her seatbelt and fought through the airbag to ease over into the passenger's seat. From there she opened the door and climbed out. I yanked her son along to go meet her at the front bumper. He bit me, drawing a scream from my lips.

"Thank you," the mother managed.

I nodded, rubbing the bite marks on my arm. A siren reached my ears. It sounded like a fire truck, not an ambulance. "Sounds like help is on its way."

She nodded and I helped stop traffic to escort them safely to the side of the road.

"Thank you," the woman said again.

The three-year-old glared at me. I glared back. "No problem." The kid's mother didn't seem to notice our exchange.

I ran back through the stream of honking traffic to check on the other driver, shocked that no one else had thought to do so by now. The whole front end of the car was smashed-in. The driver was pinned between his steering wheel and his seat. Either the airbag had failed to deploy, or his car didn't have one. Horror stabbed through me at the sight of the man's staring eyes and the blood trickling from the corner of his gaping mouth. "Sir?" I lightly shook his shoulder, and his head flopped rag-doll limp to his chest. I flinched and recoiled from the body. Turning around, I ran back through traffic to my car. The intersection was completely jammed, and everyone was sitting on their horns.

"Is everyone okay?" Kate asked, looking pale with fright.

"The kid and his mother seem fine, but the driver of the car that hit them is dead."

Kate made a strangled sound. I shut my door and put the car into reverse. Twisting around to look behind us, I raced backward up Centre street and pulled into the nearest driveway to turn back the other way. We were going to have to go around the intersection.

* * *

By the time we got to Our Lady of Sorrows School, we'd seen a couple more accidents—just fender benders, thankfully. The whole city was crawling with cops, fire engines, and ambulances, their sirens screaming in shrill echoes that never fully died. But emergency services weren't the only ones out in force on the streets. I'd seen the national guard or the military (maybe both?) driving around in Humvee convoys, blasting instructions to remain calm from megaphones on their roofs.

I parked at the school and we hurried inside with rushing streams of other parents. In the entrance, Miss Smith, the school secretary, was waiting to tell us all where to go.

"The kids are still in their classrooms," she said. I elbowed past the other parents and led the way down the hall to Rachel's Kindergarten classroom. At the door I peered in through the glass window to see Rachel sitting attentively at her desk while the rest of the class went crazy.

I opened the door and walked through. Miss Carmen's gaze found mine, but her eyes were wide and glazed, and she was biting her nails at a furious rate. She looked shell-shocked. Half a dozen kids were laughing and yelling as they ran around the room—

"Tag, you're it!" one said as he slapped another on the back.

Rachel belatedly noticed me. "Daddy! You came!" She burst out of her chair and wrapped her arms around my waist.

"Of course I did," I said, stroking her hair.

Kate came to stand beside us, looking on with a jealous gleam in her eyes. "We have to go get your brother," she said.

Rachel released me and grabbed my hand instead. We followed Kate out into the hall. I nodded my thanks to Miss Carmen, but she was still looking at me with unseeing eyes.

The chaos was more pronounced around the high school classrooms on the other side of the school. Teachers were out in the hall shouting at the kids, while the kids were either running around harassing each other, or leaning against the walls chatting to their friends. I saw a lot of boy-girl combinations. The cliche of end-of-the-world romance was playing out before my eyes on a laughably juvenile scale. One boy stole a kiss as I walked by only to have a teacher yank him away by the collar of his white polo shirt. That was when I noticed that the boy was mine. I stopped in my tracks and took over from the teacher.

Kate yelled at the man for laying hands on Alex. The teacher threw up his hands and walked away.

"Let's go!" I shouted to be heard over a hundred different babbling voices. Alex darted away from me, back to the girl he'd kissed, and stole a second one. This time I was the one pulling him away by his collar.

The girl blushed and waved goodbye. I didn't have time to ask who she was, but I was quietly impressed. I had no idea my son was such a stud.

"What's going on?" Alex asked as we left the

chaos of the high school classrooms behind. "The teachers won't tell us anything."

I glanced at him, but said nothing.

Kate explained.

"Holy crap!" Alex said.

I nodded absently. My focus was on getting us home safely so we could pack our luggage and get to the airport before mass hysteria set in and made our travel plans impossible. We had to find Kate's brother in San Antonio. The trouble was, I couldn't for the life of me remember the address he'd given me.

As we left the school and crossed the parking lot, another thought occurred to me—our money in the bank. We needed to get it out. I thought about swinging by Capital One Bank on the way home, but then I realized that everyone else would be thinking the same thing. There was going to be a run on the banks, which meant even more chaos than what we'd seen so far—not to mention the possible risk of running into opportunistic bank robbers. Best not to risk it. For now we could use our credit cards, which had combined limits well in excess of our savings, anyway.

"So what are we going to do?" Alex asked, as I held the car door open for Rachel and helped her buckle up.

"Your uncle has a place down in San Antonio," Kate explained. "We're going to go visit him for a while."

A while, I thought, shaking my head. well-meaning lies come easy when you're a parent. I thought about the government's lies and realized that it wasn't much different. We lie to protect and reassure our kids, to keep the fear from boiling over. Meanwhile, the government does the same thing with adults.

I shut Rachel's door and got into the driver's seat. Hitting the ignition button, I put the car into drive and raced out of the parking lot. Turning left onto Prospect Street, I headed back up to South Orange Avenue. After driving for just a few dozen meters, I ran into bumper-to-bumper traffic. I cursed and honked my horn in frustration. The accident we'd witnessed must have caused traffic to back up down here. I glanced around quickly, looking for a way out. There were cars to all sides. I was boxed in. I honked my horn again. "Move, damn it!"

A pedestrian walked up and rapped his knuckles on my window. He smiled and made a gesture for me to lower the window. I froze, my instincts screaming in warning. He must have seen the look on my face, because he dropped the polite stranger act and whipped out the gun he'd been hiding behind his back.

Kate screamed, then so did Rachel, and she started crying.

"Shit," Alexander muttered.

The stranger's voice reached my ears, muffled by the glass. "Lower the window and give me your phones and your wallets—now!"

CHAPTER 7

I lowered the window and eased the wallet out of my back pocket. So much for using my credit cards, I thought, as I handed my wallet to the man with the gun in my face. "I don't have my phone with me," I explained.

The robber's eyes narrowed, but his gaze roved on to Kate. "The bag! Now!"

Kate handed over her designer handbag with a grimace. "You should be ashamed of yourself!" she said in a shaking voice. "We have children in the car!"

"And I have children at home—what's your point?" he demanded as he slung her handbag over his shoulder.

Kate blinked in shock, probably surprised to hear that he was a family man.

My mind raced. Was there enough cash in our safe to buy tickets to San Antonio for the four of us? I doubted it.

The robber lingered, the crows feet around his

brown eyes pinching as he stared at my wife.

I began to worry that his mind had turned to more carnal matters. I was just about to try jumping him, when he said —

"Your rings! Hand them over!" Then he glanced at me. "Yours, too, dickhead."

I grimaced and slowly worked the wedding band off my finger. It had cost me almost a thousand dollars, and Kate's rings were worth five times that, but I doubted they would fetch much at a time like this.

"See ya," the robber said, as he pocketed the rings.

He started to leave, but I stopped him — "Wait."

Glancing back at me, he said, "What? You got something else for me?"

"I need one of my credit cards. Just one. Please. It's important."

His eyes slid away to my kids in the back of the car, then returned to me. "Sorry, no can do."

"You won't be able to use them," I insisted. "They've got my name on them."

He shook his gun in my face. "Shut up! You're rich, Mr. Mercedes. Go take some money out of the bank."

I opened my mouth to object. I was rich in

assets that I couldn't liquidate. And the bank wasn't likely to have my money for much longer.

The robber turned and ran away before I could do or say anything else. I hit the steering wheel and cursed just as the car in front of me started inching forward.

"You can call and cancel the cards, right?" Kate asked in a quiet voice as I raised my window.

I looked at her. "That's not the point. How are we supposed buy tickets to San Antonio without a credit card?" Another thought occurred to me. "Not to mention, once we get there, how am I supposed to rent a car without a license?"

Kate gaped at me, the penny dropping. "Shit."

"Yeah. Shit," I said, nodding my head.

* * *

Richard Greenhouse was at the Starbucks in San Antonio when the shit hit the fan. He saw people reacting to the news, pushing out their chairs and cursing. Coffee cups went over and splashed on the floor. Everyone hurried for the exit. A handful stayed seated, one of whom started sobbing and muttering prayers. Richard checked CNN's website to confirm what had happened while calmly sipping his coffee. It was all over the headlines. News about the true implications of "Greenhouse's Star" had officially broken.

Richard glanced at the door and thought about his pickup in the parking lot. He could bug out now and try to beat traffic on his way out of San Antonio, but it would be safer to stay put until the initial panic died down.

Looking around the Starbucks as he sipped his coffee, Richard noted that the place was completely empty now—except for the crier. She had her head in her hands, and was rocking back and forth in her chair. The baristas were chattering nervously amongst themselves, using their cell phones to look up news headlines and parrot them back in ever-rising voices.

Frowning to himself, Richard directed his attention back to his laptop. He double-checked the signal data he'd downloaded. It was all there and ready for analysis. That was the reason he'd risked coming to the city. He didn't have Internet at his place on Calaveras Lake, and three weeks ago SETI had set up a citizen science project to decode the radio signals coming from the rogue star. No one seriously believed the signals were coming from aliens anymore, but after spending the past three weeks in self-isolation, Richard was itching for something to do, so he'd come here to download the data and see for himself. But now he was stuck in a heavily populated city in Texas—Texas, the gun-owners paradise, where people don't even have to register their firearms.

Richard's thoughts jumped to his sister and her kids in New Jersey. He hoped they'd remember to fly down to San Antonio and join him, but he doubted Logan had actually written the address down. He thought about sending an e-mail to remind them of the address, but stopped with his mouse poised over the *compose* button. What if someone broke into his sister's house, stole one of their computers, and read the e-mail? Richard thought about the cell phone he'd deactivated, sitting dormant with the battery flat back at his shelter. He could call Kate if he bought a card to put some minutes on the phone, but he'd still have to get to an area with service.

No, he decided. It was a bad time to go looking for a convenience store. He hadn't gone to all the trouble of building himself a shelter just so that he could become collateral damage in an armed robbery.

Richard glanced at the door, suddenly wondering if he should worry about the Starbucks getting robbed. There were probably a hundred better targets in the area, but still...

He pulled his laptop bag down onto his lap, glanced around to make sure no one was looking, and then unzipped the front pocket and pulled out his Beretta. Richard slipped the weapon into his cargo pants pocket and closed the Velcro flap. If someone burst in waving a gun around, at least he'd be prepared.

Richard turned his attention back to his laptop and checked CNN again. One of the lower headlines was an opinion piece accusing Billionaire Akron Massey of being a part of a government conspiracy to hide knowledge of the rogue star from the American public.

Richard nodded approvingly, glad that people were starting to figure things out. The article cited the past decade of 'excessive' government funding for Starcast's Mars Colony Mission, which was on track for an early 2032 launch. The writer went on to suggest that Mr. Massey was planning to escape Earth's frozen fate and live out the rest of his days on Mars. That wasn't such a big leap, since the billionaire was on public record saying that he wanted to die on Mars.

Richard's thoughts grew wistful as he considered that. Even the most pessimistic projections left Earth more habitable than Mars, but that didn't take into account all of the wars and human-generated chaos to come.

The Mars Colony would be just like a more

extensive version of Richard's own bug out shelter. Long before even building that shelter, Richard had consulted for Starcast with a group of his colleagues from IPAC. They'd met with Mr. Massey to discuss launch sites for the Mars Colony Mission that would not be compromised by the rogue star's passing. During that meeting, Richard had jokingly asked where he could sign up for the mission. The billionaire had laughed and suggested he send a résumé. Richard had promptly sent one to the e-mail address that Massey provided, but he'd never heard back.

His thoughts came back down to Earth with a sigh, Richard wondered again about his sister and her family in New Jersey. He'd never forgive himself if something happened to her or the kids—even Logan.

There had to be a way to tell them his address safely. He was just about to ask one of the baristas to borrow their phone when he came up with a better idea: self-destructing e-mail. Gmail had a feature where he could send an e-mail that would erase itself after a certain period of time. That would be perfect.

Nodding to himself, Richard hit compose and set the e-mail to self-destruct in three days. Hopefully, either Logan or Kate would check their mail before it was erased.

CHAPTER 8

Traffic was crazy on the way home, but I managed to get us back safely. Thankfully, our home hadn't been broken into in our absence, but my suspicions were correct: there wasn't enough money in the safe to get us to San Antonio.

"You're going to have to go to the bank," Kate said.

I glanced over my shoulder as I removed the case with my revolver in it from our safe. Kate was standing with her hands on her hips, nostrils flaring and eyes flashing. She was in the middle of a full-blown panic.

"You want to send me back out there in that shit storm?" I shook my head. "Even if I do manage to withdraw some of our money, I could be followed and robbed."

"So what are you planning to do?" Kate demanded. "We can't just sit around here waiting for the end of the world!"

I shook my head. "No, we can't. We're going to stay home and lie low until the government gets this situation under control. Meanwhile, I'll call the bank to cancel and re-issue my credit cards."

"What if the bank goes bankrupt? Or refuses to give us new credit cards?"

"Our savings are safe. The government insures deposits up to two hundred and fifty thousand."

"Well, you could at least *try* the bank. Capital One has lots of branches. You wouldn't have to go far."

I frowned, wondering if maybe she was right. Or maybe she just didn't care about putting me in harm's way. Kate's infidelity had left a yawning chasm between us, and hearing my wife tell me to jump didn't make me feel any better. My gaze wandered from her to the kids. Both Rachel and Alexander were sitting on the bed, watching us. Rachel had her knees drawn up to her chest and was peering over them with big eyes, while Alexander cracked his knuckles and scowled, as if spoiling for a fight.

I slipped my revolver into my pocket and then went over and wrapped an arm around Rachel's shoulders.

"It's going to be okay," I said, and kissed the top of her head.

"No, it's not," Alex snapped. "It's the end of the world. Mom said it."

I grimaced. "Not true. Lots of places will still be warm enough to live after this..."

"Rogue star," Alex supplied.

I nodded. "After it passes, your uncle's place will still be warm."

"How are we going to get there with no money and no credit cards?" Alex asked.

There had to be a way. "Maybe..." My jaw dropped. I couldn't believe I hadn't thought of it sooner. "PayPal."

Alexander's eyebrows jumped up.

"You're right!" Kate crowed.

I turned and ran from the master bedroom, flying up the stairs to the third floor. Skidding into my office, my shoes squeaking on the hardwood floor, I flopped down into my chair. It took all of a few minutes to find a booking site and get to the point where I needed to input our traveler information. "Kate!" I yelled. "Passports!" I couldn't find a direct flight to San Antonio that was leaving today, but I did find one with a two-hour layover in Dallas. Close enough.

I was just about to yell down to Kate again, when I heard footsteps stomping up the stairs. She burst in and handed me our passports. Since we'd just had all of our other ID stolen, passports were all we had.

"Did it work?" Kate asked after a minute of hearing me type in the information.

"It will." I hadn't paid yet, but this wasn't the first time I'd used PayPal to book airline tickets. "Get our luggage and start packing for us and the kids. Take as much clothing as you can." Kate nodded quickly and turned to leave. A thought occurred to me, and I looked up from my computer. "And pack our winter clothes!"

"I will!"

It was crazy to think about packing winter clothes for a trip to Southern Texas in the middle of summer, but that was where we were at: crazy-town, next stop disaster-ville.

CHAPTER 9

After being robbed in my car just outside the kids' school, the prospect of driving to Newark Airport was terrifying. I'd hidden our passports, cash, and phones under my seat—and my revolver was in the driver's side door, within easy reach in case someone else came up to the window at a stop light. I couldn't afford to give up any of what we had left.

Thankfully, we didn't run into any difficulties along the way besides the mess of traffic on our way down to I-78.

Once we were on the expressway, it was relatively smooth sailing, and I felt myself breathing easier. Kate must have been feeling the same way, because she finally started talking.

"What's Richard's address in San Antonio?"

I winced with that question, wishing she hadn't asked. I cleared my throat. "It's on Cala-something Lake."

Kate blinked at me. "You don't know where he is?"

"When he called, *neither* of us took him seriously, remember? So excuse me if I didn't write down the address he gave me."

I could feel Kate's eyes on me. "But... then how are we going to find him?"

"I don't know. Find the lake and drive around it until we find him. Hopefully there aren't many houses on it."

"Nice plan, Dad," Alexander drawled.

"Hey, watch your tone," I snapped, glancing in the rear view mirror to give him a hard stare.

"Respect your father," Kate added.

Alex clamped his mouth shut and looked out of a window. He and I rarely saw eye to eye now that he'd hit the terrible teens. Lately it seemed like all he ever did was challenge my authority and question my decisions. Something told me I was in for a lot more of that in the weeks and months to come. Crisis had a way of provoking confrontations. I took a deep breath and let it out in a shuddering sigh. The stress was getting to me.

Kate laid a hand on my leg. I removed it just as quickly, drawing a pained look from her.

"We'll find him," she said quietly.

We reached Newark Airport twenty minutes later. I parked the car and we hurried inside with our luggage. I struggled to drag my bag on its wheels and pull Rachel along at the same time. Her little legs couldn't keep up with my pace, and I had to force myself to slow down. Our flight wasn't for another three hours, but I was still in a hurry. The sooner we got through security the sooner I could rest easy knowing that at least nobody was going to be pointing another gun at us.

The ticket counters were packed. I found the one for United Airlines and lined up with everyone else. I had our passports, phones, and cash in the laptop bag slung over my shoulder. I'd left my gun in the car. Pity there was no way to take it with us to San Antonio, but I had a feeling Richard would have a few dozen guns of his own. Rachel peered up at me as we shuffled through the ticket line. The roar of the crowds was deafening. Security guards stood all over, trying to keep order.

I glanced back to make sure that Kate and Alex were still behind me. Kate caught my eye and reached out to rub my shoulder. Alex glared. I jerked my chin at him. "What's your problem?" He was even surlier than usual.

He looked away, shaking his head. "Nothing."

I scowled and faced forward again. It felt like hours to get to the front of the line. By the time we finally did, I greeted the harried ticket agent with a tight smile and handed her our passports. She printed our boarding passes and helped us check our bags.

After that, it felt like a weight had been lifted — literally. It was a lot easier to move through the airport without our bags to weigh us down. I scooped Rachel up and hurried to the line-up for security. This line crawled even slower than the one at the ticket counters. TSA agents kept order, but barely. People were shoving and shouting to all sides. The body scanners were in full swing. I saw someone up ahead get pulled out of a scanner for having a concealed weapon—a switch blade. I frowned, watching as two TSA agents drew their weapons and disarmed him. He complained loudly about it being a gift from his girlfriend, even as the agents cuffed him and led him away.

By the time we were through security and made it to our gate fully two hours had passed. I breathed a sigh as I found a place to sit and wait with my family. Rachel sat next to me and leaned her head against my shoulder. She drew her legs up to her chest and quietly bit her nails.

"Don't do that honey. You'll chip your teeth," Kate chided.

Rachel stopped biting her nails and began sucking her thumb instead. I arched an eyebrow at that. "I thought you stopped sucking your thumb,

Rachie."

She looked up at me, but said nothing.

Kate caught my eye, and shook her head. We couldn't win both battles.

I peered around her to get a look at Alex. He was still brooding—arms crossed and eyes pinched in adolescent protest.

"What's up, Al?" I asked.

"Nothing."

"It doesn't look like nothing to me."

He didn't reply immediately, so Kate prompted, "Answer your father."

"Why do we have to go to stupid San Antonio?"

"Because I say so," I said, aware that it wouldn't be a good idea to talk about Richard's disaster shelter with so many people around to listen in.

"Why can't I stay? You guys can go without me."

I almost laughed at that, but managed to choke it down. "I suppose you're old enough to take care of yourself now. And when the snow starts to fall and the gas runs out, you won't freeze to death. You'll just bundle up, right? Not to mention food... you'll be able to walk to the supermarket and buy some. I guess that's what your piggy bank is for."

Alexander peered around Kate to glare at me again. "I'm not stupid. I can stay at Deanna's house."

One of my eyebrows jumped up. "And Deanna is...?"

Alexander didn't reply, but he didn't have to this time. I worked it out for myself. Deanna must have been the girl he'd kissed at school. No wonder he was so grumpy. He was heart-broken, thinking he'd never see her again. And he was right. He wouldn't. In fact, she'd be lucky to live through what was coming. I grimaced with that thought, and left Alex to work through his feelings. Kate and I were lucky in a way, our extended family was almost non-existent, and that meant fewer people to care for or mourn. I was an only child, and both sets of Kate's and my parents were already dead. As for friends, I'd always been too busy with work and family to maintain friendships. My wife, however... I glanced at her and my thoughts flashed back to her lover and our neighbor, Ben Fields. Maybe he'd be found among the casualties, lying in a gutter somewhere under a mountain of snow, frozen stiff.

A flash of guilt flickered through me, but my pent-up fury snuffed it out with a righteous smirk. He deserved what was coming. Then I thought about everyone else who would be affected, and my smirk died. I couldn't allow myself to be happy for what was coming just because it settled a personal score. This time the guilt lasted longer, and I forced myself to get out of my head and rather focus on the immediate future.

Looking around to root myself in the present, I noticed a stranger watching us from the row of seats across from ours. He wore a black Yankees cap and a short brown beard that made his face look fuzzy and friendly, reminding me somewhat of my brother-in-law. The stranger smiled and nodded at me as our eyes met. The crow's feet around his ice-blue eyes wrinkled.

"You got relatives in San Antonio?" he asked.

I shook my head. "How did you know..." This wasn't a direct flight. How could this stranger know where we were headed?

He jerked his head to Alex. "Your kid. He mentioned it. Smart move beating the rush down South before the snow starts to fall. I'm headed to Alamo City myself. You guys gonna stay down there?"

That gut-twisting chill I'd felt just before getting robbed at gunpoint was back. I smiled and shook my head. "Wish we could. I just thought the country will be safer right now."

"San Antonio's not exactly the country," the man said.

I shrugged. "Well, they don't land jump jets on farmer's fields."

The man snorted and inclined his head at that. "Guess you'll make your way from there."

"Yeah."

The stranger reached up and tipped the brim of his hat to me. *People still do that?* I wondered. He was wearing a brown leather jacket and blue jeans, so maybe he thought he was some kind of urban cowboy.

"Bill Summers," he said.

"Logan," I replied through a frown.

"I'm thinking of going to the country myself," Bill said. "Let this whole mess of beans sort itself out. Maybe I'll find a nice forest and go build myself a cabin like a goddamn pioneer!" He chuckled lightly, but his laughter gave me the chills. There was something cold in his eyes that I didn't like.

"Well, good luck with that," I said, and looked away, hoping he'd take the hint. Our plane was just pulling up to the gate now.

Not long now, I told myself. At least in the air there were only so many people who could cause trouble and the ways that they could do so were limited. I found it ironic that in a time of extreme crisis what worried me the most was the other people.

CHAPTER 10

People crowded around us as we hurried down the jetway to our plane, their elbows jabbing and hushed voices muttering as their footsteps resounded in an orderly stampede, muffled by the red carpeting under our feet. I held tight to Rachel's hand and tried to keep Alex in view.

Flight attendants greeted us with fake smiles as we boarded. Their eyes held the same tightness as everyone else's that I'd seen—simmering fear restrained by sheer inertia. *The routine must go on.* Even in a crisis, sometimes going through the motions is all we have left. I nodded to the attendants, and we shuffled down the aisle between seats. Due to the short notice I hadn't been able to get all of our seats together. We had two pairs of seats, separated by an aisle and two rows.

As we came to the first set, Kate said, "We'll take these." And then she busied herself by stuffing her carry-on into the overhead above her seat. Alexander kept his bag with him. It was a laptop bag like mine.

I nodded and walked on to find Rachel's and my seats. When I reached our row, I thought better of stowing my bag. It had our passports and cash in it. Best to keep that with me. I ushered Rachel in ahead of me to the window seat, thinking she might want to look outside, and then I climbed into the middle seat beside her. Balancing my bag on my lap, I thought about my phone. I'd been cut off from the news for hours and I was anxious to know what was going on. The screens in the airport all had the volume turned down too low to hear anything.

"Look!" Rachel pointed out the window. "There are people down there. What are they doing? Are they going to get on the plane?"

I smiled and shook my head. "They're loading our bags sweetheart."

"Oh. They're really small."

Nodding agreeably, I said, "Because we're high up." I unzipped my bag and pulled out my phone. Turning it on and unlocking it with my fingerprint, I swiped down and checked the notifications. There were dozens of e-mails— mostly junk mail. I went to check my inbox anyway and scanned quickly through the message subjects. One of them jumped out at me. It was from my brother-in-law. The subject was one word: *Texas*

My heart kicked in my chest and I opened the message. It read:

Hi, guys. If you want to join me, I'm at 13241 Stuart Rd, Calaveras Lake, San Antonio.

Love to all,
Richard

"Looks like we're sitting together."

I jumped at the sound of the voice and turned to see Cowboy Bill settling into the seat beside mine. He stared at my phone and nodded.

"Calaveras Lake? That's where you're headed?"

I blinked out of my shock, and quickly shook my head, turning off the phone and putting it away. "No."

Bill arched an eyebrow at me. "So you're going to San Antonio, and that e-mail is just a coincidence."

I'd had enough of this. Giving the man a hard stare, I said, "Why are you so interested in where we're headed?"

He held up his hands. "Whoa. Take it easy. I'm

just making conversation."

"My brother-in-law planned a fishing trip," I said. "He invited us before the news broke."

Bill nodded along with that. "So you're going down there to meet him. Makes sense." Bill clapped a hand on my shoulder and grinned. "Take it easy, man."

I nodded and looked over at Rachel, hoping Cowboy Bill would take the hint and leave me alone. "Are you scared?" I asked Rachel.

She shook her head. "Nope." Golden hair bobbed across her shoulders. Mine used to look like that. Now it was like salted caramel with all the white pricking through the blond.

"Good," I said. She was braver than me. I smiled and tousled her hair

"Daaad," she complained, and smoothed out her hair.

I tickled her instead, and she burst into a fit of giggles. "No more!" she said, between gasps for air. "I surrender!"

I withdrew, smiling.

"That's my seat," a woman said. I glanced in that direction.

"What? Are you sure?" Cowboy Bill asked, and then he made a show of checking his boarding pass. "Huh. Go figure. Sorry, Miss."

She nodded stiffly to Bill as he got out of the seat beside me. He caught my eye with a shrug. "Take care of your family, Logan," he said, and then walked further down the aisle to the back of the plane.

I watched him go with an icy chill prickling my arms. I had a bad feeling that Bill hadn't actually mistaken his seat. He'd sat down beside me on purpose in order to pump me for more information. How much of Richard's address had he read off my phone? And more importantly, why was he so interested in where we were going?

CHAPTER 11

I kept an eye on Cowboy Bill as we de-boarded in Dallas, but I quickly lost sight of him in the crowds. Dallas-Fort Worth was just as crowded and crazy as Newark had been, but at least we didn't have to go through ticket line-ups and security checks again. Our layover was only two hours, but it was a big airport, so I decided to head straight for our gate anyway. By the time we reached it we still had an hour and a half to wait.

After barely fifteen minutes of sitting, the kids began to get restless and started bugging each other. Rachel kept pulling Alex's ear buds out and he was getting fed up. Just as I was about to tell her to cut it out, I saw Alex cuff the back of Rachel's head.

"Dad! Alex hit me!" Rachel said, her eyes welling with tears as she looked up at me.

"Because she's screwing with my stuff!"

"Get over here," I snapped, and pointed to a seat on the other side of me.

Alex got up with a heavy sigh. Rachel stuck her tongue out at him as he went. I nudged her with my elbow. "I saw that. Behave."

"Sorry," Rachel replied in a dulcet tone.

Alex flopped down beside me and stuffed his ear buds back in.

"I'm hungry," Rachel said, suddenly no longer tearful.

"Me, too," Alex added.

Kate caught my eye across the now-empty seat between her and Rachel. She pointed to a nearby convenience store. "Why don't you go get us some snacks? I'll stay here with the kids."

Rachel bounced out of her seat. "I want to go."

"No. Stay with your mother."

"But—!"

I left the waiting area before she could come up with an argument to convince me. I wouldn't be able to hold Rachel's hand and an armful of snacks and drinks at the same time.

Inside the convenience store I grabbed candy bars, chips, and soda at random. While I stood in line to pay, I noticed a TV blaring the latest news from one corner of the store.

It was another presidential address. The president was denying claims that the government had known about the threat of the rogue star, and then she went on to detail a plan of action going forward.

"My administration is committed to meeting the increased demand for housing in the South. We will subsidize the costs and help people relocate. For those who choose to stay where they are, you will get tax credits for an equivalent value to help you prepare. You will not be abandoned. Together, we will prepare for the long winter ahead. We will shovel the streets and re-insulate our homes. We will buy warmer clothes and increase power to the electrical grid. We will grow food indoors in greenhouses, and use the latest technology to grow our crops year-round."

Applause interrupted the president's speech. She nodded and smiled winningly for the cameras. "We will do what we have always done: we will adapt. Not just to survive, but to thrive. And yes, as of 2032, we will become the first interplanetary nation in the world. Not because we are running away, or because we are afraid that the end has come, but because we *can*. We *can* live on Mars, just as we *can* live on this soon-to-be frozen Earth. We are taking nature head-on, and I assure you that we can survive anything it throws at us. This is our land, our country, our home. We will not be moved, and we will not surrender!"

The crowds roared and clapped. Some of the people standing in line with me did the same. But I just shook my head. The president had failed to address the fact that one year was not enough time to do even half of what she was suggesting. Not to mention, rising tides were projected to hit coastal cities with extensive flooding that would make even the worst hurricanes look like a joke. The tides would wash clean over cities all the way from Manhattan to Miami—probably LA and San Francisco, too.

I reached the check-out counter and paid the cashier with a twenty from the roll I kept in my laptop bag. We had just over a thousand in cash.

Heading back to the gate to join my family I passed out the snacks and drinks. Rachel and Alex fought for their favorites, but Kate settled those squabbles with arbitrary decisions. I flashed a grateful smile, and she smiled back. I was too tired to deal with the kids right now.

"Did you see the news?" Kate asked.

I nodded, frowning around a mouthful of a muffin that I'd bought for myself. How had she seen it? I looked around. There weren't any TVs around the gate. Then I noticed Alexander watching the news on his phone. He didn't have a plan, so he must have connected to the airport's

WiFi.

"What do you think?" Kate went on. "Maybe we won't have to stay with Richard for long. I mean, it's only going to be twenty degrees colder. At least we won't need air conditioners in the summer." Kate laughed lightly at that.

She had a point. Twenty degrees wasn't that much. Hope soared in my chest. Maybe we'd be able to sell the house after all. "I hope that's true," I said, even as I tried to remember what that scientist had said on the news early this morning. He'd claimed that this winter the snow was never going to melt, but that couldn't be right. Summer in New Jersey routinely hit the high eighties. Subtract twenty degrees from that and we'd still be in the high sixties. Snow would never stick around at those temperatures.

Suddenly I felt silly for running away to Texas. Richard was a survivalist nut case who'd been talking about the end of the world for years—*of course,* he'd gone off the deep end believing that this was it. As for the so-called government conspiracy and cover-up he'd mentioned, he probably saw his own shadow and thought it was somebody following him. I scowled and shook my head. Somehow, in the midst of all this, crazy Richard had rubbed off on us, and now we were running from our own shadows, too.

I sighed and regarded my family with a tight smile. "Well, at least we're finally taking a family vacation, right?"

Alex snorted at that, and shook his head. "With no Playstation, no Internet, and no TV? Nice vacation, Dad."

"It'll be fun," Kate said. "Like camping."

"Yay! Can we roast marshmallows?" Rachel asked.

"Sure, honey," I said, and kissed the top of her head. "We can roast all the marshmallows you like.

CHAPTER 12

It was a short flight from Dallas to San Antonio. Once we collected our bags and got outside, I hailed a cab and gave the Latino driver the address to Richard's place before getting in. The driver couldn't say no to a fare, but his appearance made me hesitate before loading my family into his car. He had a buzz cut and patterns etched into what was left of his hair. It made him look like he was moonlighting for a local gang. The driver flicked a glowing cigarette butt out the window of his car and arched an eyebrow at me. "Calaveras lake..." He blew out a stream of smoke. "In this traffic, you going to pay a lot."

I patted my laptop bag. "I'm good for it."

The driver glanced at me, seemed to notice my designer clothes, then nodded and hopped out to help us with our bags. I climbed in the front while Kate got in the back with the kids.

"What's your name?" the cab driver asked as he pulled away from the airport.

I glanced at him. Unlike Cowboy Bill, who thankfully I hadn't seen since de-boarding the plane in Dallas, the cab driver didn't put me on edge.

"Logan," I said. "And you?"

"Carlos. What you think of all this *mierda* about that star?" He gestured vaguely to the roof of his cab. "You think we'll see snow in San Antonio?"

I pressed my lips together. "Maybe."

Carlos grinned. *"Mis hijos van a volver locos en navidad."*

"I'm sorry?"

"My kids. They're gonna go nuts at Christmas."

I nodded, smiling tightly.

"You got a place down here?"

I hesitated. This conversation was taking an uncomfortable turn. "Just visiting," I said.

"Oh, yeah. That's good."

The conversation lapsed. Someone cut Carlos off in traffic. He slammed the horn with both hands and yelled out the window in Spanish. I heard something that sounded like *poohto*, and guessed it must be a swear word.

It took an hour and a half on the clock just to get out of the city, but after that it was smoother sailing. The wall-to-wall buildings and strip malls of the city faded to acreages and dry brown fields with clumps of green trees. Barbed wire fences walled-in Route 181 on both sides.

"That's Calaveras Lake," Carlos said as a big body of water appeared to our left. He drove on down the highway for another five minutes before stopping at a left turn light beside *Cactus Country RV Park*. The light turned green. "We're close now," Carlos said, and turned left off the highway. More brown grass and trees rolled by. The sky was carpeted in blue. The barbed wire fences closed in from both sides as the road narrowed down to just two lanes. Another five minutes passed. Carlos slowed at an uncontrolled intersection, turning left again. The street sign read *Stuart Rd.*

Just a few seconds later we passed a housing development with big homes on what looked to be half-acre plots. This was definitely the country, but I was relieved to learn that it was not completely isolated. A few blocks past that development Carlos pulled off the road in the entrance of a dusty side street. The way was blocked with a barbed wire gate and a no trespassing sign.

Carlos lowered his window and popped his head out. "You sure this is the place?" he asked.

I spied a mailbox in front of us with number 13241 on it. "Yeah, this is it."

Carlos looked back to me with a frown. "You got a key for the gate? Looks like a long, hot walk."

I noticed that there was a chain and heavy-duty padlock to secure the gate. "Nope, no key, but we're expected. You can just drop us here."

Carlos looked dubious. "There's no cell reception out here. You want me to wait? Maybe nobody's home."

"That's a good idea," Kate chimed in from the back. "If Richard got the address wrong we don't want to be stranded out here."

"All right. I'll go take a look around."

I opened my door and walked up to the gate. Grabbing it with both hands, I stepped on the wooden beam at the bottom to test it with my weight. It seemed sturdy enough. Careful to mind the barbed wire inside the frame, I pushed myself up and over, dropping down on the other side with a crunch of gravel. Casting a quick look over my shoulder, I waved to my family and then ran down the dirt road on shaky, travel-weary legs. In just a few seconds my black leather Oxfords turned white with the dust. Crickets sang loudly from the bushes. The sun glared down on me, prickling my skin with an instant sweat. The air was stifling and drier than chalk. It squeezed the moisture from my body like a sponge.

I ran on for long minutes, but there was nothing and no one in sight, just more green bushes, trees, and dry brown grass.

Before long my lungs and legs were burning, but it was my feet that convinced me to stop. The pebbles were like spikes driving through the soles of my shoes. I should have worn my runners. What was I thinking wearing city shoes on a trip to rural Texas?

Five minutes later I caught a glimpse of something shining in the sun. I wiped the sweat from my brow and held a hand to my forehead to shield my eyes from the sun. There was a massive pickup truck parked at the end of the road. I broke into a run once more, ignoring the stabbing pains in my feet. The pickup was parked in front of an old wooden house. I stopped there, beside the truck—an old F350—puzzled by the sight of the house. *This* was Richard's shelter? It couldn't even properly be called a house. It looked like a hundred-year-old shack.

I walked up to the front door and looked for a doorbell. There wasn't one, so I knocked and waited. No answer. I tried the door handle. It was unlocked. "Hello?" I called as I eased the door open with a noisy groan of rusty hinges. The house was dark and shadowy inside, but the car in the driveway gave me hope that we were in the right place. "Is anyone home?"

I heard the *chuk-chuk* of a pump-action shotgun followed by, "Hands where I can see them!"

I thrust both hands up. "Don't shoot! I'm looking for Richard Greenhouse!"

The silhouette of a man approached the door, the barrel of his shotgun dropping as he did so. "Logan?" The man stepped into the light, and I recognized my brother-in-law by his full brown beard, thinning hair, and oval face.

"You got my e-mail," he said, breathing a sigh, and pulling me into a one-armed embrace. He withdrew just a second later to peer around me. "Where's Kate and the kids? They're not..."

My mind filled in that blank, and I hastily shook my head. "They're fine."

Richard breathed a sigh, and I jerked a thumb over my shoulder. "They're waiting in a cab at the end of the driveway."

Richard's eyes pinched into angry slits. "You took a taxi? I thought I told you—"

I waved a hand to cut him off. "We didn't have a choice. Our wallets were stolen back in Jersey. We lost our driver's licenses."

"Well, I guess the driver can't have seen much from the road."

I snorted. "I can't even see much from here. Are you sure there's anything to see?"

Richard's expression became sly. "Oh, there's plenty. He walked out onto the porch with me and pointed to a dense clump of trees to my right. "Nestled in that stand of trees over there is my compound. This is the decoy house. Came with the property."

I nodded slowly, unconvinced.

"We'd better go get the others," Richard said, walking down the steps to his pickup. "You guys brought luggage I hope?"

"Yeah," I said.

Richard climbed in and stowed his shotgun in the back. I got in on the passenger's side. He fished his keys out of his pocket, started the car, and pulled a gravel-spitting turn to head back up to Stuart Road.

"You didn't tell the taxi driver why you were coming out here, did you?"

"No details."

"So no one knows you're here?" Richard pressed.

"Well..." I thought about Cowboy Bill and his strange behavior on our way down from Newark.

"Well, what?" Richard demanded. "What's *well* mean?"

I explained what had happened.

"Shit. That doesn't sound good. You think he read the whole address off your phone?"

I shrugged, and nodded. "He asked about Calaveras Lake. That's the last part of the address, so he definitely read the whole thing."

"Damn it! I *knew* it wasn't safe to send the address in an e-mail!"

I regarded him with a frown as we pulled up to the gate on Stuart Rd. Gravel crunched under the truck's tires, grinding to a stop. After watching the president's latest speech back in Dallas I was wondering if all this paranoia was even justified.

"Well, nothing to do about it now," Richard said. "If Billy The Kid comes poking around here, he's going to regret it."

Billy the Kid. I smiled. Why hadn't I thought of that?

We both got out of the truck. The taxi doors popped open and Kate and the kids spilled out, followed by Carlos. He walked around back to get our bags.

"Richy!" Kate called out, sounding suddenly like a young girl.

"Katsup!" he replied.

Siblings and their nicknames. Being an only child, I couldn't relate.

Richard opened the gate and I looked on as he greeted Kate with a big spinning hug. Alex stood off to one side looking unimpressed, but Rachel ran in and wrapped her arms around Richard's legs to make it a group hug.

"Uncle Richy!" she squealed.

"Hey there, Rach! You remember me?"

"Yes," she said.

Carlos deposited our bags beside us in two trips, then he came up to me with an expectant look on his face. "That'll be two hundred and ten."

I could feel my eyes bulge with the price he'd quoted. I was tempted to go check his meter, but thinking back over how long the trip had been, and taking into account that this was an *airport* taxi, I decided to trust him. Even if he'd tacked something onto the price, it couldn't be much. Fishing the bills out of my laptop bag, I handed them over with a grimace. "Thanks, Carlos."

He flashed a grin with a gold tooth in it, and took off like a pirate with his treasure. His tires spat gravel at us as he pulled away.

Richard led Kate and Rachel back to his truck with an arm wrapped around each of their shoulders.

On the way down the driveway, I had to hold Richard's shotgun to keep it out of reach of the kids. I flicked the safety on—privately horrified as I did so that Richard hadn't already done so, and then I hit the action release and pulled back on the action four times fast to eject all the rounds. They fell with metallic thumps at my feet and Richard glared at me.

"You could have just put the safety back on."

"I did, but having a loaded gun around kids is not a good idea—or didn't you know that?"

"I guess I'd better not show you my armory, then," Richard quipped.

"You have an *armory?*" Alexander said in an awed voice.

"You bet," Richard replied. "And now that you're going to be living here, you're going to have to learn how to shoot."

"All right!"

I frowned as I listened to their exchange. Richard made it sound like we were here to stay. I was just about to ask about that, but Kate beat me to it.

"Don't you think this is all being overblown by the media?" she asked. "The president said the temperature is going to drop by twenty degrees. That doesn't sound so bad. So we go down from eighties in the summer to sixties."

Richard pulled to a stop in front of his old

wooden 'decoy' house and unbuckled. Twisting around in his seat to face his sister, he said, "We're talking about a twenty degree drop in the global *average* temperature. The farther north and south you go, the more pronounced that drop will be. Some places around the equator will only be ten degrees colder. Others will be thirty or forty, and when the snow accumulates, we're going to start reflecting more sunlight back into space than usual. At that point, the temperature will drop some more. The oceans will cool, and then things will get much, much worse."

Kate shook her head. "Even thirty degrees less in the middle of summer isn't cold enough for ice and snow to stick around."

Richard's eyes beamed his patented know-it-all look. "During the last ice age global average temperatures were only nine degrees Fahrenheit less than they are now. Twenty degrees less puts the glaciers as far south as Northern Texas, hence why I'm in the southern part. Trust me, we ran all the data a thousand different times, looking for any excuse to hang onto hope. We didn't find any excuses."

"But the president—"

"Is lying," Richard said. "Just like she lied when the news of the rogue first broke. If she told people the truth, the country would burn itself to the ground before the rogue even gets here." Richard opened his door and jumped out. "Come on," he said. "It's time to take a tour of your new home."

Our new home. That resonated, making my stomach churn. What little hope the president had sparked with her latest speech fizzled as Richard's arguments found purchase in my brain. Like most know-it-alls, Richard had an annoying habit of being right. That meant things weren't going back to normal anytime soon.

CHAPTER 13

I soon found out why Richard called his place a *compound*. A chain-link fence with coils of razor wire ran all the way around it. Cameras peered out from the corners of the fence, each one sheltered by a small overhang of aluminum roofing. Three long, rectangular buildings with sloping roofs of glass sat inside the fence, and a concrete tower rose between them with a metal door in the base.

"How did you build all this?" I asked wonderingly, as Richard unlocked a gate in the fence and led us through. I spied a giant propane gas tank, another smaller tank beside it, as well as a vast wood pile. A gleaming platform full of solar panels lay nestled between the greenhouses and behind the tower. I turned to study the greenhouse next to me. It looked much sturdier than the standard glass and aluminum shell. Solid walls rose three feet up, and the sloping glass roof was double-glazed.

"I built it with my government pay-off,"

Richard said.

"Your what?" I asked.

"You can't silence people for free—well, not without killing them, anyway."

I shook my head wonderingly. "How do you sleep at night?"

Richard's eyes flashed. "Don't judge me. They didn't just threaten me. They also threatened you and Kate—your kids, too."

"You can't be serious," Kate said.

I blinked, taken aback. "Who's they?"

"Who do you think?" Richard snapped. "Anyway, it's too late for regrets now. Come on, let me show you to your rooms."

"Please don't tell me we're going to live in a greenhouse," Kate said.

Richard grinned. "Who better to live in a greenhouse than the Greenhouses?" He laughed, but no one else joined in. "Don't worry. The living area is below the lookout tower." He pointed to the solar panels.

That was when I noticed that those panels were mounted on top of a two-foot-high concrete structure. It was a roof. Windows with square panes of glass and thick metal frames ran around the base. The structure was at least as big as one of the greenhouses. I estimated it to be about fifteen hundred square feet. "That's a big basement."

Richard nodded and produced a ring of keys from his pocket. He opened the metal door in the base of the tower with a groan of metal hinges that were badly in need of oil.

We followed him inside, and Richard shut the door behind us. He led the way down a spiral staircase into a semi-finished basement. A long hallway stretched before us, lined with doors to either side, some of them shut, others open to reveal small bedrooms with mattresses lying directly on the floor. The floors were finished, but the walls were not. Yellow insulation packed behind plastic glared at me between wooden beams. Wires and pipes ran along an equally unfinished ceiling that was also packed with insulation. Light sliced in through sky lights and the windows that I'd seen running around the perimeter of the above-ground portion of the structure. The bare bulbs of overhead light sockets hung between the skylights.

"It's not pretty, but it will keep us warm," Richard explained, walking down the hallway.

I passed beneath one of the skylights as I followed him, and noticed that they weren't traditional glass windows, but rather reflective shafts of about a foot in length that ran through the ceiling and had a pane of glass at each end.

Richard saw me examining the skylight and nodded to the ceiling. "Light tubes," he explained. "So we don't need to use the lights during the day." From there he pointed to the nearest open door in the hallway. "There's four bedrooms," he said, turning in a circle to indicate all four doors.

He'd built in just enough space for my family and him. That realization warmed my heart. He wasn't crazy uncle Richard anymore.

"There's a shared bathroom over here," Richard said, moving on. "And this—" he turned to indicate the door opposite the bathroom. "— is the panic room."

Richard led us inside, and I noticed that there were no windows or *light tubes* in here, just an overhead light bulb.

Richard drew our attention to the door. "It's the same door as the one leading outside. You can't cut it, and it can repel a 12-gauge shotgun blast with barely a dent." Richard pointed to a chip in the door's red paint. "I know, because I already tested it."

The panic room had a couple of mattresses on the floor inside, as well as a toilet and a sink, but no privacy to speak of. *We'll just have to turn our backs whenever someone has to go—if we end up in here, that is.* I hoped we never would. Shelves full of canned food and bottled water lined the wall opposite the toilet. A second metal door was at the back of the room. "What's behind there?" I asked, pointing to it.

"The armory."

Richard went over to the toilet and retrieved a hide-a-key box from under the tank. Removing a key from the box, he opened the armory door to reveal a walk-in-closet. The walls were lined with metal shelves full of ammo, while the back wall held guns hanging from metal hooks screwed into a big sheet of plywood that spanned from the floor to the ceiling. I saw automatic rifles, shotguns, scoped rifles, handguns of all different sizes, and a few dozen metal canisters that looked suspiciously like grenades. Suddenly I felt uneasy about staying here with my family.

I jabbed a finger at the metal cylinders. "What are those?"

"IEDs."

"IE..." Kate trailed off.

"Improvised Explosive Devices," I supplied. "What if one of those goes off by accident?"

Richard shook his head. "Relax. You've got to light the fuse to set them off."

"How did you even make them?"

"Fireworks," Richard explained. "I cracked them open and poured out the gunpowder, packing it with nails and screws. They'll kill anything within a two meter radius and injure well beyond that."

"What is all of this *for?*" Kate asked. She stood barring the entrance of the armory to keep our kids out. Alex had his head tucked under one of her arms, staring wide-eyed at all of the weapons. Despite his many protests, Kate had never let me take him with me to the shooting range.

"You've got enough weapons here to start a war," I said.

Richard snorted. "Hardly. I wish I'd stockpiled more to be honest."

"*More?*" Kate echoed. "Why do you even need them?"

Richard looked at her as if the answer should have been obvious. "When everyone out there is freezing and starving to death, and they find out that we have enough supplies down here to last for the next two or three years, you better believe they're going to come knocking on our door. And when they do, they'll be armed to the teeth. This *is* Texas, after all."

Richard waved a hand at the bare concrete walls of the armory and the panic room. "I built this place like a fortress for a good reason. The windows are all barred with quarter-inch steel tubes, and the doors are custom-made with a full inch of layered steel plates. I've got a full surveillance system around the perimeter, and a twenty-foot guard tower overhead with firing angles on the entire compound. Don't think for a second that I designed all of that for nothing. This is our Alamo, and we're going to defend it with our dying breaths if we have to."

"You're going to scare the kids!" Kate left, ushering them out of the panic room before Richard could say anything else.

I winced at the comparison and fixed Richard with a scornful look. "Is that why you built this place outside of San Antonio?"

He shook his head, a grim smile lurking beneath his beard. "Just a coincidence. I didn't think about it until I'd already bought the lot. Come on, I'll show you the rest of the place."

I lingered in the armory as Richard led the way out. *The Alamo. Coincidence or fate?* I followed Richard, hoping we weren't about to repeat history.

CHAPTER 14

—ONE WEEK LATER—
June 8th

I was in the kitchen cleaning fresh-caught fish with Richard. He and I had been out on the lake all morning in his boat. The skin on my face and neck already felt tight and hot with the beginnings of a sunburn. I grimaced. My skin was going to peel for sure. Fans stood around the living area, blasting us from all sides with the combined volume of a propeller plane. Even so, it was still too hot, and the sweat was running in rivers down my front and back. I'd taken my shirt off as soon as we got back, and now it was tied around my waist, catching the sweat before it could trickle down my pants.

"There's nothing to *do* around here!" Alex whined as he flopped down on the living room couch. "And it's too hot! Can't you turn down the thermostat?"

We didn't have much in the way of air conditioning back home, but Texan summers were a lot hotter than Jersey ones. At least we were in a basement. It had to be cooler down here than it would be in an above-ground structure.

Kate looked up from where she and Rachel were coloring with crayons at the dining table. Richard didn't have any coloring books, but Rachel had packed a few of hers and her crayons from home, along with her favorite stuffed animal and doll. I marveled that Kate had managed to fit all of that into Rachel's luggage along with a full wardrobe and winter clothes. Alexander on the other hand, had much more refined interests. He'd been forced to leave his Playstation at home, and his laptop and phone were 'useless pieces of junk' without Internet.

"Why don't you go for a swim?" Kate suggested.

"Boring," Alex huffed.

"You could help us clean these fish," Richard said, holding up hands coated with fish guts.

"Gross," Alex said. His eyes flicked to me. "When are we going home?"

"Alex..." I trailed off. He knew we weren't going home. He was just looking for an argument.

"News flash—the world hasn't ended!" Alex

blurted.

"Nothing has happened yet because that star is still too far away," Richard explained.

"You're just paranoid, Richard," Alex replied.

"*Uncle* Richard," Kate corrected.

Alex went on without skipping a beat, "You've got cameras and fences, guns, and bullet proof doors, and for what? No one is trying to break in here! Why would they? *Anywhere* is better than here!"

"It might seem like that now," Richard said, "but just you wait."

"This is all your fault," Alex replied, glaring at his uncle. "It's your star that's coming to Earth, your paranoia that brought us here, and your hell hole that we're staying in!"

"Alexander Sebastian Willis!" Kate snapped.

"Screw it, I'm out of here!" He jumped up, storming toward the hallway and the curving stairwell beyond.

"Alex, you get back here, right now!" I thundered.

Richard caught my eye and gave his head a slight shake. "Let him be. He can't get into much trouble out there."

I thought about that. The media frenzy had died down over the past week. Life went on. The president had fed the people with enough comfortable lies to keep them satisfied—for now—and the national guard was out everywhere flexing their muscles, just in case. Order had been restored in the cities, and out here in rural Texas, the chaos had never really had a chance to set in. Richard was right. Alexander couldn't get into any trouble out there—besides a sun burn and some mosquito bites.

"Shouldn't you at least go lock the door behind him?" Kate asked.

Richard seemed to consider that. "Yeah, I guess I'd better." He wiped his hands on a towel and took off after Alex.

I watched them go. We were getting complacent. During the day it was easy to forget that we were sitting on enough weapons to arm a whole platoon of Marines. We pushed the truth to the back of our minds, and it festered there. Visions of a bonfire made of human bodies piled to the top of our guard tower danced behind my eyelids at night.

God help us if it came to that.

* * *

"Wait up, Al!" Richard called, breathing hard as he ran to catch up.

Alex bounded up the metal staircase, his feet

setting off echoing peals of thunder inside the tower.

Richard reached the metal door on the ground floor just as Alex was sliding the locking bolts aside. Richard leaned on the railing, gasping for air. His hairy belly shivered with each breath, dark hairs matted and glistening with sweat.

"You've got to check the cameras first," Richard said as he stumbled over to the door. He swiped the touchscreen of a tablet mounted there to wake it up. The tablet showed a live feed from the camera above the door. Brown grass waved in the breeze. Cicadas buzzed like tiny chainsaws through the tinny speakers. "Looks okay..." Richard swiped again, checking another camera, and then once more. "All right. We're good. You know where to find the key to get out of the compound?"

"In the fake rock beside the log..." Alex replied.

"Good. Don't lose it, and make sure you lock the gate again on your way out."

"Sure," Alex said.

Richard turned the mechanical lever inside the door and locking bolts slid away from all sides. "Don't be too long," he said, pushing the door open. "Your mother will worry."

"Whatever." Alex darted out, and a hot breeze

blew in. Dust kicked up by the wind made Richard's mouth taste like chalk, and the pungent aroma of cow manure made him wonder if it was just dust.

Richard watched Alexander hunt for the key beside the log, wondering if the boy's attitude was a sign of things to come.

No, he decided. Alex was a good kid. He was just blowing off steam, and there was plenty of that to go around. The solar panels weren't strong enough to run any air conditioners, and Texan summers were hot—*at least for now,* Richard thought, shutting the front door with an echoing *boom.*

* * *

Crack. Bill Summers lay low in the bushes, silently cursing his stupidity. He'd just snapped a twig. Maybe the kid wouldn't notice.

But he did. He froze and stared hard into the bushes. "Hello?"

Bill held his breath.

"Here boy!" The kid whistled a few times; then waited for a response. Bill smiled. The boy thought he was a dog! Bill's lungs burned for air, but still he held his breath, waiting.

His hand tightened around the butt of his nine millimeter Beretta. The weapon was silenced, so no one would hear if he had to use it, but now wasn't the right time to spring his trap. He wasn't finished with his recon.

The kid snorted and shook his head. Long grass rustled against his legs as he stalked away.

Letting out his breath in a sigh, Bill shook his head. That was too close. He knew better than to make noise on a recon mission. The Army had taught him all about moving stealthily, before he was discharged for *bad conduct*. That's what he got for having sex with his sergeant and assuming that it was a casual fling. All that stuff people said about a woman scorned was true and then some. After she threatened to get him court-martialed on some exaggerated assault and harassment charges, he'd sent naked pictures of her to their entire platoon.

Next stop after that was the *Big Chicken Dinner* (Bad Conduct Discharge). With those charges hanging over his head, it had been hard to find work after the Army, but he'd ultimately found his niche by becoming an enforcer with *Private Security Solutions*. That was more than ten years ago.

Bill's thoughts went to the task at hand. Something sharp was stabbing him in the ribs. He carefully eased onto his side, revealing the jagged ends of the branch he'd snapped earlier. Scowling, he pulled it out and tossed it aside. He was going to have to be more careful if he expected to get the drop on five people all by himself.

In a way, being outnumbered made things easier, though. He just had to pick off one of the kids—or maybe their sweet ass mother—and then use that hostage to manipulate the others. Bill grinned at the thought. If he played it right, they could have some real fun together before anyone even realized she was missing.

CHAPTER 15

Richard, Kate, and I all answered the door together when Alex came back. We stood barring the way with arms crossed and angry looks.

Alex was smiling as we opened the door, but his smile faltered when he saw us. "Is something wrong?" he asked.

"Where have you been?" Kate demanded. "It's been three hours! I've been worried sick!"

"You missed lunch," I added.

"I was in the neighborhood next door... the Hartfords gave me lunch."

"You left the property?" Richard demanded. "And you *spoke* to people?"

"I met a girl named Celine, and —"

Richard grabbed Alex by his collar and yanked him inside.

"Hey!" he protested.

Richard grabbed fistfuls of Alex's shirt and pinned him against the wall. "What did you tell them?" he shouted in my son's face.

"Nothing!" Alex insisted.

"Hey, lay off!" I said, and grabbed Richard by his shoulder to pull him away. He shrugged me off, and I grabbed him in a headlock. "That's enough!

"Stop it!" Kate screamed.

Richard let Alex go, and I withdrew.

"You want to explain that outburst?" I demanded as Richard shut the door, muttering under his breath.

He rounded on me. "If the people in that neighborhood realize that we have a fully-stocked shelter right here next to them, where do you think they'll go when the shit hits the fan?"

I glanced at Alex. "You didn't tell them anything about this place, did you?"

He shook his head quickly.

"What were you doing eating lunch with strangers?" Kate asked in a more even tone.

Alex turned to reveal a bloody gash in his shirt. Kate gasped and rushed over for a better look.

"I scratched my shoulder on my way through Richard's barbed wire fence," Alex explained.

Kate lifted his shirt to reveal that the wound was already bandaged.

"Who fixed you up?" Richard asked, his voice still laced with a hard edge.

"Mrs. Hartford, Celine's mother."

"The barbed wire was rusty, wasn't it?" Kate asked. "We're going to have to get you a tetanus shot."

"Are there any clinics nearby?" I asked Richard.

He shook his head. "No need for that, I have Tetanus boosters here."

I did a double-take. "You do?"

"Of course. Antibiotics and antivenins, too."

"Mommy?" Rachel's voice called up to us from the bottom of the stairs, followed by the soft ringing of her footsteps on the stairs. She stopped at the top of the stairs, clutching her favorite teddy bear to her chest. "Why is everybody shouting?" she asked.

Kate went over and wrapped an arm around her shoulders. "Because we were worried about your big brother, that's why."

"Well, come on, kid, we'd better go inject you," Richard prompted.

"Wait. There's something else—" Alex began.

Everyone looked to him.

"While I was over there, the TV was on, and I saw the news. They said something about fleets sailing through the Caribbean to Venezuela. They also said that Russia and Europe are sending soldiers to Africa and the Middle East, and that China is sending troops to Vietnam, I think."

"It's started already," Richard said.

All eyes turned to him next.

"What's started?" Kate asked.

"World War III."

* * *

That night I lay in bed with Kate, staring up at the ceiling. Ever since we'd arrived at Richard's shelter we'd begun sleeping in the same bed again—out of necessity more than choice, although I suppose I could have bunked in the panic room.

"Are you okay?" Kate asked in a quiet voice.

I rocked my head back and forth and rubbed my eyes. "I can't sleep. I've got too much on my mind."

"Oh?" Kate's lips curved wryly. "Maybe I can do something to relieve your stress?" She began running a hand lightly over my chest, then ducked it under the covers and grabbed me below my waist. My body reacted instantly, but my mind tugged the other way. The gray matter won, and I removed her hand. *You can't fix adultery with make up sex.*

"I keep thinking about what Alex saw on the news today," I said. "All the nations with the biggest militaries are getting ready to invade their smaller, weaker neighbors."

"Will that affect us?" Kate asked.

"I don't know. Richard's place is built completely off the grid, and we're far enough from major cities that I don't think we'll become collateral damage. I suspect we'll be fine as long as our supplies last, but after that..."

Kate nodded slowly, and I rolled over to look her in the eyes. "I guess some small part of me was still clinging to the hope that Richard is wrong about what's coming, but if our government is willing to invade Venezuela, then this isn't just about colder winters and shorter summers. It's about our survival and where we're going to put three hundred million people when they're all forced out of their homes."

Kate bit her bottom lip, looking both vulnerable and sexy at the same time. On impulse I reached a hand behind her ear and stroked the back of her neck. Her eyes widened and her lips parted, but she said nothing. I locked my hurt and anger away for the moment, and leaned in for a kiss. It was one of those melt-my-insides kind of kisses that came once in a while to remind me how much I loved my wife.

Kate pulled away sharply, her eyes suddenly wide.

"What's wrong?"

"I thought I heard something."

I glanced at the door. "It's probably just Richard getting up for a midnight snack. Or one of the kids going to the bathroom."

Kate sat up and shook her head. "No," she whispered. "It was metallic, like footsteps on the stairs."

"Well, maybe it was Richard going up to the lookout tower?"

"In the middle of the night? Why would he do that?"

My mind raced. I thought about the panic room; then I thought about the fact that Rachel's and Alex's rooms were close to the stairs. If someone had broken in, they'd reach our kids first.

More rational thoughts chased those fears away. How could someone break in? The door was too strong and it was locked from the inside.

"I'm going to go take a look."

"Logan... be careful."

I opened the drawer in the nightstand beside our mattress and withdrew a nine millimeter pistol that Richard had given me. "Stay here."

* * *

Bill waited for the boy to get out of earshot before creeping in through the open gate in the chain link fence. He'd brought wire-cutters, but why ruin a perfectly good fence if he didn't have to? He might need it later. Swinging the gate partially shut behind him, he made sure to leave it in exactly the same position that he'd found it. When that boy came back from whatever he'd gone out to do, Bill wanted to be sure he found everything just the way he'd left it. Creeping up to the red door in the base of the tower where he'd seen that kid emerge a few minutes ago, he tried the door handle. To his amazement, it turned and the door popped open. The door was *heavy,* and obviously custom made. The hinges groaned as Bill swung it open. He winced, and quickly stepped inside. His feet *clanged* on the metallic landing of a spiral staircase behind the door. *Shit.* He eased the door shut behind him and worked hard to control his breathing. He froze and listened for any sign that the people inside had heard him. His silenced Beretta felt suddenly cold and heavy in his hand. Stairs leading down revealed what he'd already guessed—this was some kind of bunker. Stairs leading up must give access to the top of the tower. A lookout post. Bill had to hand it to whoever had built this place. It was highly defensible—*assuming you keep the doors locked.* Bill smirked at that. He was just about to start down the stairs to find his hostage when he heard a door opening, followed by muffled footsteps. Bill thought about dashing outside, but that would be the first place they'd look when they found the door open. Instead, he crept up, making sure to keep his footsteps perfectly quiet. He encountered a locked metal hatch at the top. It was locked from the inside with a series of sliding bolts, so he could definitely open it, but he thought better of that. Opening the hatch would make too much noise.

Relying on the shadows at the top of the stairs to conceal him, Bill sat on the second-highest step and peered through the railing to the landing below. Someone was standing there, at the front door. A yellow bug light revealed that it was Logan, and he had a gun of his own.

Bill tightened his grip on his pistol. If Logan decided to come up the stairs he'd have no choice but to use it.

* * *

Holding my gun in both hands, I peered up the stairwell from the bottom to check for intruders. I couldn't see anyone, so I stalked quietly up the stairs to the landing. The first thing I did was check the door. It was slightly ajar and unlocked. My heart kicked inside my chest and adrenaline tingled in my fingertips. Feeling watched, I spun around, looking for whoever had broken in.

The stairs were made of two separate spirals spanning three floors, one below and two above to reach the top of the guard tower. I looked up, but I couldn't see anything at the top of the stairs. It was too dark. I aimed my gun through the center of the stairwell and started up the stairs.

"Hello?" I called. "I have a gun!"

No answer.

If there was someone hiding at the top of the stairwell, they could definitely see me, but I couldn't see them. That put me at a disadvantage.

"Logan!" Kate yelled up to me. "Alex is not in his room!"

I lowered my gun, and stopped climbing the stairs. "Damn it. He must have sneaked out!"

Footsteps rang on the stairs below. I went back down and met Kate on the landing. Setting the safety on my Smith and Wesson, I slipped the gun into my pajamas pocket. It lay cold and heavy against my thigh. I grabbed my shoes from the rack beside the door and pulled them on. Gesturing to the door, I said, "He left the door open on his way out." Not that he had a choice. He didn't have his own key, and there was no way to lock the door behind him without one.

"Where do you think he went?" Kate asked.

I only needed half a second to think about that. "To see that girl again, where else?"

"In the middle of the night? What could they possibly be do..." she trailed off. "You'd better find him. If he gets some girl pregnant we're going to have a whole new set of problems to worry about."

"No kidding." I pushed the door open, and moonlight swept in.

Richard came pounding up the stairs, bare-chested and brandishing his pump-action shotgun. "What's going on?"

"Mommy?" Rachel asked from below the stairs.

"It's okay, sweetheart, go back to bed!" Kate called back.

"Well?" Richard intoned. He jerked his chin to the open door. "What's going on?"

I explained what we'd heard and Alex's absence from his room.

Richard blew out a sigh. "Fantastic. The world is ending and our biggest threat is a horny teenager."

"I've got to go find him," I said.

Richard nodded. "Good luck. Hit the buzzer when you come back and I'll open up for you."

"Got it," I said, and then darted out into the night.

CHAPTER 16

I found the chain link gate unlocked and cracked open, just like the front door, but since Alex *did* have access to a key for the padlock, he'd left the gate open out of negligence, not necessity.

As I ran through the moonlit field around Richard's place, my gun bounced in my loose-fitting pajamas pocket. I withdrew the weapon with a grimace, suddenly wishing I'd thought to give it to Kate. Busting up my son's midnight tryst with a loaded gun in my hand was bound to make its way to the ears of the girl's parents. If I was lucky maybe she wouldn't say anything in order to avoid having to explain what she was doing sneaking out in the middle of the night.

As I ran, it dawned on me that Richard's property was almost five acres, and my son could be literally anywhere on or around it. For all I knew he'd sneaked into the girl's house. If that was the case, I'd have to go knocking on doors until someone could tell me where she lived. Except that walking down the street of some rural Texan neighborhood in the middle of the night, with a gun, was a good way to get my head blown off.

Besides, I wasn't a hundred percent sure that I wanted to ruin the one good thing my son had found here. Not until I knew more, anyway. Slowing my pace to a brisk walk, I tried to put myself in Alex's shoes. If I were a horny teenager, where would I go? What would I do?

It didn't take me long to come up with an answer. The lake. It was a good excuse to get a girl to take off her clothes. I turned down toward the lake and ran.

* * *

Bill waited until the door shut with another rumble of protest. The bare-chested ape pulled a lever on the inside of the door and locking bolts slid into the frame on all sides. He'd gotten lucky. He'd been planning to hide inside the compound until morning, to wait for someone to come outside and then ambush them, but finding the door open had accelerated his plans. Now he was inside, and the occupants of the bunker thought they were safe. It was perfect.

Both the hairy ape and Logan's hot wife descended the stairs. Bill listened to the woman reassuring her daughter. There was nothing to worry about, she said. They were perfectly safe. Bill heard an interior door click shut, but the voices continued. The ape had gone back to bed. Another door *clicked*. The voices were muffled now. Bill started down the stairs, being careful to keep his boots from clanging on the metal steps. Different scenarios raced through his head. The safest thing would be to shoot them all now and then finish off Logan and his son when they came back.

But that left no room for more enjoyable pursuits. Logan's wife would make for good company while the world went to shit. Her daughter looked to be about six years old. She'd be a dead weight, but the thought of shooting a little kid made his insides twist. Besides, the mother needed a reason to behave. Bill nodded to himself. The girl and her mother would live.

He reached the landing at the front door and continued down into the bunker. A hallway with doors on either side came into view. All was silent, and the hall was dimly lit. One of the nearest doors opened, and Bill froze. Logan's wife hadn't seen him yet. She was backing out of the room, her eyes still on her daughter.

Don't turn around, he thought at her. *Don't—*

But then she did. Their eyes locked for a frozen instant, and then she screamed and darted back inside her daughter's room. Bill cursed under his breath. Another door opened. *Chuk-chuk.*

"Kate?" Ape-man's hairy chest and belly came into view. Instinct took over, and Bill squeezed off two shots in quick succession—*plap, plap.* The silencer did its job.

Ape-man took a bullet in the shoulder and one in the leg, jerking in time to each. *BOOM!* He fired the shotgun, but his aim was off, and the slug ricocheted off the stairs behind Bill. His ears rang painfully from the noise. Ape-man collapsed, struggling to reload the shotgun with one hand. Bill grinned as he swept in for the kill. He reached the wounded man's side. Ape-man's eyes were squinting from the pain, his chest rising and falling with shuddery breaths. His shotgun lay on the floor beside him. Bill aimed his gun at the man's head. "Night night."

"Wait," the man said.

Bill arched an eyebrow. Then came another deafening *BOOM!* and his left foot exploded with a searing heat. Bill fell over, howling from the pain.

* * *

When I reached the pebbly excuse for a beach around Calaveras Lake, I had to crawl through the barbed wire fence and ended up scratching my leg. I bit back a curse and went jogging down the beach until I heard laughter and chattering voices. I picked out Alex's voice, as well as a girl's. Walking toward the sound, I spied two heads bobbing and splashing in the water. Then I came upon two mounds of clothes. They'd gone skinny dipping. A smile touched my lips as I remembered my own youth. In my experience, skinny dipping in cold water didn't result in anything else. The cold was a good inhibitor, and I could see even from here that my son and the girl were keeping some distance from each other—probably treading water to stay afloat. I didn't need to break this up and embarrass Alex. Not yet, anyway. Instead, I walked up the beach and sat down in the shadows of an overhanging tree. My pajamas were dark gray and black, so I doubted they'd see me skulking there.

The laughter and chattering went on for a while. It quieted a few times and I saw the two bobbing heads come together in what I assumed to be a kiss. They broke apart just as quickly, however. It was all quite innocent as far as I could tell—besides the fact that they were naked. I'd have to have a talk with Alex about abstinence, and then give him some protection—because me talking to him wasn't going to be enough.

After about five more minutes the two of them came swimming in to shore and darted out of the water, yelping and laughing from the cold. I looked away to give them some privacy, even though I couldn't see more than their silhouettes. This time I *heard* them kissing. I glanced back in their direction to make sure there wasn't anything more happening between them. They were both still half-naked. Romeo was at second base, and Juliet showed no signs of stopping him. This was getting into dangerous territory. I was just about to go break them up when Juliet showed some sense and pushed my son's hands away.

"I have to go home," she said.

"Are you sure?" Alex asked.

"Yes." She pulled on what looked like half of a shirt. "But this was fun. Thank you."

Alex pulled on his shirt next. "I'll walk you home." They walked right by me, oblivious, and I saw that they were holding hands. Oddly cutesy after what I'd just seen.

I waited and trailed behind, giving them plenty of space, both to give them some privacy and to make sure they didn't hear my footsteps. Eventually we came to a cul-de-sac. Massive homes flanked that street on either side. A pang of envy hit me, and I thought about my own big house, sitting empty in Jersey and squatting on all of our cash.

Alex said goodbye and started back across the empty field between Richard's place and Juliet's neighborhood. I hurried after him, no longer taking pains to be quiet. He stopped and turned at the sound of my thumping footsteps just as I ran up behind him.

"Hey," I whispered.

"Dad? What the—"

"You left the door open."

"What are you doing out here? Did you *follow* me?"

"Not exactly. I went looking for you."

He spotted the pistol in my hand. "With a *gun?*" he demanded. "Are you insane?"

I smiled and shook my head. "We heard you leave and we thought it was an intruder. I took the gun with me by mistake."

Alex snorted. "Nobody wants to break *in* to Alcatraz, Dad."

I laughed lightly at that, and we started walking again. "Well, you might have a point there," I said. "So who's the girl?"

"Were you watching us?"

"I didn't really have a choice. It was that or break you two up, and I figured you'd rather I wait."

Alex made an irritated noise and shook his

head. "You could have just gone home."

"And leave you to impregnate some girl?"

"Seriously? I'm not stupid. And we didn't do anything."

"Well, I hope not. But it's better to be safe—if you know what I mean?"

"Even the frogs know what you mean."

They were chirping loudly along with the crickets.

I shrugged. "Better to have protection and not use it than need it and not have it. That said, you're way too young to even think about using it."

"Dad! Seriously!"

I laughed again, nervously this time. "So who's the girl?"

"Celine."

The way that name rolled off Alex's tongue, I could tell that he was smitten. He might be a dumb, horny teenager, but he wasn't as cool as he liked to think.

I nodded. "I'm glad you've found something down here to keep you going. This hasn't been easy for any of us, but... it's going to get better."

"You mean before it gets worse?" Alex demanded. "That star hasn't even arrived yet and we're already hiding underground."

We reached the barbed wire fence around

Richard's property. "Alex." I turned to face him, my tone deadly serious. "You saw what they were saying on the news today. World War III is about to start. I can't think of a better place to be when that happens than an underground bunker with enough supplies to last for a few years. We're the lucky ones, even if it doesn't seem like that now."

"What about Celine? Her family seems to be doing okay. They're going to put bars on their windows and fill their garage with food. Why couldn't we get a place like theirs and do the same thing?"

"Because we already have a house, and we won't make any money if we try to sell it now. And I don't have a job, so no bank will give us a loan. We don't have any way to buy a house like theirs. But anyway, Celine's home needs electricity, and it relies on municipal water. I'd be willing to bet they don't even have indoor heating. It's going to be hell for them when the temperature starts to drop."

"Isn't Texas supposed to stay warm?" Alex asked.

I nodded. "Warm enough to survive, but that doesn't mean you won't get cold. Look, just trust me. It doesn't get any better than where we are right now."

Alex snorted and I held the barbed wire fence

open for him to climb through. He did the same for me on the other side, and we started across Richard's property. I wrapped my left arm around Alex's shoulders—the one not holding the gun. "We're going to be okay, son."

He just sighed, resigned to his fate. I suppose I couldn't blame him for complaining. He was grieving the loss of our old life. Truth be told, so was I.

* * *

Bill cursed violently. His foot was okay, but he'd lost the tip of at least one toe. He could see the white of bone gleaming through his ruined boot. "You dumb fucker!" Bill pushed himself up into a sitting position and grabbed the shotgun barrel to yank the weapon away from Ape-man. It didn't take much. He was obviously too weak to put up a fight. Unlike Bill, he'd probably never been shot before.

Using the shotgun like a cane, with the barrel facing the floor, Bill got up and hopped over to Ape-man's side. His squinting eyes widened and flicked to the shotgun.

"Don't even think about it!"

Leaning against the wall and balancing on the heel of his injured foot, Bill lifted his good foot and stomped on the man's face. Ape-man's nose went *crunch* and more blood gushed. He cried out weakly, but then his head lolled to one side—either unconscious or dead.

Turning around, Bill came face to face with Logan's wife. She was standing behind him, holding his Beretta.

"Drop the gun!" she said in a trembling voice. Using her free hand she swiped trickling tears from her eyes.

Bill was about to do as she said, but then he noticed how she was holding his gun—one-handed—and she wasn't even aiming at him, although she probably thought she was. He smiled and shook his head. Leaning against the wall once more, he yanked his shotgun cane up and pumped the action—*chuk-chuk.* "You first," he said, and began hobbling toward her.

"Stay away!" She brushed away more tears. "I'll shoot!"

"No you won't." He took a long step toward her, wincing at the blinding burst of pain from his injured foot.

Plap. The woman pulled the trigger. He was surprised she'd had the strength with just one hand on the gun. The bullet nicked Bill's arm. He hissed and gritted his teeth.

"Mommy?" A little girl's head popped out into

the hallway behind her.

The woman glanced over her shoulder. "Get back in your room, now!"

Taking advantage of her distraction, Bill lunged. Blinding pain erupted in his foot, but he managed to grab the pistol and wrestle it away. Pocketing the weapon, he delivered a roundhouse slap that sent the woman sprawling. The little girl screamed and slammed her door. Bill loomed over the sobbing woman. She began scuttling away, and he hobbled after, using the shotgun as a cane once more. When he grew tired of the chase, he jerked the shotgun up and aimed it at her chest. "Enough."

The woman froze. "What do you want?"

Bill smiled and produced a roll of duct tape from his cargo pants. Her eyes widened with horror. Funny how the thought of becoming a hostage scares people more than getting killed.

"At least you're going to live," he said.

Glancing at his injured foot, she jumped up from the floor and made a run for it. She reached the door to her daughter's room and jiggled the handle.

It was locked. Sobbing, she pounded on the door. "Rachel!"

Bill smiled anew and dropped the duct tape at

his feet to aim the shotgun properly once more. "Get back over here."

She stepped away from the door just as her daughter opened it. A tear-streaked face popped out. "Mommy?" The girl saw him and froze.

Bill leaned against the wall again and kicked the tape toward the woman. "Tie up your daughter."

"No," she said in a shaking voice.

Bill aimed the shotgun just over her head and pulled the trigger.

BOOM! The sound was tremendous in the enclosed space. The mother jumped, and the kid screamed.

"Now!" Bill yelled to hear himself over the ringing in his ears.

CHAPTER 17

We reached the chain link fence around the compound and this time I made sure I locked it behind us. Alex went to put the key back in the fake rock by the log.

"I can't find it," he said.

"Look harder," I suggested.

Not waiting for him, I walked on to the guard tower. Moonlight gleamed on the pebbly ground. I rang the buzzer to let Richard know we were back and then waited for him to come open the door. That door was too thick to hear much on the other side, but I could have sworn I heard the *chuk-chuk* of Richard's shotgun.

I froze. Why would he answer the door with a loaded gun? He always checked the cameras first to see who was there, so he'd know whether or not it was us. I heard locking bolts sliding away. Coming to a quick decision, I darted around the corner of the tower. I saw Alex crossing over to the door and waved to him. He stopped and stared at me. Then came the groan of hinges, followed by, "Don't move a muscle, kid." Horror sliced through me. That voice was vaguely familiar, but from where? The guy from Newark. My insides churned and adrenaline sparked in my extremities. Kate and Rachel were inside with him. Richard, too. My mind raced through a dozen horrible possibilities in the span of just a few seconds.

Alex couldn't have been more than twelve feet away from me, the intruder even less, but I was hiding around the corner and behind the door, so he couldn't see me. I raised my pistol and flicked off the safety.

"Where's your father, kid?"

"Who are you?" Alex demanded.

"You don't remember me? I'm Bill. Now answer the damn question."

"I don't know. I thought he was here."

"Well, he's not. Walk toward me. Real slow, with your hands up."

Alex did as he was told, his eyes flicking to me as he started forward.

I gave my head a slight shake.

"What are you looking at? Come to think of it, how'd you ring the doorbell from all the way over there?"

"Dad, run!" Alex said. He hit the ground.

BOOM! The shotgun went off, and my heart seized in my chest.

But then Alex bounced up, his shoes spitting gravel. *Chuk-chuk.* The door swung wide, and a shotgun barrel swept into line with my head. I ducked behind the corner of the tower. *BOOM!* A chunk of concrete exploded beside me, the pulverized debris pelting my arm with a fierce wash of fire.

"Come out and play, dickhead!"

I ran around the side of the tower, my heart pounding. Where was Alex? Was he okay?

I stopped at the back of the tower and listened. My ears were ringing and the crickets were the only thing I could hear. I couldn't stay where I was. Bill could come around from either side and he'd see me right away, whereas I'd have to turn my head in both directions to be sure of seeing him. Spying the roof full of solar panels in front of me, I remembered that it was about two feet off the ground. The solar panels added an extra foot. That was enough to provide cover.

I ran along the side of the roof, crouching as I went.

"You're louder than an elephant!" Bill crowed.

BOOM! I braced myself for a slug to go tearing through me, but instead I heard a metallic shearing noise. He'd shot out one of the solar panels. *Chuk-chuk.*

I darted around the back of the shelter and peered over the top. He was standing where I'd been a moment ago at the back of the tower. I could see that he was leaning heavily against the wall.

Richard. He must have got in a shot before giving up his gun. I grimaced at the thought of what that might mean for my brother-in-law.

"I've got your wife and your little girl down stairs," Bill said. "If you want to see them alive, you'd better throw your gun away and come over here."

I was just taking aim with my gun when he pushed off the wall of the guard tower and ducked down behind the solar panels.

"By the way, at this distance, and in this piss poor lighting, a gun like yours isn't going to kill me. It's just gonna make me mad. Mine on the other hand, will gut you like a fish."

I heard a tell-tale metallic groan, followed by a heavy *thunk. The door. Good thinking Alex!*

"Shit!" Bill popped back out of cover and went limping around the tower, using his shotgun like a cane. I jumped up too and took aim at his back.

Bang! His right shoulder jerked with the

impact and he fell over cursing. A split second later he was back on his feet. *BOOM!*

"What did I tell you!" he screamed. "Now you're dead you dumb fuck!" *Chuk-chuk.* He fired again and concrete exploded in my face. The fragments stung my eyes and blinded me. I dropped my gun and clawed at my eyes to clear them. The gun was useless if I couldn't see to aim it.

My ears were ringing too hard to hear, but through my tears I saw a blurry shape appear standing over me. I groped around for my gun, but Bill kicked it away and thrust the barrel of the shotgun in my face.

"Say cheese!" *Click.* Bill dropped another f-bomb and threw the weapon away. "Your lucky day, maggot. I'm gonna have to do this the hard way." He shifted his grip on the weapon, wielding it like a club. "Batter up!"

Just then came the echoing report of a rifle. Bill's left arm jerked with an impact, and he spun around like a ballerina.

"Get him, Dad!" Alex called down to me from the tower. He'd gone up and found the hunting rifle that Richard left up there for emergencies.

I jumped to my feet, but Bill spun back the other way, whipping his shotgun around so fast that it whistled. *Clack!*

A home run. I was outta there. Darkness folded around me, and sucked me under.

CHAPTER 18

I awoke to the sound of screaming sirens. My eyes cracked open and pain erupted in the side of my head. Kate and Rachel were there in the back of the ambulance with me.

"Kate," I mumbled. "You're okay."

Kate grabbed my hand.

"Daddy!" Rachel bounced over to me and tried to give me a hug, but one of the EMTs pushed her back.

"Please keep your daughter away, ma'am."

Kate nodded and quickly moved to restrain Rachel.

"What happened?" I searched my wife's face. Her eyes were red and puffy from crying. I felt a tickling around my head and reached up to scratch the itch. That was when I noticed the thick bandage.

Another EMT pulled my hand away. "Don't touch the dressing, sir."

"What happened?" I asked.

"You don't remember?" Kate asked. "Alex said that monster hit you in the head with Richard's shotgun."

I didn't remember getting hit in the head, but I did remember Bill. "Did Alex... kill him?"

Kate shook her head. "He got away."

"How? We locked the fence."

"He shot the lock with his pistol."

"Damn it." Then again, I was glad that he'd decided to make a run for it. Better that than stay and have a shootout with my son. Come to think of it—"Where is Alex?"

"He's in the other ambulance with Richard." Kate's mouth turned down, and she looked like she was about to start sobbing, but she pulled it together. "He feels responsible for what happened."

"And Richard?"

"Please try to save your strength," one of the EMTs chided. Rounding on my wife, the EMT said, "You shouldn't be talking to him right now. There's a reason I didn't want you to ride in the back."

"We don't have another way to get to the hospital!" Kate snapped.

"Your husband's welfare is my primary concern. Not family reunions."

I felt my ire rising with that exchange. I was just about to give the pimple-faced kid a piece of my mind when a stabbing headache stopped me. I gasped from the pain. I'd probably better save all the pieces of my mind for now.

"You see?" pimple-face said, noticing the look on my face. "Please sit down, ma'am."

"Richard got shot," Kate replied, ignoring the kid and staring at me with trembling lips and welling eyes. "In two places. And that monster stomped on his face. His nose is shattered. He's in critical condition."

"Shit. And they let Alex ride with him?"

"Up front, not in the back," Pimple-face chimed in. "Sir, I need you to relax and stop talking, right now. Your vitals are rising, and that's only going to put more pressure on your brain. Do you understand?"

I nodded once.

"Good."

A burning need to urinate struck me. "How far is it? I have to use the bathroom."

"That's the diuretics doing their job. We're about twenty minutes away. Can you hold it? If not, we have a bucket you can use."

I was bursting. Twenty minutes sounded like an eternity. "Bucket," I croaked.

EMTs scurried about, and I winced as the ambulance went over a bump that sent a jolt through my aching head. When it came time to use the bucket Kate turned Rachel away so that I'd have some privacy. One of the EMTs held me steady while the other one pulled down my pants. The sheer indignity of it was infuriating, but I had bigger things to worry about. The EMTs sealed the bucket and went back to checking my vitals.

It seemed like a *long* ride to the hospital. When we arrived, I was whisked straight on through, while my family was forced to stay in the waiting room. I overheard the doctor talking to the EMTs as they walked me down the hall. Pimple-face said that I should go to the ICU. Something about a subdural hematoma. Another gurney went racing past mine. It was Richard. I caught a glimpse of his injuries. He was all bandaged up—head, shoulder, and leg. My guts clenched when I saw how pale and waxy his skin looked. He went directly into surgery while I went on to the ICU. I remembered Kate had said he'd been shot. They probably still had to remove the bullets. How long had it been since he'd been shot? How much blood had he lost? What if he didn't make it?

My thoughts twisted with horror for more than just the sentimental reasons. Richard was our guide and mentor for the dark times ahead. He was the survivalist, not me or Kate. I didn't even know how to grow food in his greenhouses, let alone what to do to keep the shelter warm when the snow started to fall. We hadn't gone over any of those things with him yet.

Come on, Richard, I thought. *Don't die on us now.*

CHAPTER 19

"**Y**ou're a very lucky man, Mr. Greenhouse," the doctor said.

I looked on with Rachel and Alex as the doctor gave Richard and my wife care instructions for his injuries. Richard's broken nose was set, his shoulder and leg bandaged and the bullets removed.

I'd been discharged just this morning, thank God. We didn't have the money for a longer stay. As it was, I was going to have to get to a bank and withdraw a good chunk of our savings to pay for this.

A nurse wheeled Richard out of the hospital and waited with us for a self-driving Uber. When the vehicle arrived, the nurse helped us get Richard inside. The hospital had provided him with a cane, but he wasn't strong enough to walk around with it yet.

The ride back to Richard's place was a long one, as usual, but thanks to the self-driving car we had all the privacy we needed to talk.

Richard's eyes found Alex and he glared. Like most self-driving vehicles, the seats in the back faced each other.

"I'm sorry, Uncle Richard," Alex said for the umpteenth time.

"Not sorry enough." Richard's voice was nasal and muffled by his broken nose. He nodded slowly and his jaw clenched. He was definitely holding a grudge, or maybe it was the pain-killers wearing off. "I'd give you each your own key, but then what happens if one of you gets taken hostage?" Richard's gaze flicked to Kate. She'd already told me how she and Rachel had been tied up with duct tape. The thought of whatever Bill had been planning for them made my blood boil.

"We need a plan to avoid these types of situations going forward," I said. "That guy is still out there, and not only does he know where we live, but now he also knows how well we've prepared."

"So do the police and the EMTs," Kate said.

Richard glanced sharply at her. This was obviously news to him. "What do the police know?"

"They came to question me. I had to tell them what happened and where," Kate said. "It's hospital policy to report gunshot wounds."

"Did they go investigate?"

Kate hesitated, and then shook her head. "I don't know."

"Let me guess, you left the front door wide open."

"Because we don't have the key," Kate replied.

"You could have taken it out of my pocket!" Richard roared.

Tears welled in Kate's eyes. "We were in a hurry. I was arguing with them about letting us ride in the ambulances, and you were both unconscious. You almost died!"

"And now you've killed us all," Richard said, nodding agreeably.

"Hey, take it easy," I said. "It's not her fault."

Richard rounded on me, eyes flashing. "Don't you get it? Billy the Kid found out about our shelter and look what happened next. Now a handful of EMTs and who knows how many policemen know about it too."

"They're *police*," I said. "Not thugs."

"What happens when their backs are to the wall?" Richard challenged. "Don't fool yourself.

Police make great thugs." Looking back to Alex, he said. "From now on, we have a curfew. No one goes out after dark."

"What? That's ridiculous!"

"If you don't like the rules, you're welcome to find someplace else to live." He glanced my way. "That goes for all of you."

I bristled at that. "Hey, if you don't want us, just say the word and we'll be gone."

Richard shook his head. "I didn't say that, but having a couple of years' worth of food and supplies stored up isn't going to do us any good if we're all dead in a couple of months. From now on, the rules are simple. No one goes out after dark. We always lock the doors behind us. The keys will be hidden, not kept on us—in case we run into trouble while we're out. And finally, we always check the cameras before opening the door. Is everyone clear?"

I nodded. Kate's head bobbed along with Alex's, and Rachel said, "Crystal clear," in a tiny voice that sounded far too serious for her age.

I didn't like Richard's attitude or his tone, but I had to admit his rules made sense. The world was gearing up for war, and so were we.

* * *

Hours later we were all sitting in the living

room, *sans* the kids, who were in their rooms resting. We were all grateful to come home and find that there wasn't any police tape waiting for us. It didn't look like they'd been by to investigate either, despite Richard's concerns. I figured since no one had been killed, they might not be allowed to search the scene without our permission. Either that, or local law enforcement was overrun and our case was a low priority—again, probably because it wasn't a homicide case.

Richard was sitting on the couch, busy with his laptop. He'd been there for over an hour already, staring fixedly at his screen. I wondered what could be so absorbing and went over to take a look.

His screen was filled with a colorful graph and numbers as well as a black box full of scrolling text, or maybe that was computer code.

"What is that?" I asked.

"Radio waves detected from the rogue star," Richard replied. "I'm running a pattern matching algorithm to see if I can find something."

I shook my head. "I don't get it. What kind of pattern?"

"One that might indicate intelligent life."

Kate came over to join me in looking over her brother's shoulder. "But it's not, right? They found a natural explanation."

"It can be hard to rule out natural causes. The signal is periodic and it seems to have structure, which was enough for people to assume it was ETI before they knew about the rogue star."

"ETI?" Kate asked.

"Extraterrestrial intelligence," Richard said. He went on, "The rogue may be naturally emitting EM in the radio spectrum, but there could also be intelligent aliens in orbit around it who are transmitting. In that case, the radio waves would overlap and blur together across different frequencies, exactly like we're seeing here. In my opinion, the only way we'll know for sure if someone's out there is if we send our own message. If we get an answer, we'll know it's ETI."

I considered that. "Wouldn't it be just as hard to classify a subsequent message?"

Richard shook his head. "Not necessarily. The first message might not have been directed at us, in which case the information it carried was designed to be interpreted by them, not us. Even considering all of the potential barriers to communication between us and an intelligent alien race, it should be easy enough to send a message that cannot be mistaken for natural emissions. Interpreting the message might well prove to be impossible, but the very existence of the signal would say something all by itself, the cosmic equivalent of—Hello, I am here."

It all sounded pretty far fetched to me, but I could hear the excitement in Richard's voice. He believed this was a real possibility, and more than that, he was hoping for it. "You want it to be aliens. Why?"

He glanced over his shoulder, grinning out of the corner of his mouth. "Because if they can survive in the cold, dark void between stars, then they've perfected a way to live without solar radiation, and that's exactly what everyone on Earth needs right now. If they come visit us here, maybe they can help."

I snorted and shook my head. "You mean if they don't decide to kill us all and take our planet for themselves."

"Well, yeah, there's that," Richard conceded. He put his laptop aside with a sigh, and then used his cane to ease himself up from the couch, grunting and panting as he did so.

"Let me help you," Kate said and rounded the couch to grab his arm.

Richard's gaze found mine. "You probably think I'm crazy."

I smiled. "A little."

"Well, if it makes you feel better, I probably

am."

"What do you need?" Kate asked. "You don't have to get up. I can get it for you."

"I need the toilet," Richard replied.

"Oh. I'll help you get there."

Richard nodded agreeably, then glanced at me. "Can you believe that jackass shot the arm I use to wipe?" He shook his head ruefully. "You'd be surprised how hard it is to re-learn such a simple task."

I frowned at the scatological talk, and my gaze slid away, back to Richard's computer. A message popped up on the screen.

"Richard, something popped up on your screen."

"What's it say?" he asked.

"It says *Match Found.*"

Richard hobbled back over to the couch faster than I'd thought him capable. Flopping down, he grabbed his laptop and clicked past the message to study a series of single digit numbers with lots of decimal places on a black and white screen.

"This is unbelievable," Richard whispered.

My heart began to race. "What is it?"

"The signal. The time interval between high-energy pulses was exactly the same as the propagation delay. In fact..." Richard busied

— 162 —

himself with what looked like a math program on his computer, typing in numbers furiously.

"Yes!" He whooped and laughed, slapping his good leg.

Kate and I traded a look. "What's going on?" I asked.

Richard twisted around in his seat, wincing as he did so. There were tears leaking from the corners of his green eyes, and they were dancing with child-like wonder. "The delay between the pulses," he began breathlessly. "Initially it was one point zero nine five days. That's the same amount of time it would have taken for the second pulse to travel from them to us. The interval between the second and third pulses was a little less—one point zero nine *one* days—and that difference corresponds *exactly* to the reduction in signal delay due to the rogue star's velocity and the distance it traveled during the first delay."

My brain hurt just thinking about what Richard was trying to say. I couldn't see the significance, but I could see from Richard's reaction that this must have something to do with clarifying whether or not the signals were natural.

"The pulses are ongoing," Richard said when we didn't immediately react with whoops of delight as he had. "The intervals vary so slightly that it was easy to assume we were looking at interference from some kind of orbital debris around the star, but the interval is decaying at a set rate that's directly proportional to the velocity of the rogue. That's too much of a coincidence. Those high-energy spikes are messages from ETI! They have to be."

I still wasn't buying it. "Is there any way you can put that in layman's terms for us?"

Wide-eyed and pale, Kate nodded slowly.

Richard appeared to think about it for a second. "They sent their first message, right? Then they waited the exact amount of time it would take for us to receive that message before sending a second one. They did the same thing with the third and the fourth messages, waiting just over a day between messages. They've done that for the past month, ever since we started picking up the signals.

"They used the interval between transmissions to communicate with us. The physical nature of the signals, regardless of their possible content, is encoded with information that we should recognize: their distance from us, which we can calculate using the speed of light and the delay between pulses, and their relative inbound velocity, which we can calculate by how much the delay between pulses is changing over time."

"But what does that *mean?*" Kate pressed.

Richard's eyes sparkled on either side of his nose splint. "If I had to translate, it would go something like this: Hello, if you can read this, then you know we're coming, and how soon we'll be there, so get ready."

CHAPTER 20

Déjà vu struck me as I sat at the gate with my family, waiting for our flight at the San Antonio International Airport. A little more than a week ago we'd arrived here from Dallas, and now here we were, on our way out again.

Immediately after his discovery that the radio signals from the rogue star couldn't be the result of natural processes, Richard had told us that he was heading up to San Francisco and from there to Mountain View where he would present his findings to the SETI Institute in person. He wanted us to stay, but after what we'd been through with that psycho stalker, none of us liked the idea of staying behind. This was the perfect chance to get away.

I managed to convince Richard to fly us all up to San Francisco *and* foot the bill for it by arguing that the police wouldn't be able to get permission to search his property if we weren't there to open the door for them. He agreed on the condition that I withdraw the remainder of our savings on our way back and use them to help re-stock the shelter.

So here we were, on our way to San Francisco. Richard was typing away on his laptop to one side of me, Rachel sitting quietly on the other. I discretely peered over Richard's shoulder to see what he was doing now. He was logged into Gmail and busy drafting an e-mail to...

akronreevemassey@gmail.com

I did a double take. The body of the message confirmed it. The e-mail was addressed to Akron Massey. Reading the message over Richard's shoulder, I discovered that he was writing to the billionaire about an occasion in which he and Mr. Massey had met and exchanged contact information ten years ago. He went on to describe his findings about the alien signal, and he said that he was sharing the information even before he shared it with SETI in the hopes that Mr. Massey would reconsider him as a candidate for the Mars Colony Mission.

Richard hit the send button and looked up

from his computer. He cracked his knuckles and rolled his shoulders. I was still staring at his screen, too shocked to look away.

Richard noticed. "What did you see?" he asked, his green eyes pinching to either side of the steel splint that held his nose together.

"You know Akron Massey?" I asked.

"I've met him before."

I pointed to his screen. "You asked to join the Mars mission. You'd do that? Run away and leave us to fend for ourselves?"

Richard shook his head. "It's not very likely that Massey will take me up on it. Everyone assigned to the mission will have been training for years already. Since I haven't, I'm not a good fit for a plus one."

I smiled at the party reference.

Richard went on, "Besides, it's been a long time since Massey gave me his email. For all I know he'll never even get the message."

I nodded along with that, wondering if the long odds should make me feel better or worse. The fact that Richard had sent the message in spite of those odds meant that he was desperate — desperate to escape Earth.

"Rick," I began in a low voice. "A few hours ago you were excited by the idea that this might be

ETI." I used the abbreviation to obscure what I was saying from potential eavesdroppers. "Now you're looking for a way to escape. What aren't you telling us?"

Richard glanced around, obviously uncomfortable to be discussing this in such an open place, but after our run-in with Bill, I'd chosen an empty row of seats far away from everyone else waiting at the gate. Richard's gaze returned to mine. "I hope that first contact will be a mutually rewarding experience that somehow elevates us and saves us from what's coming."

"But?" I pressed.

"But..." Richard shook his head. "If this is ETI, then we already know one thing about them with absolute certainty—they're a lot more advanced than us.

"In our history, whenever a more advanced society met a less advanced one, the result was always the same: the destruction or assimilation of the lesser race. So unless our visitors are a lot more peaceful than we are, it's safe to say we already know what's going to happen when they arrive."

I nodded slowly. It was a chilling conclusion, and one which I had already drawn for myself. The only thing holding me back from the brink of a full-blown panic was the hope that Richard was wrong about the nature of the signals. Maybe SETI would be able to prove that when he shared his findings with them.

I felt Rachel tugging on my sleeve and turned to see her peering up at me. "Yes, sweetheart?"

"What's ETI?"

We hadn't shared Richard's discovery with the kids yet. As far as they knew, this was a family vacation. I pasted a smile on my face and shook my head. "Nothing important, honey."

Alexander was looking at us, too. "It means extraterrestrial intelligence," he said. "What are you guys talking about?"

I grimaced. Richard and I had been careful to keep our voices down, but Rachel hadn't.

Richard traded a glance with me and shrugged. "He's going to figure it out sooner or later."

Later would have been better, but I nodded my consent.

"Watch my computer," Richard said as he went to sit beside Alex and Kate.

I listened with half an ear to Alexander's hushed exclamations as I did so.

After about a minute, I saw something pop up on Richard's screen. It was a Gmail chat window from *Akron Massey.* The message read—

Can we meet?

"Uh, Richard, you need to see this."

He came back over to see what I was talking about. His eyes widened at the sight of the chat window. I could actually see his hands shaking as he sat down and typed his reply.

Meet where? I'm on my way to speak with SETI in Mountain View. My flight leaves for San Francisco in half an hour.

Three green dots appeared to indicate Mr. Massey was typing.

How about my place in Bel Air?

Richard hesitated, and the three green dots reappeared.

Give me your flight number, and I'll have someone waiting with a private jet to take you to LA. When you get here we can discuss your suitability for life on Mars.

I elbowed Richard in the gut, and he flinched. "Ask if we can come—not to Mars, to Bel Air."

Richard glanced at me, then nodded and typed the question.

Absolutely. The plane sleeps ten.

"Sleeps?" I echoed. It's crazy to think how much money some people have—soon to be *had*. Disaster is the great equalizer. Pretty soon Massey's billions would be worth more as kindling than currency.

How do we find your guy? Richard typed.

He'll be holding a sign with your name on it. Greenhouse, right?

That's right, Richard replied. *We're arriving on flight AA75 from Dallas Fort Worth at 11:05 PM.*

Good. See you soon.

Richard and I traded shocked looks. "So much for long odds," I said. Turning to Kate, I added, "Change of plans. We have a new connection from San Francisco to LA."

She flashed a puzzled look at me. "What? Why LA? I thought Richard was going to Mountain View?"

"We're going to meet Akron Massey at his mansion in Bel Air. He's flying us down from San Francisco on his private jet."

Kate's eyes widened in disbelief.

Saying it aloud made it all the more real to me. My heart beat faster in my chest, and sweat prickled between my shoulder blades. I couldn't help feeling hopeful, like maybe the billionaire would offer to help us out with some of his money. He was going to lose it all to crashing economies soon, anyway, so why not throw a few million our way? Part of me knew better, but the other part of me clung to that delusion like a life raft. Akron Massey was going to save us. I was sure of it.

CHAPTER 21

—SIX HOURS LATER—
June 11th, 12:34 AM

I settled into my plush white leather chair on Massey's plane. It was fully reclinable, and comfortable enough to make my bed back home feel like it was made of nails. An air hostess who could have been a model came by to introduce herself.

"I'm Vera Lopez," she said. She had no accent to accompany the name, so I guessed that she'd been born here in the USA. "If you would like anything to eat or drink, I can take your orders now and serve you as soon as we are in the air."

"Sweet!" Alex said.

"Shh," Kate added. "Rachel is sleeping."

"What do you have that's hot?" I asked in a whisper, glancing at Rachel in the seat across the aisle from mine. It was past midnight, and she was fast asleep. From the sound of the light snoring coming from the front of the plane, so was Glenn Reese—the balding no-nonsense brick wall of a man that Mr. Massey had sent to pick us up at San Francisco Airport.

"We have Salisbury Steak or Lasagna for tonight, as well as an assortment of cold deli sandwiches."

"I'll have the Lasagna," I said.

"Me, too," Richard added.

Alex ordered the same, while Kate went with the steak. Vera nodded graciously. I heard the engines whining and then the plane jolted into motion. Vera reminded us to buckle in, and excused herself, saying that she'd come back for our drink orders once we were in the air. She went to take her seat beside Glenn, and I took a moment to recline mine, thinking no one would try to stop me with the oft-repeated *please make sure your trays are locked and your seats are in the upright position.*

I could see runway lights flashing through the window as we taxied around. The plane stopped just a few minutes later. Before we'd boarded this luxury aircraft, Glenn had picked us up from San Francisco International in a big black suburban and driven us to a smaller airport more suited for private planes.

Massey's plane sat there on the runway, idle

for a moment; then the whine of the engines turned to a sudden roar, and we rocketed down the runway. Rachel woke up and started crying. I felt myself sliding backward out of my seat, and suddenly I realized why airlines made people put their seats up.

I reached across the aisle for Rachel's hand and used my other hand to hang onto my seat. "It's okay, Rachie. You fell asleep. We're taking off now." She squeezed tight, and choked back her tears with muffled sobs. Kate glanced over her shoulder at us. The sensation of sliding out of my seat got worse as the plane nosed sharply up. I hurriedly raised my seat to the upright position. I was glad I did. The plane banked sideways and San Francisco appeared through my window. High rises shone bright, illuminated docks hedged the dark expanse of water in the bay, and the Golden Gate Bridge lived up to its name. From there, countless city blocks swept by. Streetlights pooled in luminous grid lines around the empty black spaces that were the rooftops of shorter buildings.

About fifteen minutes later the plane leveled out and Vera made good on her promise to come back and take our orders for drinks. I asked for a beer, then thought better of that—this was a billionaire's private jet. I asked for a glass of the best whiskey they had instead. She came back wearing silk gloves and holding a decorative crystal decanter and a matching glass. The bottle and the glass were pieces of art, and I suspected the gold embellishments on them might actually be real.

"Sixty Year Old Tullibardine Scotch," Vera said with a smile.

Sixty! "Ah, on second thought, I'll have the beer. I wouldn't want Mr. Massey to find out I drank all of his good Scotch."

Vera smiled and shook her head. "His good Scotch is a hundred years old. This is the bottle he reserves for guests. You're more than welcome to have some."

"Well, when you put it like that..." I trailed off and nodded. Vera poured two fingers into the glass she'd brought and handed it to me. I didn't dare to ask for ice. Raising the glass to my lips, I was greeted by the spicy, fragrant smell of oak. I took a sip. The flavor was even more luscious than the smell. Rich-tasting, and ever-so-smooth going down... "I think Mr. Massey has just ruined whiskey for me," I said through half-lidded eyes.

Vera laughed politely and went to go put the priceless bottle back.

I felt guilty for drinking something so

expensive. All of Hell was about to be unleashed on Earth, and here I was sipping liquid gold distilled straight out of Heaven.

Then again, it would be a crime not to enjoy this. Smiling to myself, I reclined my seat by a few degrees and laid my head back with a sigh. Guilty pleasures were the only kind the world had left.

* * *

—THREE HOURS LATER—
June 11th, 3:27 AM

I didn't sleep on the plane, but by the time we deplaned and climbed into the self-driving Tesla waiting for us in LA, I was lapsing in and out of consciousness. I fought it for a few minutes; then I heard car doors opening and felt Kate shaking me.

"Wake up, Logan. We're here."

"Already?" I lifted my head from her shoulder and wiped the drool from the corner of my mouth. "Sorry," I mumbled, noticing the dark patch on her blouse.

We climbed out of the car in front of a massive three-story house. A giant fountain thundered beside the car. Glenn led us up a stairway to a pair of twelve-foot black doors with golden handles. Two men in black suits flanked the doors with semi-automatic pistols highly-visible in holsters at their hips. They barely glanced at us as we approached. We were expected.

Glenn asked us to look the other way as he typed in a security code and then provided an audible password. Something inside the doors *clunked* and they opened automatically for us, parting to reveal the entrance hall of a modern-day palace with gleaming hardwood floors, white wainscoting and intricate moldings. A curving marble banister rose to a balcony that overlooked the entrance. While I was still staring at that, one of the guards from outside brought us our bags.

Richard whistled softly. "So this is how the other point zero zero zero one percent live."

I smiled at that and shook my head. Glancing behind me, I saw Glenn shut the doors behind us from a panel on the wall.

The doors swung shut and locked behind us with another *clunk.* "System armed," a pleasant female voice announced. "Welcome to the Massey residence."

Glenn turned to face us. "Mr. Massey has not arrived yet, but he has arranged for you to spend the night here. Please follow me upstairs to your rooms."

Glenn took Richard's luggage, since he was injured, and the rest of us carried our own up the stairs—except for Rachel. I carried her backpack over one shoulder, mine over the other, and my laptop bag with our travel documents and cash around my neck.

The rooms upstairs were fantastically large. Kate expressed concern about letting the kids sleep alone, and Glenn showed us to one of the rooms that Massey's kids used when they visited him on weekends. It had two beds in it.

"He won't mind?" Kate asked.

Glenn shook his head, but offered no further explanation. After we all knew where to sleep, Glenn dismissed himself, saying that he would be just down the hall if we needed anything.

"You can also reach me through the Echos."

"The Echos?" Kate asked.

Glenn pointed to one of the black cylinders sitting on the nightstands beside our bed.

"Say *computer,* to wake it up, then say, *call Glenn Reese.*"

I nodded along with that.

"Thank you," Richard said, and then walked like a zombie to the room across from ours. The wheels of his luggage dragged loudly on the hardwood floor.

Glenn nodded to us and then walked away. Kate and I went to put the kids to bed, ushering them down the hall ahead of us. Alex rolled over and went to sleep almost immediately, but Rachel was wide-awake thanks to all of the naps she'd taken along the way.

"Where are we?" she asked.

"At a friend's house," Kate said, while brushing blonde hair away from Rachel's forehead.

"This is a *house?* It's huge!"

I nodded, smiling at her.

"Can we stay? I like it better here."

My throat closed up in a painful knot. "No, honey, we can't."

"Why not? It has lots of rooms."

"Because it's not our house," Kate replied.

"Neither is the basement where we live. That's Uncle Richard's."

Basement. I supposed that was a good way to describe it. Kate looked to me for help, her eyes red with exhaustion. I took over for her. "That's true, but Richard is family. Mr. Massey isn't. And Richard invited us to stay with him for a long time, while Mr. Massey only invited us to spend the night."

"So we have to get on another plane tomorrow?"

"The same one, I think."

Rachel gave us a big yawn and rubbed her

eyes. "Good. This time I'll stay awake. Alex said they have donuts. I'm going to get one."

"Sure," Kate said through a smile. "Now go to sleep, honey."

Rachel shook her head vigorously. "I don't wanna."

"Why not?" I asked.

"I had a bad dream."

Kate looked to me with a pained grimace. "About the bad man?" she asked. "You're safe here. Don't worry."

Rachel shook her head again. "No. I dreamed that you and Daddy don't love each other anymore, so Daddy left us alone."

I blinked, taken aback by that. "Sweetheart... I'm not going anywhere."

"You promise?" Rachel's blue eyes glistened, bluer than ever in the pale blue light bleeding through the lampshade of the lamp beside her bed.

"I promise. Now go to sleep. It's been a long day." I kissed her on the forehead, and then Kate did, too. We turned out the lights and eased the door shut behind us.

We walked down the hallway to our room in an uneasy silence. She shut the door and then we both changed out of our clothes and took turns showering in the en-suite bathroom.

When we finally crawled into bed, exhaustion hit me like a tidal wave. The room was spinning as though I were drunk.

"Is it true?" Kate asked.

Fighting to hold heavy eyelids open, I glanced at her. She was on her side, staring at me. Her features were fuzzy in the pale wedge of moonlight spilling through the window on her side of the bed.

"Is what true?" I asked.

"That you don't love me anymore?"

The knot in my throat was back. "No," I said simply.

Kate nodded. "Good, because I still love you."

I wondered if that was a lie. "What about Ben?"

"What about him?" Kate asked slowly.

"He's probably going to die, you know. That doesn't break your heart?" I couldn't keep the bitter edge from my voice.

"I don't want anyone to die, but I won't be heartbroken. I told you. We weren't in love."

I accepted that with a frown, but nodded and leaned over to give my wife a kiss. It was meant to be a peck on the lips, but she pulled me close and made it last. I felt a corresponding reaction from my body, and for the first time in over a month I was actually tempted, but far too exhausted to do anything about it.

"Let's get some sleep," I said.

I rolled over and Kate spooned me awkwardly, hooking one of her feet between mine. Seconds later, I fell into a deep sleep.

I saw the open door of Richard's shelter before me, gleaming with moonlight. It was swinging impossibly in the wind, as if it were made of wood and not steel.

I crept toward the open door with my heart in my throat. There was a pistol in my hand. As I looked at it, the magazine fell out. I hurried to pick it up and slot it back in, but it wouldn't click into place. I held it there with my other hand, hoping it would still shoot.

The door swung wide, and two pinpricks of light appeared—eyes peering at me from the shadows of the stairwell.

I brought my gun up quickly, rattling the slide. "Who's there?! I'll shoot!"

"So will I."

Billy the Kid stepped out of the shadows, pushing both Kate and Rachel ahead of him. He held a pistol to the back of each of their heads. Their mouths and wrists were duct-taped, and their cheeks were stained with tears.

"Let them go!" I screamed.

Bill's lips spread impossibly wide, revealing far too many teeth. He grinned at me like a shark. "Didya miss me, Logan?"

CHAPTER 22

—SIX HOURS LATER—
June 11th, 9:49 AM

I woke up screaming.

"What? What's wrong?" Kate sat up quickly, her blue eyes wide and blinking as they darted around the room.

I stared dead ahead, horror churning inside of me. My mind drifted slowly back to the here and now, and I shook my head to clear it. "I had a nightmare."

Kate looked at me. "About what?"

I told her, and she smiled reassuringly and rubbed my back. "It was just a dream, Logan. He's long gone. Probably recovering in a hospital somewhere."

"Or dead, if we're lucky," I added with a scowl. "What if he comes back? He knows where we are now."

Kate frowned. "Now you're making me scared.

Maybe we should have stayed and let the police investigate."

"Maybe..." I rubbed my eyes and sighed. "Or maybe you're right. Maybe he's not coming back."

Sunlight streamed in through the window on Kate's side of the bed. My stomach growled, forcing my thoughts in a new direction—breakfast, coffee...

I glanced at the black device sitting on the nightstand beside Kate, and wondered if I should try calling Glenn for room service.

That didn't feel right. Was it his job to get coffee for Mr. Massey's guests? Somehow I doubted it. I could get my own coffee—probably, assuming the coffee maker wasn't some kind of fancy cappuccino machine.

I got up and fished clean clothes out of my luggage.

"Where are you going?" Kate asked as I changed out of my pajamas and into a pair of slacks and a button-up shirt.

"I was just going to see if I could find some coffee," I said as I sat on the edge of the bed to pull on my worn out black leather Oxfords.

Kate nodded and climbed out of bed wearing nothing but her underwear. "I'll come with you." She pulled on a pair of jeans and a shirt, then slipped into her sandals, and straightened her hair with her fingers. I marveled at how quickly she could go from jet-lagged, sleep-deprived zombie to drop-dead gorgeous. She had an effortless kind of beauty that I'd always admired.

Kate grabbed my arm for support and leaned her head on my shoulder as we staggered out the door and into the hallway. Richard's door was open, the bed empty. We went to check on the kids, but their beds were also empty.

"Are we the last ones up?" Kate wondered aloud.

"Maybe."

As we walked down the hall, I heard distant voices coming from downstairs. The air was laden with the smells of breakfast and coffee. We hurried down the winding staircase together. There was a guard in a black suit standing just inside the doors, beside the security panel.

"Morning." I nodded to him.

He nodded back, but said nothing. We turned and walked down a short hallway from the foyer, and emerged in a vast living room that looked out on a sparkling Olympic-sized pool. The chain-link cage of a tennis court lay to one side of that. We followed the sound of the voices and of cutlery scratching on plates through an open door in the far side of the living room and emerged in a breakfast nook surrounded by windows. Everyone was already sitting around a big circular table. The kitchen adjoined the nook, and I glimpsed at least two people in black and white service uniforms busy in there.

A man I recognized but had never actually met looked up from where he sat beside Richard. "Welcome," he said. "Please sit down. Are you hungry?"

"Yes, thank you," I replied, nodding. Kate took my hand and led me to a pair of empty seats beside Alex.

"I'm Akron," our host said.

I nodded, smiling at the pointless introduction. "Logan," I replied, watching as he raised two fingers and waved to a woman in a maid's uniform who was just emerging from the kitchen.

"Camila, would you please bring them each some breakfast, please?"

"Yes, sir," she said, and disappeared into the kitchen once more.

We didn't get a chance to order, so I assumed we'd be getting a bit of everything.

I saw the remains of pancakes, eggs, and bacon on Alex's plate, and my mouth began to water.

Akron's gaze found my wife. "And you are?"

"Kate. Richard's sister."

Akron nodded, and the woman in the uniform returned with two steaming plates of food. A second member of the staff entered the dining area pushing a silver cart. She poured us each a cup of coffee and a glass of orange juice, and then asked what we'd like in our coffee.

"Nothing for me," I said, already raising the steaming cup for a sip. "Thank you."

"I'm full!" Rachel announced and pushed her plate away.

"Me, too," Alex said.

Mr. Massey regarded my kids with a smile. "Would you two like to go watch TV in the living room? Or maybe play some video games?"

Both Alex's and Rachel's eyes lit up with that suggestion.

"Can you adopt us?" Alex asked.

Still smiling, Mr. Massey called over their shoulders to the living room. "Glenn!"

Our guide from last night emerged wraith-like from the living room. "Sir?"

"Would you please set these kids up with some entertainment? Take them to the theater in the basement."

"Yes, sir."

The theater—of course, there's a theater.

Glenn escorted my kids from the room. They practically bounced on their way out.

My gaze returned to Mr. Massey. "They've been deprived lately."

"I can imagine," he said, smiling tightly at me.

An awkward silence descended over the table. Kate and I took advantage of it to dig into our breakfast.

"Richard," Mr. Massey began. "I assume your family already knows what you've discovered?"

"They do," Richard confirmed between popping grapes into his mouth.

"Good. In that case, we can discuss everything openly. Do any of you need anything else from the kitchen?"

We all shook our heads.

"In that case—Camila, Valeria—"

The sound of dishes being washed stopped, and the two women who'd served us a moment ago emerged from the kitchen. "Yes, Mr. Massey?" one of them asked.

"Please see to your duties upstairs. You can come back and clean the kitchen later."

"Of course, Mr. Massey." Both women left in a hurry, and suddenly the four of us were alone.

Mr. Massey propped his elbows on the table and rested his chin on a bridge of clasped hands. "I understand you've been staying with Richard during these troubled times."

"He was kind enough to invite us," Kate confirmed.

Turning to Richard, he said, "I double-checked your findings on my way here. How did you even think to check for such a thing? It's not an obvious pattern."

Richard shrugged. "I set up a program to look for a lot of different relationships in the data. All of the parameters I gave were ones that I would use myself to contact an alien race. You have to think about context. The only common point of reference we have besides math and physics, is the fact of their arrival. Given that, it makes sense that they would encode the physical characteristics of the signal with some or all of the data that pertains to that arrival."

"Have you had any luck deciphering the messages themselves?" Massey asked.

"I haven't tried."

"Why not?"

"Because it's a waste of time. We don't know what they might be trying to say, let alone how they've encoded the data. It's like trying to solve an algebra equation that's all variables. You could find a million different solutions, but who knows which one is correct?"

Mr. Massey nodded along with that. "Still, we have a year before they arrive. If we could even decode a tiny piece of one of the messages, we might be able to get some advance warning about the nature of the beings we're about to meet."

Richard looked skeptical. "Even if we could do that, how would it help to have advance warning? We can't prepare for an invasion in one year."

"No, we can't," Massey replied. "But we can run away before they get here."

"You're talking about Mars."

Mr. Massey nodded. "The Colony Mission is ready to go. We can leave either before or after the rogue passes us—after will be easier due to the elongation of Earth's orbit, but if we're in the middle of an alien invasion by then, we might not even get off the ground."

"We," Richard echoed. "You're planning to join the colonists?"

"I wasn't, but now I'm considering it."

I couldn't keep quiet any longer. I was bursting with curiosity. "If you weren't planning to leave Earth before, then where were you planning to live?" I wanted to know about this billionaire's preparations. Where was *he* hiding? Did he have room for more? Whatever preparations he'd made over the past ten years would undoubtedly make Richard's shelter look like an old storm cellar by comparison.

"I have a refuge where I can stay," Mr. Massey said. "It's stocked to last for a decade or more." Turning back to Richard, he said, "And that brings me to the point of this conversation. You obviously have a refuge of your own."

"We do," Richard confirmed.

"But the fact that you showed up here with a broken nose and two gunshot wounds tells me that it's probably not as safe as you would like. You need a real haven. *The* Haven."

Richard's brow furrowed, and he shook his head. "The Haven?"

Mr. Massey hesitated, then looked around as if to make sure that we were alone. Apparently not satisfied, he wiped his mouth on a napkin and got up from the table. "Let's go sit outside."

He walked over to a pair of floor-to-ceiling windows behind him. They proved to be French doors leading out onto a spacious terrace. He opened the doors and gestured for us to join him. We did so, filing out one at a time. The air smelled of dew and fresh-cut grass, and I heard a lawn mower moaning in the distance. We took our seats across from Mr. Massey on a couch facing the grounds.

"Before I say anything," Massey began, "we need to get something straight. Everything I'm going to tell you is in confidence, and I'm trusting you all in good faith to never share it with *anyone* else. Do you agree?"

Our heads bobbed, and he went on, "Good. Haven is an underwater colony that I've spent the past ten years building. It uses much of the same technology that was pioneered for the Mars mission, and it is where I currently reside with my family, along with nine hundred and twenty-six of the smartest and most skilled individuals that I could find."

"Underwater?" I echoed. "Why under..."

Massey pointed to Richard's nose. "Because no matter how well-appointed or provisioned a shelter is, once others start to find out about it, they'll try to take it from you. Underwater the chances of discovery and unauthorized entry are much lower."

"How do you grow food without sunlight?" Richard asked. "And what about supplying fresh-air for all those people?"

Mr. Massey hesitated. "We use UV lamps and a floating solar sheet to supply power, but I'm afraid I can't disclose anything else about the facility or how it operates. I've already taken a big risk just by telling you that Haven exists."

"So why did you?" I asked.

Mr. Massey looked at me, then back to Richard. "I want you to come to Haven with me and join a team dedicated to decoding the alien signals. I also want you to keep what you know about those signals to yourselves. In exchange, I'm offering permanent quarters at Haven—" Mr. Massey's gaze slid back to mine. "For all of you."

CHAPTER 23

We sat in shocked silence. I couldn't believe it. I was right. Akron Massey *was* going to save us.

Kate broke the silence. "When do we leave?"

"Not so fast," Akron said. "Unfortunately, all of the quarters in Haven have already been assigned. For now, only Richard would be able to join me, and even that will probably mean him having to sleep in a utility room."

My heart sank, and anger took the place of hope. "So what are we even talking about this for?"

"Simple. My ex-wife wants compelling evidence that these aliens are not friendly before I take her and our kids to Mars. Once we leave Haven, there'll be more than enough room for all of you."

"And then we'll be stuck with the unfriendly aliens?" I asked.

"There's only going to be so much room on Mars. Besides, Haven is the next best thing. If I'm wrong and aliens don't invade, or they find a way to peacefully co-exist with us, then you'll be much better off staying here on Earth."

Richard looked uncertain. He scratched one cheek through his thick beard. "What makes you think I can come up with the evidence you're looking for?"

"Because you've already found it. You just need to help me draw one or two more conclusions from the data that will tell us something about whoever is sending these signals.

"I'm already convinced that Mars will be safer than Earth. You and your team just have to help me convince my ex-wife of that. And even if your team fails, there's a chance she'll agree to leave anyway."

Richard nodded along with that. "There's one thing I don't like about this. You said we have to keep what we know a secret. I've had enough of keeping secrets. The time for secrecy is over. People need to know what's coming. Why not share my findings?"

Mr. Massey raised a finger to make a point. "Because if you do, the governments of the world will start preparing for war with these aliens, and their citizens are going to panic again. Knowing that aliens are coming won't do any good, but it could do a lot of harm."

"Like drawing unwanted attention to your Mars Colony Mission?" I guessed. The billionaire looked at me, and I went on, "People who are thinking like you, that Earth won't be safe for us after aliens arrive, will want to find some way to join the colonists, and those who can't might lash out because of it. You're worried that the mission could be sabotaged if people learn the truth."

"It's a legitimate concern," Mr. Massey replied. Turning back to Richard, he said, "Well, do we have a deal?"

* * *

"I'll do it," Richard said.

"Excellent," Massey replied.

I wasn't sure whether to feel relieved or concerned. Now we'd be going back to Richard's shelter without him. We'd have one less man to defend it, and we would lose all of his accumulated survivalist expertise.

"How are we going to get in contact?" I asked.

Massey's gaze slid over to mine and his eyebrows darted up.

"We don't know where Haven is, so how will we know to go there after you and your family leave?"

Understanding dawned in Massey's eyes. "Do you have a shortwave transmitter?"

I shook my head. "A what?"

"A HAM radio."

"We do," Richard replied.

"Then you just have to point your antenna in the right direction and set your transceiver to the right frequencies," Massey said.

I frowned. I didn't know a lot about HAM radios, but I suspected that wouldn't be the most reliable means of communication. "What if we miss the message? We can't sit with our ears to the radio all day for the next however many months."

"We could set dates for check-ins," Richard said.

Akron Massey nodded. "Good idea. Today is the 11th of June, so let's set the first check-in for six months from now. December 11th. We'll set the second one for just before the rogue's closest approach. How far can we can push that?" The billionaire looked to Richard for an answer.

"A week before?" Richard replied. "That would be April 25th, right before the shit hits the fan."

"Does that sound acceptable to you, Logan?" Massey asked.

I nodded slowly.

"Good. Richard, you'll stay here with me until we're ready to leave. Glenn will take the rest of your family back to the airport and my plane will fly them anywhere they need to go."

I raised a hand. "Hold on. I don't know how to operate a HAM radio."

"I can show him," Richard said, speaking to Massey. "But I'll need to go back to San Antonio with them to do that."

Akron Massey stroked his chin as he considered that. "I suppose we can all leave LA together. I'll stop in San Antonio and wait there for you."

"Sounds like a plan," Richard said, grinning.

Kate looked at me, her blue eyes big. I saw hope sparkling in her gaze, and felt it when she reached over and squeezed my hand, but I couldn't bring myself to share it. A billionaire's private shelter might be safer than our poor man's equivalent, but our invitation to go there hinged on a big caveat. Richard had to convince Massey's ex-wife that everyone on Earth was doomed. And if he could do that, then it meant we were doomed right along with them.

CHAPTER 24

We had to catch an Uber back to San Antonio International from the small airport where Akron Massey's jet had landed. We picked up Richard's truck from the airport parking lot, and he paid a hefty parking fee. I drove us out, because Richard's injuries were still too painful to handle a steering wheel. I insisted we stop at the nearest branch of Capital One before going back to Richard's place on Stuart Road. We might need our money while he was away at Haven with Akron Massey.

There, in downtown San Antonio, I finally managed to withdraw all of our savings—forty-five thousand two hundred and change in cash. I stuffed it all into my laptop bag and carried it out with me at a harried clip. Thankfully, the doors of the bank were guarded, and we'd parked in clear sight of them.

I climbed back into the truck and opened the glove compartment to stuff the money in there. A gleaming pistol and a box of ammo gave me pause.

"You have a gun in here?" I demanded.

Richard just shrugged. "Yeah, so?"

I shut the compartment. "Never mind. Just put this down at your feet, okay?" I handed him the laptop bag, and he nodded.

From there, it was a long, quiet trip back to Richard's place. We were all too tired for small talk.

I felt the heat pressing in through the windows, even though the truck's air conditioner was on the lowest setting. The highway shimmered like water on the horizon. At times like this it was hard to believe that an ice age was coming.

After about forty minutes of driving down US 181, I turned off onto Stuart Road. Five minutes after that, I saw the barbed-wire gate and the mailbox with Richard's address on it. Richard got out to open the gate, I drove through, and he locked it behind us. As soon as he climbed back in, I drove us down the dusty dirt road to his decoy home. The old wooden shack came swirling out of the clouds of dust that we were kicking up. I parked in front of it, and Richard climbed out again.

"Let's go," he said, his voice still nasal from the splint. "The sooner I teach you how to use that radio, the sooner I can get started decoding those signals for Massey."

I stumbled out of the truck, my legs cramping from spending so much time in cars and on airplanes over the past twenty-four hours.

We each grabbed our own luggage, except for Rachel and Richard. Alex helped Richard with his satchel, while I slung Rachel's backpack over one shoulder and mine over the other. I clutched my laptop bag full of money to my chest like a life preserver.

We followed Richard across the overgrown grass around his decoy home to the stand of trees beside it that concealed his shelter.

"Can I go?" Alex asked.

"Go where?" Kate replied.

"Next door, to see Celine."

"Don't you want to change and shower first?"

He shook his head. "I don't need to."

I could have begged to differ.

Kate looked to me, and I hesitated before nodding. "All right. Go on, but don't stay there all day."

Alex flashed a rare smile at me. "Thanks," he said.

"What about your bag?" Kate asked. "Don't you want to leave that with us?"

Alex shook his head. "I might need it if we

decide to go for a swim."

"Hey, kid—" Richard stopped and held out a hand, making a *gimme* gesture. Alex stared at him, uncomprehending. "I don't think my clothes will fit you," Richard explained.

Alex appeared to notice Richard's satchel dangling from his shoulder. "Oh, right, sorry," he said, and walked back to pass the bag to him. Richard grabbed Alex's hand instead and pulled him into a tentative embrace. Alex didn't seem to know where to put his hands.

"I might not be here when you get back," Richard said. "Take care of your family for me, okay?" He withdrew to an arm's length, and Alex nodded. "And keep practicing your shooting. You never know when you'll need it again."

"I will," Alex said.

"Not a word about this place to your girlfriend, her parents, or anyone else, all right?"

Alex nodded again. "I'll be careful. Goodbye, Uncle Richard."

"See you."

Alex turned to leave, and we watched him go.

Richard sighed. "Lurking somewhere under all those hormones is a good kid."

"Am *I* good kid?" Rachel asked, squinting up at me, her blue eyes sparkling in the sun.

"The best," I replied with a lop-sided grin, and tousled her hair. I was surprised by Richard's admission. We all had Alex to thank for Billy the Kid getting into the shelter, but Richard was the one who'd suffered the most as a result. Then again, we also had Alex to thank for driving that psycho off, so maybe it evened out.

We started toward the shelter once more. Long grass whispered past our legs. Cicadas buzzed, and the trees clapped their leaves as a hot wind blew, bringing with it the smell of cow manure. I sighed. Somehow that was beginning to smell like home. It felt like months, rather than weeks, had passed since we'd first arrived.

"Can we go fishing?" Rachel asked.

"Sure, Rachie," I said.

"Yay!" She tugged one of my hands away from my laptop bag and held it in her own, swinging it back and forth as she skipped along beside me.

We reached the gate in the chain link fence around the compound. Richard opened it, and we all walked through after him, heading for the red door at the bottom of the guard tower.

In that instant, a flashback tore through my mind's eye—that red door silver with moonlight, opening to reveal dark gleaming eyes.

Didya miss me, Logan?

I flinched and shivered with the memory of that nightmare.

"Ow!" Rachel said, and I noticed that I was unconsciously squeezing her hand.

"Sorry," I replied.

Kate cast a curious glance our way, but I shook my head, as if to say—*it's nothing.*

Richard reached the door and opened it with his key. I pulled Rachel aside as the door swung wide, half-expecting to see Billy the Kid waiting for us in the shadows of the landing.

But there was no one there.

Richard walked through, but Kate hesitated, her eyes on me. "Logan?"

She walked over to me and Rachel. "Hey," she whispered. "It was just a dream. The door would have been locked from the inside if someone was in there, and Richard's key wouldn't have opened it."

I nodded slowly. She was right. Richard frowned at us from the landing. "Are you guys coming, or what?"

I hesitated. "Maybe you should check to make sure that it's safe first."

"Safe from what?" Richard asked.

"From me," a dark voice suggested.

My veins to ice, and electricity sparked in my

fingertips. Richard's eyes widened. I heard boots crunching on gravel, and turned to see Billy the Kid limping toward us from one of Richard's greenhouses. He hadn't been waiting for us inside the shelter. He'd been waiting for us to come back and open it. He held a silenced Beretta pistol in both hands, and his lips were curled in an ugly sneer.

"Did you have a nice trip?" he asked.

CHAPTER 25

Richard slammed the door shut, and I heard locking bolts *thunk* into place.

"Shit!" Bill said. He limped the rest of the way over to me and grabbed me roughly by the arm, pressing the barrel of his silencer to my head. "Open the door, Richard!"

Shock rippled through me. How did he know Richard's name?

Rachel screamed and kicked him in the chins. "Leave my daddy alone!"

"Rachel!" Kate yelled.

"Buzz of, kid!" Bill said, and kicked Rachel in the chest. The tip of his boot hit her in the chin. She screamed and fell over.

Unthinking rage took hold of me, and I rounded on Bill, pushing his gun aside and aiming a swing at his face. He leaned away, dodging the blow; then caught my arm and pulled me into a headlock. I felt my eyes bulging. I couldn't breathe. "Nice try, old man," he said, and cold steel pressed against my head once more. "Richard!"

I heard the hatch opening on top of the guard tower and saw the barrel of a rifle appear. Black spots danced before my eyes and my vision narrowed swiftly. Bill ducked behind me, his breath rancid and hot on the back of my neck.

"Drop the gun!" Bill said.

"You first!" Richard replied.

Kate stood off to one side, hugging Rachel against her legs. Rachel's muffled sobs made my heart ache. I battled Bill's arm with both of mine, inching it away just enough to suck in a desperate breath before he tightened his grip again.

"Well?" Bill prompted. "If you don't drop it, I'm going to shoot him."

"You shoot him, and I won't have any reason not to shoot through him to get to you. This is a high-powered rifle, loaded with full metal jacket cartridges. I could shoot through a bear and still hit you."

Bill barked a laugh. "So why haven't you? Go on, shoot him!"

I braced myself for the searing flash of heat of a bullet tearing through me.

But Richard didn't shoot.

"That's what I thought!" Bill said. "You're bluffing! FMJ rounds are a dumb choice when it comes to bringing down a target. A survivalist asshole like you would buy only the deadliest rounds he could find."

"Are you willing to stake your life on that?" Richard challenged. "Drop the gun, and we can all still walk away from this."

"I don't think so. I have a counter proposal. You're going to come out here, unarmed, and with your hands up."

"If I do that, you'll just kill us anyway. You can't risk any of us leaving here and reporting you to the police. And speaking of the police, they're already on their way, so if I were you, I'd get a head start."

Hope surged inside of me, and I struggled to stay conscious despite the steady pressure on my windpipe.

"You called the police?" Bill asked, his voice quavering. "Oh man, oh man! Shit! I guess your cell phone gets better coverage than mine! Or maybe your land line is underground, right? That's why I didn't see one. No, wait, I know! You used the shortwave antenna on the roof of your tower! I saw it when I was up there yesterday on your ladder."

Dread sliced through me. If he knew about the antenna, then he'd already cut it off.

"What ladder?" Richard demanded.

"The one you left around the back of that shack at the end of your driveway," Bill said.

"What do you want from us?" Kate cried.

Bill glanced at her, and I caught a peripheral glimpse of him looking her up and down slowly. "Maybe you and I can talk about that a little later."

"Go fuck yourself!" I gritted out, struggling to elbow Bill in the gut.

"Why would I do that, when your whoring wife can lend a hand instead? Right, Kate? You know what I'm talking about."

Horror stabbed through me again.

"How do you know my name?" Kate asked in a trembling whisper.

"Oh, sweetheart, I know a lot more than that. For instance, I know what your ass looks like when that dress comes off."

"What?"

"Oh yeah, you're a real tease. You shouldn't fuck the neighbor with the blinds open."

"What is he saying?" Richard called down to us.

I didn't have the stomach for a reply.

"You've been stalking me?" Kate asked.

"*Surveilling*—let's keep it classy—and don't make yourself feel too special. I've been watching all of you. It was just a job, and they paid me well. Don't you think I'd have shown my face sooner, otherwise? I'm not some psycho stalker."

Distracted by the conversation, Bill had eased his grip around my throat enough that I could breathe.

"Who's they? Who paid you?" I asked.

"Who knows? They closed up shop after all this shit started to go down, but if you ask me, that says it all. Richard told you on the phone that the government wanted to keep him quiet, right? I was the threat in case he didn't. Someone disposable that they could burn if they had to."

"Is that what this is? Revenge for Richard warning us about what was coming?"

Bill snorted in my ear. "No, man. I told you, my gig dried up weeks ago. I'm a free agent now, just looking for a way to survive, like you assholes."

"I have money," I said, desperate to turn this around somehow.

"Oh yeah?"

"In that bag." I pointed to the laptop bag I'd been carrying. It was out in the open with the rest of our luggage. Hopefully Richard would be able to get a good angle to shoot at Bill if he tried to reach it.

"Nice try."

"It's true!" Kate said.

"Shut it! Richard! You have one minute to surrender and come down here. After that, I start shooting."

"No," Richard said. "If I go down, you'll just shoot us anyway. I need a guarantee that you'll let us leave."

"How's this for a guarantee?" Bill asked.

His gun left my head, and I saw him aim it at the ground. I realized what he was doing just a split second before I heard the muffled *plip.* Blinding pain tore through my toes, and I screamed.

"Logan!" Kate cried out, sobbing, but I heard her as if from a great distance. Between the pain and lack of oxygen flowing to my brain, I was just about to pass out.

"The next bullet goes through his head!" Bill screamed beside my ear. "You have thirty seconds left!"

CHAPTER 26

"Ten seconds, Richard!" Bill called out. "Maybe the next bullet should find little Rachel, what do you think? Maybe that will motivate you!"

"All right! Enough! I'm coming down."

"You better hurry!"

Adrenaline sparked through my veins, keeping me conscious. I fought Bill's hold on me, but he just tightened his grip until I couldn't breathe again. "Don't do anything stupid!" Bill muttered in my ear.

My heart thundered in my chest, and my lungs burned for air. There had to be a way out of this. Maybe if we all made our move at the same time, we'd have a chance. It would be five against one—four if we didn't count Rachel.

But no, that wasn't right. There were only three of us. Bill's arm eased and I sucked in a deep breath. Alex was still with Celine. Bill had forgotten about him.

Hope stirred inside of me even as the door at

the bottom of Richard's tower opened with a rusty screech, and Richard came out with his hands up.

Bill shuffled to keep me between him and Richard. "Stop right there, and turn around slowly," he said.

Richard did as he was told.

"Stop!" Bill said again as soon as Richard's back was turned. "Pull up your shirt—slowly!"

Richard hesitated.

"Come on!"

Richard did as he was told, revealing a pistol tucked into the waistband of his pants, hiding between the folds of fat at the small of his back.

"Nice try. Pull it out slowly and throw it in those bushes over there. You make any sudden moves and Logan gets an earful of lead."

Richard pulled out the pistol and threw it into the bushes. My heart sank. Now Alex was our only hope.

"Turn around and get over here," Bill said.

Richard walked over very slowly. "Stop dragging your feet, fat ass! You think I don't know what you're playing at? Trust me, your nephew isn't going to save you this time. By the time he gets here, you'll already be dead."

That hit me like a bolt of lightening. Bill knew about Alex going to see Celine. He must have overheard us talking. And Richard's suspicions were right. Bill had no intention of letting us go.

"Please. Don't do this," Kate sobbed. "We won't report you to the police. I promise we won't. Just let us go!"

Bill snorted. "Sure you won't, because you're not going anywhere, sweetheart. But don't worry. You and your daughter will live."

"She's just a child!"

"What kind of sicko do you think I am?" Bill demanded. "She's insurance. You're the entertainment. You behave, she lives. Simple as that." Richard came within five feet of us, and Bill took a quick step back. "Stop right there." Then he released me and gave me a shove. My foot erupted with a sharp spike of pain, and I stumbled and fell in front of Richard.

Before I could try to get up, Bill said, "Get on the ground, face down beside him."

"You're going straight to hell," Richard said as he sank to his knees.

Bill snorted. "A godless scientist like you trying to send me to hell? That's rich. Kiss the dirt, heathen."

"Fuck you," Richard spat.

"You'd rather die on your knees? No problem."

I pushed off the ground, coming up to a sitting position. Bill's aim shifted to me. "You want to go first?"

I hesitated. I'd just caught a glimpse of the gate in the chain-link fence swinging open behind Bill. It was Alex. I watched him creep through, holding a pistol in both hands, and I held my breath. Where had he found a gun? Then I remembered—the glove compartment of Richard's truck.

Bill seemed to notice that I was looking at something over his shoulder. His brow furrowed and he began to turn. "What are you..."

"Alex, shoot him!" Richard said.

Bill tucked and rolled. Alex tracked him with his gun, but nothing happened.

"What are you waiting for!" I screamed as Bill came out of that roll in a crouch, his own gun sweeping up to aim at my son's chest.

"I can't pull the trigger!"

Bill jumped up and lunged. Alex backed away hurriedly, still trying to shoot. Bill snatched the weapon away from him and held it up sideways while covering Alex with his own gun.

"It's a Beretta, like mine. Thing is, kid, Berettas have safeties, and you forgot to turn yours off."

"Shit," I muttered.

Richard sprang off the ground with a sudden

roar, and I stumbled to my feet, limping toward Bill with gritted teeth. Startled, he spun around and took aim, dropping Alex's gun at his feet so that he could use both hands.

That was when Alex made his move. He tackled Bill from behind and clawed at his eyes. Bill's gun went off with a muffled *plip*, but the shot went wide and dug into the dirt. Rachel screamed in terror, and Bill cursed viciously as he tried to throw Alex off. Then Richard reached him. He grabbed Bill's wrist and wrestled with him for the gun.

Still limping toward them, I bent down and picked up a rock. Bill elbowed Alex in the gut and he fell off Bill's back, landing with a *crack* on top of something in the long grass.

Bill's gun inched ever closer to Richard's head. "You're fucking dead!" he roared.

I tried to run, but my injured toes wouldn't let me. I wasn't going to make it.

But Kate did. She ran in and slammed Bill in the side of the head with her own rock. He stumbled away, his eyes wide and gun waving around blindly as blood streamed down the side of his face. We all just stood there, frozen with horror and wary of the gun in his hand. Bill blinked, and his eyes appeared to focus once more.

"You bitch!" His gun swept into line with her. "Say good—"

I lunged, but Alex was faster and cracked him in the head with a broken branch. Bill stumbled again, his gun tracking toward Alex. Kate screamed and slammed her rock into his head one more.

This time Bill's eyes rolled up, and he collapsed, limbs flopping like a rag-doll.

I limped the rest of the way to reach him, arriving just in time to see Richard stomp on Bill's face with a sickening *crunch.* The man groaned, blood running in rivers down his cheeks. His nose looked like a smashed tomato.

"Feel good, doesn't it?" Richard bent down to retrieve something from the ground, and he came back up holding Bill's silenced Beretta.

"Look away," he said, but didn't wait for me to do so. He pulled the trigger twice—*plip, plip.* Bill's head jumped in time to each impact. The rock in my hand fell from limp fingers with a *thump.* There were two dime-sized red holes in Bill's forehead.

"You killed him," Kate said in a shaking whisper.

"Damn straight," Richard replied.

"We should have tied him up and called the police!" she said.

"Why? So they could come poking around here and see my setup? Or maybe so they could investigate a little deeper and find out about his contract to watch your family and my government pay-off." Richard shook his head. "No, it's better this way. Trust me, Kate. Grab his feet. We're going to bury him under the wood pile."

To my surprise Kate did as he asked. I watched, nauseated and shaking with spent adrenaline as she and Richard dragged him over to the wood pile.

"Lean on me, Dad," Alex said as he came over and wrapped my arm around his shoulders on the side of my injured foot.

"Thanks." I heard a familiar sniveling sound and looked around quickly. "Rachel?"

"Daddy!" she cried, but I didn't see her pop out of hiding. I tracked her voice to one of the greenhouses and limped over with Alex. We found her sitting in the long grass, wiping her eyes with dirty hands and leaving muddy streaks behind.

I tried to crouch down beside her, but my injured foot wouldn't let me, and I fell on my ass instead.

"Mommy—" Rachel broke off to suck in a shuddering breathe.

I pulled her into a hug and kissed her head.

"She's fine, Rachie so is Uncle Richard."

Alex came and made it a group hug.

"Everyone's fine." Rachel went on sobbing. "Shhh," I whispered, as I rocked her back and forth. "Everyone's fine. You're safe."

"What about the bad man??" More sniveling.

I shook my head. Not seeing the point of sugar-coating it and keeping her fears alive, I said, "He's dead, Rach. He won't be bothering us again."

To my amazement, Rachel's sobbing quieted at that, but we kept on holding each other, anyway.

"How's your foot?" I withdrew from my kids, to see Kate on her haunches beside us.

"I don't know," I said, shaking my head. "It hurts. Where's Richard?"

"Digging. I'm going to take your shoe off, okay?"

I winced at the thought of that.

"If the bullet's still in there, we'll have to take you to the hospital."

"And tell the police how I got shot?" I asked. "They'll find the body and arrest us for hiding it."

"Why do you think I need to see your foot?"

Kate tugged my shoe off, and I bit back a cry as the movement disturbed my injured toes. Kate gasped at the sight of my blood-stained sock. She took that off next, revealing an ugly, blood-crusted and swollen mess around my big toe and the one beside it. Kate gingerly touched my big toe, and I cried out in pain.

"Damn it, Kate!"

"Sorry... you're lucky. None of your toes is missing. It looks like the bullet just grazed them both. We'll be able to fix you up here."

Nodding slowly, I blew out a shuddering breath and leaned my head against the side of the greenhouse with a hollow-sounding *thump*. At least there was some good news in all of this.

I caught a glimpse of something gleaming in the grass beside us and turned to look at it—long metal poles arranged in a crosswise pattern.

"Is that Richard's shortwave antenna?" I asked.

Alex went to retrieve it and held it up for us to see. "Looks like it," he said.

"Hopefully Richard can re-attach it," I replied.

"I'm sure he can," Kate said. "If not we'll buy the parts he needs. I'm going to go get something to clean your foot. Stay here."

I nodded along with that and laid my head back against the greenhouse again. Rachel curled up against me, and Alex sat down on the other side of me, holding the antenna. The sun beamed down from a bright blue sky. A breeze blew, feeling hot on my skin, but cold in my sweat-soaked hair.

This whole mess with Bill just underscored the need for us to find a safer place to live. If we had this much trouble repelling one invader, what would we do when the desperate masses found us?

Not to mention aliens. But somehow the thought of their arrival inspired more hope than fear. Maybe Massey was wrong and they would turn out to be friendly. If they'd found a way to live around a dead star, then surely they could help us live here on our soon-to-be frozen Earth. Hope swelled in my chest, and I sighed.

"Are you going to be okay, Daddy?" Rachel asked, her eyes on my foot.

I squeezed her shoulders. "Don't worry, Rachie. I'll be fine. We're all going to be just fine."

PART 2 - ARRIVAL

CHAPTER 27

—TEN MONTHS LATER—
April 25th, 2032
7 DAYS BEFORE THE ROGUE'S ARRIVAL

I sat at a desk in the shelter's utility room, nestled between the giant batteries for the solar array, and the shelter's dormant gas boiler. On the desk in front of me was Richard's shortwave radio. Static hissed and buzzed from the radio, mingled with the muffled voices of dozens of different radio sources, most of them speaking in urgent tones and relating horrors that I could only guess about. The world was in chaos, but we were in a bubble of relative ignorance—no Internet, no TV, not even a connection to the electrical grid for us to keep track of outages.

The only ways we could learn about the outside world were via reports that came to us second hand from Alex's girlfriend, Celine, and via the radio I was listening to now.

After burying Bill under the woodpile and fixing his antenna, Richard had shown me and Kate how to work his radio. He'd given us a list of emergency channels to listen to between waiting to hear from him at Haven, and we'd done plenty of listening in the months since he'd left.

When spring never came and the snow didn't melt, all the people who were still clinging to their lives up north began a mass exodus to government housing projects in the southern states. And some of them didn't stop there. Last I'd heard, armed convoys of American refugees were waging a war on the Mexican border. Meanwhile, the actual war in Venezuela was on-going, and no one could move down there yet. Their infrastructure had been in shambles even before we'd invaded. As far as I was concerned, that made it a dubious option in the first place. There was bad, and there was worse. Texas, with its food shortages, power outages, shanty towns, tent cities, and government projects that slept twelve to a room was *bad*, but Venezuela was infinitely worse. It was a bombed-out war zone. The situation in the rest of the world wasn't much better either. Russia and Europe were battling over the Middle East and Africa, while China had almost fully occupied South East Asia and Indonesia.

As all of the news filtered in through my radio, I'd been tempted to ask for more information, but Richard had warned me not to transmit unless it was an emergency. He'd explained that our location could be derived from our signals, and HAM radio operators were prime targets at a time like this. People would assume that anyone with a HAM radio was a prepper with a cache of supplies, and they'd go looking for those supplies. It was a dog eat dog world out there.

"Hey there, handsome," a warm voice said. I turned to see Kate come in with a steaming cup of coffee. "You probably need this."

Smiling I held out a hand for the cup. She sat on my lap before reluctantly prying her hands away to give it to me. I didn't have to wonder about her reluctance. The cup was a source of warmth. April in southern Texas should have been *hot*, but here we were at nine o'clock at night, wearing jackets *inside* our shelter. I was trying to save our firewood, so the wood stoves weren't running, and the only other sources of heat we had were the in-floor systems. The electric one drained our batteries too much at night, and I was saving gas for the hydronic system until we really needed it.

"Still nothing?" Kate asked, while running her hand through my hair. It was growing long. So was my beard for that matter.

"Not yet," I said, and raised my cup for another sip. She went on playing with my hair. She'd encouraged me to keep it long, saying it made me look dangerous. At a time like this I supposed the more dangerous I looked the safer she felt. That, or she'd meant her comment in purely carnal terms.

Kate and I were closer than ever. It had taken me a few months to finally get over myself and forgive her, but now the biggest issue keeping us apart was that Richard, being a single guy, had forgotten to stockpile birth control in his shelter. In the beginning I'd risked driving without a license to get to the nearest pharmacies and buy out their supplies, but now that it was too dangerous to venture out, we had to ration ourselves.

A sudden burst of noise issued from the radio, pulling me out of my thoughts. I waited for it to pass, my ears straining for a discernible message.

Going in, I had zero experience operating shortwave radios, so Richard had simplified the process for me. Haven Colony's frequency was set to channel one. All I had to do was keep the radio turned on and tuned to that channel, and of course, stand by all day to listen.

Kate and I had already been listening for twelve hours straight, taking turns to give each other a break, and we hadn't heard a peep from Haven Colony. The day was almost over and our hopes had already died with the light, but Richard made us promise not to leave the radio until the clock struck midnight, and maybe not even then. Bouncing radio waves over the horizon could be elusive, he'd explained, and there were a lot of false positives in the form of muffled broadcasts from other stations. Thankfully, we were listening for something very specific—one of two messages that I had written down on a pad of paper I kept on top of the radio. The first message was: *This is T95C calling M1ARC - code QRV.*

That was the message we really wanted to hear. The last part—*QRV*—was the key. Richard had told us it meant *are you ready?* If for whatever reason Haven wasn't ready for us, then we'd get the second message—the same one that we'd received back in December: *This is T95C calling M1ARC - transmitting 73.*

Seven three was radio code for *best regards.* That seemed like a sarcastic message to get when we were waiting anxiously for the green light to get out of this hell hole, but Richard had explained that messages were best kept brief, since there was no guarantee that our connection would last, and longer messages might lead to unwanted attention.

Regardless of which message we heard, we were supposed to reply with a brief message of our own.

This is M1ARC. You're five nine.

Five nine meant that we'd heard them loud and clear, so that they would know to stop transmitting. If we didn't hear the message clearly, then we were to send back *one one* instead.

Overall, it wasn't a method of communication that inspired a lot of confidence, but right now it was the only one we had, and not just because Richard had built his shelter off the grid. According to Alex's girlfriend, the cell networks were down, electricity was spotty, and Internet and cable likewise. Even when the electricity did come back, the cable and Internet were usually still out. Getting both services to work at the same time required a miracle that Celine's parents were no longer willing to pay for, but that was the last that I'd heard on the subject.

Alex hadn't been able to visit Celine for more than a week now. Her parents had her on lock-down after an RV gang cruised through her neighborhood breaking into homes. Besides stealing all of the supplies that they could, they'd killed at least six people who were home during the raid, and raped several women. Celine's house had escaped by virtue of the burglar bars and security doors her father had installed. That, and he'd fired back with his shotgun from one of the second-floor windows.

Hearing that account made me glad that Richard had built his compound far enough from the road that no one could see it.

Another burst of noise came over the radio, and Kate leaned suddenly toward it. "Can you turn up the volume?"

I arched an eyebrow at her over the rim of my coffee mug. "You want that racket to be louder?"

"No, but... listen..."

I did. The muffled voices were as indecipherable as ever. If we tried scanning for the frequencies they were using we would probably be able to hear them clearer, but we couldn't risk missing a message from Haven.

Shaking my head, I said, "I can't make anything out." All of the hissing and popping was drowning out the voices.

"Don't you hear it?" More popping. "It sounds like gunfire."

I blinked. "What? Who would fire a gun while

using a radio?" Kate just looked at me, and I figured it out for myself. "Right. Dumb question." The military and police used shortwave radios all the time. Either of them would have a good reason to fire their weapons while transmitting. I listened harder to the noise. Kate was right. Those popping sounds did sound like weapons fire, but they were coming in rapid bursts. That didn't sound like police weapons to me. "I wonder what's going on?"

Muffled voices were shouting at each other between the gunfire; then I heard something else—a screech of what might have been electronic interference, but for the agonized screams that followed.

"What was that?" Kate asked, her eyes big and staring. Another screech came, followed by another burst of noise from the radio, this one rumbling and roaring. The window in the utility room rattled in its frame. My gaze skipped up to that dark pane of glass, my heart suddenly pounding in my chest.

"Was that an explosion?" Kate asked, her eyes widening still further, until they looked like they might fall out of her head.

"I need to go check on something." I patted Kate's thigh urgently to get her off my lap. She got up and turned to watch as I ran out of the room.

"Where are you going?" she called after me.

"Upstairs, to the tower!" I called back.

"Why?" came her distant reply.

Alex opened the door to his room and I almost ran into it. "What's going on?" he asked as I ran past.

Rachel opened her door next, rubbing sleepy eyes with her fists. "Daddy? Why are you running?"

I didn't have enough breath to spare for a reply. Taking the stairs two at a time, I used my hands to pull myself up faster. My palms were slick with sweat and sliding on the cold metal railing.

One thought echoed over and over through my head: the speakers in our radio weren't powerful enough to rattle windows. As if to confirm that, another *BOOM* sounded, and the staircase shivered. I reached the hatch at the top of the stairs and slid the locking bolts aside. Pushing the hatch open, cold air came howling in—with a flurry of... *snowflakes.* I stared at them melting in my palms, horror bursting inside of me.

This was April! San Antonio was supposed to stay relatively warm, not plunge into an ice age with the rest of the planet. The rogue star wasn't even here yet, and that meant temperatures were still going to drop.

A flash of light brought my gaze up to the sky, and I gasped. Meteors were falling, drawing fiery orange streaks through the night. *Boom.* The tower shook. A much smaller streak appeared, racing *up*, followed by another flash of light.

I heard footsteps on the stairs behind me, heard an echo of my gasp, and turned to see Kate covering her mouth with both hands.

"Shit!" Alex said from where he stood on the stairs just behind her.

"What's happening?" Kate asked in a crumbling voice.

Another *boom.* I looked away, back up to the sky. Again I saw a tiny streak of light, followed by a bright flash. The meaning of all that crystallized in my brain, and I realized what I was seeing. Those smaller streaks were missiles, and the meteors weren't meteors at all. They were spacecraft.

"They're here," I said.

CHAPTER 28

We stayed up there, watching like idiots as the sky fell. Falling snow soaked into our clothes.

First the temperatures dropped below freezing, and now this: our interstellar visitors were a month early, and on today of all days. We were supposed to be leaving the shelter today. Instead, I was contemplating an indefinite stay. We couldn't go out now, not with aliens invading Earth and our country waging war on them. Maybe that was why Haven hadn't contacted us. They didn't want to draw attention to themselves by broadcasting radio signals.

Another missile streaked through the night, and another explosion shuddered through the tower, this one closer and more powerful than before. Flaming debris rained down, and I wondered how many alien lives had been lost. Kate reached for my hand, and Rachel hugged my legs harder.

"Why are they firing?" Alex asked.

I was wondering the same thing myself. Having been completely cut off for the past week, there was no way to know how the initial exchange with our alien visitors had gone. Did the president try to shake hands, and they somehow misconstrued that as an act of war? Did they fire the first shot or did we? It seemed beyond foolish to attack an alien race with superior technology unless there was no other option.

Another spaceship streaked down, this one larger or closer than the rest. I peered up at it through squinting eyes, waiting for the inevitable flash of a missile exploding against its hull.

But this time that didn't happen. The envelope of orange fire that wreathed the falling spacecraft dimmed to a faintly glowing silhouette, and I noticed that the vehicle was streamlined from nose to tail. This was not some gravity-defying spaceship with mysterious technologies that could somehow bend or break the laws of physics.

This spaceship was gliding down. The white cone of a sonic shock wave appeared, wreathing the vehicle, first at the nose, and then the tail, followed by a thunderous *boom*.

"Dad, what's that?" Alex asked.

I turned to see him pointing behind us. Another spaceship was coming down, but this one was even closer and far larger than the speck I'd been tracking across the sky. It was coming down for a landing tail-first somewhere behind Celine's neighborhood. It couldn't have been more than half a mile away.

"I think we'd better go downstairs," I said. Just then, a pair of jet fighters streaked overhead, so close that the roar of their thrusters was deafening and wind of their passing staggered us. Missiles shot out, racing on thick white plumes of propellant, but before they could reach their target, they exploded like fireworks right over Celine's neighborhood. Seconds later, both fighters broke apart. The flaming pieces tumbled from the sky and crashed with dazzling flashes of light somewhere over the horizon. The thunder of those blasts belatedly reached my ringing ears, and I snapped out of it.

"Downstairs!" I yelled. Not trusting anyone to be able to hear me, I physically ushered my family down the stairs. Rachel was sobbing and holding her ears. Alex looked like he'd seen a ghost, and Kate was screaming things that I couldn't hear. I hoped my hearing loss was temporary.

I made sure my family was on their way, then shut and locked the hatch behind us. More explosions thundered through the tower, shaking it

— 237 —

hard. By the time we were downstairs again, I was relieved to find that my hearing was returning.

Kate grabbed fistfuls of my jacket and shook me. "We can't stay here!" she said, her eyes flashing with panic.

"You want to go out there?" I demanded, pointing back to the stairs. "There's a war going on above our heads!"

Kate released my jacket and subsided, slowly shaking her head and backing away. She fetched up against the wall and slid down it to the floor.

"My ears hurt!" Rachel screamed.

I went down on my haunches beside her. "Let me see," I said, and pulled her hands away.

"What?" Rachel shouted in my face, and I realized that she still couldn't hear.

I rubbed her ears as if that would make a difference. "They'll get better soon," I said.

"I can't hear you!" she shouted again.

I repeated myself, this time using the same volume as her. She nodded slowly and wiped tears from the corners of her eyes.

"Where did Alex go?" Kate asked.

My brow furrowed, and I glanced about, looking for him. He wasn't with us in the hallway anymore.

"Alex!" I shouted.

But he gave no reply.

Giving up, I went to look in his room. It was empty. "Alex!" I called again as I returned to the hall. I couldn't see him in the living room either. Maybe he'd gone to hide in the panic room, or to get a gun from the armory. I scowled at the thought of him grabbing an automatic rifle off the wall. Right now the safest thing for any of us to do was to stay put, not grab a gun and go join the fight.

Running down to the panic room I yanked the heavy metal door open with a screech of hinges. I'd already filled my lungs to blast Alex with a lecture, but the air whistled out in a frustrated sigh. The panic room was empty. I went to check the door to the armory. It was still locked.

Where else would Alex go? To listen to the radio in the utility room? To hide in one of the storage rooms? Or maybe he'd gone back upstairs to watch the battle in the sky.

But then a new thought hit my brain like lightning, and I ran for the stairs. Even from the bottom of the stairs I could see that the front door was cracked open, and moonlight was pooling on the landing. A flash of orange light briefly illuminated the stairwell, followed by the distant boom of an explosion.

Alex had never followed us downstairs. With our ears ringing from the explosions, we hadn't heard him unlocking and opening the door. After seeing the battle raging outside, he'd run off to go rescue Celine.

I ground my teeth. Even if he made it there and back safely and convinced Celine to come, she would bring her parents with her. That meant we would have three more mouths to feed.

I had to stop him. Dashing back to the panic room, I found the key under the toilet tank and used it to open the armory. I zeroed in on an automatic rifle hanging there—an old M16A2. Taking a magazine off one of the shelves, I slotted it into the weapon. Pulling back on the charging handle, I released it, chambering the first round. Being careful to mind the trigger, I checked to make sure the safety was *on*.

"What is it?" Kate asked, and I turned to see her standing in the open doorway. She sounded like she was snapping out of it. "Where's Alex?"

I frowned. "Playing the hero for his girlfriend." I slung the strap of the rifle over my shoulder and stalked toward my wife with the weapon aimed at the ground. Kate barred my exit, her eyes on the gun. "What are you doing with that?" she demanded.

"What do you think I'm doing with it? It's a war zone out there! If I go out empty-handed, I might not come back."

Kate didn't look happy, but she moved out of the way. I held her gaze a moment longer. "You need to lock the door behind me—and don't open it for anyone that isn't me or Alex."

Kate nodded, and I hurried by her. I ran into Rachel next, biting her nails and peering up at the open door from the bottom of the stairs. I jerked the gun away from her as I approached. Her blue eyes swiveled to me, then dipped to the rifle. They grew big and round as only a child's could.

"You're leaving us?" she asked in a quivering voice.

"Just for a minute," I said. "I'll be right back. I promise." Glancing back to look for Kate, I found her standing right behind me. Nodding once, I vaulted up the stairs and shouted back down to her as I left the shelter. "Lock the door!"

CHAPTER 29

I ran through the empty field between Richard's property and the adjacent neighborhood of Lakeview Ranch. Tall grass swished past my jeans. Explosions rumbled in the distance, accompanied by steady flashes of light. I wondered if this invasion was limited to San Antonio, or if the entire world was being carpet-bombed with alien landers.

My heart raced thinking about what might be inside those vehicles. I'd watched enough movies to conjure horrifying pictures of deadly predators, along with a plethora of humanoid-looking aliens that could easily be played by humans in monster suits. But what did real aliens look like? I couldn't even begin to guess. I didn't particularly want to find out, either.

Coming to a cul-de-sac lined with luxury homes, I skidded to a stop in the grass. I had an assault rifle, and I was approaching a neighborhood that had been raided by armed robbers little more than a week ago.

With a grimace I shrugged out of the rifle's carrying strap and laid it down carefully in the grass. I'd come back and retrieve the weapon as soon as I found Alex.

Taking off at a run, shadowy lawns scrolled by. One and two floor houses peeked out between hedges and trees. Somewhere in the distance I heard gunfire popping in a stream of steady bursts. Military? I wondered. Or civilians defending their properties? Fighter jets roared, sonic booms cracking in their wake.

I looked at each of the houses, trying to find one with the lights on. I didn't know which house was Celine's, but I could ask one of her neighbors to point me in the right direction. The problem was, no one was advertising their existence right now. Not one of the houses had their lights on. A penny dropped in the shallow pool of my distracted mind, and I realized the neighborhood was probably suffering from a blackout.

Then I remembered that Celine's house had burglar bars. I began checking the windows of every house that I passed, trying to distinguish actual bars from window frames. Fully half of the houses looked like they had bars.

So much for that idea...

Maybe I should have just let Alex go and come back with Celine's family. Intercepting him early no longer seemed to be an option, anyway. But the rattling roar of a machine gun set me straight. There was a battle raging somewhere within just a few miles of here. I had to get Alex home before the fighting got any closer.

Up ahead I saw the lights inside a car flick on. Car doors slammed and headlights illuminated a garage door. The car began backing out of the driveway, and I sprinted toward it, catching up in seconds. The driver saw me coming and her eyes flared wide. I could see two kids in the back hurriedly putting on their seat belts.

"Hey!" I yelled, and slammed into her door with my momentum. I heard the doors lock. Slapping on the window with both palms, I said, "Wait! I just need to ask you..." I trailed off. Her face was cut and scabbed in places. Ugly bruises colored both cheeks and one eye. Was this one of the rape victims from last week?

Tires squealed and she raced down the street before I could say or do anything else. But then I noticed something. The street ended in another cul-de-sac up ahead. Brake lights blazed crimson and she began backing into someone's driveway to turn around.

My pulse pounded in my ears as I waited for her to come back. Headlights turned my way, and I raised both hands, waving as if I was signaling to an aircraft. Just then, a sharp whistling noise split the air. Before I could wonder what it was, the car exploded in a fiery ruin. Flames licked through broken windows, surging high into the night. I gaped at the sight. A flaming car door hit the street with a metallic *thud*, and I snapped out of it. I had to get those people out! My shoes smacked pavement, drawing sharp pains from my knees and feet as I ran.

By the time I reached the vehicle, I could see that I was far too late. Blackened flesh that might as well have been charcoal peeked through the lapping flames, and no one was moving. Beside me someone's porch lights snapped on, and a door flew open. I heard cursing, followed by a man's voice. "Get over here!"

Thank God. I turned and ran toward the voice. A buzzing sound reached my ears just as I leapt up the man's steps to his front door. I heard loud *pops*, followed by men screaming, and the sound of car doors slamming. A heavy *thud-thud-thud* followed, along with the rumble of a truck's engine.

"Get inside!" The stranger who'd called to me grabbed me by my jacket and pulled me through the open door. I stumbled and fell on my hands and knees. The man shut and locked the door behind me. Dark eyes flashed at me in the fuzzy gloom, followed by a glint of moonlight on the steel barrel of a handgun. "I don't recognize you. What are you doing here? What's your name?"

"Logan," I said, picking myself up. "I'm from 13241, next door."

"Uh huh," he said. "No one lives at 13241."

I grimaced. Maybe we'd done too good a job of keeping a low profile over the past year. I shook my head. "We do. I promise. My son has a girlfriend who lives here. He ran over to look for her, and I came looking for him."

"What's his girl's name?"

"Celine," I said.

"Celine Hartford?"

Alex had never given me a last name and I'd never asked, but how many Celines could there be in one neighborhood? "Yeah," I said. Finally someone who could point the way to her house.

The man lowered his gun. "I'm Duncan Mayfield."

"Nice to meet you," I said. I jerked a thumb to the door just as the rumble of another explosion came rattling through Duncan's house. "Do you have any idea what's going on out there?"

"Have you been living under a rock or something?"

"Or something," I confirmed.

"There's aliens landing all over the planet! We're shooting down as many as we can, but they're shooting back."

"But why? Did they shoot first?"

Duncan holstered his gun in his pants pocket and adjusted his jacket to conceal the weapon. "Maybe we'd better go sit down," he said. He led the way to an adjacent living room, and I went to sit on a couch beside a bay window. Through the gauzy white curtains I saw that the car fire was still burning bright.

"Are you crazy?" Duncan asked just as I sat down. He stood beside a door at the far end of his living room. "Down here," he said as he opened the door. I crossed over to him and saw an unfinished plywood staircase vanishing into a shadowy basement. "Go on, hurry up."

I could barely see Duncan's face, let alone the stairs. Grabbing the railing I began to feel my way down. Duncan shut the door and what little light there'd been vanished entirely. My eyes widened in a vain attempt to let in more light, and I turned to look behind me. My instincts were screaming at me for following this stranger into his basement.

"Duncan?" I asked.

"Yeah?" A penlight snapped on, peeling back the shadows and blinding me at the same time. "Keep moving," he said as he started down the stairs.

The penlight was barely enough to keep me from tripping. The basement smelled dank and moldy. My instincts were still screaming. This was a bad idea. "You know I just need to find my son. If you could point the way to Celine's house..."

The hairs on the back of my neck stood up, and I turned from the bottom of the stairs to peer up at Duncan. The penlight bobbed as he ambled down the stairs. He walked by me and flicked something with a *click*. A desk lamp snapped on, revealing a table filled with ammunition and guns.

He gestured to an old BarcaLounger with the stuffing coming out that sat in front of an ancient TV set. "You want to find your son? Sit down and listen. It's not safe out there. If your son is smart, he's hiding in his girlfriend's basement with the lights off."

Duncan eased down onto a stool beside the table of guns. I went to sit in the BarcaLounger as directed, and swiveled it to watch him in the gloomy yellow light of the lamp. Seeing him clearly for the first time, I was taken aback. Duncan was wrinklier than an elephant, and the patches of peach fuzz on his head were white as silk. I'd just assumed from the way he'd pulled me inside so easily that he was a young man. But despite his age, Duncan didn't look frail.

He fixed me with a hard look. "So you don't know anything?"

I shook my head. "Just about the rogue star and the signals. Nothing about what happened when they arrived."

Duncan grunted and pulled the gun out of his pocket. Laying it on the table beside him, he leaned forward and clasped his hands between his knees. "To answer your question earlier, *they* didn't fire the first shot—not with guns, anyway. A little less than a week ago they came down with a handful of ships. They went straight for all the warmest parts of the planet. One of them landed right here in Texas, another in Louisiana, another in Florida. By some miracle we got to watch it on TV and hear about it on the radio—maybe all the technicians whose job it is to fix things finally got off their asses and fixed the networks for a day, or maybe the government did it for them."

I nodded for him to go on. "What happened after they landed?"

"Nothing. They just sat there and waited for

our response. They must have sat there for a whole day before the president herself flew down to say hi. I bet a whole lot of people tried to stop her, but—" Duncan snorted and shook his head. "Women. Once they get a thing in their heads..."

"What happened?" This story was dragging on. I needed to find Alex.

"Well, once they saw the president standing there with her bodyguards, calling to them with a megaphone, the lander opened up, and their ambassador came out. It had two arms, two legs, a head, clear white skin, and these dead blue eyes. It looked just like one of us, except that it had to be eight feet tall, and it walked like it had a stick up its butt. It came alone and stopped within a few feet of the president; then its mouth gaped open, and this screeching sound came out."

I remembered the noise I'd heard over the radio—the one that silenced the soldiers' screams. "Then what?"

"Half a dozen hovering disc things came racing out of its ship. The president's bodyguards pulled her back and whipped out their guns, but the ambassador didn't seem to mind. Those hovering disks came together in a circle to project images in the air between them, right in front of the president. The first image showed Earth from orbit.

The second one showed our planet, but as it will be in a few years, when glaciers cover eighty percent of the planet. A big snowball. You could see that the oceans had dropped, but everything around the equator still looked green and brown."

"Go on," I said slowly.

"Then they highlighted everything from southern Texas to Brazil in a bright green band. The water, too. The Earth rotated, showing that the green went all the way around.

"By this point I was thinking to myself, great! They know what we're up against. That must mean they're here to help, right?" He shook his head in dismay.

As the former editor-in-chief of a big publisher, I wanted to take a red pen to this guy's mouth. "You can skip the editorializing."

Duncan's eyes pinched into wrinkly slits. "You want me to tell the story or not?"

I swallowed my annoyance and waved a hand for him to go on. "Sorry."

"As I was saying, the planet rotated to show everything they'd highlighted. Then the ambassador pointed at President Fowler with a long, skinny finger, and another image appeared. It showed the sorry masses of humanity, all bundled in blankets and coats, walking from this lush, green field with trees and flowers and birds into a snow-covered wasteland." Duncan broke into a bitter peal of laughter. "You had to see the look on Fowler's face!" He chuckled darkly for a second longer, but then subsided with a sigh that sounded more like a sob.

He went on, "The camera panned back around to show the field, and then it hovered up so you could see all these big silvery spaceships sticking up between the trees. I don't know if that was intentional or not, but we got the message loud and clear. The damn *Screechers* were kicking us out of the only place left on the planet where we'll be able to live, and flipping us the bird to wave goodbye."

CHAPTER 30

None of it made any sense to me. "So, they're kicking us out."

"Trying to," Duncan replied, nodding. "But we're giving them hell. It's not like the movies. They didn't come with ray guns and energy shields. They came with rocket ships armed with high-powered lasers, missiles, and hyper-velocity projectile weapons. Not to mention, there's a lot fewer of them than there are of us."

"So... we're winning?" I asked.

Duncan shrugged. "Hard to say. We haven't had power for the past week, and that means no cable. I've been listening on the radio, but the signal's bad."

I pointed to the lamp beside him. "If there's no power how do you have working lights?"

Duncan smiled and glanced up at the ceiling. "Solar panels on the roof. I've got just enough juice to turn on the lights and keep the fridge running."

I chewed my lip. "What are they?"

"Machines. Robots."

"That look like *us?*"

Duncan barked a laugh. "Some of them. I guess they thought we'd take the eviction notice better if it came from a friendly face. Only the ambassadors have skin, though."

"But how did they know what we look like before they arrived?"

Duncan shrugged. "Maybe they've been watching us from afar. They say it must have taken them hundreds of years to get here. That's a lot of time to prepare."

I puzzled over that, wondering how they could possibly see us from that far. Something told me a telescope wouldn't cut it. "What do the rest of them look like?"

"There's all different kinds—some big, some small, some with legs, some with wheels—others that fly. It's the flying disks you've got to watch for, if you ask me. They're smaller, so there's lots more of them, and there's no way to see them at night. They can see us just fine, though. They track infrared signatures."

"Is that what destroyed that car?"

"No, that had to be one of the bigger *Screechers.*"

"That's what they're called?"

"A nickname from TV, yeah. I think it stuck. Hard to say. Anyway, it fits. That's what they sound like when they're trying to talk. They screech. Must be their language."

"If they're all robots, where are their creators?"

Duncan arched an eyebrow at me. "Maybe they killed them. That's why everyone's so scared of AI, right? The rise of the machines."

"All right, but then why kick us out of the warmest parts of the planet? In fact, why come to Earth at all?"

Duncan shook his head. "More resources? Easier access when they're not buried under miles of ice? Or maybe they're just looking for a change of scenery."

All these maybes weren't getting me anywhere. I got up from my chair. It was time to go. "I need to go find my son."

Duncan held a finger to his mouth and cupped a hand to his ear. "Shh. Listen."

I did. The rattling pops of machine guns drifted to my ears.

"They're still fighting out there. You should wait."

"I can't. What if they find him before I do? I need to get my son to safety."

Duncan snorted. "There's no such thing. With

any luck our boys will beat them, but until then, the best you can do is hide in your basement and stay away from the windows."

"Thanks for the advice, but I'm going. I'd appreciate it if you could point the way to Celine's house."

Duncan held my gaze for a long moment, his jaw visibly clenching. "Damn it. Fine, have it your way." He stood up and grabbed his pistol. Slipping it into his pocket, he grabbed another one from the table beside him and held it out to me. "You know how to handle a firearm?"

I nodded and checked the gun in the light. It was a Glock. I pressed the button to eject the magazine and check that it was loaded. Pushing it back in until I heard a click, I pulled back on the slide to chamber a round. I made sure to keep my finger far away from the trigger. Unlike most guns, I knew that Glocks had a hair trigger.

Duncan nodded approvingly. "Don't shoot unless you have to. The Screechers track sounds just as well as heat." With that, he turned out the lamp beside him, and used his pen light to lead the way back up the stairs.

Once we reached the front door, he opened it and I walked out into the night. My eyes flicked every which way, looking for those hovering disks that Duncan had mentioned. Keys jingled, and I turned to see Duncan locking the door behind us.

"You're coming with me?" I whispered.

He answered with a flash of white teeth. "You're going to get yourself killed if I don't. Come on," he said, and led the way across his lawn. He held his gun in both hands and swept it around, scanning the sky for targets. He looked like he had combat training of some kind. I followed as closely as I could, and mimicked his movements. When we hit the sidewalk, he broke into a light run.

Up ahead I saw headlights pooling on a cross street, but they weren't moving. The idling rumble of a truck's engine reached my ears along with the distant popping of more gunfire. We reached the cross street and found the truck attached to the headlights, standing just a few feet away from us. It was an armored Humvee. The windshield was spidered with cracks around multiple bullet holes, and splashed with blood. A dark shape was draped over the roof, the barrel of a machine gun turret angled up at the sky.

I stopped and stared at the truck. Those soldiers had come here to protect us, and they'd lost their lives in the process.

A strong hand grabbed my jacket and yanked me toward the Humvee. "They're coming,"

Duncan hissed beside my ear, and I noticed a buzzing noise cutting through the distant sounds of battle, approaching fast.

CHAPTER 31

Duncan bolted over to the side of the Humvee. I ran after him, and we crouched together beside the idling engine. The buzzing grew quickly louder, then faded into the distance. Thinking that meant the way was clear, I began to stand, but Duncan yanked me back down. "Don't move," he hissed.

I glared at him through the shadows. Getting jerked around like a dog on a leash was getting old.

"Their sensors are 360 degrees," Duncan whispered. "The slightest flicker of movement on their infrared will send a bullet whistling through your chest faster than you can blink." Duncan's eyes flicked up. "How do you think those soldiers died?"

"We can't stay here forever," I objected.

Duncan held up a hand and mouthed for me to *wait*. A few seconds later he peeked up over the hood of the car. I held my breath and listened.

"Clear," Duncan whispered. He made a

follow-me gesture, and then sprang out of cover. I raced after him as he cut across the front lawn of a big corner house a few dozen yards away. A full moon turned the grass to a gleaming silver carpet under my feet.

Duncan went straight for the front door. I saw the bars on the windows, and my heart jumped inside my chest. This had to be Celine's house. Duncan reached the door and crouched down in the shadows of Celine's front porch. He waved me over as I bounded up the steps. I crouched in the shadows beside him, gasping for air. Duncan clamped a hand over my mouth, pinning me to the wall. The buzzing sound was back and quickly growing closer.

He cursed under his breath and reached up to try the door handle. Before I could ask, he shook his head. Of course it was locked. He stood up and fired his gun into the lock three times. A ricocheting bullet crunched through the siding beside my head, and I leapt out of cover. I could see the lock on the door was mangled by the bullets. Duncan kicked the door. *Thud.* It shook with the impact, but showed no signs of yielding.

The buzzing noise became a roar, and booming sounds followed in a steady rhythm. They sounded like *footsteps.* Duncan turned to me with wide eyes.

A shrill *screech* drew our eyes away from each other to a disc-shaped drone hovering a few feet away from us and gleaming in the moonlight. It screeched again, and Duncan answered with an inarticulate roar. He fired his pistol at the drone, three times fast. Bullets *clinked* off its armor, then came a metallic shearing noise, followed by a *crunch,* and the buzzing abruptly stopped. The disc fell to the grass with a *thump* and lay still.

I let out a shuddery breath, thinking we were in the clear. Another *boom* shook through us, followed by what sounded like a tank cannon swiveling, and then a deafening *BANG!*

Duncan exploded like an over-ripe tomato. So did the door behind him. A blast of heat, shrapnel, and gore slammed me against the wall and clacked my teeth together. Sharp stinging pains throbbed in my face and neck. My ears rang and ached, making it impossible to hear, but I could still *feel* those heavy plodding footsteps shuddering through the wooden beams beneath my feet. Blinking in shock, I saw the source of that earthquake—a massive four-legged machine with articulated arms. One of those arms was pointed at me, and the tip was glowing white-hot.

I dived through the shattered door, sliding in a puddle of gore that I thankfully couldn't see.

A muffled *BANG* reached my injured ears. The shock-wave carried me inside and sent me sprawling with another blast of heat. I scrambled to my feet and ran deeper inside the house. Another blast chased after me, splintering the wall beside me and knocking me into the opposite one. Stumbling on with my momentum, I reached the end of the hall and emerged in an open living space. Desperate for cover, I turned sharply to duck into the kitchen, but my shoes slipped on the tiles and I went down hard. Just as well. Another projectile whistled by, right where I had been standing, and blew out the French doors at the back of the house. Shards of glass zipped by me, like needles to my already battered face.

I crawled around the corner and hunkered down between kitchen cabinets. Patting myself down in the dark, I checked for any serious injuries that might have escaped my notice with all the adrenaline pumping through my system. The worst was a six-inch splinter lodged partway into my thigh. I pulled it out, and staunched the flow of blood with my hands. Empty hands. Somewhere along the way I'd lost the gun Duncan had given me.

Grief and guilt washed over me at the memory of the old man. It was my fault that he was dead.

He'd warned me not to go out.

A door swung open between the kitchen and the living room, and a man popped out, the barrel of a shotgun sweeping through the gloom. The weapon found me and the man's gleaming eyes narrowed. "Who the hell are you?" he hissed. "And how did you get in here?"

"Logan Willis," I replied.

The barrel of the shotgun wavered. "Alex's father?"

I nodded, and he waved me over. I eased up to my feet and limped over to him, suddenly noticing that every inch of me either stung with shrapnel or ached with bruises. Blood ran down my leg in a warm trickle, soaking into my jeans. Walking through the open door, I saw a shadowy staircase leading down into a dimly-lit basement. The man with the shotgun shut and locked the door behind us. A flashlight swept up to greet us, momentarily blinding me as it parted the shadows in a wide swath.

"Harry?" a woman called out in a trembling voice.

"Quiet!" he snapped.

"You're Celine's Dad, right?" I whispered, turning to him at the top of the stairs.

It was his turn to nod. "Yeah." He jerked his

head sideways. "What's going on out there?"

Ground-shaking footsteps interrupted us, and I glanced at the door Harry had just locked behind us. It was a simple wooden door. "That's not going to hold," I said.

CHAPTER 32

I found Alex and Celine hugging each other on a couch in the basement of the Hartfords' house. A flashlight sat between them, aimed at the ceiling to provide diffuse light. My gaze lingered as I saw my son's girlfriend clearly for the first time. She was a stunning girl with dark hair and perfect golden skin. I wondered if that was all Alex saw in her, or if he had a better reason for risking his life (and mine) by running out after her in the middle of a war zone. My eyes found Alex, and I glared, but he probably couldn't see that in the darkened basement.

"Where's mom?" he asked.

"Back at the shelter with Rachel—where you should be right now," I snapped.

Harry Hartford moved between us to get my attention. "Your son mentioned that. He said you've got a place that's safe. Is that true?"

I hesitated, wondering how safe it would be after everything I'd seen tonight. A four-legged tank like the one standing on the street outside could blow open the front door of our shelter just as easily as it had blown through Harry's. The only hope we had was that the Screechers wouldn't find Richard's complex. It seemed like a scant hope to hold onto, but Duncan had said there weren't that many of them compared to us, so maybe they wouldn't be able to conduct a thorough search.

"Well?" Harry prompted. "Is it safe there or not?"

"Safer than here, especially since one of the big Screechers blew your front door apart."

Harry cursed and his wife made a strangled noise. "So that's how you got in here," he concluded.

I nodded. "We should lie low for now. We can't go outside with that thing waiting for us, but it's too big to come inside, so we should be safe down here."

"What about the flyings discs?" Harry asked.

He made a good point.

Harry turned to his wife. I noticed that the beam of her flashlight was shivering. "We can run out the back and head for the lake," he said. "They hunt us by our heat signatures, but we might stand a chance of concealing those signatures in the water."

"Good idea," I said.

"They'll still see our heads," Alex pointed out.

"So duck if you hear one coming," Harry replied. "Besides, bullets don't travel far underwater. We'll stand a much better chance."

"What if they see us running to the lake?" Celine asked.

I shook my head. "I didn't see any more discs out there, and the one that found us didn't shoot. I think it was out of ammo. They might be re-arming, or maybe they moved on after they killed the soldiers."

"Us? Soldiers?" Harry asked, shaking his head.

I told him about Duncan and the Humvee full of dead soldiers we'd found.

"If they killed soldiers, what chance do we stand?" Harry's wife shrieked.

"Quiet!" he hissed, and held up a hand to emphasize the need for silence. His gaze strayed to the ceiling.

The basement was shaking with muffled thunder. Dust trickled down from the ceiling with each impact, shimmering in the light of Mrs. Hartford's flashlight. Gradually, the sound grew softer. The Screecher outside was moving on.

Harry let out a controlled sigh. "All right. We wait until those footsteps are gone, and then we run like our tails are on fire. Got it?" He turned in a slow circle to make sure we were all on the same page. No one voiced disagreement this time.

When Harry's eyes grazed mine, I nodded. "You have another gun?"

"Yeah. Over here." He led me to a wall with rifles mounted on it. Taking an AR15 off the rack, he loaded it with bullets from a chest of drawers below the rack, and then handed the gun to me. "You know how to use it?" he asked before letting go.

"I brought an M16 on my way over."

"So where is it now?"

I shook my head. "I didn't think it would be polite to come knocking on your door with an assault rifle."

Harry snorted. "Too bad."

"We can't swim with guns, anyway."

"Sure you can." Harry withdrew a rolled up strap and clipped it onto the back and front of the rifle he'd given me. Then he withdrew a second strap for himself and clipped it to his shotgun. Slinging the gun over his shoulder, he began slotting extra shells into slots in the strap. "No sense leaving our guns behind," he said. When he was done loading ammo into his gun strap, he handed me a bandoleer of ammo. I strapped it on, watching as Harry cocked his head to the ceiling and held a hand to his ear.

I listened with him. The thundering footsteps were so soft now that they were almost indiscernible.

"It's gone," Alex said.

"Almost," I replied.

"It's the best chance we're going to get," Harry added.

"Maybe we should just stay here," his wife added. "If they moved on that means it's safe, right?"

I wondered if she was right, but Harry shook his head. "They'll be back." Harry turned to me. "Did they go into any of the houses?"

I thought about that. "Not that I saw. They shot up some lady's car when she tried to escape, but that was it."

Harry nodded as if I'd just confirmed his suspicions. "They're prioritizing. They'll take out the military and people on the streets first. After that they'll come back for a more thorough sweep. We don't want to be here when that happens."

That made some sense, but it didn't make me feel any better about hiding in Richard's shelter. What if they found us there, too?

CHAPTER 33

Harry Hartford insisted he go up first to make sure that the way was clear. I waited with the others in the basement, in the dark with the flashlights off, sitting on the edge of the couch beside my son. Mrs. Hartford's silhouette paced back and forth through the silver glow of moonlight spilling in from the windows at the top of the basement walls. She was a nervous wreck.

"Mom... save your energy," Celine said. "You're going to need it to run."

She stopped and stared wide-eyed at her daughter. Something shifted behind her eyes, and she snapped out of it. "You're right." She came and sat on the other arm of the couch.

I glanced at her. "What's your name?"

"Deborah."

"Nice to meet you," I said. "I'm Logan."

The door at the top of the stairs burst open, and we heard hurried footsteps thumping down the stairs. Deborah clicked her flashlight on and shone it in that direction.

Harry's head popped between the ceiling and the posts of the railing. "Let's go!" he said in an urgent whisper.

We didn't wait to be asked twice. Alex and Celine were the first ones up. I followed, walking fast, with Deborah beside me. As we ran up the stairs, I kept a firm grip on my rifle to keep the barrel from swinging into line with anyone.

Before we could leave the stairwell, Harry barred the way and nodded down to his wife. "Turn off the flashlight, Debs."

I heard a *click,* and the shadows came rushing in. "Follow me," Harry whispered, and then dashed out.

We raced through the kitchen and through the twisted, molten remains of the French doors. Following Harry we cut across his backyard and into an unkempt field between Lakeview Ranch and Calaveras Lake. As we went, I strained to listen for buzzing sounds, but the only thing I could hear was nature's orchestra of crickets and frogs. I was surprised the cold hadn't shut them up, but maybe these were their dying gasps.

Long grass swished by our legs as we ran. Up ahead I caught a glimpse of moonlight shining on the water. We were almost there.

The grass parted, and we hit the gravel access road that ran around the lake. Still I didn't hear any buzzing sounds.

Harry stopped running and we all slowed to catch our breath.

"I think we made it," I breathed.

"Don't rejoice yet," Harry said. "We still have a long, cold swim ahead of us."

I hadn't thought about that. Right now the activity and my winter clothes were keeping me warm, but the lake would be freezing. Not to mention, I wouldn't be able to swim with my boots, jeans, jacket, and gun all weighing me down.

"Maybe we should walk," I suggested. The possibility of masking our heat signatures in the lake seemed to pale in comparison with the risk that we could all freeze to death in the process.

We reached the pebbly beach, and still there were no buzzing sounds to indicate that we'd been spotted or followed. "All right," Harry said. "But we should walk close to the water, just in case we need to run in and hide."

"Fair enough." I turned to see Alex and Celine holding hands as they hurried down the beach ahead of us.

"You'd better lead the way," Harry said. "I don't know how to get to your place."

"Sure." I nodded and took off at a run, forcing the others to run to keep up. Pebbles crunched and skittered under our feet, making me wince. The frogs and crickets did a pretty good job of covering for us, but they couldn't completely mask all of the noise we were making. I thought about what Duncan had said, that the Screechers could hear us, too, and wondered how far the noise would carry.

I stopped and turned to address the others.

"What's wrong?" Harry asked as he ran up beside me.

"We're making too much noise. We should stick to the grass if we're not going to swim."

Harry nodded and glanced back the way we'd come. I noticed his body stiffen, and then he raised his shotgun to his shoulder.

"What is it?" I asked.

"I thought I saw something..." he said slowly.

I brought my own gun up and sighted down the barrel. A flicker of moonlight winked at me through the grass.

"There..." Harry said. "Did you see it?"

I had. "Alex, take the others to the shelter."

"But—"

The grass parted and a small version of the four-legged tank I'd seen earlier came creeping through. Six articulated arms unfolded and bright green lasers sliced through the dark, seeking targets.

"Alex, run!" I yelled.

I heard a girlish scream, followed by a burst of skittering pebbles as everyone except for myself and Harry fled.

Harry fired his shotgun with a deafening *bang* that terminated in a metallic *crunch*. All six arms and lasers converged on his chest. The beams hovered there for a second, and I was too horrified to react. The metal monster shrieked at us. Harry screamed in reply. *Chuk-chuk.* He reloaded his shotgun, and I experienced a flash of deja vu. The same thing had happened before Duncan exploded in a sticky wave of gore on Harry's front porch.

"Wait!" I reached out and pushed Harry's shotgun down. At the same time I lowered my rifle and held up my hands.

Three of the six lasers diverted from Harry's chest to mine. Another shriek sounded from the metal beast, but still it didn't fire on us.

"It's trying to talk to us," I said. "Put your gun on the ground." I shrugged out of my rifle strap and laid the AR15 at my feet. Harry did the same with his shotgun.

The lasers disappeared, and another shriek reached our ears, but this one sounded less urgent.

The alien robot came slinking out of the field toward us, pebbles crunching under splayed metal feet.

I held my breath as it approached. The articulated arms were still tracking us, even without the lasers, making me wonder if the lasers had been for our benefit—a visual warning.

The Screecher came to within just a few feet of us, revealing a sleek, aerodynamic design that gleamed in the moonlight. The machine might have passed for a robotic dog if it weren't for the six long, spider-like arms that sprouted from its back, and the fact that it's head was nothing but a gleaming black ball mounted above its shoulders on a long, skinny neck. I stared into that gleaming black sphere and felt it looking back at me. It was like a giant eye. I wondered if that was its function and if the machine would be able to see us without it. Directly below the sphere, where a real dog's head and neck would have been, was what looked like the barrel of a powerful cannon.

"We are unarmed," I said. "We mean you no harm."

All six lasers snapped back on. Three for each of us. The emerald beams connected us to the alien machine in some perverse way.

"I don't think it understands the concept of

surrender," Harry said.

What *would* it understand? There had to be a way to communicate that we were not a threat. Taking a chance, I got down on my knees. Pebbles ground against my knee caps with sharp stabs of pain.

"Please," I said, with my hands still raised in surrender. "I have children. They need me."

The Screecher shrieked at us again. I wished I could understand whatever it was trying to say. "We're not a threat." Harry got down on his knees beside me.

The lasers vanished once more, and metallic clicking noises followed as the Screecher's six arms folded away against its sides.

I nodded encouragingly and smiled. The Screecher turned and slunk away. Beside me, Harry shifted his stance. The shotgun swept up, moonlight flashing off the barrel.

"Harry, no!"

He fired into the bulbous head of the Screecher with a deafening boom. The head exploded with a sound like shattering glass, and the robot gave a piercing wail. Metal arms deployed once more, sweeping every which way and firing bullets with muffled reports. One of them zipped by, so close to my ear that I could feel the wind of its passing.

Another grazed my shoulder with a searing flash of heat. I twisted around and fell over backward with the imparted momentum of the projectile.

Harry reloaded, firing again and again at the alien machine. Metal crunched loudly with each impact. I sat up, feeling faint as I tried to staunch the hot sticky river of blood pouring from my shoulder.

I saw the robot collapse, arms and legs thrashing. Pebbles skittered away from it in waves, and bullets zipped blindly through the night. Harry reloaded and fired again, and this time the machine lay still.

"What were you thinking!" I demanded.

Harry walked over and kicked the robot to make sure it was actually disabled. The arms and legs didn't even twitch. Turning back to me, he said, "We need to get out of here before another one comes to investigate."

* * *

Harry took a moment to check my injury. "It doesn't look too bad. Keep pressure on it."

He held out a hand to help me up, but I couldn't spare one of my own. My injured arm was too weak, and my other hand was busy keeping pressure on the wound.

Harry realized his mistake and moved to lift

me up under my arms instead. He grunted and heaved to get me on my feet. Once standing, I turned and glared at him. "What the hell did you shoot it for?"

"It turned its back," Harry replied as he bent to retrieve my AR15 from the ground.

"Because it was going to leave us alone!"

Harry snorted and shook his head. Leaving his shotgun to dangle by its strap, he held the rifle in both hands and started jogging down the beach.

I caught up to him, walking fast on trembling legs. "Are you going to explain yourself?"

Harry sighed. "That one might have left us alone, but then there'd be a record of it finding us. If the Screechers are coming back for a second sweep, it would be better if they don't already know where to look."

I shook my head and brushed by Harry, taking the lead. "It might not matter. If they come back for a thorough search, they'll find us anyway."

Harry appeared walking alongside me, and glanced over his shoulder. "Yeah maybe. How defensible is your shelter?"

"You'll see in a minute," I replied as I angled up from the beach. We had to crawl through a barbed wire fence—no small feat with the gunshot wound in my shoulder.

Cutting across the back of Richard's property, the decoy house came into view, and I heard a snort from Harry. "You're joking, right?"

In lieu of an explanation I led him around the back to the stand of trees that concealed the real shelter.

"Oh, I see," Harry said as we came to the chain fence that ran around the compound. Alex had left the gate open. I nodded to Harry. "Help me lock it, would you?" He nodded and left his guns to dangle from opposite shoulders while he wrapped the chain and clamped the padlock through it. That done, we both hurried over to the door in the base of the tower. I hit the buzzer beside the door and waited. A few moments later I heard locking bolts clunking as they slid aside.

Kate burst out and wrapped me in a painful hug. "Ouch!" I complained.

She withdrew sharply and saw me holding my shoulder, my hand glistening blackly in the dim yellow light spilling from the shelter. "You're hurt!" she said.

"It's not too bad," I said. "The bullet only grazed me." At least I hoped that was true. It was hard to tell in the dark.

"You got shot?!"

"Shhhh," Harry hissed. "They could hear you."

We piled into the shelter, and Kate shut and locked the door behind us. As soon as the door was secured she came to look me over. The blood drained from her face and tears sprang to her eyes. "Oh, Logan... what happened to you?"

I frowned and looked to Harry. He was also staring at me like he'd seen a ghost. This was the first time that Harry and I had been able to get a good look at each other since we'd met. He was a big man with a barrel chest, dark hair, a broad jaw, and a thick black beard. I could see that he wasn't injured. As for me... after all the near misses with that tank-sized robot, it was hard to say.

"What? What is it?" I asked, my eyes darting between them.

"How the hell are you still alive?" Harry asked.

CHAPTER 34

I went straight to the bathroom to check myself in the mirror.

"Logan, wait!" Kate called after me. "Let me help you down the stairs."

"I'm fine," I said.

At the sound of our voices, Rachel came running from the living room. "Daddy!"

Alex trailed behind her at a more reserved pace. Rachel stopped abruptly, and horror flashed in her eyes when she saw me. Her mouth popped open and she screamed before turning and running back the other way. Harry's wife, Deborah, emerged from the living room as well. She and Alex stood off at a distance in the hallway, staring at me like I was some kind of monster.

Fearing that might actually be the case, I darted into the bathroom and hit the lights. My mind instantly rejected the face in the mirror. I stood blinking in confusion at my own reflection. My entire face was stained red. Chunks of clotted blood were stuck in my beard and hair. Sparkling bits of glass pocked my cheeks, and one and two-inch-long splinters protruded like spikes from a dozen different places. My coat was shredded and drenched with blood, dark red stuffing oozing out everywhere.

Kate caught up to me in the bathroom. "Where did all the blood come from?" she asked.

I turned to her with a grimace. "Not mine," I said simply.

"But you are hurt," Kate said.

I nodded, wincing as the full measure of those hurts hit me for the first time. Now that we were safe, at least for the time being, my brain was free to nag me about all the niggling injuries I'd sustained—and the not-so-niggling gash in my shoulder.

"I need you to get undressed," Kate said, looking me over once more.

"Yeah," I replied.

She pointed over my shoulder. "Get in the shower. I'll be back."

I stripped down, peeling away layer after layer until I was naked and shivering. I went to stand in the shower, and Kate came back with the first-aid kit. She opened it on top of the toilet. It was the size of a toolbox. Taking out a sheet of gauze, she doused it in rubbing alcohol and turned to me.

"This is going to hurt," Kate said. Finding a concentration of a dozen minor cuts on my chest and stomach, she wiped the gauze over them. Alcohol seeped in and trickled down my front. I screamed and slapped the wall. But I'd forgotten about my shoulder. The resulting flash of pain from that injury put me on my ass in the shower.

"Logan! Are you okay?" I nodded and leaned my head back, feeling sick and light-headed. "Maybe I'd better stay seated."

Kate nodded and quietly went about cleaning my cuts. The puncture wound in my leg was deep and had already clotted, so I told her not to bother. There was no way to sterilize it after the fact. When Kate got to my face she had to use a pair of tweezers to remove the splinters and the bigger chunks of glass. Seeing how bloody the sheet of gauze already was, she laid it aside and soaked a hand towel with alcohol instead.

"Close your eyes." I did as I was told and gritted my teeth against the searing pain that erupted as she wiped the towel all over my face. When she was done, the towel had turned bright red.

Kate moved on to my shoulder next, checking the bullet wound there. The blood had dried and mostly clotted, staunching the flow, but as she cleaned it, hot rivers poured down my back and side. Fortunately the bullet had mostly missed, so it wasn't as bad as it looked. Tears dripped down Kate's cheeks as she cleaned the wound.

"How did this happen?" she asked, shaking her head.

"Which part?"

"All of it!"

Deciding to skip over Harry's part in things for now, I went on to explain about Duncan and the alien tank; then I related what he'd told me about the invaders.

Kate wrapped my shoulder tight with gauze, and then sat back on her haunches to wipe her cheeks. I reached out with a shaking hand to help, but ended up smearing her face with blood.

"Sorry," I said.

"This doesn't seem real," she said. "How can this be happening?"

I heaved a sigh and shook my head. I didn't have any answers. A violent shiver tore through me, drawing a cascade of protests from my battered body. "Could you get me some clothes? It's freezing in here."

Kate shook her head. "Not yet." She grabbed her tweezers and scooted forward to set to work on my face, picking out all the smaller bits of glass. We must have spent an hour like that, with her picking and poking at my face and neck. I was too tired and weak to say much, and she was too focused on the task at hand. About halfway through the process Alex poked his head in.

"Dad?"

"Go to your room, Alex!" Kate snapped.

He retreated hurriedly, and I scowled. Wondering what kind of punishment was called for, and *how* to punish him when he had so little to begin with. This was all his fault—his and Harry's. They were both loose cannons as far as I was concerned, but in Alex's case, this was the second time that he'd gotten us into trouble because of his connection with the Hartfords, or rather, because of his connection with Celine.

When Kate finished, she helped me to take a shower—hot, thankfully—to wash away the rest of the blood. She stood in the shower with me, fully clothed, and heedless of how wet her clothes and hair were getting. We had to be careful not to get my shoulder dressing wet, but all of my other injuries were minor enough that it didn't matter— except for the puncture wound in my leg. It began bleeding again. That put an end to the shower. Kate ushered me out and dried me with a towel before setting to work dressing my leg with alcohol and more gauze. When she was done, she handed me a pill and filled a glass of water from the sink. I eyed the pill speculatively.

"Antibiotics," she explained. "It's that or an injection."

I took the pill and gulped water from the glass, only then realizing how thirsty I was.

"I'll get you some clothes. Hold on."

Shivering again, I was so weak that I had to sit on the toilet to not fall over while I waited for Kate to return. She came back a minute later with fresh clothes and helped me to get dressed. Finally, Kate led me out into the living room and eased me down into an armchair. I noticed the clock on the wall showed that it was half past midnight.

"I'll be right back. I need to go change into something dry," Kate said.

The Hartfords sat huddled together, staring vacantly into the darkened vault of Richard's wood stove. There was another one at the other end of the shelter, beneath the spiral staircase.

"We should light that fire," Harry said.

I just looked at him. He figured out why a second later. "Oh, right. They're heat seekers."

I nodded and looked away, searching for my kids. Alex, miraculously, must have listened to his mother and retreated to his room. Rachel was also nowhere to be seen. "Rachie?" I called.

A door opened, and I heard the pitter-patter of hurried footfalls. Finding me in the chair, and no longer drenched in blood like some primordial monster, she launched herself into my lap. I had to bite my tongue not to cry out from the pain. A tear leaked from the corner of my eye, but I smiled and kissed Rachel's head as she hugged me tight.

"You're not dead?" she asked, her voice muffled by the sweater my wife had helped me put on.

I shook my head, smiling ruefully. "No, honey. I'm okay." I stroked her hair, taking a slow, deep breath and letting it out in a sigh. Kate returned a minute later. Seeing me and Rachel sitting there, she smiled fondly at us and went to sit in the other armchair across the wooden chest that served as a coffee table.

No one spoke for a long moment. Harry looked somehow smaller now, sitting between his wife and daughter, his arms draped over their shoulders like a blanket. The look on his face was equal parts horror and shock.

"Harry," I said quietly, aware that Rachel was well on her way to sleep.

He looked at me, eyebrows raised.

"I need you to tell me everything you know about the Screechers. You were watching the news when they came, right?"

"We were listening to it on the radio. I thought that guy you ran into already told you what happened."

"Maybe there was some detail he missed, or something that I didn't pay proper attention to at the time. What I really need to know is, what are they after? Are they just evicting us from all the warmer regions, or are they trying to exterminate us as well?"

Rachel looked up from my chest to regard me sleepily. "Exterminate? What does that mean? What are Screechers?"

"Shhh. Nothing honey. Go back to sleep."

She buried her face in my sweater again, and I nodded to Harry. "So?"

"You just said it. They're kicking us out, and we're resisting."

I considered that, and thought back over everything I'd seen tonight, trying to answer my own questions. "That Screecher that you took out was willing to leave us alone after we laid down our guns. I think that says more about their intentions than anything. It's like what we did in Venezuela. We invaded because we needed their land, and all the people who died defending their country died because they refused to give it up without a fight. They were collateral damage, not the target."

"So..." Harry shook his head. "What are you saying?"

"I'm saying that we need to take our supplies and head back up north—peacefully—before we become collateral damage."

CHAPTER 35

"Leave? We just got here!" Deborah Hartford said.

Kate was watching me with big eyes and shaking her head. "We'll freeze to death, or starve. At least here we have power, heat, gas, and food... Richard didn't build this place for nothing. Without it we won't last long."

"And how long do you think we'll last against the Screechers?" I countered. "A few seconds, maybe, while they cut through the front door."

Harry shook his head. "You can leave if you want, but we're staying. If the Screechers are so peaceful, then I'll wait for them to come and evict us peacefully. Leaving now versus then shouldn't make much difference if they're not actually trying to kill us."

"He's right," Kate said. "Besides, it's a war zone out there. The best way to avoid becoming collateral damage is to keep our heads down and wait for the fighting to end."

I was about to mention Haven Colony as a potential destination, but then I remembered Massey's warnings about not sharing the knowledge of Haven's existence with anyone. Besides, we didn't even know where Haven was, let alone how to get there, and Richard had never called. My eyes found the clock. It was twelve forty-five. Had Kate been listening to the radio while we were gone? Before we'd been interrupted by the sounds of war bleeding through our radio, we'd still had a few hours of listening to go before we were supposed to give up on hearing from Richard.

My thoughts circled back to the explanation I'd given myself for his silence: he couldn't afford to send a message now. The Screechers would trace the signal and find Haven.

But did that mean that Richard had given us up for dead, or would he try to contact us later? My eyes found Kate's, and I nodded, coming to a decision.

"We'll stay here for now, and keep listening to the radio in case things change out there."

Kate nodded back. Richard would find a way to contact us. If not... my thoughts went to the rendezvous Richard and Akron had set for us. We were supposed to meet up at Starcast's launch

— 291 —

facility in Memphis. There, the same plane that had brought Akron Massey and his family over from Haven Colony would be waiting to fly us back to whatever boat or helicopter would take us the rest of the way.

"It's late. We should get some sleep," I said.

"Where are *we* going to sleep?" Harry asked.

I pointed to the couch that he and his family were sitting on. "It's a pull-out."

Harry grimaced, but said, "Thank you."

It would be a tight squeeze with all three of them, but right now comfort was a secondary concern. They were lucky just to be alive.

* * *

—THE FOLLOWING MORNING—
April 26th
6 DAYS BEFORE THE ROGUE'S ARRIVAL

I sat at the top of the tower, wearing gloves and a parka along with one of Richard's winter coats, since mine was now shredded, blood-soaked, and in the garbage. Kate was downstairs trying to use the radio to reach Richard, while the Hartfords and my kids slept in.

I watched the rosy hues of dawn gradually transition to fiery reds with the rising sun. Frost sparkled on the grass below and in the skeletal tops of the trees around the compound. I blinked in shock, and shivered, realizing for the first time that the trees were losing their leaves. Our tower and the surrounding compound would be visible now—a beacon drawing the huddled masses to us, or worse, the Screechers.

I breathed out a sigh and my breath turned to clouds as I exhaled. Reaching for the thermos of coffee beside me, I popped open the spout and took a sip. The chill in my bones retreated somewhat.

I grabbed my binoculars next. They were sitting beside the scoped rifle I'd brought up from the armory. I pressed the binoculars to my eyes and gazed through the crooked fingers of half-naked branches to the rooftops of the houses in Lakeview Ranch. They all looked to be intact. I breathed another sigh. Maybe the Screechers weren't hell-bent on wanton destruction.

But even as I thought that, my gaze wandered, and I found no less than a dozen thin white tendrils of smoke rising in the distance. My eyes tracked right, out over Calaveras Lake to San Antonio, and I gasped. Dozens more columns of smoke were rising there—dark and angry, and feeding into a churning black cloud that looked like it had erupted from a volcano. Even from this distance I could see bright orange flames flickering through the black. The city was burning.

I tracked my eyes back the other way, and this time I noticed the massive towers rising out of ranchers' fields on the outskirts of the city. Each of them was like a gleaming mirror. Those landers looked far more familiar than alien. I wondered how they compared with Starcast's landers for the Mars mission.

Muffled footsteps came clomping up the stairs behind me, followed by a metallic squawk as the hatch opened. I turned to see Harry standing there with the hatch propped open on his back. "Brr! It's freezing out here!"

"Yeah, pretty chilly." I could feel warm air wafting out from the open hatch. The in-floor electric heating was set with a timer to come on at sunrise, just as soon as our solar panels could handle the extra power draw. "What's up?" I asked.

"No sign of the Screechers?"

"None," I confirmed, shaking my head. That was the first thing I'd checked for when I came out. I was still on the lookout for them, but the skies were clear, and the surrounding area was free of the four-legged tanks and their smaller cousins that we'd encountered last night.

Harry propped the hatch open and crawled out beside me to look for himself. He kneeled in front of the low wall around the roof and gaped at the sight of San Antonio.

"Shit," he said.

"Yeah," I agreed. "Deep shit."

Harry shivered and hugged his shoulders, rubbing them vigorously; then he rubbed his hands together and blew into them. "Damn it's cold. I'm going back downstairs."

Before he could leave, more footsteps sounded on the stairs. We both turned.

The sound of my wife's voice preceded her—"Logan!"

The urgency in her voice set my heart pounding at once. "What's wrong?"

She rose into view. As our eyes met, she stopped and leaned heavily on the railing to catch her breath. "The radio."

"Richard?"

"No, I couldn't reach him."

"Then—"

"I tried scanning for a news station. I found one. Apparently we surrendered last night," she said.

"What? That fast?" Harry demanded.

Kate nodded slowly. "The Screechers took out Washington, New York, and a handful of other major cities."

I gaped at her. "With what? Nukes?"

She shook her head. "Something even more powerful, I think. Whatever it was, we surrendered before they could use it again."

"You got all of that in just a few minutes?" I asked. "What about Richard? You need to get back down there and listen."

Kate held up a hand. "The Mars Mission is leaving in a week."

"What? They're still planning to leave with aliens in the sky waiting to shoot them down?"

She shook her head. "None of them landed north of Mississippi."

"Then how did they hit DC?" Harry asked.

"They launched a missile from somewhere in Florida. Anyway, it doesn't matter. We've surrendered, and they're not attacking us anymore."

Harry rubbed his hands together and blew into them again. "Well, now what? We just roll over and freeze to death?"

Kate looked at me. "I think it's time to tell them about Haven."

I gave her a warning look, but it was too late.

Harry's gaze found me. "What's Haven?"

Kate replied before I could: "Somewhere that we'll be safe, where the Screechers won't find us."

"Haven..." Harry trailed off, shaking his head. "If it's so safe, why aren't you already there?"

"Because we don't know where it is, and we were waiting for an invitation. My brother-in-law was supposed to call us on the radio so that we could meet him in Memphis and go from there."

Harry arched an eyebrow at me. "Isn't that where our rockets are launching from? I'm guessing that's not a coincidence."

I shook my head and explained about Akron Massey's involvement and the deal he'd cut with us and Richard. By the time I was done, Harry's lips had turned blue from the cold, and even Kate was shivering.

Harry looked skeptical. "So you think a survivalist billionaire would risk leaving Haven in the middle of an alien invasion?"

I took a moment to consider that, taking into account what I knew of Massey and his previously-stated goal of escaping to Mars. "Yes," I decided. "Especially now that the Screechers have stopped attacking us."

"And we know exactly where to find him," Kate said. "Maybe Richard can't tell us where

Haven is, but we can go to Memphis and ask Mr. Massey for directions."

CHAPTER 36

We all gathered in the living room to discuss our options. The adults sat around the dining table while the kids lounged on the couch. From where I sat, I could see Alex sitting beside Celine, her head resting on his shoulder, and Rachel curling up on the other side of him. I frowned and looked away. Alex and I hadn't said a word to each other since last night. I was still waiting for an apology, but perhaps a spontaneous apology was too much to hope for with a teenager.

"How the hell are we supposed to get from here to Memphis in a week?" Harry asked.

"We have Richard's truck," Kate said.

I nodded. "And plenty of diesel in storage. We'll have to find a way to load spare fuel in the back, but we should be able to make it. It can't be more than a day's drive from here to Memphis."

Harry grunted. "Under ideal conditions maybe. Not in the middle of some robot-driven exodus. You know how crowded the roads will be with everyone going North?"

I shook my head. "I don't think there's enough gas to go around. The pumps have been dry for months thanks to all of the people who relocated down here."

"Great, so we'll find their vehicles abandoned in the middle of the road," Harry said. "That's even worse."

"We can go off-road to get around them. That's the advantage of all-wheel drive."

"That won't work in the snow. We'll get stuck."

Harry made a good point there. If it was this cold outside San Antonio, it was bound to get a lot colder before we reached Memphis.

"And what about the fact that there's three of us and four of you? That's seven people for a five-seater."

"I guess we'll have to take turns sitting in the back," I said.

"We'll freeze to death," Harry replied.

"We could cover the steel frame at the back with a tarp and use sleeping bags. That would be enough to keep us warm."

Harry frowned and shook his head. "It's too risky. Best case we're forced to turn back. Worst case, we freeze to death somewhere on the side of the road between here and Memphis."

Deborah began chewing her nails beside him, clearly overwrought just thinking about it.

Kate turned to me, and I could see the resignation in her eyes. "Harry is right, but we're going to have to leave sooner or later, and it's only getting colder. By the time we're forced to leave, things will be much worse."

I looked at Harry. "I don't suppose you know how to fly a plane or a helicopter?"

He shook his head.

"You know anyone who can?"

"You mean assuming we find one we can steal? Duncan was a pilot in Afghanistan," he said. "But according to you, now he's a puddle on my porch."

I grimaced. *Great.* "All right, let's think out of the box for a minute...." Everyone waited for me to go on while I wracked my brain for answers. If the problem was running into obstacles on the road that we couldn't go around, then the solution would involve removing those obstacles. I already knew from touring Richard's compound what kind of equipment he had that could help us. "We can put chains on the tires," I began. "And Richard has a tow bar and a winch on his truck. We can probably use those to move any obstacles we can't go around."

"Suppose you find an obstacle that can't be moved?" Harry asked.

I looked him in the eye. "Harry. You and your family are welcome to stay here, but we're leaving."

I could see the wheels turning in Harry's head. He looked to his wife, and Deborah suddenly stopped biting her nails. "What do you think?"

She slowly shook her head. "I don't know."

Harry looked back to me. I secretly hoped he would take me up on my offer. After he'd gotten me shot with his recklessness, I wasn't sure I trusted him not to do something else to compromise our safety.

"You mind if we sleep on it?" Harry asked.

I nodded. It would take at least a day to prepare for the trip, anyway. "On the condition that you help us prepare regardless."

"No problem. What do you need?"

"Containers for fuel. Lots of them."

* * *

—THREE HOURS LATER—
April 12th

"It's not enough," I said, shaking my head as I

looked over the supply of diesel we'd packed into the back of Richard's old Ford F350. By my calculations we needed at least fifty gallons of spare fuel. That meant ten five-gallon containers. We'd found three in the form of water cooler tanks and four more in the form of five-gallon jerry cans that Richard had in storage.

"We're out of containers," Harry said, grabbing the steel frame rising from the truck bed and peering in.

"What about your house?" I asked.

Harry looked at me like I'd just lost my mind. "You want to go back there?"

"We surrendered, so it should be safe. Besides, I didn't see any Screechers out there earlier."

"You might have missed them."

"If they were out patrolling, then they should have found us here already."

Harry didn't look happy. "I don't know, Logan. I think it's a bad idea."

"We're going to be out there on the road soon enough, anyway. Better we find out how the Screechers react to us now than later—just don't go shooting any of them this time."

"And what if they shoot us first?"

"Duck."

"That's not funny."

"No, it's not, but we have to risk it. It beats running out of fuel a hundred miles from Memphis and having to walk the rest of the way."

Harry sighed and grabbed his shotgun from where he'd left it leaning against the side of the truck. I took the AR15 he'd given me out of the back. Richard had better weapons, but I hadn't shown Harry the armory yet, and I wasn't sure that I wanted to. If he was trigger happy with a pump-action shotgun, I didn't want to know what he'd do with a fully-automatic assault rifle.

I glanced back toward our compound, catching a glimpse through the trees of the chain-link fence and the guard tower. "Maybe we should go back and lock the fence before we go," I said.

Harry shook his head. "Bad idea. What if we're being chased on our way back?"

"Good point. All right let's go."

* * *

We were nervous crossing the field to get to Lakeview Ranch. Our eyes tracked the sky and field, looking for Screechers, even as we strained to listen for telltale buzzing sounds or clunking footsteps.

Coming to the cul-de-sac where I'd entered the neighborhood the night before, I retrieved my dew-soaked M16 and slung it over the opposite shoulder from Harry's AR15.

Harry nodded approvingly, and we started down the street to his house. If I'd known last night that Harry's house was on the corner of the same street I'd started on, I could have saved myself a lot of trouble—and also saved Duncan his life.

Down at the end of the street, beyond the now silent Humvee, I saw the burned-out wreck of the car I'd seen get blown apart last night. I shuddered at the memory.

The street in front of Harry's house was buckled in a trail of giant claw-shaped indentations from the Screecher tank I'd encountered last night. The span between those footprints was almost the same as the width of the whole street.

Following Harry up his driveway, I stopped at the bottom of the steps leading to his front porch. Duncan's remains glared accusingly at me in the light of day. The porch was splattered with bloody chunks lying in a thick black puddle between us and the gaping hole where Harry's front door should have been. Harry looked away with a grimace, cursing under his breath.

My stomach churned, but I couldn't look away. Duncan had undoubtedly saved my life by sacrificing his. If he hadn't drawn the attention of that tank, Harry's front door would have remained standing, and I'd probably have died looking for a way to get in.

"Let's go around the back," Harry suggested.

I followed him around the side of his house, keeping a firm grip on my M16 and scanning for targets. The air was crisp and quiet. The calm after the storm.

When we got to the back of Harry's house, we found the French doors lying in a twisted mess on the grass. We crept through the gaping hole where they'd been, our eyes scanning the darkened, rubble-strewn interior. Broken glass crunched under our boots.

I turned to Harry. "Let's not stay longer than we have to. We need containers for the fuel. Where are they?"

"This way."

Harry led me down the hallway that tank shells had chased me through last night. The wall was splintered to the point that I could see straight into Harry's garage through a collapsing frame of two by fours. He walked *through* the wall, ducking under a buckled beam and jumping down into the garage. When I landed beside him, he pointed to the walls around the black SUV that was parked there. Those walls were lined with open metal shelves. I saw cans of food, bottles of water, jerry cans of gas, toilet paper, blankets, sleeping bags, flashlights, batteries...

"We're lucky. No one's been here to loot the place yet," Harry said, and walked straight over to the jerry cans.

I stayed where I was, staring at his SUV. "Is that car four-wheel drive?"

"No. That would have cost an extra five thousand, and at the time I thought, why bother? I live in the South, and I'm not going to do any off-roading." Harry snorted. "Looks like that came back to bite me in the ass."

"Still," I said, shaking my head. "We could use a second vehicle."

"We'd need twice the fuel," Harry pointed out.

"We'd also have twice the room."

"True." Harry grabbed two five-gallon jerry cans off the shelf, and I could hear the gasoline sloshing around inside of them.

"Do you have enough?" I asked.

He glanced at the storage rack beside him. "Maybe, yeah, I think so."

"Then let's do it. That way we won't have to freeze our asses off in the back of the truck."

Harry flashed a lop-sided grin at me. "I thought you said we'd be warm enough with a tarp and sleeping bags."

"I lied."

Harry chuckled. "All right. Help me load her up, and let's get out of here."

I nodded. Harry fished the car keys out of a drawer in a standing metal tool chest and opened the back of his SUV. He folded the rear seats for extra storage, and then we loaded all of the jerry cans into the back. There were ten of them—exactly the fifty gallons we needed for the truck. The SUV would get far better mileage than Richard's Super Duty F350, however.

Harry threw three empty water cooler tanks on top of the jerry cans to satisfy the reason we'd come here—spare containers for diesel. He pointed to the row of remaining water tanks on the floor. "Should we take a few? We're going to need something to drink."

I nodded, but as we strained our backs to lift those sloshing five-gallon tanks off the floor, I was beginning to think that we should empty them instead. My original fuel estimate for the truck didn't seem even close to good enough, especially not if we were going to have to stop and tow cars and debris out of the road along the way.

I expressed those concerns to Harry, and he agreed. We began tipping the tanks to pour the water out on the concrete floor of his garage. Water *glugged* out noisily. That sound was almost enough to drown out the ones we heard next: the crunching of broken glass and the whisper of creaking floorboards. Harry's eyes widened with alarm and he placed a finger to his lips. We both righted our water jugs and stood up slowly, readying our weapons.

We listened, staring through the splintered remains of the wall between Harry's garage and his house. My heart hammered in my chest, and my hands grew slick with sweat on the cold metal casing of my M16.

Muffled footsteps thumped on carpet, coming closer, and then the whirring of robotic joints joined that sound. Harry raised his shotgun and sighted down the barrel. I did the same with my rifle.

A Screecher came stalking into view—all gleaming silver. It looked disturbingly human with two legs, two arms, a head... My finger tightened on the trigger of my rifle as that head turned to us. Two black eyes gleamed at us, and the Screecher held up its hands, palms out in a gesture of... *surrender?*

I turned to Harry, blinking in shock, just in time to see the barrel of his shotgun flash with a deafening *BOOM!*

CHAPTER 37

Chuk-chuk. BOOM! Chuk-chuk. BOOM!

The Screecher staggered backward with each impact. Shells crunched through its armor—one flaying open its chest, the other tearing a ragged furrow through its face, and a third ricocheting off the wall beside its shoulder.

The Screecher made a strangled sound as it collapsed in the hallway. *Chuk-chuk.* Harry took an extra second to aim this time. I saw the Screecher thrashing to get up, and I snapped out of it. I tackled Harry to throw off his aim. *BOOM!* The shell tore through the ceiling.

"Are you crazy?" he demanded as we fell over and I pinned him to the floor. "Get off me! It's going to get away!"

"It wasn't going to attack us!" I spat. I jerked my head sideways to indicate the struggling machine.

"So what?" Harry said as he pushed me off.

The Screecher was back on its feet, staring at us

and making more strangled sounds. Harry scrambled to his feet and took aim. I wrestled with him. "Stop it! We surrendered, remember? You want to get us killed?"

"Fuck off!" he roared, and elbowed me in the gut.

The alien robot pointed at Harry and fired a shot of its own with a muted *p-plip*. A pair of rods appeared in his chest, flashing in time to electrical zapping sounds. He jittered and fell over, his limbs twitching and eyes rolling.

I gaped at the humanoid Screecher as it ducked inside the garage and stalked toward me, both arms raised and aiming at me now. It made another distorted, strangled noise, and I saw that the speaker grille, which was located exactly where a human's mouth would be, had been ripped open by one of Harry's slugs.

"I'm sorry," I said, holding up my hands, palms out the way I'd seen the robot do. "We don't mean you any harm." That probably sounded like an empty assurance after Harry's shooting spree.

The Screecher stopped within easy reach of me, fully two feet taller than I was. It made a hissing noise that sounded frustrated to me, and then it made a show of looking around. The robot's eyes were like two camera lenses. Its arms dropped to its sides and weapon barrels slid into concealed compartments in its forearms. The robot's hands clenched and unclenched restlessly as it surveyed the garage. I saw *five* fingers on each hand. Shock rippled through me. My eyes tracked down to the robot's feet. They were less human. No toes, just four splayed metal prongs for stability.

Turning back to me, the robot aimed one of its arms at the ground between us and I saw weapon barrels sliding out of concealment once more. A bright green laser hit the floor. The concrete instantly began sizzling and smoking as the laser evaporated the water we'd poured out a few moments ago. I took a step back, watching as the Screecher traced a smoking pattern on the concrete.

Harry groaned and mumbled something. I glanced at him. He rocked his head from side to side, obviously still dazed.

The sizzling noise of the laser stopped and the green glow vanished. The robot waved me over, and I suppressed a shiver, chilled by how familiar this alien's appearance and body language were.

I saw the pattern on the scorched concrete, but I couldn't make sense of it in the dim light of the garage. "I'm sorry. I don't understand."

The Screecher's eyes glowed to life, dazzling me with their light and peeling away the shadows.

Suddenly the pattern of scorch marks at my feet became clear. It was a two-dimensional image. To one side I saw one of the four-legged Screechers with its ball-shaped head, and its six spider-like arms raised in a threatening posture. Beside that were three people. One of them was taller than the rest, with thinner legs and arms, and it was standing between the four-legged robot and the other two people. It was hard to tell from such a limited image, but I got the distinct impression that two of those people were me and Harry, and that the taller one was this Screecher. I pointed to it and then pointed to the robot. "Is that you?"

To my amazement, the machine nodded.

"You understood me?" I asked.

The Screecher made another strangled sound, and then cocked its head to one side.

Maybe it understood my gesture and not my words. I pointed to the other two human figures and then to myself and Harry. He was still lying on the floor, trying to get up, but every time he did, the stakes in his chest electrocuted him again.

"And that's us?" I asked, turning back to the robot.

Another nod.

I shook my head. "What does it mean?"

The robot took a hesitant step forward, then

held up a hand, palm out, as if to reassure me. Another step. I peered up at the robot, squinting into the light pouring from its eyes. I couldn't help leaning away. This thing could probably rip out my throat faster than I could blink.

Just then, its arms swept up, and its body arched over me. I cried out in alarm, and tried to get away, but it wrapped one arm around me and curved its body over mine, trapping me where I stood. I glimpsed the robot's other arm sweeping around the garage with weapons deployed and bright green lasers tracking.

I got the message loud and clear: this Screecher was on our side.

CHAPTER 38

"A little help here," Harry said through gritted teeth.

I strode over and bent down to pull the stakes out of his chest, but the robot pushed me aside.

I gave it a dark look. "You have to let him go."

The machine studied me for a moment before nodding its head and plucking the stakes out. Electricity leapt over its chassis as it did so. It tossed the stakes aside and they went skittering and crackling along the wet floor.

This robot had just saved me from a nasty shock. I smiled and yanked Harry to his feet. He eyed the robot warily, one hand resting on the action of his shotgun, and his other drifting toward the trigger.

"It's friendly," I explained, and pulled his trigger hand away.

"How do you know that?" he snapped. "Did it say that?"

"It tried. Look—" I pointed to the picture on

the ground.

Harry snorted. "That could also mean it wants to escort us peacefully off his land."

I regarded the robot, and it cocked its head at me.

"I don't think so," I said. "It's not trying to get us to leave. It's waiting to see what we do next. I think... I think it might be hiding here."

"Hiding? From what?"

"From the other Screechers."

"You're telling me this robot is a conscientious objector?"

"Why not? Just because they're robots doesn't mean they can't have personalities and individual traits. Any real AI would have that potential."

Harry snorted again.

The robot in question looked from Harry to me and back again, as if trying to figure out what we were saying. It said something in a strangled burst of static, and I wondered what it would sound like if Harry hadn't damaged its speakers.

An idea came to me. "Do you have something to write with?"

Harry was watching the robot with a wary frown. "Maybe." He backed away slowly, heading for his car. "Keep an eye on that thing, would you?" He said as he reached the side door of his car and turned his back.

"Sure."

He opened the car and rifled around inside for a moment before retrieving a pad of paper and a pen. He came over and handed it to me. There was a shopping list on the first sheet of paper. I tore it off and then held the items out to the robot.

"Go on," I said. "Write something." The Screecher hesitated, cocking its head curiously as if it had never seen paper before. Maybe it hadn't. I demonstrated the purpose of it by scribbling on the pad with the pen. "Look," I said. "Just like your lasers."

The robot reached out with one over-sized hand and dexterously grabbed both the pen and the pad of paper. Using its other hand, the robot grasped the pen as I had done and furiously wrote something on the pad. Turning it around for us to see, I saw a string of simple symbols, just two different kinds. One was a horizontal line, the other a vertical line. They weren't ones and zeros, but they may as well have been.

"It's a binary code!" I said, a thrill of excitement coursing through me.

"Yeah, but what does it say?"

I frowned. This was a breakthrough, and it was a good starting point, but we wouldn't be able to translate anything until we could sit down and create a dictionary. Morse Code is also binary, but if you don't know how to translate it to letters, it's equally incomprehensible.

The Screecher pointed to himself, and then to the string of symbols on the pad, and I got it.

"I think that's his name," I said.

"Great," Harry scoffed. "We can call him OneZero for short."

"OneZero. That's not bad." I pointed to the robot. "OneZero."

He pointed at himself, and another strangled sound escaped his speaker grille.

I introduced myself and Harry next. The robot made another strangled sound in response to each of our names. This time, through the static I could have sworn I heard a garbled version of our names.

"We need to go," I said, turning back to Harry. "Let's load up the rest of the supplies and get back to the shelter."

"And I suppose we're going to take this thing with us?"

"Why not?"

"Because it could be a trick to find out where we're hiding!"

I considered that. "OneZero could have killed you instead of shooting you with those stun bolts.

Or he could have stunned us both and dragged us out of here. I think he's earned some measure of trust. Besides, we're going to be leaving the shelter soon anyway."

Harry pressed his lips into a fine line and shook his head, watching OneZero with a knitted brow. "I don't like this."

"Just think about how useful he could be if we run into trouble from Screechers or other people along the way. Not to mention he could probably tow us out of a ditch all by himself."

"He's a robot, not superman," Harry replied.

"Maybe, but the point is, we shouldn't be too quick to dismiss his help. And while we're at it, maybe we can learn more about the Screechers. If we can find out why they're here and why they want all of the land around the equator, maybe we can come to some kind of understanding."

"Uh-huh."

"He'll ride with us," I said. "In the back. If he's planning a double-cross, you'll see it coming and you can run away if you want."

"Unless he shoots me first," Harry growled.

I opened my mouth to offer further argument, but Harry stopped me with an upraised hand. "Let's just get out of here before another one shows up and turns this trip into a circus."

* * *

"Logan... why would you bring that thing here?" Kate asked. Her eyes never left OneZero's gleaming, slug-scarred face. We were all standing in the living room while OneZero stood in front of us, his head grazing the ceiling, and body blocking the only exit. I frowned at that positioning, but tried not to let Harry's paranoia get to me. I wanted OneZero to be on our side. I *needed* him to be.

"Is he safe?" Rachel asked, peering up at him from around my legs. She held out a hand as if to poke him with a finger, and OneZero mimicked that gesture, reaching back for her.

"Rachel!" Kate yanked her back before their hands could touch.

"Ow! Mom!" Rachel complained, rubbing her shoulder.

"No, he's not safe," Harry said. "He shot me."

"Where?" Deborah said.

He patted his chest.

"It stunned him," I explained. "The wounds are only surface-deep."

"Still counts," Harry complained, wincing and scratching his jaw through his black beard.

I glared at him. "I'm the one who got shot, remember?"

But Harry refused to meet my gaze.

"Why does he look so much like us?" Celine asked. She brushed an overgrown lock of hair out of her face. "I thought they were *alien* robots."

"Yeah," Alex agreed. "It doesn't make sense."

"I've been wondering the same thing," I said. "As for whether or not he's safe, OneZero has had a thousand chances to kill or capture us already."

"Actually, this is his first chance to catch all of us together," Harry pointed out. Like Kate, his gaze never left the robot, and he held his shotgun in both hands, ready to fire at a moment's notice.

OneZero didn't seem concerned by that.

"Well, he's still not doing anything," I pointed out. "If all he wanted was to catch us in one place, now's the perfect time for him to act."

Harry glanced at me. "Maybe he's waiting for backup."

"He's right, Logan," Kate said. "We can't trust it. I can't believe you brought it here. Why would you do that? Just last night one of them shot you! You almost died out there!"

I turned to her, and related the part of the story that I'd withheld last night—the part about me getting shot because Harry had turned on that spider-dog robot after it had decided to leave us alone.

"Is that true?" Kate asked, her gaze straying to Harry.

"I was just covering our tracks," Harry said. "If I hadn't, we'd have been ambushed in our sleep."

"The Screechers aren't the aggressors here," I argued. "Think about it. They didn't come down shooting. We fired the first shot."

"Passive aggression is still aggression," Harry replied. "They expected us to take the eviction notice lying down. When we didn't, they blitzed us with war machines and weapons of mass destruction, and now that we've surrendered, *they're* acting like the victims." Harry snorted and shook his head. "I don't buy it."

"This one is different," I insisted. "That picture he drew clearly showed his intent to defend us from the other Screechers."

"What picture?" Kate asked.

I explained, and she appeared to relax.

"They're individuals," I added. "They're capable of resisting their orders just like any human soldier."

OneZero regarded me steadily, his black eyes inscrutable.

"I like him," Rachel said, waving to the robot. OneZero's gaze shifted to her, and he waved back. Rachel giggled, and I smiled. Turning to take in the group, I said, "We should finish packing and go. It's still early. There's no reason we have to wait until tomorrow."

Worry lines creased my wife's face. "Are you sure?"

"I am," Harry said, surprising us all with his eagerness. "I'm not going to be able to sleep with that thing down here with us. Let's hit the road."

I smiled and nodded. "OneZero." The robot looked at me. "Could you help us load the rest of our supplies?"

No reaction. The language barrier was still alive and well. I turned and waved for him to follow me to the storage rooms at the back of the shelter. Clomping footsteps trailed after me. At least he understood my gestures.

CHAPTER 39

We left the shelter at midday, rolling down Richard's driveway to Stuart Road with OneZero in the back of the truck. We hid him and our supplies by tying a bright blue tarp onto the cargo rack. I didn't think it would be a good idea to leave our supplies uncovered, and based on OneZero's stated allegiance, it would probably also be best if other Screechers didn't see him riding with us.

When we reached the end of the dirt road leading from Richard's decoy house to the street, I realized that I'd forgotten the key to the padlock on the barbed wire cattle gate. I could probably just drive through it, but that would scratch the truck to hell. Not that it mattered, but old habits die hard. I got out with my M16, flicked off the safety and set the gun to single-fire mode. Taking aim from a safe distance, I squeezed the trigger.

Bang! The stock slammed into my good shoulder, and the lock flew apart. Not bad for such a small target. I flicked on the safety, opened the gate, and then climbed back in beside Kate. I handed her the rifle, and she took the weapon without so much as a frown. My wife was getting used to seeing weapons by now. The back of both Harry's car and my truck were loaded with enough guns and ammo to start a war—besides food, water, clothes, and fuel.

I turned right onto Stuart Road with Harry's black SUV close behind us. We cruised past Harry's neighborhood. Just as before, I could see that the houses were all still in good condition, but I could also still see the black cloud of smoke hovering over San Antonio. I suspected that we'd escaped the worst of the fighting by being so far out in the country.

Right after Harry's neighborhood, we reached an intersection, governed by a rusty stop sign. In the distance I could see one of the silvery landers jutting above the trees. I turned to Kate who was busy organizing a bundle of maps in her lap.

"Well? Which way do we go?" I asked.

"Give me a second."

"Kate..." I glanced out the window, checking the sky for Screechers. I remembered the car they'd blown up last night as it tried to leave Lakeview Ranch, and I wondered if our surrender would make that much of a difference to their levels of aggression.

"Left," Kate said.

I turned left onto the cross street, and leaned over the steering wheel to study the sky. I wished I'd taken more time to study the maps for myself. "When is our next turn?"

"Ummm..."

"Just look at the path Harry and I highlighted. We need to get up to the I-30 and head East." I remembered that much at least.

"Right... it looks like you can just stay straight until you reach it. Or... hang on. Logan, there's a faster route. You could just keep going until you hit the I-35."

I shook my head. "Stick to the highlighted route, Kate."

I could feel her eyes on me, silently asking why. I'd already seen that the I-35 was faster while looking over the maps with Harry, but that route would take us through San Antonio, Austin, and eventually Dallas, and we'd both agreed that it would be better to avoid major cities wherever possible.

Kate gave up and went back to her maps. "Well, for the I-10, just keep straight and turn off when you see the signs."

I nodded. "Good. Start looking for the next

turn."

"Uhh... 130 What's that?"

"A state highway," I said. "Thanks Kate."

She flashed a tight smile and laid a hand on my thigh. We were in this together. It's funny how our marriage had been about to fall apart until this crisis drove us together. Now we were closer than ever. I guess there's always a silver lining.

We drove on for the next twenty minutes in relative silence. We saw a few cars on the road with us, which I took to be a good sign, but there were also a few burned-out wrecks. I had to brake hard to avoid a collision with one on two separate occasions. Thankfully Harry wasn't riding on my bumper so he didn't pile into us from behind.

"I need to use the bathroom..." Rachel said.

I glanced in the rear-view mirror to make eye contact. "How urgent is it?"

"I need to go now!" Rachel said, bouncing her knees as she pinched them together.

Beside her Alex sighed and yanked his headphones out of his ears. He had an old phone loaded with some of Richard's favorite music. "This music sucks!"

"We're going to have to pull over," Kate said, her hand moving to my biceps and giving them a squeeze. "Better now than later. It looks safe."

I nodded and flicked on my hazard lights to get Harry's attention. He flashed his headlights at me, as if to ask what was wrong, and I turned off the hazards to indicate right just before pulling off onto the shoulder.

"Pass me the rifle," I said.

Kate handed it to me, and I got out. Harry rolled to a stop behind us, and Rachel opened her door in a hurry.

"Where's the bathroom?" Rachel asked, while hopping up and down on one leg.

"There isn't a bathroom," I said. "You'll have to pee here."

"Where?"

A car came whistling by and blasted us with a frigid gust of air. Startled that I hadn't seen it coming, I looked around quickly. Not seeing anything else in the near vicinity, I wrapped my left arm around Rachel's shoulders and guided her around the front of the truck. "Here," I said. "I'll stand next to you so no one can see."

Rachel made a pouty face. "I'll hold it."

"You can't hold it. I don't know when we'll be able to stop again."

"But—"

"No buts. Hurry up. It's dangerous out here."

Rachel heaved a sigh that was halfway to a

sob. "Turn around."

I nodded and busied myself with scanning the horizon. In the distance I heard a rumbling sound. Glancing back the way we'd come, I saw the sun glinting off the windshield of another car. No, not a car—a semi-truck. Grabbing my rifle in both hands, I flicked off the safety, and held it at the ready and out of sight, hidden behind the hood of the truck.

Harry honked his horn behind us.

"Rachel..." I said.

"Done!" I glanced over my shoulder to see her pull up her pants, then led her back around to her door. Being careful to keep the barrel of my rifle away from her, I opened the door, and Rachel hopped in. I slammed the door behind her, and the semi blasted its horn again as it drew near. I hurried to my door and climbed in just as the semi rolled to a stop beside us with a noisy *tsss!* from its air brakes.

The driver lowered his window before I could shut my door. "You folks headed North?" he asked in a drawling southern accent. A thick blonde beard shadowed a craggy face, and a furry bomber hat with the dangling ears topped his head.

I nodded. "Yeah."

The driver appeared to notice my rifle. "Nice

piece." From there his gaze tracked over to his side mirror. "Looks like y'all are well-prepared."

I smiled tightly.

"Where y'all headed? Maybe we can travel together."

There might be safety in numbers, but we couldn't afford to share our supplies, and I didn't particularly trust Harry, let alone a complete stranger.

"Thanks for the offer, but we're good."

"Oh, sure. No problem. Y'all take care then. Be careful of 'em Screechers. I hear they're crawling all over the interstates."

I did a double take. "What? How do you know?"

The trucker patted his dash. "Heard it on my CB. The I-35 is packed with cars, people, and Screechers alike. The bastards are drivin' us North like cattle."

"So how do we get around them?"

"I don't know if you can, but I'm sure as hell gonna try. Stick to the state highways. That's my advice. Well, y'all take care now."

As the semi rumbled off, I found myself wondering if that trucker wouldn't actually make a meaningful addition to our convoy.

A sudden hiss of static followed by Harry's

voice drew my attention to the walkie-talkie sitting in the cup holder between me and Kate. "What's up? Over." Richard's utility room had four of the handsets, plus chargers and adapters for the car. The walkie-talkie squawked at the end of Harry's message as he released the transmit button, a feature which made saying 'over' superfluous.

I flicked the safety *on* for my rifle and grabbed the handheld radio. Holding the button on the side of the device, I said, "Trucker says the interstates are packed with Screechers driving people North."

"What? So what are we going to do? Over."

"Give me a second." I shut my door and motioned to Kate. "Pass me the maps."

She handed them over, and I spent a minute looking for alternatives to our highlighted route. In order to go around the interstates we'd have to take a path that was much less direct, and consequently a lot longer. That would eat through our fuel supply in no time. It might not be a problem if we could find fuel along the way, but somehow I doubted the pumps would be flowing. We had what we had for fuel, and that meant we couldn't take anything but the most direct route to Memphis. But if things were bumper to bumper on the interstates, even that might not be good enough.

Another burst of static issued from my handset. "Well?" *Squawk.*

I slowly shook my head, feeling suddenly cold all over even though heat from the engine was blasting us through the vents.

"Logan? Did you copy? Over."

I held the transmit button. "I copy. Listen, the only way around the interstates is to take country roads, but that means two things: one, we could get lost really easily. And two, we'll add days to our trip and run out of gas along the way. Over."

A hiss of static that might have been a sigh reached my ears. "I told you we should have stayed in the shelter."

"It's not too late to go back," I said, daring him to do just that.

"All right, let's turn around. Over."

"Wait." It was my turn to sigh. "The trucker said the Screechers are driving people North."

I paused to gather my thoughts, and Harry was quick to interject. "So what?"

"So, they're not killing people, Harry. They're escorting them out of their territory. We could join the exodus. We have to go North anyway. Over."

"You don't know that they're not killing people." Another squawk signaled that Harry had released the transmit button.

"If they just wanted to kill us, the military would still be fighting them," I reasoned. "If the Screechers weren't honoring the surrender, we'd know about it. Over."

"How? Have you been listening to the radio? Over."

"No," I admitted. "But that trucker has."

"So have I," Alex put in, and I glanced over my shoulder at him. He held up the phone in his hand and waggled it around. He had one ear bud in, and was clearly listening to something. "Dad's right. They're not killing us."

I'd been holding the transmit button while Alex spoke. Turning my head to speak into the handset, I said, "Did you hear that? Over."

"Yeah, okay. Fine. Keep the radio on, and let's go join the rest of the cattle. Over."

I nodded and passed the maps back to Kate. I felt a lot less intrepid and optimistic as I pulled out onto the road. Rumors were one thing, but I was putting my family's lives on the line. Until I saw for myself what was actually happening, I wouldn't be able to relax.

CHAPTER 40

The ramp leading to the I-10 was right up ahead, but I could see that there was something blocking the way. Silvery metal gleamed in the midday sun, and six spidery arms tracked us with bright green lasers. Two hovering discs flanked the four-legged Screecher, tracking us with more lasers. The inside of our truck took on an eerie emerald glow from the combined focus of those beams.

Kate's nails bit into my thigh. "Logan, maybe we should turn back,"

"They might shoot if we try to turn around now. We're going to have to go straight."

My radio crackled to life. "I don't like the look of this. Over."

I grabbed the walkie as we rumbled past the Screechers. "Relax. You don't see them shooting, do you?"

"The Nazis didn't shoot all the people they rounded up on trains, but that doesn't change the fact that they gassed them later." A radio squawk punctuated Harry's concerns.

My heart jumped, and an acid burn began creeping into my throat as I thought about what he'd just said. He could be right. What if we were heading straight into a trap? We were armed, but that wasn't much comfort. How much would our guns do against alien war machines? Harry had shot OneZero twice at point-blank with a shotgun and caused only minor damage.

We continued down the road, heading North to the I-35. No Screechers tried to stop us, but all the subsequent turns that appeared to our right were similarly guarded. Farmland and pasture for cattle blurred by us in orderly squares of green and brown, hedged with bare, skeletal trees. Black smoke roiled on the horizon. We were heading toward San Antonio.

"This is a bad idea, Logan," Kate said, her nails digging into my thigh again.

I glanced at her, but said nothing. The Screechers weren't giving us a choice.

We drove on a while longer, and the smoke grew thicker. We began to smell the acrid stench of it through the vents, even though I had the car's climate controls set to circulate the air inside the truck. My eyes burned. Fat black flakes of ash came twirling out of the sky like snow, sticking to our window. I turned on the wipers and made a smeary black mess. As the visibility worsened, we had to drop our speed. We passed suburban neighborhoods and broken-down cars on the sides of the road. People waved and yelled for us to stop as we drove by. I glimpsed a green road sign indicating a right turn to Randolph AFB.

An Air Force base, I thought, and glanced right, trying to see through the swirling gloom. No wonder there was so much smoke. This must have been where those jet fighters had come from.

As we reached the exit to the Air Force base, I saw more Screechers guarding it. A pair of blackened shells that looked like they might have been Humvees were pushed to the side of the road, one of them overturned. An equally blackened tank came swirling out of the darkness just beyond that, also sitting at an odd angle beside the road. We hit a section of buckled street leading to the tank in two parallel lines that looked suspiciously like they'd been torn as the tank had been pushed or dragged off the road. Then we raced up onto a bridge that crossed the highway below.

Red tail lights came swirling out of the darkness. My brain made the connection a second too late.

"Logan!"

I slammed on the brakes. Rachel screamed, and our chain-bound tires skidded with a horrible grinding noise.

We hit the vehicle ahead of us with a sickening crunch that sent our heads whipping forward and clacked my teeth together. I heard fuel containers thumping around, followed by a metallic clattering that might have been OneZero.

I sat there, stunned and blinking at the never-ending line of cars ahead of us. The line was moving, but slowly. Meanwhile, the car we'd run into had stopped, and the driver was busy getting out. I glanced in my rear-view to see Harry had stopped safely behind us. He had his hazards on—probably smart considering I hadn't been able to see the car ahead of me until its brake lights came on.

A man appeared at my window. Knuckles rapped on the glass. "Hey!"

I reached for my rifle, but the stranger produced a pistol from behind his back before I could. *Not again,* was all I could think as he aimed it at my head.

CHAPTER 41

"**W**hat have you got?" the man asked as soon as I lowered my window. Acrid smoke poured in, making my nose and eyes burn. This guy had his mouth buried in a scarf to filter out the smoke, but I could still see how young he was. Despite that, his eyes were cold and dark. His head was shaved on both sides and long on the top, hanging over one side of his head like a mop. I glanced at the crumpled back of his car. It looked like a seven-seater. The bumper sticker on the back depicted a couple with three kids and a dog. That hit me with a jolt. This kid didn't fit in that picture. He'd stolen the car. I wondered what had happened to the family who had owned it.

"Hey, dipshit! I'm talking to you." The slide on the pistol rattled as he shook it in my face.

I grimaced and looked back at him. "What do you want?" I asked.

"You fucked up my car, dipshit. Insurance sure as hell isn't going to pay, so you're going to have to figure it out with me. What have you got to compensate me for my loss?"

"That's not your car," I said.

"Logan," the warning tone in Kate's voice was enough to send a chill down my spine. I cringed, waiting for a bullet to go through my head. Cars were driving by on the other side of us, none of them stopping or seeming to care that we were being held up at gunpoint.

"Not my car? Well, shit, Sherlock! I guess I should go look for the owner then. Don't worry. I'll get right on that after you pay up."

"I've got some money here," I said, reaching for the roll of bills in the back pocket of my jeans. My mind flashed back to the twenty thousand dollars I had stashed under the lining on the floor beneath my seat, but there was no way he would know about that unless I told him.

"Hey, hands where I can see them! Money's gonna be useless soon if it ain't already." The boy's eyes flicked to the back of the truck. "What you got under that tarp? Supplies?"

I shrugged, but a flicker of hope swelled in my chest. The kid snapped his fingers at me. "Hand me that rifle—slowly!" I turned to Kate and she did as she was asked. The barrel of the gun came out facing the kid. As I passed it over my lap, I heard a *click* as Kate tried to pull the trigger. I winced. The safety was on.

"Oh you're gonna wish you didn't do that!" the kid said, grabbing the barrel of the rifle and yanking it out of my hands. It clattered to the asphalt beside him, and he aimed his pistol at my wife's chest. "Cover your eyes kiddies! Mommy's goin' to a better place."

I leaned in front of her, blocking his aim.

"You want to die, too? Fine, eat—"

Clink!

He never got to finish that sentiment. The pistol flew out of his hand. He gripped his wrist in a white-knuckled fist and screamed as blood spurted from a missing trigger finger.

Plip, plip, plip! His body jerked three times in quick succession. Stumbling backward, the kid's eyes slid to me, and the scarf fell away from his mouth. I was wrong about his age. This kid couldn't have been more than sixteen. Old eyes, young face.

He fell over, stiff as a board. I caught a glimpse in my side mirror of OneZero's gleaming arm retreating into the tarp at the back. I got out and grabbed my M16. Checking the safety, I passed it to Kate, and then hopped back inside. I shut the door and locked it. Just as I was about to put the window up, my radio crackled.

"Shit, Logan! Are you guys okay?"

I glared at the handset, then answered, "No thanks to you."

"I was about to get out and do something," Harry said. "Debs stopped me."

Sure, blame your wife, I thought. Maybe it was true, but I was beginning to think the Hartfords might be dead weight.

"Let's go check his car," Harry suggested when I didn't reply.

"Yeah. How about *you* do that? I'll stay and guard the vehicles with OneZero. Over." It was a test.

"I'm not sure he needs your help. Over."

"All the same. You go. I'll stay and watch your back. Just like you were watching mine a minute ago. Over."

"Logan, I swear I wouldn't have let him do anything. Over."

"He was just about to shoot Kate in the head! If it weren't for OneZero, she'd be dead right now."

A hiss of static burst over the handset and I saw Harry climb out with a semi-automatic shotgun. As he reached my door, he leaned in and said. "Let's not turn on each other, okay? It was a bad situation, and it happened fast. There was no way for me to judge the right moment to intervene."

"The right moment to intervene was when you saw him pull a gun."

Harry grimaced. "All right, fine. You win. I'll do better next time. I promise."

"I hope so." I frowned and raised my window as he turned and walked over to the dead kid's stolen car. Right now *everything* was a bad situation. We were fresh out of good ones, and I had a bad feeling that Harry was only in this for himself. If I wasn't careful, he was going to get us killed. But at least I had OneZero. I'd have to find a way to thank him when I got the chance.

Cars were still rolling by us, none of them stopping. Up ahead traffic was moving, except for the crumpled SUV blocking the way in front of us. I watched Harry rummage around inside the vehicle, pulling out sleeping bags and luggage. Before he even got around to the trunk, I saw a giant, gleaming metal disc come flying over the smoke-clogged horizon.

I pushed the button on my handset. "Harry, look out!" He looked up sharply, and spun around with his shotgun up and tracking.

The disc stopped right above Harry and dropped a pair of bipedal Screechers in front of him. They looked just like OneZero. Bright green lasers snapped out from their arms, and he raised his hands in surrender.

One of the Screechers lowered its arms and walked around Harry. It went right up to the SUV, bent its legs, and lifted. To my amazement, the vehicle tipped up on one side. The Screecher heaved and it went over with a crash. It did the same thing once more, this time rolling it over the concrete wall along the side of the bridge. The SUV landed with a distant crash, and then both Screechers turned and stalked away. The one still aiming its guns at Harry kept him in its sights, backing away slowly until the hovering disc above them deployed metal clamps on retractable lines and yanked them back into the sky. The big hovering disc drifted off, carrying them away.

I slowly raised my walkie-talkie and pressed the transmit button. "Well, at least we don't have to worry about towing cars out of the way."

Harry didn't reply. He didn't have to. It was clear that the Screechers were eager to keep traffic flowing North. The most direct way to travel North would be to stay on the I-35 as soon as we reached it, but that meant crossing through several major cities along the way. That thought gave me pause.

If we'd already run into an armed

confrontation on the outskirts of San Antonio, what else were we going to come up against along the way? And even after we left occupied territory, we'd still have to head East to reach Memphis. At that point the Screechers wouldn't be there to help keep order, and the situation would devolve into a total human free-for-all.

Harry ran by my door, banging on it with his hands. "Let's go!" he shouted into his radio.

I caught a glimpse of a dark shadow above us, and leaned over my steering wheel for a better look. Another one of those big discs was hovering above us, and this time we were the ones blocking the road.

Visions of us being thrown over the side of the bridge raced through my head, and I hit the gas. Maybe a human free-for-all wouldn't be so bad.

PART 3 - FINDING HAVEN

CHAPTER 42

The I-35 was packed with cars, but they were all moving steadily at thirty miles an hour. The Screechers quickly dealt with the ones that broke down, stopped, or ran out of gas. Five minutes seemed to be about the limit for a car to stay in one spot before the Screechers took action and pushed it out of the way. The displaced occupants of those vehicles were left to join the flow of traffic on foot. It seemed like the pedestrians were allowed to stop for longer breaks, which told me that the Screechers understood the limits of our biology versus our technology. The pedestrians were left alone just as long as they didn't try to leave the interstate. We'd seen an unlucky group make a run for a stand of trees only to get shot in the back by the hovering discs. The message was clear. Keep going North, or else.

As we rolled along, the crackle and hiss of the car radio kept us company. We had to keep scanning as we went, but a few of the FM frequencies had emergency government broadcasts on them, as well as the occasional update from civilian broadcasters. What we'd gleaned so far was that the Screechers had set up a border just below thirty-five degrees latitude. I'd already figured out from the map that the first major city due North of us at that latitude was Oklahoma City, but before we reached it we would cross Austin and Fort Worth. Signs for Austin kept popping up, and I saw another black cloud of smoke like the one we'd seen over San Antonio hovering in the distance. Traffic started to slow down, and Harry's voice crackled through my walkie-talkie: "Keep your guns close. We could run into some trouble from pedestrians trying to steal our vehicles if traffic stops. Over."

"Copy that," I said.

"I'm thirsty!" Rachel whined. "And hungry!" She'd been stuck on a loop, repeating that like a mantra for the last ten miles.

We had a cooler full of drinks and snacks on the back seat, sitting between her and Alex, but drinking meant peeing, and we couldn't risk a pit stop.

"Not yet, honey. You'll have to wait."

"But—"

"No buts," Kate intoned.

She and I traded worried glances. We had already estimated the distance from Austin to Oklahoma City using the scale on our maps. It was about four hundred miles, and at thirty miles per hour, that meant we had more than twelve hours of driving ahead of us. There was no way we'd be able to avoid stopping between now and then. At an estimated 10 miles per gallon, our 48 gallon tank would get us to Oklahoma City without the need to refuel—but only if we didn't run into too much traffic along the way.

I wondered if my kids could pee out the windows. Alex could, but how would Rachel manage? Or Kate? A five minute stop would be enough to pee, but I wasn't sure I wanted to risk drawing attention from the Screechers—let alone the desperate and weary-looking pedestrians stumbling along the sides of the interstate. Seeing the covered back of our truck, they were already shouting for us to stop and pick them up as we drove by. Some of them threw rocks. Rachel's window was spidered with cracks, and so was the windshield.

I shook my head and clenched my teeth. It was too dangerous to stop. The logistics of this trip were fast becoming a nightmare, and it was only going to get more crowded and more dangerous when we reached Austin. There had to be a way to keep moving North safely. Our fuel should last. Bathroom breaks were the problem.

The obvious solution came to me, and it didn't involve mooning any would-be hitchhikers as we drove by.

"Okay guys, here's the drill. You can drink and eat to your hearts' content, but—"

"Yay!" Rachel said.

"Finally!" Alex opened the cooler and pulled out a juice box and a sandwich. Rachel hurried to do the same.

"Hang on!" I shouted to be heard over the commotion in the back. "There's a catch. You're going to have to pee in cups. And if you have to go number two..." I trailed off, shaking my head. "Best if you can hold it until we have to stop and refuel." At least we'd thought to bring toilet paper.

I saw my kids' reactions in the rear-view mirror. Rachel's eyes widened, and Alex's lips twisted with disgust.

"Eww," Rachel said.

"That's the rule," I insisted.

"We'll make it," Kate whispered, patting my thigh.

"Yeah," I agreed, my knuckles turning white

on the steering wheel as my eyes darted around for threats. We had to make it.

CHAPTER 43

The situation in Austin and Fort Worth was almost identical to what we'd found in San Antonio. Traffic slowed to a crawl as we drove through. We took advantage of the moments when traffic seized up completely to refuel and empty our bladders. The cup system had worked so far, but there was no point in using it if we didn't have to. Each time we got out, I took my M16 with me, and Harry took his shotgun. We took turns covering each other as we emptied our bladders. Within a minute of exiting our vehicles, Screecher discs would begin buzzing around us, a warning for us not to delay. Each time we refueled, I took the opportunity to check in on OneZero, but he just stared at me with those black eyes, not moving or trying to communicate. He didn't seem to mind the long, lonely trip in the back of the truck, and I was glad to have him. He'd already saved Kate's life, and I had a feeling he had a lot more life-saving in his future.

Thankfully, however, we didn't run into any more problems with our fellow travelers. I noticed that some of those travelers were with the military and the national guard, and I suspected we had them to thank for the civilian cease-fire.

Our armed forces joined the creeping lanes of traffic with their guns, trucks, Humvees, and even their *tanks*, but the latter quickly ran out of fuel and joined the cars pushed to the sides of the interstate. Somehow the Screechers paid no special attention to the soldiers. Likewise, I didn't see any of our guys opening fire on the hovering discs, big or small, that shadowed both sides of the interstate as far as the eye could see.

Now, fourteen hours after we'd set out from San Antonio, all three cities between us and Oklahoma City were far behind us. It was after two AM and pitch black outside but for the river of red tail lights ahead and the white running lights of disc-shaped Screechers to either side.

Warm air blasted me from the vents. I'd been forced to turn the heat on after the sun went down. A few inches of snow piled to either side of the interstate told me that it was below freezing outside.

A green sign shone bright under my headlights—

Oklahoma City
20 Miles

I breathed a sigh and worked some of the kinks out of my shoulders and neck. Fourteen hours of driving practically non-stop had left me tense and beyond exhausted. Kate had offered to trade places with me a few times, but she had a tendency to get sleepy behind the wheel. I didn't want to risk her veering off the road and getting us shot to pieces by Screechers.

Besides, Kate was already asleep. I glanced in my rear-view mirror to see that the kids were, too. We went over a bump in the road—some piece of rubble or debris that I hadn't seen. We were lucky it wasn't the kind that could rip open our tires. Kate flinched and woke up suddenly, covering a yawn with one hand.

"Where are we?" she asked, looking around with big, blinking eyes.

"Close," I said, nodding to another road sign that listed the exit number for the city of Norman.

"Norman?" Kate asked as we passed the sign.

"It's just below Oklahoma City."

"Where do you think we'll stop?"

"Oklahoma City," I said. "It's just above thirty-five degrees North on the map." That's where the radio broadcasts had said that the Screechers had set up their border.

Kate nodded agreeably, but her gaze held a world full of doubt and worry.

We passed through the city of Norman, and traffic slowed again. We ended up inching along for another hour. *Fifteen hours and counting...*

I wondered what the Screechers' border would look like. Would they have patrols watching it? Would they shoot people trying to cross it from the North?

Next up on the road signs was a city called Moore. Kate checked the maps and found that it was part of the greater metropolitan area around Oklahoma City. *Just a little farther,* I told myself, blinking the sleep from my eyes and shaking my head to stay awake.

"Logan... what is that?" Kate pointed to one side of the interstate.

I could see a long line of pinprick-sized lights hovering in the sky, all evenly spaced and stretching on as far as we could see.

"I think that's the border."

CHAPTER 44

April 27th
5 DAYS BEFORE THE ROGUE'S ARRIVAL

The lights turned out to be more of the hovering discs that had flanked us all the way from San Antonio. Border guards. I glanced up at them as we drove underneath, wondering if they ever ran out of power, or if they could just hover there indefinitely.

Immediately after we crossed the border, the Screechers flanking us peeled away, leaving us to drive on by ourselves. City lights glowed on the horizon, spreading a blanket of hope and warmth. Lights meant infrastructure. Civilization. Heat. They meant that we hadn't lost everything. Not yet, anyway.

Even as I thought about that, darkened buildings swept by on both sides. Here, within striking distance of where the Screechers had drawn their line in the sand, everything was abandoned. Had the people fled or had they been killed?

"Look—" Kate said, pointing out her window to a cluster of illuminated multi-story buildings up ahead. A sign identified them as *Mission Point Apartments*. Right after that came a strip mall. My eyes picked out familiar signs and logos—

BEST BUY. JCPENNY. WHATABURGER. BED BATH AND BEYOND.

Traffic slowed to a crawl. A green overhead sign appeared with cars peeling off to the right under it.

EXIT 116

S. 19TH ST

I merged right and joined the line of peeling cars.

"Where are we going?" Kate asked. My walkie-talkie crackled to life with the same question from Harry.

I grabbed it and said, "That shopping complex. The parking lot. We can stop there and get some sleep."

"What about a hotel? Over."

"Everyone else will be thinking the same thing. We're not going to find any rooms."

"Well, you think we should stop so close to the border? Over."

I saw military vehicles waiting in line for the same exit as us. That made me feel better about it. "I'm falling asleep at the wheel, Harry. The Screechers all left us at the border. We should be safe."

"All left except for one," Harry replied.

"Ex-nay. Someone could be listening on our frequency."

"Right. Over."

We passed the exit and rolled down a one-lane off-ramp that looped around to an internal street in the city of Moore. Traffic was bumper to bumper. It took about twenty minutes just to reach the end of the exit. The kids woke up, and Rachel began complaining that she needed to pee. I grimaced. "Can you hold it?"

"Maybe," she replied.

"See if you can wait until we're parked. I'm sure one of those stores will have a bathroom we can use."

"I'll try..."

We turned right onto the internal road and then took the first left into the parking lot of the shopping complex. The glowing blue sign for Ross lay dead ahead, and the red one for OFFICE DEPOT beside it. WHATABURGER rolled by to my right. I could see that the parking lot was already packed with cars, even though it was the middle of the night and everything was closed. Between ROSS and MAURICES there was an empty grass lot with at least a hundred cars parked in it. A matching grassy space sat opposite that in the parking lot, also clogged with vehicles. Despite the cold, and the fact that it was the middle of the night, people were standing around and walking all over the parking lot. There were thousands of them.

We rolled by a broad section of sidewalk in front of FIVE BELOW and JUSTICE - JUST FOR GIRLS! that was double and triple-parked with cars.

"We're never going to find a space," Kate said, shaking her head.

I had a bad feeling she was right, but said nothing as I continued to circulate with the snaking lines of traffic. Even the little grassy curbs were filled.

Just as I was about to give up, I caught a break. Red tail lights appeared in a space ahead of us. I stopped to let the car out. A driver on the other side thought the space was for him, and we ended up bumper to bumper, blocking each other's way. I lowered my window.

"I indicated, you didn't," I said.

"I didn't see anything," the man replied.

Cars began honking behind us.

"Whether you saw me or not, I did, and you didn't," I said reasonably.

"Well, I'm not moving," the other man said.

"Yes, you are," I replied, and revved my engine with an impressive roar. He was in a sedan. Pushing him out of the way wouldn't be hard. He'd be lucky if we didn't roll right over him.

I saw him reaching for something in his glove box, and I reached over Kate's lap for my gun.

"Logan!" Kate said in a warning tone. I whipped the rifle up and aimed it at the other driver. "Freeze, or I'll shoot," I said.

Not hearing me, or not believing the threat, the other driver whipped out a gun of his own—a revolver. His eyes widened at the sight of my gun.

"If you shoot me, I'll probably live," I said, nodding to his gun. "But if I shoot you, there'll be a hole in your chest the size of my fist."

"Fuck you!" the driver said, and shook his gun at me. It went off with a *bang* and I felt something hot whiz by my ear. I pulled the trigger—

Nothing happened.

The safety was on. My heart thumped painfully in my chest as a jolt of adrenaline went lancing through me. The driver of the sedan gripped his gun in both hands this time, and the barrel swept into line with my chest.

BOOM! The car's windshield exploded and blood spattered the inside. I blinked in horror and shock. Wondering if that was OneZero's handiwork again, I checked my mirror. Harry was leaning out his window with his shotgun, looking dazed at the result of firing it.

Cars were no longer honking their horns at us. A terrible silence accompanied the ringing in my ears, but for the sound of nearby pedestrians screaming and fleeing for their cars. Kate was shaking me and holding something to my ear. I turned to look at her, blinking in a daze. She had her jacket off and was pressing it to my ear. It was slick with blood. That driver hadn't entirely missed me. I noticed a corresponding bullet hole in Kate's window. Thank God she hadn't been hit. Rachel sobbed in the back, and I could see that she'd wet herself. Alex was saying something about needing a gun of his own.

"I'm okay," I said slowly.

Kate stopped trying to staunch the blood trickling from my ear and looked at me with scalding eyes. "No, you're not!"

I eased my foot down on the gas and pushed the dead driver's car out of the way; then I pulled into the empty space. There was some extra room on the grassy curb behind it, so I pulled all the way up there and motioned for Harry to double park behind me.

People were back to honking their horns, and I noticed that the car I'd pushed out of the way was clogging both sides of the street behind us. One irate driver honked his horn and yelled curses out his window at us.

I shut off the engine and grabbed my M16.

"What are you going to do?" Kate asked.

"Tell him to shut up," I said as I opened my door.

"Don't." Kate grabbed my arm to stop me. "Someone could kill you this time."

"I have to go check on the other driver. He might not be dead."

"Forget about him! He tried to kill you!"

"Even so. Lock the doors." I slammed the door as I left. Harry got out in front of me and we both walked around back of his SUV with our guns at the ready. This time I flicked *off* the safety, and hefted my rifle to make sure it was highly visible as I approached the screaming driver.

"You can't just go around killing people! He's blocking the whole street!" the driver said as I approached.

I walked straight up to his door, not aiming the rifle at him, but making damn sure he could see it.

"Hey buddy. It's been a long day. Calm down. I nodded to the sedan in front of him. "In case you missed it, he shot me first," I said, and pointed to the rivulets of blood trickling down my neck from my ear. "I'm going to go check on the other driver. One way or another we'll move his car, okay?"

"Fine. Whatever."

Harry and I walked over to the sedan. The sight that greeted us turned my stomach—dead eyes staring, chest flayed open. Everything inside the car was glistening blackly with the driver's blood.

"Shit! I killed him," Harry said in a shaking voice.

"Yeah. Thanks, by the way. He was aiming lower with the second shot."

I heard a stampede of footfalls and looked up to see four soldiers running toward us. When they saw me looking, all four of them stopped and swept their rifles up. The leader shouted, "Put your weapons on the ground now!"

I carefully laid my M16 down, and Harry did the same with his shotgun. The soldiers approached us slowly. "Hands where I can see them," the leader said.

We both raised our hands, but I shook my head. "It was self-defense!"

They stopped within just a few feet of us, close enough that I could read the *U.S. ARMY* patches sewn into their uniforms.

The leader took one look inside the car and then swept glaring eyes back to me. "Baker," he said, nodding sideways to one of the others.

"Sir?"

"Collect their weapons."

"Yes, sir."

"Hey, we need those." Baker stepped forward and retrieved both my M16 and Harry's semi-automatic shotgun from the ground.

"For self-defense, right?" the leader said through a sneer. "Fields, move that car! Let's get traffic flowing again."

"Yes, sir!"

"Ask the driver behind us," I said, and turned my head to show off my injured ear. "He shot first."

The soldier appeared to consider that before shouting to said driver. "Who shot first?"

"The dead guy!"

The soldiers in front of us gradually lowered their rifles. The leader looked to Baker, and spent a moment studying our guns. "Where did y'all get these? They're military-issue. Do either of you have a Federal Arms License?"

I hesitated before shaking my head. The world was ending and this guy was worried about gun licenses? "They belonged to my brother-in-law."

"Uh huh. So I guess you didn't steal them off any dead servicemen."

That's why he cares. "No, sir. And even if I had, it wouldn't be because I killed them. There were a few dead soldiers in our neighborhood the night the Screechers attacked, but I didn't have time to take their weapons."

The dead guy's car started moving, and traffic began flowing around us on both sides again. The lead soldier waved us over to one side, and we went to stand beside Harry's bumper. Kate and Deborah were there waiting for us, both of them hugging their shoulders for warmth.

"It's true," Kate said, blowing out white cloud of condensing air as she spoke. "The guns belonged to my brother."

The soldier didn't look happy, but he gave in with a nod. "All right, but I'm still going to have to keep them. We don't need any more dead people in this parking lot tonight."

I was about to argue, but the way the soldier said *any more dead people* gave me pause. This wasn't the first casualty they'd seen tonight.

All the more reason we need our guns. "How do

you expect us to protect ourselves?" I demanded. "You can't go around taking people's guns at a time like this!"

"Watch me," the soldier replied.

I wasn't ready to give up yet. We had other guns with us, but none as powerful as the ones that had just been confiscated. "We have children," I explained, and pointed to our cars. "And we still have a long way to go. Those guns have saved our lives more than once already."

"Yeah, but how many lives have they taken?"

"Just the one you saw," I replied. OneZero's kill didn't count. "You really want to leave us defenseless on the open road with two women and three children?"

The soldier just shook his head. "You want to stay safe? You can tag along behind one of our vehicles in the morning. I'll get you set up with an escort if I can. We have convoys heading South, West, and East, so take your pick. Where are you headed?"

"Memphis."

The man's eyebrows darted up and beetled together. He reached up to scratch an itch under the brim of his army hat. "Why Memphis?" he asked slowly.

"We have family there," I lied.

"Well, you're in luck. What's left of my platoon is headed there, too."

The coincidence made me suspicious. "Why Memphis?"

"Because that's where the president is, and she's recalled six whole divisions to protect the city."

I frowned. "The president? I thought DC was wiped out."

"It was. That doesn't mean the president was sitting in the White House when it happened."

It was my turn to ask: "Why Memphis?"

The soldier looked around conspiratorially. "Officially? Because it's as far south as you can get without crossing the Screechers' border, and its far from the coast, so no danger from the rogue when it arrives. Unofficially, because our illustrious leader has booked herself a ticket to Mars. Word is that she and that billionaire are in cahoots and they've known what's coming for years. They're both holed up at the launch facility with a few thousand of our boys patrolling the perimeter."

CHAPTER 45

I couldn't believe what I was hearing, but not because of the rumors that the president was fleeing Earth. This soldier had unwittingly validated the very reason we'd left San Antonio.

"Are you sure Akron Massey is there?"

"Oh yeah. Hell, I don't even blame him. His company built the rockets. He's got to feel some sense of ownership." The soldier snorted. "Of course he built them on tax payers' dollars, but who's counting, right?"

Cars flowed by beside us, horns honking, and drivers shouting out their windows at each other. A pair of soldiers were directing traffic and watching our backs with their guns.

"What time are you leaving in the morning?" I asked.

"Oh six hundred. If you want to come, I suggest you get some sleep."

I checked my watch and grimaced. It was four in the morning. San Antonio and Oklahoma City were on the same time zone, so that gave us exactly two hours to sleep. "We'll join you. How do we find you?"

"Hey!" a driver shouted out his window to catch the soldiers' attention. "You guys have any idea where we can park?"

The soldier speaking to us turned and glared at the man. "Do I look like a traffic cop, to you? Move along!"

The driver's head popped back in, and the soldier's gaze swept back to us. "I'll swing by here before we go. Make sure you're ready to leave."

"We'll be waiting."

"Good. No more shootouts, you copy?"

"With what guns?" I asked. We still had plenty, but he didn't need to know that.

The soldier smiled crookedly at us and turned to leave.

"What's your name?" I asked before he could get away.

"Corporal West. Or KW if you prefer."

I hesitated before offering my own name. *West.* The soldier was black. *KW?* Kanye West popped into my head, and I wondered if it was racist of me to make that connection.

"Before you say anything—yes, that's what KW stands for, and no, I am not related to the man."

One of the corporal's troops snickered, followed by—"How's Kimmy and the kids, KW?"

"Can it, Fields!"

I smiled at the exchange. "I'm Logan. This is Harry." I pointed to my wife. "That's Kate and Harry's wife, Deborah."

"Nice to meet y'all. See ya in the morning," he said. "Squad, move out!" he said in a parade ground voice, and started jogging back the way they'd come.

I heaved a weary sigh and looked to Kate. "Let's get some sleep."

"Roger that," Harry said.

* * *

Beeeep. Beeeep. Beeeep.

I woke up with a pounding heart and a thousand aches all over my body. Every muscle felt torn. My head seemed like it was stuffed with cotton. I fumbled sleepily for the Beretta I'd hidden in my side door. It was still dark out, but the first blush of dawn was on the horizon.

I sat up and righted the driver's seat. Seeing that the only threat in sight was the alarm Alex had set on his cell phone, I relaxed and put my gun away. I found the cell phone and shut off the alarm with an angry swipe of my finger. It hadn't woken anyone else. Alex and Rachel were still fast asleep in the back, somehow both sharing the bench seat as if it were a twin mattress. Alex was half on, half off, his legs bent and dangling over the improvised footrest that was our cooler.

I turned to Kate, but she was sleeping too, curled up against her window in a fetal position. I rubbed my aching eyes and tried to stretch in the small confines of the truck. I saw the people in the car next to us sleeping, too. The urge for me to go back to sleep was almost overwhelming.

Coffee. I would have traded all of our fuel and guns for just one cup. Maybe we'd be able to buy some along the way.

I heard a door slam and saw Harry getting out in my side view mirror. With a sigh, I grabbed the Beretta and opened my door. The cold hit me like a gut punch, and I gasped. It seared my exposed skin and made my nostrils stick together. I was awake now.

I jumped down and slipped my gun into the waistband of my jeans at the small of my back. I didn't want Corporal West to see it and confiscate it, too.

"How'd you sleep?" I asked, stopping in front of Harry. He was blowing into his hands and rubbing them together vigorously. I began to do the same. We couldn't wear insulated gloves and still fit our fingers through the trigger guards of our weapons, so we'd opted not to use them. I had a feeling that pretty soon we were going to have to give in and wear them anyway.

"Not good." Harry glanced behind him and shook his head. "Where are they?"

I checked my watch. "It's still five minutes to six. They'll be here. We should re-fuel while we wait." Harry nodded and went around the back of his SUV. I went to the back of the truck and untied one corner of the tarp at the back to pop my head in.

OneZero was in the exact same position I'd seen him in when I'd checked on him last night before going to sleep. I waved a hand at him to catch his attention and make sure he was still alive—or *powered on*, in his case.

OneZero raised a hand and waved back.

"You need to stay out of sight," I said.

He cocked his head at me like a dog trying to figure out what his master was saying. The language barrier was about the same as it would be with a dog, but we still hadn't properly established which one of us was the master.

"Just keep doing what you've been doing," I said, and grabbed two jerry cans full of diesel.

Setting them down at the back, I went around to my side of the truck and pulled the lever to open the gas tank door.

The tank sucked down all ten gallons, and there was still plenty of room for more. I was about to reach in for another jerry can when I heard rumbling engines and men's voices. Booted feet came clomping toward us, and I heard Harry speaking to someone. Footsteps approached me at a steady clip. I threw the empty jerry cans in the back with OneZero and spun around to face whoever was headed my way.

It was Corporal West.

"All set to go?" he asked, nodding to me.

I nodded back, slowly, fumbling for a reply in my suddenly dry mouth.

"Good." His eyes tracked past me to the open gas tank door. "You've got spare fuel with you?" His gaze found mine again.

"Yeah," I managed.

"Diesel?"

I nodded again.

"Can you spare some? We're running on fumes."

"Uh..." I glanced at the back of my truck. If I reached in to get more fuel, the corporal might see OneZero. How would he react to that? A vision of a shootout that ended with our army friends drowning in their own blood flashed through my head.

"Oh, I get it," the corporal drawled. "You want our help but you think it's a one-way street."

"No, that's not it."

West shrugged. "Then prove it." Corporal West took a step toward the back of my truck, but I moved to block his way.

"You got something in there you don't want me to see, Logan?"

My mouth popped open, but no sound came out. I needed to come up with a good excuse and fast.

West touched something on his uniform and yelled, "Fields! On me! Over," into a radio that I couldn't see.

Think! Damn it!

CHAPTER 46

Another soldier came running. Fields, presumably. I heard a door opening, followed by, "Logan?" It was Kate.

"Step aside," Corporal West said, his eyes on me.

"I don't have anything to hide," I said and stepped aside reluctantly.

"We'll see about that." Corporal West nodded to Fields as he arrived. "Open the back."

"Yes, sir."

I watched, frozen with terror as Fields stepped forward and peeled open the tarp. He recoiled in a hurry and his rifle swept up. "Woah! Contact!"

Corporal West's rifle snapped up and he joined his squad mate aiming into the darkened back of the pickup.

"Wait!" I said. "My kids are in the back!" If they fired their guns at OneZero, the bullets would shoot straight through into the cab.

"Scratch that," Fields said. "It looks to be

offline."

Corporal West peered in and then rounded on me. "You brought a Screecher with you?"

I shrugged, my eyes darting to see that OneZero was doing a good rag doll impression. "It's dead."

"Yeah? And what if the others want to bury it or something? What if they're tracking you?"

I frowned. "Then they would have confiscated it by now. We were flanked by Screechers the whole way from San Antonio. If none of them figured out we have one of theirs in the back, they're not about to figure it out now."

Corporal West sighed. "Still. You should ditch it."

"We should study it," I said. "Imagine what your division commander will say when you deliver this to him. You'll probably get a promotion."

"My division commander is dead."

"Well, show it to whoever else is in charge, then."

Corporal West seemed to consider that. "All right, but keep it hidden. Fields, grab a can of fuel—you too," he said, snapping his fingers at me.

I nodded and waited for Fields to withdraw a blue water tank full of diesel, and then I grabbed the last two jerry cans full of fuel, grimacing as I did so. *There goes our last fifteen gallons.*

"We're going to need to find more fuel," I said as we lugged them over to the soldiers' vehicles. I was expecting to see a whole convoy, but there was just one Humvee waiting behind Harry's SUV, along with the other two soldiers we'd seen before going to sleep.

"Where is everyone?" I asked.

Corporal West smirked. "You were expecting the cavalry or something?"

"I saw at least a dozen military vehicles pull in here last night."

"I bet you did, but they're all out of fuel. Assuming they haven't gone AWOL, they're probably still siphoning civvies' tanks. Regardless, we can't wait around for them. And speaking of waiting, are you going to do something with that fuel, or what?"

I nodded and hurried over to pass the jerry cans to Fields, who was busy trying to figure out how to pour diesel from a five gallon water jug. I solved his dilemma by passing him one of the funnels from the jerry cans. As I did so, Harry came over and whispered to me. "How much do you have left?"

"Not enough to get to Memphis," I said, and

winced at the pins and needles coursing through my frozen hands.

"Neither do we," Corporal West said, proving that he could still hear what we were saying. "But we just need enough juice to get us to the next working set of pumps."

Harry and I traded glances. With so many people pouring out of the South, I had a bad feeling we weren't going to find any gas stations that still had fuel—and here I was dumping the last of mine into an even less efficient engine than Richard's old F350.

When we were done, we piled into our vehicles. Richard and I reversed out of our space and followed Corporal West's Humvee through the parking lot. Fortunately, almost everyone was still sleeping in their cars, so we didn't run into any trouble getting out, but beyond the shopping complex I could see that the interstate was still clogged with bumper to bumper traffic. We inched along, wasting precious fuel. I fantasized that Corporal West's Humvee was a tank and that he could just push everyone out of the way. Instead his Humvee just sat there, idling away its fuel the same as us. I wondered who would run out first. We'd given them fifteen gallons, and I'd only re-fueled with ten.

"We're never going to get out of the city," I said, shaking my head.

Kate's hand found my arm and squeezed. "At least we're alive."

I caught her eye. She was smiling, her blue eyes full of hope. I marveled at how she managed to keep her spirits up in the middle of all this. Something tight unwound inside my chest, and I smiled back.

Traffic seized up completely and we sat there for fully ten minutes before one of the soldiers jumped out and came over to my door. I lowered my window. It was Fields. I recognized him by his freckly face, yellow teeth, and the weathered creases around his eyes.

"The interstate is blocked for miles," he said.

"But we're not even on the interstate!"

"This street leads straight to the on-ramp," Fields replied, pointing way off into the distance. "We're not going anywhere anytime soon."

CHAPTER 47

"We could ride down the curb," I suggested, and pointed to a snow-dusted grassy slope beside the road that led down into a concrete ditch for run-off.

"That might work," Fields said. "Let's try it." He ran back to his vehicle. Moments later we were kicking up clods of grass-covered dirt and racing past the frozen traffic. A few people caught on and pulled out behind us.

We had to ride up and over the turnouts into parking lots, pushing through traffic along the way. Coming to a set of traffic lights, we turned right, still rolling down the curb. Off-roading like that wasn't hard for either the soldiers or us, but I felt bad for Harry. He had a two-wheel drive, not four. If he got stuck along the way, they'd have to pile in with us.

We drove by a McDonalds, and my stomach growled. "Do we have any food back there?" I asked.

"Let me see," Kate replied. "Alex! Wake up!"

He groaned. "What? What is it?"

"Get a sandwich for your father, please."

In the rear-view I saw him sit up with a grumpy face and start digging through the cooler. A moment later, he passed a sandwich to Kate. She unwrapped it and passed it to me. I ate one-handed, trying not to bite my tongue as we jumped over the concrete abutments at the side entrance of the shopping center where we'd spent the night.

Up ahead, I spotted an oddly-shaped water tower, all white metal, with a bulb at the top and *Moore* scrawled across it in blue letters. To the left of that was a Shell Station. I grabbed my walkie to tell Harry.

"I saw it. You think West did? Over."

"I think so. It's hard to miss."

A few seconds later, the Humvee rolled to a stop in the grass and everyone but the driver got out. Fields came up to my window with the other two—Baker and... I noticed that the fourth soldier looked Chinese, but I couldn't recall hearing his name.

"Time to fill up," Fields said as soon as I lowered my window. I nodded and jumped out to get the empty fuel cans from the back of the truck.

Harry did the same, carrying two of his own

empties over to us. We each grabbed two containers, except for the Chinese soldier.

"Chong, watch our backs," Fields ordered. "Let's move out!"

We crossed traffic together to reach the station. The sun was rising over the top, staining the sky crimson.

"We'll have to make several trips," Harry said, and hefted the two jerry cans he was carrying.

"Assuming they have any fuel," I replied. But there were lots of cars lined up at the pump. I took that to be a good sign.

When we got to the station, Fields raised his voice and said, "Everybody stop what you're doing! We have priority."

I heard people grumbling and cursing as we approached. Chong held his gun at the ready, eyes scanning for threats.

But to my amazement people stepped away from the pumps and let us fill up first. We never would have gotten away with that if it weren't for our army escort. Even the station manager facilitated, keeping a record of the purchases for reimbursement, but not charging for them.

It took us half an hour to fill all of our empty containers and our tanks. By the time we were done, my back was aching and my arms were shaking, but we had enough fuel to get to Memphis.

Getting back into our vehicles, we started down the curb again, jumping over abutments and pushing through traffic on the side streets. As the buildings thinned out, so did the traffic, and pretty soon we were back on the road.

Hope swelled in my chest as I saw that we were making forty miles per hour. If things stayed that way, we would be in Memphis by nightfall.

"Dad, I need to pee!" Rachel said.

"So do I," Alex put in.

"Why didn't you go while we were fueling up?"

"Mom wouldn't let us," Alex explained. "She said it was too dangerous to get out, and you weren't there to ask."

"Use the cups!" I suggested, and flashed a grin in the rear-view mirror.

I had to laugh. We were in the middle of an alien apocalypse and our biggest problem was relieving our bladders.

But then I remembered our other problem. We had an alien soldier in the back of our truck, and we were escorting him through enemy territory. We could be arrested as collaborators, or shot and killed in a shoot-out with our own military. Not to mention, what was OneZero after? Why had he joined us, and where was he trying to go? It was reassuring to ascribe benevolent motives to the machine, but what if I was wrong?

* * *

I had to hand it to Corporal West. He really knew how to navigate. He managed to avoid traffic and slow-downs by sticking to country roads. It was only when we started running low on fuel that he took us into the little town of Ozark on the Arkansas River, where we stopped to refuel, eat, and use the gas station's restroom.

That had been almost seven hours ago. Now it was long past sunset and we were stuck in traffic on the I-40, waiting our turn to cross a bridge over the Mississippi River and into downtown Memphis.

"I can't believe we made it!" I said.

Kate nodded, smiling tightly at me, but not saying anything. The kids were asleep again, and I guessed she didn't want to wake them.

While we waited, snow began to fall in fat, tumbling flakes that stuck to the windshield, blocking my view. I turned on the wipers. This wasn't the first time we'd had to deal with snow along the way. It took an hour for us to reach the bridge, and by the time we did, I saw why. There were dozens of soldiers and their vehicles parked up ahead, restricting the flow of traffic into the city. Cars were pulled off the side of the interstate, being searched by soldiers. Whole families and lone travelers alike stood around, shivering in the snow as the soldiers rifled through their belongings.

Another half hour passed, and we were down to a quarter tank. If this kept up we'd have to shut off the engine and re-fuel. But then the last two cars ahead of us rolled through the road block. Corporal West's Humvee stopped at the road block. I saw him lean out to speak with a soldier there. I hoped we wouldn't have to submit to a search because we were traveling with him.

West leaned farther out to point at us. One of the soldiers came over and I lowered my window. Falling snow swept in with a blast of frigid air.

"Hello," I said.

"You need to pull over and submit to a search." He pointed to the side of the road.

"Sure thing." I nodded agreeably and smiled as I pulled over, but my heart was thumping hard in my chest. What would they say when they found OneZero in the back?

I had a bad feeling our robot guardian was about to be seized by the military, and I was pretty sure that this time he wasn't going to play dead.

CHAPTER 48

"**W**hat the hell are you doing with that?" the corporal searching our truck demanded.

"It's deactivated." I pointed to the damage Harry had done with his shotgun when we'd first encountered OneZero. "I thought we could learn something from it."

"You can't take it into the city," the man replied. "It's a secure area."

Falling snow was landing in my hair and accumulating. I struggled to come up with an excuse to keep the robot with us.

Meanwhile, the corporal waved a few more soldiers over. I peered around the back of our truck looking for Corporal West. He was standing outside his Humvee, talking with one of the other soldiers. He saw me just as another two men came jogging over. "Corporal!" I called out. "Could you come here for a second?"

He arrived just as the one searching our truck ordered his subordinates to climb into the back and pull OneZero out.

"Is something wrong here?" West asked the other corporal.

"Nothing wrong. We're seizing illegal assets, including this Screecher."

"Hold on," West said. "I'm under orders to deliver it to General Harris of the 29th Infantry."

I blinked, wondering if it was true. Maybe West had made radio contact with one of his superiors on the way over from Oklahoma?

The corporal searching us took West aside and they talked in private for a minute while I stood shivering in the dark with snow melting in my hair. The two soldiers who'd been ordered to pull OneZero out hadn't climbed in yet, but they were watching him with knitted brows and gloved hands flexing on their rifles. Thankfully, OneZero hadn't so much as twitched. Somehow I knew he was watching and listening, but I doubted he understood any of what was happening.

A third soldier came over, and I suspected from the way the two corporals deferred to him that he was in charge. The three of them conferred for a minute before striding over to me.

"How did you come by this piece of hardware?" the one in charge asked. I noticed an extra chevron on his upper sleeve and realized that he was a sergeant. The crows feet around his squinting eyes made me think he was about my age.

I sucked in a frigid breath and briefly recounted the story of how we'd found OneZero in the ruins of Harry's old home. But instead of describing the encounter as it had actually happened, I said we'd found him lying motionless in the rubble.

"What made you think to load it up and carry it across the border?"

"I thought it might be useful for our side to study."

The sergeant grunted. "Maybe so, but hopefully having it in our custody doesn't violate the cease fire. Either way, I suppose it's too late now. We'll have to move it to Corporal West's vehicle."

My heart sank, but I nodded. I felt bad for OneZero, but there wasn't anything I could do. For the first time I wondered what he'd been hoping to accomplish by joining us on this trip. Surely he'd known that there was a chance he'd become a prisoner once we crossed the Screechers' border.

West nodded to me, and the other corporal motioned for his soldiers to get in the back of our truck. "Search it while you're in there."

"Yes, sir," they said in unison.

The sergeant nodded to me before turning and walking back to a green tent behind the road block.

I watched as soldiers pulled clothes out of our luggage, rifled through cases of food and water, and unfurled our sleeping bags. Finally they found the wooden box full of guns and ammo that I'd hidden under all of that other gear. One of the two soldiers retrieved an impressive hunting rifle and held it up for his corporal to see.

"They've got a case full of guns and ammo, sir."

The corporal turned to me, and I noticed a name patch peeking out from under the butt of his rifle. *Johnson.* He had a square jaw and a mean look in his eyes. "Who are you delivering those guns to?" he demanded.

"No one," I protested, shaking my head. "Those are for our protection."

"Not anymore. Bring them out," he added, waving to his men.

West slowly shook his head, as if disappointed in me. He probably thought he'd already confiscated all of our guns when he took my M16 and Harry's shotgun.

Once the soldiers had our case of guns on the ground, Corporal Johnson ordered his men to get everyone out and search them and the rest of the truck. Johnson patted me down himself. I'd left my Beretta in the side door on the driver's side. The soldiers found it and the spare magazines in the glove box. They also lifted the back seat and found the hidden storage box underneath. They ordered me to open it with my keys. I did so, revealing my laptop bag and Alex's, along with a shotgun and two more pistols. They took the weapons, but left our laptop bags alone. I wished I'd thought to hide a gun in one of them. Moving on, the soldiers searched Harry's SUV, coming up with another handgun—a Smith and Wesson, and two more rifles.

By now, I couldn't feel my toes or my fingers. Rachel started to cry and complain about the cold, even though she was wearing thicker gloves than I. Picking her up, I held her close to keep her warm and quiet her sobbing. She promptly fell asleep against my shoulder, making it impossible to put her back down. My arms and back began to ache. She was a lot heavier than she used to be.

Alex went over to speak with Celine, while Harry and Deborah oversaw the search of their vehicle. I heard Deborah complaining loudly as the soldiers unpacked her bags and made a general mess of things.

Finally, Corporals Johnson and West returned.

"Get the Screecher out," Johnson said to his men; to me, he added, "You're cleared to enter Memphis. You have a place to stay?"

"We do," I lied, keeping half an eye on the soldiers as they dropped my tailgate and began removing containers of fuel to get better access to OneZero.

"Then I suggest you head there without stopping," Johnson said. "There's a lot of unrest in the city right now."

I nodded slowly, wondering what that meant. Grunting noises drew my attention to the soldiers in the back of the truck, and I watched them struggling to drag OneZero out by his feet. Cursing loudly, they gave up after moving him just a couple of inches.

"Sir, it's too heavy."

"Put your backs into it!"

"We're trying, sir."

Johnson shot an accusing look at me before climbing in and grabbing a foot. The three of them heaved and cursed, dragging OneZero out one inch at a time. Corporal West reached in to help them as they got to the tail gate. Kate and I backed away to give them space. They yanked OneZero out and he fell on the side of the road with a loud *thunk.* Rachel woke up with a start and looked around with wide eyes.

"Daddy?" she asked, sounding confused.

"Shhh," I whispered in her ear.

She popped her thumb in her mouth and laid her head back against my shoulder.

"How the hell did you get that bastard in there?" Johnson asked.

My back spasmed painfully, and I was forced to put Rachel down. She stood beside me holding my hand and sucking her thumb. She saw OneZero's limp body, and I braced myself, thinking that she would say that OneZero had climbed into the back of our truck all by himself. What would that make us? Guilty of collusion with the enemy?

I shrugged and gestured vaguely to Harry and his family. "We all helped."

Johnson glanced at them, then back at me, his eyes pinching into suspicious slits.

Rachel tugged on my arm. "Dad, what's OneZ—" I squeezed her hand so hard that the bones ground together. Rachel cried out and yanked her hand away from me. "Owww!"

"Are you okay, honey?" I asked, as if confused by her reaction. I dropped to my haunches in front of her, taking the opportunity to give her an urgent look. There'd be time for apologies later.

Rachel rubbed her hand and scowled at me.

Kate caught on. "Come sweetheart, let's leave Daddy to talk to the soldiers." She led Rachel away, and I straightened to regard Corporal Johnson once more.

"Is she okay?" he asked.

"She'll be fine. She hurt her hand the other day."

"You were saying about how you got the Screecher into your truck...?"

"There's six of us, not counting my daughter," I explained. "We managed to lift him in together."

Johnson seemed to accept that. He called for assistance over his radio, and I noticed that it took exactly six soldiers to lift OneZero and carry him into the back of Corporal West's Humvee. They were probably a lot stronger than us, but thankfully Johnson didn't come back over to question us again.

Kate and Rachel got back into the truck while I re-packed our luggage and containers of fuel, securing them with ratchet straps. By the time I was done, my extremities were all stinging with pins and needles, and I was shivering uncontrollably.

Jumping down off the tail gate and landing on numb feet, I waved Alex over and called out to Harry: "Let's go!"

He nodded and gave me a mock salute. I went to speak with Corporal West while Alex climbed in. OneZero lay limp and folded up in the back of West's Humvee. I wondered when he was going to decide to wake up—or could he? Maybe he was out of juice. I supposed that would be better for him in the end. Best not to be awake when they dissected him and analyzed him for weaknesses.

Moving on, I walked up behind Corporal West. "I guess this is where we part ways."

He turned from where he and Corporal Johnson were busy studying a map on the hood of his Humvee. West stuck out a hand. "It was a pleasure."

I shook his hand, and nodded sideways to the truck. "Where are you taking the Screecher?"

"To General Harris of the 29th Infantry," West replied in a dull voice.

"Right. I forgot. Well, see you around, Corporal."

He nodded, and I saluted as I left. I climbed into the truck beside Kate and turned the engine on with a throaty roar. I hesitated with my eyes on the back of the Humvee.

"Everything okay?" she asked.

"Yeah." I pulled out onto the interstate and rolled up to the boom blocking the bridge. Corporal Johnson waved us through, and I glanced in my rear-view mirror to see Harry rolling along behind us. The bridge was almost empty thanks to the road block tying up traffic, and we zipped across at forty-five miles per hour. I saw the lights of downtown Memphis. Skyscrapers peeled back the night with their lights. A giant glass pyramid gleamed at the end of the bridge, the sloping sides illuminated by bright spotlights.

I'd never been to Memphis, but the city looked inviting with all those lights. Now all we needed was to get lucky and find a hotel where we could spend the night.

"What do you think they're going to do with him?" Kate asked.

"OneZero?"

She nodded.

"I don't know. Probably crack him open and see what makes him tick."

"He saved my life," Kate said.

I looked at her. "He's just a machine. Besides, there's nothing I can do about it now. We need to focus on our own survival."

A heavy silence fell following that statement.

"They're not going to hurt him, are they?" Rachel asked.

"No, honey," I said, shaking my head. "Robots don't feel pain."

"How do you know?"

"Because they don't."

"But how do you—"

"Honey, be quiet," Kate said. "Daddy needs to concentrate."

I took the off-ramp into downtown Memphis, and immediately saw what Corporal Johnson meant about *unrest* in the city. The streets below were literally on fire.

CHAPTER 49

We drove past the flaming wrecks of broken-down cars along the sides of the road. Shadowy clumps of pedestrians walked down the sidewalk on the river side of the street, and down railway tracks on the city side.

"Logan, lock the doors," Kate said. Some of those shadows were glancing at us.

I hit the appropriate switch and all four doors locked. We came to an intersection and stopped at a red light. Beside us was a blue sign pointing right to the *Welcome Center.*

Just then, a pair of youngsters on bikes went racing through the intersection in front of us. One of them held a flaming bottle high in his hand. He threw it, and it exploded beside my door with an audible *whoosh* of flames. Kate and Rachel screamed.

"Logan!" Kate prompted.

I floored it through the intersection, narrowly missing one of the kids. Harry raced through after me. The truck bounced over something I didn't see, our suspension rocking, and then I heard a loud thumping noise that sounded like it was coming from the back.

"What was that?" Kate whispered sharply.

I thought about the open tarp at the back, and wondered if someone had jumped in to raid our supplies while we were at the light. I cursed under my breath and grabbed my walkie-talkie.

"Harry, did you see anyone climb in the back of my truck?"

"No. Why? Over."

I breathed a sigh. "We heard something, but it must have been some of our fuel containers breaking loose."

"Must have been. We would have seen it if someone jumped in. If they had, though, I'm not sure what we could do about it without any guns. We need to find somewhere safe to spend the night. Over."

"Copy that. Any ideas?" I asked, while scanning both sides of the road. To our right was a park with trees and benches along the Mississippi River. There were tents pitched in the snow-covered grass beneath those trees. We had tents and sleeping bags of our own, but I doubted that squatting in the park would be either warm enough or safe enough for us. To our left, the tops of skyscrapers peered down on us with the glowing names of banks and big companies.

"What about Beale Street?" Harry asked. "We're bound to find hotels there."

"I don't know where that is."

"Follow me," Harry said, and pulled into the oncoming traffic lane to get ahead of me. I let him get by, and he promptly took the next left, heading away from the river toward a tower with a sign that read *I bank* at the top.

We drove down a street full of broken shop windows and drifters warming their hands over garbage can fires. Rolling past the bank tower, Harry hung a right, and we rumbled past more broken windows and burnt-out cars. To my surprise, people had pitched tents along the sidewalks, too. Reaching the next intersection, we stopped for a red light, and I spotted a large building with a glowing red sign at the top.

The Peabody

That name clicked with some distant memory in my brain. This was a famous luxury hotel. I followed Harry through a left turn, drawing ugly looks from street-bound pedestrians standing on the corners watching us. Somehow we were the only cars on the street besides the scattering of wrecks we'd seen. What had happened to all the other vehicles who'd crossed the bridge ahead of us?

Maybe they never left the interstate, I reasoned.

Up ahead Harry stopped at the front doors of the Peabody Hotel. To my surprise those doors were guarded by four soldiers. Harry hopped out and spoke briefly to one of them before waving me over.

I got out and hurried over to him.

Harry explained, "They don't have any rooms, but there's space on the roof if we're willing to pay."

"On the roof?" That sounded just as cold as camping on the sidewalk. "How much?"

Harry nodded to one of the soldiers, deferring the question. "What's the rate here?"

"One thousand per tent, per night."

"What?" I thundered. "That's insane!"

The soldier laughed darkly at me. "Why do you think there's so many people camping on the streets?"

I was about to argue some more, but Harry grabbed my arm and shook his head. "Just for tonight. We've been driving for sixteen hours straight. At least we know it will be safe with these guys guarding the doors."

I had the last twenty thousand dollars from our savings stashed under the seats, but this seemed like a stupid way to blow through it. "And what do we do with our cars?" I asked. "We can't just leave them out here. You saw what happened to everyone else who parked on the street."

The soldier who'd spoken a moment ago overheard our discussion. "There's valet parking."

"And how much will that cost?" I snapped.

"Hey, it's not my hotel. Take it up with the manager."

"Come on," Harry said. "One night. There's bathrooms and hot showers."

"Where? On the roof?"

"In the spa."

"Can *you* pay?" I challenged.

He nodded. "For one room and one night I can."

"You mean one *tent*."

"Right, that's what I meant."

I sighed. "All right. Let's go book a spot." I went back to my truck and lifted the lining on the floor under my seat to withdraw a stack of twenties.

"They have room for us?" Kate asked, sounding relieved.

"On the roof," I explained.

"What?"

"Yeah, we'll be camping in the cold, but at least we'll be safe. Wait here."

Not bothering to explain further, I shut the door and walked up to the front entrance of the hotel. Harry was already waiting there. I nodded to the soldiers.

"Watch our vehicles please. We have kids inside."

"No problem, sir."

As we walked through the doors, a welcome gust of warm air greeted us. My eyes closed to half-lidded slits. Maybe we could just sleep in here. I glanced around. It was like a whole other world inside the lobby—a world where aliens had never invaded, and people weren't out camping on the streets between the blackened skeletons of vandalized cars.

The muted strains of Blues music trickled to my ears. And even though it was past two in the morning, people were lounging on plush chairs and couches, drinking cocktails. Marble floors and columns sparkled in the light of ornate crystal chandeliers hanging from ceilings with dark wooden moldings and what looked like stained glass murals. Water trickled from a fountain in the center of the lobby. Flowers grew on top, and a pair of live ducks were sleeping on the edge of the fountain. My gaze strayed back to the people in the lobby. Some of them were asleep, too, others nodding off with their cocktails in hand and dazed looks on their faces. They were all well-dressed.

"What the hell?" I whispered, shaking my head. "Who *are* these people?"

"Government officials and rich jackasses is my guess," Harry muttered back. "Or maybe just weary, desperate travelers like us."

We reached the front desk and expressed our desire to rent a piece of the Peabody's roof.

"It is *very* expensive, and we're almost out of room," a snooty hotel clerk replied while slowly shaking his head.

"We can pay," I insisted, and slapped my stack of twenties down on the desk. Harry did the same with a smaller stack of his own.

The clerk's eyes widened. "Very well. You have your own tents and sleeping bags, I suppose? Rentals cost extra."

"We do," I confirmed.

"How many tents?"

I thought about that. There was no way we'd all fit into one. "Three tents."

"Any vehicles?"

"Two."

"Will you be requiring our valet service for them?"

"Where's the parking lot?"

"One block down, but it's somewhat risky to park there yourself, I'm afraid. Our valets are all armed soldiers and well equipped to deal with any threats that might arise."

I grimaced. "Fine. We'll valet park them, then."

"Okay..." the clerk's eyes dipped to his computer screen. "That will be—forty-two sixty, and yes—that's all dollars and no cents."

I couldn't believe it. My cheeks bulged with indignation. "I thought it was a thousand per night per tent!"

"Who told you that?" the clerk replied, blinking slowly at us.

"That's fine. We can pay," Harry said. To me he added, "We'll split it—one third two thirds. Fair enough?"

I gave in with a reluctant nod and began counting out two thirds of 4260, which I roughly calculated to be 2900. Harry paid the rest, and then the clerk called over his valet parkers—two privates with the national guard. A bellhop followed us outside with a golden baggage cart. The cold hit me like a slap to the face. My eyes flew wide open and I shook my head to wake up. The heat and the Blues music in the lobby had turned me into a sleep-walker.

Anxious to get everything done in a hurry so we could get some sleep, I hopped into the back of my truck and began unloading our bags. In the process, I tripped and fell over something at the back. I knocked my chin on whatever it was, and cursed under my breath.

"Is everything okay back there, sir? Do you need some help?" the bellhop asked, peering in.

"No, I'm fine," I said, feeling around in the dark for whatever I'd tripped over. My hands grazed cold metal, but it wasn't the wheel well or the side of the truck. It was cylindrically shaped. I stared hard into the darkness, frozen and uncomprehending. Then an invisible, icy hand closed over mine. I yelped and recoiled from it, stumbling backward and falling against our spare fuel supply.

CHAPTER 50

My mind flashed back to the *thump* we'd heard earlier, and I realized that it hadn't been a fuel container breaking loose. They were all still strapped in place.

"Sir? Are you okay?" the bellhop asked.

I glanced over my shoulder to see him standing on my back bumper and leaning in to reach me, as if to help me up. The private acting as my valet was peering in, too, but there was nothing to see except for the empty space that OneZero had vacated almost two hours ago.

And yet, somehow, that space wasn't empty. OneZero was back, and he was as invisible as any ghost.

"I'm fine," I said, belatedly snapping out of it. "I just slipped that's all. I'm going to pass you the first bag. Hold on."

"Of course," the bellhop replied.

I passed our bags out one after another, this time being careful to mind OneZero's invisible limbs. I couldn't believe that he'd escaped. Maybe I was hallucinating? I felt around for one of his invisible limbs, and my hand once again closed around a cylindrical metal object. A smile sprang to my lips. Corporal West was going to be disappointed when he delivered an empty truck to his division commander.

But why had OneZero come running after us? What had we done to deserve such loyalty from an enemy soldier? Was it because I'd tackled Harry to stop him from shooting OneZero again? Or was he riding along with us because of some hidden agenda that just happened to coincide with ours?

What did he want? Somehow, I needed to find out. Tomorrow I'd take the time to sit down with OneZero in private and start working on a dictionary to translate his binary codes into something I could understand.

Once the bellhop had all of our luggage and the Hartfords' loaded on his cart, we watched from the sidewalk as the valet drivers took our vehicles to whatever parking lot the desk clerk had mentioned. I watched the tail lights receding into the distance, wondering if OneZero would stay in the back of the truck and wait for us to return. I hoped so.

"Let's go, Logan," Kate said, tugging on my

arm. I turned to see our kids walking ahead of us with Harry's family, just now passing through the doors of the lobby.

* * *

By the time we finished pitching our tents on the trampled, snow-covered roof, I realized that I couldn't even remember how we'd gotten up to the roof, let alone how we'd pitched the tents. My mind had shut off already.

We crawled into our tents, my kids taking one, Kate and I the other, and the Hartfords a third. I fell asleep in seconds, but what felt like just a few minutes later, I woke up with a gasp, and lay staring up at the blue fabric of our tent. Kate's breathing was still slow with sleep, but mine was suddenly shallow and rushed. My heart pounded with adrenaline. I'd been running on it for so long that my adrenal glands didn't know when to shut off. Somehow, I felt exhausted and wide awake at the same time.

Carefully removing Kate's arm from my chest, I crawled out of my sleeping bag to the flap of the tent, and unzipped it. Snow fell inside the tent. It had been piled against the flap. I had to crawl through the snow to get out. The two or three trampled inches I remembered from before were now covered with an additional twelve. Snow squeezed into my fur-lined leather gloves, melting against my skin and trickling past my wrists. I stood up and walked over to the edge of the roof, my boots crunching through the snow. A faint glow swelled over the horizon, out beyond the Mississippi river.

I watched as the sun came up, turning the rosy blush of dawn to a golden fire. Now, in the light of day, I saw that the city had taken some serious damage. One of the high-rises close to the Peabody was collapsing and leaning against another that was still under construction. The majority of the city's towers were still standing, but several had their windows blasted out.

In the distance, across the river, I spied a group of massive towers reaching for the sky around squat buildings with flat, snow-covered roofs. I realized that those weren't towers. They were rockets.

For a second, I thought those were the Screechers' landers, and that they had moved their border north into Memphis, but then I realized that those were *our* rockets. I was looking at Starcast's launch facility. We'd crossed the bridge into Memphis for nothing. Now we'd have to cross it back the other way. I counted nine rockets in all. Vast fields of green tents surrounded the facility.

Army camps.

How were we going to get through all of them to speak with Akron Massey? Despair clutched my heart just as a frigid wind blew, cutting through my jacket and drawing a shiver out of me. I tucked my hands into my armpits for warmth and turned to regard the tents behind me. Everyone who'd checked into the rooftop was still fast asleep. *Lucky them.*

Kate's head popped out of our tent. "What are you doing up so early?"

"Couldn't sleep."

"Come back to bed," she insisted. "You had a long day. You need your rest."

I gave in with a sigh and took a step toward her. Just as I did that, a distant roar came rumbling to my ears. I turned and saw Starcast's launch facility engulfed in fire and billowing clouds of smoke.

I gaped at that. Tents unzipped behind me, barely audible through the on-going roar. Alex and Rachel came trudging through the snow to stand beside me and watch the spectacle. Kate's hand slipped into mine, and we traded worried glances.

"Is that..." she trailed off.

Three rockets lifted off amidst roiling clouds of smoke and fire, taking all of our hopes with them.

The Mars Colony Mission was launching ahead of schedule. We'd traveled all this way for nothing.

CHAPTER 51

"Now what are we going to do?" Harry asked, as he squinted up at the dwindling streaks of light. His gaze came back down to Earth to glare at me. "I told you we should have stayed in the shelter."

"So let's just go back," Deborah said.

Harry scowled at her and shook his head. "And I suppose we'll just ask the Screechers politely if we can cross their border? They'll probably shoot us on sight. No, Logan's plan is bust, and now we're no better off than anyone else—except we don't even have a place to stay anymore."

"We have a house in New Jersey," Kate said. "You could come stay with us."

"Yeah? And how are we going to stay warm? What are we going to do when the snow is piled up to your roof? Dig tunnels? There's no sugarcoating this. Your husband screwed us all."

"He did the best that he could! And no one

held a gun to your head. You could have stayed. We all knew that this was a long shot, but we went willingly."

I placed a hand on Kate's arm. "No, he's right," I said. "This is my fault. I convinced them, and you. You didn't want to leave either."

"We're all adults, responsible for our own actions," Kate objected. "Don't put this all on yourself."

"Does this mean we're not going to go live with the fishes?" Rachel asked, tugging on her mother's sleeve.

Kate flashed a smile at our daughter. "Don't worry. We're going to find someplace even better!"

I grimaced and turned to leave. There were lots more people on the roof now, standing outside their tents and murmuring amongst themselves as they watched the rockets climb steadily into the sky. I wove around them on my way to the exit.

"Where are you going?" Kate called after me.

"I need to go get something out of the truck," I said.

"Get what?"

"My laptop!" I shouted back. That was true, even though it wasn't the real reason I was leaving the roof. I hadn't told anyone about finding OneZero last night, but now it was more important

— 414 —

than ever to find a way to communicate with him. Maybe he would have some idea that could save us, or maybe he could find a way to get us back to Richard's shelter.

I figured if I could charge my laptop in the lobby and catch a WiFi signal from the hotel, then I'd be able to search for images online. I'd download as many as I could, and then show them to OneZero. We could match words with their binary counterparts to develop a dictionary of sorts. It might be slow going, but it would work—assuming that the hotel's Internet was still working.

* * *

The walk to the parking garage was nerve-wracking with all the drifters on the streets. They all looked mean and dangerous—even the scattered families that I saw. But unlike last night where I'd felt their eyes glaring as we drove by, today they barely gave me a second glance. I suspected that it had something to do with the fact that now I was walking around like them rather than riding high in my truck.

All the same, I kept my head down until I reached the entrance of the garage. There I came face to face with four more soldiers, just like the ones guarding the entrance of the hotel. I showed them my keys and valet stub, and they let me through.

The garage was massive, just like the hotel, and I realized too late that I shouldn't have refused the desk clerk's offer to have one of the valets show me to my vehicle. But if I had accepted that offer, I wouldn't have the privacy I needed to talk with OneZero.

Wondering where to look for my truck, I thought about the fact that we'd arrived last night to find the hotel (and roof) already full. Based on that, I decided to check the top floor of the garage.

I got lucky and found both Harry's SUV and my F350 double-parked near the ramp.

Poking my head into the back of the truck, I whispered, "OneZero!"

But I couldn't see anything. Maybe he'd left. Or maybe he was still hiding.

"Hey, are you there?" I tried again.

The air shimmered and a dimly gleaming silhouette appeared, translucent as if it were made of water or glass.

I marveled at the technology it must have taken to accomplish that.

"It's okay," I said. "There's no one else around. The coast is clear." I doubted he'd understand any of that, but maybe he'd catch something from my tone of voice.

OneZero's body went from transparent to opaque. "Coast is clear," he said in a crisp, female tone.

I blinked in shock and slowly shook my head. "You can talk?"

"Talk," he said. Once again that voice clashed with my concept that this robot was a *he*, and I realized that I'd simply defaulted to my own gender out of some ages-old patriarchal bias.

"You're a she?" I asked. Did robots even have a gender?

"She."

I frowned. Was that confirmation, or was OneZero just copying what I said? For all I knew it simply preferred the sound of a woman's voice.

I glanced over my shoulder to make sure there was no one around to listen in, but the garage was empty, and I couldn't hear anything except for the distant whistling of a frigid wind.

Pulling myself up inside the truck, I arranged the tarp behind me to cover the entrance from prying eyes. Taking a seat on the fuel containers, I nodded to the robot. "OneZero."

It cocked its head at me.

"We need to work out a way to understand each other. I'm going to go now, but I'll be back soon with something that we can use to communicate."

"Communicate," OneZero said.

"Exactly. I'll be back, okay? Don't go anywhere."

OneZero just looked at me, and I smiled reassuringly as I left.

Walking around the back, I opened the rear door on the driver's side and lifted the back seat to reveal a lockable under-seat storage box. I unlocked it with one of the keys on my keyring and slid it open to reveal my laptop bag and Alex's. I thought about the remainder of our cash stashed under the lining below the front seat and wondered if I should move it to here. I discarded the idea a few seconds later. If those soldiers had found this compartment and forced me to open it, so could a gang of robbers on the highway.

On my way back to the hotel I was considerably more nervous now that I had something of value slung over my shoulder. Fortunately, no one seemed to notice or care about the laptop, and the hotel entrance was only a block away from the garage.

Back in the warmth of the lobby I breathed a sigh of relief and went to the front desk to ask about the WiFi and an outlet I could use.

There was a new desk clerk there this morning, and she was much friendlier than the man who'd greeted us last night.

"Of course. The password is—" the woman appeared to hesitate. Doubt flickered across her face as her gaze dipped to my toes and back up to my battered face. There were plenty of scabs peeking through my shaggy beard from all the shrapnel and glass Kate had picked out of my face three nights ago. That, and my long, unwashed hair had to give this woman pause. Maybe that was why the people on the street hadn't bothered me—I looked worse than them.

"You're staying at this hotel?"

I nodded slowly. "Yes. On the roof. We came in last night."

"I see. And what's your name?"

"Willis. Logan Willis." I tapped my foot impatiently while I waited for the clerk to look me up.

"Of course. I apologize. You'd be amazed at how many people try to sneak in here."

"I can imagine." If it weren't for the soldiers standing outside, everyone would probably be in here. Of course, give them a few more days out in the cold without food, water, or plumbing, and they'd probably storm the entrance anyway. We

— 419 —

had to move on before that happened.

The clerk smiled tightly at me. "The network is the only one around, and the password is Stokes88, like the musician."

I nodded my thanks, and went to look for an outlet. I found one by the windows facing the street. The chairs around the outlet were filled with snoring people, so I sat on the floor with my back to the wall. I watched the people in those chairs as I waited for my computer to start up, wondering how much the Peabody charged per night for a spot in the heated lobby.

My laptop's welcome screen appeared, along with a cheerful tone, and I typed in my password. Logging into the hotel's WiFi with the password the clerk had given me, I opened a browser window and typed *dictionary of pictures* into Google to see what would come up.

The first result was "Visual Dictionary Online." I clicked through to that site and scanned the page. Seeing a *downloads* tab, I tried that, and found that they had an offline version. I started the download. This was going to be easier than I'd thought.

While I waited for the download to finish, I thought about what else I could accomplish now that I finally had an Internet connection. I went straight to CNN and began scanning the headlines.

Screechers Building Border Wall

Refugee Crisis Worsens as Screechers Drive Millions North

The Fight Continues in Africa

New Estimates Put Death Toll Over One Billion Worldwide

Coastal Cities Turn Into Ghost Towns Anticipating Tidal Waves

Rogue Star Arriving Early - April 28th at 5:30 PM

Mars Colony Mission Leaving Early, Initial Launch Set for April 28th

The wording of that final headline hit me—*initial launch*—and I thought back to what I'd witnessed from the roof. We'd seen three rockets taking off, but I'd counted nine on the ground. That meant there were still six more waiting to launch.

My heart began beating double time in my chest. There was a good chance Akron Massey was still at the launch facility. We might not be too late to ask him where Haven was, after all.

CHAPTER 52

I clicked the headline and hurriedly scanned through the article. It talked about three separate launches, each one separated by twelve hours. The first one had been at 6:00 AM local time. The second would be at 6:00 PM tonight, and the final one would take off at 6:00 AM tomorrow.

Wondering about the timing, I remembered another headline—the one that said the rogue star was arriving early, and I clicked back in the browser window to check that headline.

Rogue Star Arriving Early - April 28th at 5:30 PM

What day was it today? Checking the date and time in the corner of my screen, I blinked in shock. The rogue was arriving *tonight,* just before the second rocket launch.

I took a moment to stop and think about that. What did that mean for us?

My mind drew a blank. Memphis was so far from the coast that it didn't really matter. The rogue would pass us by and we probably wouldn't even notice. The long-term effects of its approach and departure were what concerned us—the disruption of Earth's orbit and the dropping of temperatures around the world. And we'd already begun to feel those effects: snow in Memphis in the middle of Spring. It was absurd, and things were only going to get worse. What would we do when the warmest place we could go was well below freezing? Where would we go when we ran out of money for hotels? Would we end up camping on the streets like those people outside? How long before hunger drove people insane and drove them to cannibalism?

Darkness and despair gathered, dragging me down and threatening to snuff out the fragile hope that I was still clinging to—Haven. We had to find Haven.

I shook myself out of my dark musings and forced myself to focus. We still had time to catch Akron Massey. The second group of rockets wasn't launching until 6:00 PM. My gaze returned to the date and time in the corner of the screen. It was 7:38 AM right now. We had just over ten hours to reach Massey and convince him to tell us where Haven was.

"There you are!" I looked up to see Kate and the kids approaching at a hurried pace. "There's a

— 423 —

complimentary breakfast in the hotel restaurant," Kate added as they stopped in front of me.

I jumped up off the floor with my laptop in my hands. "You have to see this!"

Kate's brow furrowed. "What's wrong?"

I clicked the headline that read *Mars Colony Mission Leaving Early, Initial Launch Set for April 28th* and turned the screen around for my family to see. Kate peered at it, slowly shaking her head.

"We already know about the launch. We just watched it with you, remember?"

"Yes, but that was only *one* of the launches." I showed her the headline and explained my deduction; then I pointed to the part where the article described three separate launches. "What are the odds that Massey would go in the first wave? Think about it. The Screechers could still decide to shoot those rockets down. He'll want to hang back and wait until he's sure it's safe."

"So we might still catch him," Kate said, her eyes widening.

I nodded. "Yes, if we can find some way through the soldiers guarding the facility."

"How are we going to do that?"

"I don't know, but we have to try. Maybe they'll give us security clearance because you're Richard's sister, or else they might give us some way to contact Mr. Massey."

"So what are we waiting for?" Alex asked.

I checked the status of my dictionary download. It was done. "Nothing," I said. "Where are the Hartfords?"

"Harry is up on the roof guarding all of our stuff," Kate said. "Debbie and Celine are getting breakfast."

"Go round them up and meet me on the roof. We need to leave right away."

Rachel's eyes flashed and her bottom lip popped out. She stomped her foot and crossed her arms. "No," she said. "I'm hungry."

"We should eat first," Kate said.

My stomach growled, and the possibility of hot coffee sealed it. "All right, but let's be quick."

* * *

After breakfast and three cups of coffee, I went to the front desk with Harry to get his keys so that we could retrieve our own vehicles. We got his keys, despite the desk clerk's protests that we'd already paid for the valet service and might as well use it. Harry walked grudgingly beside me as we walked down the snowy sidewalk to the garage.

"I don't see why you couldn't just use the valet. Are you afraid they'll scratch the paint?"

"No, I'm afraid that they'll spot OneZero in the

back."

Harry looked at me with sudden interest. "I thought those soldiers confiscated him?"

I explained what I'd found last night and how OneZero could apparently cloak himself in plain sight.

"That's unbelievable!" Harry said, shaking his head. "Why do you think he came back? He could have just run away and hid somewhere on his own."

"I've been wondering the same thing."

We showed our keys and valet parking stubs to the soldiers guarding the garage. They let us through, and I led Harry up to the top floor. Stopping at the back of my truck, I opened the tarp and waved. "I'm back, OneZero."

But OneZero gave no reply and made no attempt to de-cloak.

Harry peered in beside me. "Are you sure you didn't just imagine the whole thing? You've been running on little to no sleep for days."

I gave him a sharp look. "He was here. In fact..." I stared into the back of the truck again. "He's probably still here. Maybe he's scared of you."

"Me? Why would he be scared of me? *He's* the killing machine who invaded my planet and kicked me out of my home, not the other way around."

"Maybe because you shot it?" I suggested. "OneZero, it's okay. Harry knows about you. You can reveal yourself."

The air shimmered and that transparent silhouette appeared once more.

"Holy shit," Harry breathed.

The silhouette became fully opaque, and gleaming black eyes stared back at us.

"Harry's a friend, remember?"

"Friend," OneZero said in that feminine register again.

"He can talk? He's a she?" Harry asked.

"Seems like it," I said, and hopped into the back of the truck with my laptop. I pulled the computer out and showed her how to work it, and also how to navigate the dictionary I'd downloaded. She caught on quickly, and seemed to understand the purpose of the application. I searched the word *dictionary*, and a picture of a physical dictionary appeared. I grimaced, thinking that wouldn't be very helpful, but OneZero grew animated and pointed excitedly to the book.

"That's what this is—a dictionary," I said, pointing to the application window.

OneZero nodded slowly, and I left her to it.

Meanwhile I withdrew a car charger for the laptop and strung it through the rear window to reach one of the truck's electrical sockets. When I finished, OneZero caught my eye and shook her head.

"Logan," she said.

"What's wrong?" I went to look at the screen. She'd typed some gibberish into the search box. Of course she couldn't search for words like I'd done.

I showed her how to click on categories and sub categories instead. She tried it, and randomly came up with the image for a stove—a device that she would never recognize because robots had no need for food or cooking. I sighed. This was never going to work.

If only I had Rosetta Stone in English on my laptop. I'd downloaded the Spanish version last year to help Alex with his Spanish homework. He'd gone from C's and B's to A's by the time the school year ended, so I knew first-hand how effective it could be. Plus, it did exactly what I was trying to do with the visual dictionary by associating pictures with words. The difference was that it also taught sentence structure, grammar, and pronunciation—not just vocabulary.

"You ready to go?" Harry asked.

"Yeah," I replied in a dull voice.

"Something wrong?"

I explained the problem.

"So why don't you use the Spanish version?" he asked.

"Because I don't know Spanish, for one. We'd just be transitioning from one unknown language to another."

"But not an unknowable language. I know a little bit of Spanish," Harry said. "Maybe I can translate."

I blinked, and the penny dropped. "So does Alex."

"So he can translate. What's the problem?"

"No problem. I wasn't thinking." All those A's were about to pay off. I loaded the program and showed OneZero how to work it. She got excited when she saw the images and written words to accompany them. She pointed to a picture of a boy drinking a glass of water and repeated after the program's audible description.

"*El niño está bebiendo!*" OneZero said in a perfect Spanish accent.

"Exactly," I replied.

"*La niña está bebiendo!*" OneZero went on, repeating after the program again.

"You just keep that up," I said, already wondering how fast she would learn. Unlike us, she probably had perfect recall, so once would be enough to burn everything into her mind. I remembered that Alex had spent at least a hundred hours using Rosetta Stone before he started getting A's in class. Of course, later I'd found out that he was only interested in learning because of a Colombian exchange student at his school. Regardless, if we were lucky, the one hundred hours that it had taken him to learn would end up being more like twenty for OneZero.

"*La niña está saltando!*" OneZero declared.

"Sounds like it's working," Harry said.

"Yeah," I said, as I crawled out over the fuel containers and then the tailgate. "It would be nice if I knew what she was saying, though."

"That's what Alex is for."

"Right." I just hoped he would remember enough of what he'd learned to be able to communicate with the robot. He'd dropped out of Spanish right after the Colombian girl had left.

* * *

It took us two hours to pack up our things, check out, and return to the bridge we'd crossed last night. Now we were sitting in traffic on our way back across the Mississippi. I told Alex to open the back window and tell OneZero to hide.

"I don't know how to say *hide* in Spanish," Alex objected.

"Then rephrase it! She can't let them see her this time."

"Okay, okay—let me see." He slid the window open. "OneZero?"

"*Sí, Señor* Alex?"

"She knows my name?" Alex asked.

"Just tell her."

"Ahh... *t-tenes que...*"

"*Tengo que...?*"

"Hide," Alex said.

"Hide," came OneZero's polly-parrot reply.

"No, I mean. *Tenes que no...*"

"I thought you knew Spanish?" I demanded, glancing in the rear-view mirror. OneZero's head appeared between my kids. Rachel peered up at him and waved.

"I *do* know Spanish!" Alex objected. "Kind of. *Tienes que no dejar tu ver. Entiendes?*"

"Tengo que no dejarme ver?" OneZero replied. *"Si, exacto."*

She covered her eyes with her hands. "No dejarme ver."

"Ahhh..." Alex trailed off.

Something had definitely gotten lost in the translation.

Alex was still trying to get her to hide herself by the time the army roadblock appeared. There were just two cars left between those soldiers and us.

"OneZero," I said and jabbed a finger at those soldiers. "You remember the men from last night? The soldiers?"

"Soldiers," she replied.

"They're looking for you," I pointed at her, then at my eyes, and then back to the soldiers. "They're going to take you away and hurt you if they find you. Do you understand me?"

She stared at me for a moment longer, then looked to Alex. "*No dejarles verme*," she said.

"What does that mean?" I asked.

"I think she just corrected my Spanish," Alex said.

And with that, OneZero vanished into thin air. "Perfect, OneZero! Just like that. Hide."

"Hide," she replied.

I shook my head wonderingly. "You spent a hundred hours learning, and she's spent two. How the hell does she know more Spanish than you?"

Alex shrugged. "She's an alien robot, I'm not. Maybe she hacked into the computer and memorized the whole thing already."

I frowned, wondering if that was what she'd actually done. A cold draft brushed my neck, and I nodded to Alex. "Close that window. You're letting out all the heat."

"Sure." He slid it shut.

The car ahead of us moved to the front of the line, and I rolled into position behind it. As soldiers searched the vehicle, my thoughts went to what I was going to say to get past the next road block — the one around Starcast's launch facility. I remembered the field of tents I'd seen around the facility. There had to be thousands of soldiers camped there. I doubted they were going to let us through.

Kate's voice interrupted my thoughts: "Logan, if they search the truck like they did last time, won't they find OneZero anyway? That's how you found her, right?"

I chewed my lower lip, thinking hard about that. Hiding in plain sight might not be good enough.

CHAPTER 53

I stood at the back of my truck, peering in with the pair of soldiers who'd come to search it.

"What is all of this?" the corporal asked, rapping on one of my improvised water-tank fuel containers and nodding to our stack of luggage behind that.

"Supplies for our trip," I said, trying not to look as nervous as I felt.

The corporal gave me a hard stare. "Where did you say you were headed?"

I hesitated, wondering briefly if I should tell him the truth. Best case, he'd point us in the right direction, but more likely he'd interrogate us and perform an even more thorough search before ultimately telling us that the launch facility was a restricted area. I'd have better luck showing up there in person and looking for a ranking officer to speak with.

"Do you have a destination in mind?" the corporal asked.

"A family farm in Idaho," I said, coming up with that on the spot. *Idaho?* I wondered.

The corporal frowned. "That's a long way from here, and it's going to be a lot colder come winter time. You should stick to the South if you can."

I nodded along with that. "Maybe we will."

The corporal nodded back. "Good luck," he said.

"You're not going to search my vehicle?"

"Should I?" the corporal challenged.

"Well, no," I said, mentally kicking myself for suggesting it.

He nodded and smiled reassuringly. Pointing to the license plate on my bumper, he said, "According to our records you came through here last night."

"Yeah, we did."

"Then you've already been searched. Carry on."

I couldn't believe our luck. Hurrying back to the driver's seat, I hopped in and started the engine.

"That's it?" Kate asked.

"That's it," I confirmed as we rolled through the road block. I went slowly to wait for Harry, but his vehicle wasn't searched either, and we were on our way again just a few minutes later.

* * *

Even though I knew roughly what direction to head in, it took an hour to find the launch facility. We ended up going in circles for a while before I decided to follow a pair of army trucks. They led us straight to the camp around the facility, but the road leading in was barred by a boom and a guard house. The trucks in front of me cruised right through, but when the soldiers standing guard saw me and Harry waiting in line, they dropped the boom and came rushing out with their rifles aimed.

I lowered my window as they arrived.

"This is a restricted area," one of them said. "Turn around immediately."

"We have an appointment to see Akron Massey," I replied.

The soldier's brow furrowed as if considering the possibility, but then he shook his head. "You're not on the list."

"Just call Mr. Massey and tell him that Logan Willis and his family have arrived."

"I'm sorry, sir, but you're going to have to leave."

"Can't you call him for us and ask? Mr. Massey will be very upset if he learns that you turned us away."

"My orders come directly from General Davis.

Mr. Massey is a civilian and has no authority to contradict those orders."

"Then get him to come to the perimeter. Can you do that?"

"I'm sorry, sir, but I do not know Mr. Massey personally, nor do I have any way of reaching him. You're going to have to turn around. If he is expecting you, then you should be able to call him or reach him via e-mail. If he authorizes you at the gate, then we'll let you through."

E-mail. Why hadn't I thought of that? I struggled to remember the e-mail address that Richard had used to contact Akron. I vaguely recalled that it had something to do with Akron's name, but it had been almost a year since Richard had contacted him from the airport in San Antonio. Besides, even if I could figure out his e-mail address, what if he didn't check it before his rocket launched?

"Sir? Are you listening? You have to turn around right now. If you don't, I'll have to confiscate your vehicle and have you arrested."

I bristled at that. "Arrested? You're not a policeman."

"We're under martial law, sir. And even if we weren't, this is an army camp, so we arrest whoever we like."

"All right, we'll leave."

"Come back when you're authorized."

"Sure," I said, smiling thinly as I put the truck into reverse and backed up. I pulled a U-turn and came alongside Harry's SUV. He lowered his window.

"They won't let you through."

"No."

"Now what?"

I shook my head. "I don't know, but we have to leave before those soldiers get any twitchier."

Harry nodded slowly, scowling at me. I couldn't blame him for being upset. We'd come a long way just to get turned around now. There had to be another way to get to Massey.

Farmers' fields swept by to either side, their crops flattened under a blanket of snow. Ice glistened on the road as the Sun soared high into a clear blue sky. Long minutes passed as we drove back the way we'd come.

"What about OneZero?" Rachel asked. "I bet she could help us."

My eyes widened and I slammed on the brakes. The truck's chain-bound tires skidded with a noisy roar.

"Logan!" Kate scolded.

Harry barely managed to stop behind us. My

walkie-talkie crackled to life. "What the hell did you do that for?"

I ignored both Harry and my wife as I twisted around to stare at Rachel. "You are a genius, did you know that?"

"I am?"

"Yes."

Alex's brow furrowed, but then he appeared to get it, too, and his jaw dropped. "OneZero is invisible."

"Bingo," I said.

CHAPTER 54

We were far enough from the army camp that I figured we could risk pulling off to the side of the road to speak with OneZero. Just in case, however, I decided to speak with her through the back window rather than by climbing in the back.

"OneZero, we need your help."

"Help?" came the robot's reply.

"Alex?"

"Ummm... help that's *ayuda,* I think. *Necesitar ayuda.*"

"*Necesitan, ayuda? Como les puedo ayudar?*"

"What did she say?"

"I think she's asking *how* she can help," Alex replied.

"Good. Tell her we need to speak with a man named Akron Massey. We need her to get past the soldiers and find him for us."

"Okay..."

My walkie-talkie crackled. "So? Is she up for it?" Harry asked.

"We're working on it," I replied.

Alex was muttering under his breath, as if practicing what he was about to say before he actually said it.

"So?" I prompted.

"*Necesitar hablar con* Akron Massey," Alex said. "*Poder tu... jalar esta hombre?*"

"*Necesitan que busco Akron Massey y que lo llevo a ustedes para que puedan hablar con él?*"

"Yes—I mean, *sí,*" Alex said, but he didn't sound too sure.

"*Cómo se ve?*" OneZero asked.

"What did she say?" I prompted.

"She's asking what he looks like," Alex replied.

"Damn it." We needed a picture of him. Akron's face was always plastered all over the news. It would be easy to find him if I could get my laptop to another WiFi connection. "Tell her that we'll get a photo for her."

I indicated left and pulled back out onto the road. Harry contacted us again, and I told Kate to explain.

I headed back down to the interstate and joined the flow of traffic heading West. A sign for West Memphis appeared, and I took the next exit to get there. We cruised down a road beside the I-40 and I spotted a *Days Inn* to our right. Indicating right, I turned toward the Inn and doubled-parked on a curb in the parking lot. A big red *no vacancy* sign glared at us from the Inn's sign, but fortunately we weren't looking to stay the night. I hopped out and went around the back to get my laptop from OneZero. Harry joined me at the bumper as I came out, and soon we were striding across packed snow to reach the front of the Inn.

An armed man in civilian clothes stood at the entrance with a shotgun in one hand and a glowing cigarette dangling from the other. When he saw us coming, he popped the cigarette in his mouth to grab his shotgun in both hands, covering the entrance.

"Didn't you see the sign? No vacancy," he mumbled around his cigarette.

"We don't need a room," I explained, and held my laptop up for him to see. "I just need to use the Internet."

"Internet is for paying guests only. Go find a diner."

"We can pay," Harry insisted. "We just need to use it for a few minutes."

"Fifty dollars a minute."

I blinked. "You're joking."

"You see me laughing?"

"Fine," Harry said, already pulling out his

wallet and fishing out twenties.

The guard eyed the money speculatively. "There's also a twenty dollar entrance fee."

"You just made that up," I said.

The man held his shotgun one-handed and pinched his cigarette between two fingers, dragging so hard it sucked in his cheeks. He tossed the smoking butt at his feet and blew out a chimney's worth of smoke. "You don't have to pay," he said. "Just like I don't have to stop someone from siphoning your gas or slashing your tires."

Harry scowled and fished another bill out of his wallet. "Take it," he said, thrusting a twenty at the guard as we crossed the remaining distance to the doors.

"Smart choice," he said.

We hurried inside. A welcome blast of heat hit us, along with the unwashed stench of at least fifty people.

The lobby of the Days Inn was even more crowded than the lobby of the Peabody had been. People were sitting and lying all over the floor with backpacks for pillows. Others were standing and leaning against the walls, their eyes vacant and staring. We pushed through the crowds to the front desk. The guard outside hadn't been joking about the usage fee. The clerk asked for one hundred dollars for two minutes. Harry grudgingly handed over five twenties, and we found an empty corner to stand in. It took me three minutes to find and download a few pictures of Akron Massey from old news headlines, and then we were on our way.

"Hey!" the desk clerk called after us. "You didn't pay for all your minutes!"

We hurried out the doors before he could catch up with us. I climbed into the back of my truck and turned the laptop toward the empty space where I assumed OneZero was sitting. "This is what Akron Massey looks like," I said, flicking through images one after the next.

"Akron Masey," OneZero replied.

"Exactly."

"*Exactamente.*"

"Can you help us?"

"Help. *Ayuda. Sí. Voy a jalar Akron Massey.*"

I didn't understand much of what she'd said, but I understood *sí* just fine. OneZero was going to help us. I flashed a grin at her and passed my laptop into thin air before climbing back out of the truck. It was time for us to pay those soldiers at the camp another visit.

* * *

We didn't go all the way back to the

checkpoint, since I had a feeling the soldiers guarding it would be less than receptive if we showed up there again without authorization. Instead, we stopped about a mile from the road leading into camp, within sight of the tents, but far enough away that I hoped we wouldn't get into any trouble for loitering.

"Tell OneZero she needs to get out here," I said to Alex.

He relayed that as best he could.

"*Salgo aqui?*" OneZero replied.

"Sí, exacto," Alex said.

"Don't forget—Akron Massey," I added.

"Sí, jalar Akron Massey."

With that, we heard clunking footsteps, followed by a sudden release in the truck's suspension as OneZero jumped out. I checked my mirrors for any sign of her, but I couldn't see anything. I let out a breath I hadn't realized I was holding.

My radio crackled. "Invisible or not, she's going to leave footprints in the snow. Over."

I grimaced. Harry was right. Grabbing my walkie-talkie, I said, "Hopefully she sticks to tire tracks or trampled areas."

"And walks quietly. Over," Harry added.

"Yeah," I replied slowly, my eyes scanning the

city of green tents in the distance. Even invisible, OneZero would need a miracle to get through there undetected. And even if she did, she still had to find Akron Massey, figure out how to tell him that we were here, *and* somehow convince him to come out and speak with us. I imagined her trying to tell him all of that in Spanish, and shook my head. There was a lot of room for failure in this plan. I had a bad feeling this was not going to go the way I hoped.

CHAPTER 55

As soon as I heard the air-raid sirens, I knew that OneZero was in trouble. "They must have seen her," I said, shaking my head and blowing out a breath.

Kate looked to me, her eyes wide. "Can they trace her back to us?"

I thought about that. "Maybe—if she feels like naming her accomplices, and if they can find someone to translate what she says. Finding a translator won't be hard, though. With so many people in that camp, one of them is bound to speak Spanish."

"Then we need to leave."

"But we *can't* leave without OneZero," Rachel whined.

"I'm sorry, honey. I don't think we have a choice."

My walkie-talkie crackled. "You hear that alarm? We'd better get out of here. Over."

"Copy that," I replied.

"Maybe it's a coincidence," Alex said. "They could be running a drill. Or maybe they're under attack."

I twisted around to look at him. "If they're under attack, then that's even more reason for us to get out of here. Whatever it is, it's too dangerous for us to stay here on the side of the road with a camp full of soldiers just across the field from us."

I started the truck with a throaty roar, and a welcome blast of heat came through the vents.

Just as I was pulling out onto the street, Kate leaned over my lap and pointed out the window. "Look!"

I stopped and stared, open-mouthed in shock. It was OneZero, running impossibly fast through the snow-covered field between us and that camp full of soldiers. She couldn't have been going any less than forty miles per hour. About the same speed as the convoy of trucks and Humvees racing after her. But the most shocking thing of all was that she was giving a piggy-back ride to a full-grown man. I couldn't see who it was from this distance, but I could definitely guess.

"Shit!" I said. "She abducted him!"

* * *

By the time I snapped out of it, OneZero had already reached us. She rapped on the window with one hand, and I lowered it.

My walkie-talkie crackled with Harry's voice. "What are you waiting for? Let's get the hell out of here!"

"*Aqui está Akron Massey,*" OneZero declared. "*Debemos irnos. Me estan siguiendo.*"

I didn't get any of that. "OneZero what the hell were you thinking? Alex! Did you tell her to abduct him?"

"I don't know!"

Akron Massey glared at me as OneZero set him down beside my door. "You..." he said. "*You're* behind this? They're going to arrest both you and your wife when they get here." He turned and nodded over his shoulder to the approaching horde of vehicles.

I grimaced and shook my head. "There's been some kind of misunderstanding."

"I told her to *jalar* Akron Massey," Alex said. "That means to find him!"

Akron's eyes darted into the back of the truck, and he smiled. "Kid, *jalar* means *to grab. Hallar* means *to find*."

"Shit," I muttered.

"They sound similar in Spanish if you don't pronounce them right."

I latched onto that excuse. "You see? It's a

misunderstanding. We didn't mean for her to abduct you. You have to explain that to those soldiers when they get here."

"Your robot held me and my family at gunpoint!"

"I'm sorry about that," I said. "But all we wanted was to talk with you."

"So talk. You've got about five seconds."

"Where is Haven? And where's Richard? We never got a message from him."

Akron Massey glanced at Harry's SUV behind us, then back at me. "I thought I told you not to mention Haven to anyone?"

"You also said you'd call us before you left."

"There's isn't enough room for all of you," Akron added.

I gritted my teeth. "It's just three extra people. We can make it work! Where is it?"

Akron hesitated, and then a megaphone blasted us from one of the approaching trucks. "Surrender your hostage, and come out of your vehicles with your hands up—and tell the Screecher to stand down!"

"We can trade. You tell me how you made friends with the robot, and I'll tell you where Haven is," Akron suggested.

I shook my head. "I don't know how."

"How did it learn to speak Spanish?"

I shrugged. "I gave her a laptop with Rosetta Stone on it, but I have no idea how she learned that fast."

Akron's brow furrowed, and he glanced at the robot. "Well, she speaks like a native."

The pursuing vehicles from the camp ground to a halt in the snow-covered field, and armored soldiers boiled out with their rifles at the ready.

"I repeat, surrender your hostage and come out of your vehicles with your hands up! Tell the robot to stand down, or we will open fire."

"Logan, I think we'd better do as they say," Kate put in.

"One second!" I snapped. "Massey, I answered your questions. Now it's your turn."

"What does it matter?" he snorted and gestured to indicate what we were up against. "They're never going to let you leave, and it won't matter whether this was a misunderstanding or not. The fact that you have a Screecher on your side means you're going to spend the next however many days or weeks answering their questions and helping them replicate a friendly response from the others."

That hit me like a bucket of cold water. Akron was right. Then again, spending time in the Army's custody might not be so bad right now. "Tell us where Haven is, and we'll surrender. We can go there after we've answered all of their questions."

"All right, fine. You have something to write with? Look for an oil rig off the coast of North Carolina. It's at thirty-five degrees and thirty minutes north latitude by—"

"Hang on!" I turned to Kate, snapping my fingers. "Pen! Paper!"

The army's megaphone boomed out another warning: "You have ten seconds to comply!"

"Logan, *te está mintiendo*," OneZero said.

"What did she say?" I asked.

"Nothing. You'd better get out," Akron said.

"She said he's lying!" Alex put in.

The megaphone sounded once more: "Your time is up!"

"Get out of the truck now, Logan," Akron Massey urged. "This isn't worth dying over."

Grimacing, I opened the door and came out with my hands up.

"Step *away* from the vehicle!"

I did as I was told.

"Everyone else needs to come out, too!" the soldier with the megaphone said. I heard doors opening and turned to see my family getting out, followed by the Hartfords.

Akron was right. We were all going to be arrested. And then what? According to OneZero, Akron had just lied about the location of Haven. Even if we could get another answer out of him, there'd be no way we could trust it. And if we couldn't find Haven, we were as good as dead.

My mind raced, trying to come up with a solution even as I saw soldiers running through the field to reach us.

Rachel came up to me and hugged my legs. "Are we in trouble, Daddy?"

I looked down at her and smiled tightly. "I'm afraid so, Rachie."

"But we didn't do anything wrong."

An idea struck me then. She was right. We *hadn't* done anything wrong.

"Alex," I said slowly, not daring to turn around. "Tell OneZero that she needs to *jalar* all of us and take us to the Screechers' border."

"Uh, are you sure about that?"

"You've lost your mind!" Akron said. "They'll kill us!"

"No, they won't," I said, and hoped that was true.

"*Necesitar jalar todos nosotros a la frontera tuya, entiendes?*" Alex said.

I didn't wait for OneZero to confirm before

hamming it up on my end. "The Screecher says she's going to kill us all if you come any closer!"

CHAPTER 56

The soldiers stopped advancing. The one with the megaphone said something else: "Move away slowly from the robot!"

"We can't! She'll shoot!" I said.

"That's a lie!" Akron Massey added.

I glanced back at him, glaring. Then my eyes darted to OneZero, willing her to play along. "Alex, tell her she needs to pretend that we're her prisoners."

"*Ummm... nosotros necesitar ser tus prisioneros,*" he said.

OneZero's posture straightened at that, and her arms came up in a threatening posture. Green lasers snapped out, aiming at each of us. Before the soldier with the megaphone could say anything else, she spoke in an amplified voice of her own.

"*Estas son mis prisioneros! Voy a llevarles a la frontera! Si tratan de impedirme, se les voy a matar.*"

I understood something about prisoners, and frontier, which I guessed meant border. Whatever she'd said, it drew an immediate reaction from the soldiers. They began conferring among themselves, and the one with the megaphone passed it to someone else, who replied in Spanish.

"What did he say?" I asked.

Akron Massey ground out a reply, "He asked why it wants *me.*"

OneZero said something else.

"And that?" I prompted. My arms were getting tired from holding my hands up.

"She said it doesn't matter why. All that matters is that she's going to kill us if they try to interfere."

"Logan, are you sure about this?" Kate asked.

"No," I replied.

Harry stared at us in shock.

The soldier replied, again in Spanish, but this time Akron didn't have to translate. I saw the soldiers retreating to their vehicles, and I felt cold steel jabbing me in the back. "Márchense!"

OneZero pushed us along to the back of the truck along with my family and Akron Massey.

"Todos adentro!" OneZero said, and gestured for us to get in. I waited for my kids and Akron Massey to go first. As I helped Kate up, one of OneZero's arms strayed to the Hartfords, and her targeting lasers found each of them. "Ustedes también!"

"What did she say?" Harry asked.

"She wants you to get in the back with us," Akron replied.

The Hartfords climbed in, and Harry glared at me. "Nice job. You've just killed us all."

I was about to join them in the back, but OneZero pulled me away and pushed me along to the front of the truck. I guessed she needed a driver.

"Hey, ease up," I said, but she just shouted at me in Spanish.

This charade was getting too real for my tastes.

* * *

I drove away from the launch facility with OneZero sitting hunched over in the passenger's seat beside me. Glancing in my side mirror, I saw the convoy of army vehicles following us at a respectable distance.

If they somehow managed to neutralize OneZero without killing us, we'd be arrested for sure. Or at least *I* would. Akron Massey was witness to the fact that I'd put the robot up to this. I racked my brain trying to come up with an escape plan that didn't actually involve crossing the Screechers' border. Maybe the army would give up when they saw us getting close?

My heart pounded and I shook my head. What had I done? I'd made a bad situation worse and turned myself into a wanted criminal in the span of just a few seconds. Desperation and pressure were a bad mix. Maybe it wouldn't be so bad if I just pulled over now and surrendered.

The window at the back of the truck slid open, interrupting my thoughts. Akron Massey's head appeared. I wondered how he'd managed to open that window from the outside; then I noticed the charging cable dangling over the backseats.

"I have a family, too, you know," Akron said.

"Tell us where Haven is and I'll let you go."

"Why? So you can lead the Screechers straight to it?" Akron demanded.

"We'll be careful," I promised.

"You can't reach it, anyway. Haven is in the Gulf of Mexico. You'd have to cross the Screechers' border just to get there."

I wondered if that were true, and looked to OneZero with my eyebrows raised. I tried to remember the word she'd used for lying. Minty-something. "Minty...?"

OneZero managed to guess what I meant.

"No," she said.

At least that word was the same in both Spanish and English. I nodded to Akron in the rear-view mirror. "Well, then I guess it's a good thing I'm headed for the border."

"They'll kill us before we can cross it."

"OneZero is one of them. She'll convince them to leave us alone."

"Are you willing to stake your family's lives on that?" Akron asked.

I grimaced and shook my head. "Let me figure out where to go from here. The only thing you have to worry about is answering my question. Where in the Gulf of Mexico?"

"You think I have the coordinates memorized?" Akron demanded.

"If you don't, then you're going to have to come with us."

Akron made an irritated sound. "Look, it's approximately three hundred miles south of the Mississippi River Delta. There are two deep sea drilling rigs that mark its location."

"How did you leave?"

"I took a submarine to New Orleans and drove North from there with everyone else."

"So the submarine should still be in New Orleans?"

"No, the captain took it back. Like I said, there's no way for you to get to Haven now."

"We could steal a boat," I suggested.

"Sure, assuming you can get there safely, and assuming that the Screechers don't sink it or follow you after you leave the harbor. And I'm guessing you know how to skipper a ship?"

This plan was sounding worse by the second.

"Anyway, that's your problem. I told you where Haven is. It's your turn. Let me go."

"How do I know you're not lying?" I asked as I rejoined the I-40, heading west.

"You're just going to have to trust me," Akron replied.

I glanced in my side mirror and saw army vehicles racing up the on-ramp after us in a long line.

"Not good enough," I replied. "Besides, I can't stop yet. We're being followed."

Akron Massey blew out a frustrated breath and withdrew into the back of the truck. Before long, we were driving through West Memphis again. I passed the Days Inn and kept on going until we were through the city. I needed to figure out which road would take us South. Reaching over OneZero's lap, I found our road maps in the glove box and pulled them out. I swerved dangerously a few times before finding the right map and arranging it in my lap. The nearest highway that would take us south was the AR-147. I took the exit to reach it at a place called Lehi, and the trucks pursuing us followed.

As I turned left down the AR-147 and drove through the truck stop that was Lehi, I checked the fuel gauge and saw that we were running on empty. It would have been smart to fill up while we'd been sitting there waiting for OneZero to come back. Unfortunately, I hadn't imagined myself becoming the getaway driver in a car chase at the time.

I grimaced, hoping the Screechers' border wasn't far. I zeroed the trip counter to track the distance we traveled. We wouldn't get more than fifty miles out of what was left, and that was under good conditions, but conditions were far from good. Snow covered the highway, and even after switching over to four-wheel drive, I couldn't make more than twenty-five miles per hour without the truck threatening to swerve off the road.

About ten minutes later we passed the town of Midway Corner, and then ten minutes after that, we passed another one called Anthonyville. At that point, I could sense that we were running on fumes. We wouldn't make it more than a couple more miles.

I looked to OneZero, about to express those

concerns to her, but she was pointing to something on the horizon. I turned to look and saw a ragged line where the horizon should have been. *What is that?* I wondered.

As we drew near, details began to emerge. It looked like some kind of wall. OneZero said something in Spanish that I didn't understand. Before long I saw that it was made of snow-covered cars, their windows broken and doors falling off. This was what had happened to all the vehicles that hadn't made it North. That wall stretched clear across the horizon from one side to the other as far as I could see. The wall rose at least two stories. One of the large four-legged Screechers stood over the highway, blocking a gap in the wall with a pair of the big hovering discs. OneZero held out one of her hands to me, palm up, as if to indicate that I should stop here. I applied the brakes and came to a halt some fifty yards from the wall, peering up at it, and marveling at the sheer number of vehicles before me. I wondered if the barrier stretched all the way from coast to coast already. It had only been a few days since the invasion began. How had they moved so many vehicles in such a short time?

Behind me, I heard a familiar megaphone voice call out to OneZero in Spanish, and saw the army vehicles behind us fanning out across the highway, blocking the way back.

I glanced at the Screecher tank in front of us, and despair gripped me. The army had called our bluff, and now we were trapped between them and the Screechers.

CHAPTER 57

OneZero made herself invisible and then opened her door. I watched the empty space where she had been, slowly shaking my head. What was she doing?

"OneZero?"

No reply came. I looked away, and all of a sudden saw her materializing in front of our truck, between the Screechers guarding the border and us. One of the hovering discs came down, growing rapidly in size as it approached. The center of the disc appeared to be a giant rotor blade, while the circumference formed a thick ring. The disc stopped just a few feet above the ground, and landing struts dropped down. A ramp lowered, and I saw one of the smaller dog-like Screechers emerge. It shrieked at OneZero, and she shrieked back. Six articulated arms unfolded to extend high above the robot's spherical head. Green targeting lasers snapped out—one of them shining through the windshield to land on my chest. A dozen more targeted the army trucks behind us.

OneZero and the dog-like Screecher shrieked back and forth for a while before OneZero turned and waved to me, as if to indicate that I should come. Hope rose inside of me, and I sucked in a quick breath. Maybe she had convinced her people to grant us some kind of asylum.

"What's going on?" Harry asked.

My eyes flicked to the rear-view mirror, and I saw him staring back at me.

"I think she wants us to drive across the border," I said.

"No way. Don't do it."

"We don't have a choice."

"Yeah we do. Give yourself up and let us go."

I hit the gas instead.

"Hey!" Harry said.

"If you get out now, the Screechers might shoot you," I explained.

"As opposed to them shooting me later, when I'm their prisoner? Stop the truck, Logan. We're leaving."

"I agree," Akron put in. "We need to go back before it's too late."

Maybe they were right. My foot left the gas and hovered over the brakes, hesitating. A flicker of movement in the side mirror caught my eye.

One of the Army trucks was following us.

Just then, a thunderous *boom* cracked the sky, followed by a second one, and a flash of light in my side mirror. The truck behind us was a slumping ruin of molten metal, belching fire and black smoke from broken windows.

* * *

Thick black smoke poured into the sky, and no survivors emerged from the ruined army truck. I drove on, but more slowly now that I knew what lethal force the Screechers would apply for non-compliance. I heard Harry and Akron cursing in the back, but they didn't ask me to stop again so they could get out.

I reached OneZero in a matter of just a few seconds, and then I was forced to stop anyway, because that disc-shaped aircraft was still blocking the highway.

OneZero came up to my side door and tried to open it, but it was locked, and the handle tore away in her hand. She tossed it aside and made a gleaming fist. I blinked in shock, and leaned away from the door just as she punched out the glass. Pea-sized fragments rained down in my lap, and OneZero opened my door from the inside. That done, she reached in and cut my seatbelt with a previously unseen accessory on one of her fingers.

I landed hard in six inches of snow.

"What the hell was that for?" I demanded, struggling to get back up.

She kicked me in the gut and the wind left me in a rush. I lay there with my diaphragm paralyzed, desperately trying to suck in a breath. Horror clawed inside of me like a living thing trying to get out. Had I somehow misread OneZero's intentions all this time? Or had she grown tired of our alliance and decided to flip back to her side again?

The dog-like Screecher walked over and trained some of its weapons on me with bright green lasers, while OneZero went around the back of the truck, her feet crunching in the snow. She said something in Spanish that I didn't understand, and then yanked someone else out with an audible *Oompf*. I twisted around slowly, mindful of how many different guns were trained on me.

Akron Massey was lying in the snow, face-down, with OneZero's claw-like foot planted on his back. The others piled out in a hurry to avoid being forced out like him. OneZero yanked Akron to his feet and shoved everyone along to reach me. I stood up carefully, catching dirty looks from both Akron and Harry—the billionaire's face was red, and there were clumps of snow clinging to his eyebrows, lashes, and sweater. He wasn't even wearing a jacket, and his loose-fitting slacks couldn't have provided much warmth either.

"Nice j-job, Logan," Akron said, shivering violently. "You've j-just made us p-prisoners of war."

Before I could think of something to say to that, OneZero jabbed my wife in the back, and she cried out in pain, stealing my attention. She picked her way through the snow, holding both of our kid's hands.

"I'm hungry," Rachel complained as they walked by me.

There were dry snacks in the cooler, and plenty of canned food in the back, but I doubted OneZero would give us a chance to get it.

I looked to the robot and scowled. "Traitor." She screeched something at me, giving new meaning to her species' nickname. In the background behind her, through the billowing clouds of smoke from the ruined truck, I saw the army convoy speeding off. They'd given up.

OneZero screeched again and gave me a shove, forcing me to turn around and start marching toward the border with the others. Alex was walking with Celine now, instead of his mother, so I caught up to Kate and grabbed her free hand. She squeezed so hard that I felt my bones grinding together.

"What are they going to do with us?" she asked.

I just shook my head. I wondered the same thing. And why were we being made to walk on foot? The border crossing, even with that giant four-legged Screecher straddling it, looked more than big enough for our truck to drive across. Instead, we were trudging through six inches of snow to get there. I could feel it soaking through my pant legs, icy water trickling into my boots.

We reached the disc-shaped aircraft that had landed on the highway to speak with OneZero, and a buzzing roar thundered through the air. The aircraft hovered up with an icy gust of wind that made us stumble. I squinted up at the aircraft. Freezing wind continued to blast us from its rotor as it roared overhead. I twisted around to watch as it passed over us, despite OneZero's prodding weapons and shrieking protests. The disc hovered over my truck and dropped articulated arms around it like tentacles. It looked like a jellyfish.

Those tentacles writhed, punching through windows with noisy bursts of breaking glass and twined around the truck's roof and chassis.

"Hey!" I said, watching helplessly as it lifted

our truck and all of our supplies into the air. The hovering disc rose swiftly. I gaped up at the bright blue sky, unable to tear my eyes away as the only home we'd known for the past three days dwindled to a speck.

I had a bad feeling about where they were taking it. The disc zipped high over the wall of piled cars and then dropped ours on top. It fell with a *crash* and began rolling to the bottom, spewing containers of diesel, luggage, food, water, and everything else we desperately needed right now. By the time the truck came to a stop, it was a total wreck—roof flattened, chassis twisted, tires flat...

I stared hard at that twisted ruin, and slowly shook my head. This was a nightmare.

Another shriek pierced my ears and I felt OneZero jabbing me in the back again. This time she accompanied that jab with a violent shove that sent me sprawling, face-first into the snow. I emerged to the sound of Akron's laughter.

"Karma's a bitch!" he crowed.

"You would know," I replied.

"Shut up! Both of you!" Harry snapped.

"*Muévanse!*" OneZero added, and fired a whistling stream of bullets over our heads to emphasize her point.

CHAPTER 58

April 28th, 3:15 PM
2 HOURS AND 15 MINUTES BEFORE
THE ROGUE'S ARRIVAL

We marched between the legs of the four-legged tank that straddled the highway. The monstrous machine was easily two stories high, and our heads cleared the bottom of the chassis with ease. I wondered if it was autonomous, or if it had other Screechers inside to control it.

On the other side of the wall buzzing black clouds flowed from piled cars to what looked like the foundation of a second wall, except that this one was solid and made of gleaming metal just like the Screechers themselves. Akron figured out what was happening before I did.

"They're using the cars for p-parts to build a new wall," he said, still stuttering with the violence of his shivers.

I marveled at how thick those swarms of bug-sized Screechers were. "If the entire border is like this, there must be trillions of the little ones," I added.

"There's no way all of them fit inside those landers," Harry added.

He was right. But the explanation was right in front of us. "If they have assembler bots that can build a wall from cars, then they probably started by mass-producing themselves first. They've been stripping our civilization for parts to build their own."

OneZero stopped pushing us and looked up just as a buzzing roar split the sky. One of those giant discs, maybe the same one that had trashed our truck, came hovering down and landed on the highway in front of us. A ramp dropped, and a humanoid Screecher model came out and waited at the bottom. OneZero pushed us forward again, and I realized that she meant for us to board the aircraft.

Akron stumbled and cried out as his foot caught on some piece of debris hidden in the snow. It turned out to be a car's bumper. He cursed and limped the rest of the way to the ramp.

A guilty lump rose in my throat as I watched him. Right now he should be with his family preparing to leave this mess behind and start a new life on Mars. And right now my family and the Hartfords should have been looking for a new shelter where we could weather the coming winter. In my desperation to find the shelter we'd been promised, I'd doomed us all. If I hadn't told OneZero to pretend to take us all hostage, she'd never have had the chance to actually do so. Or would she? If that was her intention all along, had my scheming really changed anything? I couldn't have stopped her from taking us hostage. I shook my head to clear it. I wasn't going to let myself off that easily.

OneZero shouldered past us as we reached the bottom of the ramp, and she shrieked something at the other humanoid model. The four-legged we'd seen emerge the first time the disc had landed walked past us and up the ramp, folding its six spider-like arms against its sides to fit through the door.

We waited and looked on as the two humanoid robots conversed in shrill tones.

I felt a tug on my jacket. "Daddy, what are they talking about?"

"I don't know, Rachie," I said.

"Do you think they're talking about supper? OneZero hasn't had anything to eat either."

I shook my head. "No, sweetheart. Robots

don't need to eat."

"But we do. Can't you ask them if they have something? My stomach hurts."

I winced at that and nodded, offering my daughter a tight smile. "I'll try."

Kate was watching the exchange, biting her lip with tears gleamed in her eyes. As our eyes met, she looked away shaking her head. She might not have said it, but I knew she blamed me for this, too. Whatever happened next was on me.

OneZero turned and gestured for us to walk up the ramp. She said something in Spanish to accompany the gesture, to which the other humanoid model cocked its head curiously.

Akron started up the ramp, but the second robot stepped in front of him, blocking the way. OneZero turned and said something else to the second robot, and they spoke for another minute in their screeching language, leaving us shivering at the bottom of the ramp. They finished speaking, and the second one turned to regard us with gleaming black eyes. It said something to us.

It was speaking Spanish now, too. Somehow OneZero had shared her knowledge of the language with it.

"He says to get inside," Akron said, as the second Screecher stepped aside. Akron led the rest of the way up the ramp, and we emerged inside the ring of the aircraft. It was the same gleaming metal on the inside as it was on the outside. I noticed that the inner wall of the ring was lined with metal clamps, and that the four-legged Screecher model was clamped against the wall. These were the Screechers' equivalent of seat belts. Everywhere else that I could see the clamps were empty, but I estimated that this disc could carry at least twenty Screechers.

A groaning sound started up behind us and I turned around. The landing ramp was rising into place. Now facing the other way, I noticed that the outer wall was transparent, or else lined with some kind of digital display. It gave us an unobstructed view of the snow-dusted highway and the wall of cars to either side.

Both OneZero and the other humanoid model pointed to the inner wall. OneZero said something, and Akron translated: "They want us to secure ourselves for transit," he said, and I noticed that he was no longer shivering. It was almost as cold inside as it was outside, but at least here we were sheltered from the wind.

I glared at OneZero. "Transit where?"

"*Dónde vamos?*" Akron asked.

"*Vamos a Haven.*"

I didn't know a stick of Spanish, but I didn't need to know what those other words meant to understand what she'd just said. Somehow OneZero had gleaned enough from our conversations with Akron Massey to realize why we had wanted to speak with him, and where we were trying to go.

The implications of that hit me hard. I hadn't just doomed the eight of us. I'd doomed everyone in Haven Colony, too.

CHAPTER 59

"**D**o you have any idea what you've done?" Akron demanded as OneZero and her partner forcibly clamped us against the wall by our wrists and ankles.

"Yes," I said. I didn't know what else to say. An apology would sound hollow at this point.

"I told you that robot was trouble!" Harry added.

Kate caught my eye as she was clamped to the wall beside me. To my surprise there was no accusation in her gaze—only fear and apprehension.

"Daddy!" Rachel screamed when the second humanoid robot grabbed her by her wrists.

"Get off of her!" Alex said. He took a run at the Screecher, but before he even reached it, the robot lashed out and sent him sprawling with a back-handed slap.

"Alex!" Kate sobbed, but he picked himself up just a few seconds later.

Rachel continued to struggle, and blood seeped between the robot's fingers as metal bit through her wrists. "Stop it!" I yelled. Tears stung my eyes. "Let her go!" I yanked hard against my restraints, bruising my wrists in an effort to break free. "Rachel! Stop struggling!"

But she was hungry and tired. She was beyond reason. She screamed and cried, tears streaming down her face. "OneZero! Help!"

My gaze snapped to the robot. She just stood there, watching, and I glared at her with pure hatred.

The second robot finally succeeded in clamping Rachel against the wall, and then stepped away, shrieking softly, as if muttering under its breath. It pointed to OneZero and then indicated the others. Deborah and Celine were huddled to one side, hugging each other and crying softly. Alex stood a few feet away, stunned into silence.

The second robot went over to Akron and began speaking to him in Spanish while OneZero secured first Alex and then Celine and her mother against the wall. This time no one resisted. My eyes tracked back to Rachel. She was sniveling more quietly now, her eyes wide with shock. Thankfully her wrists were no longer bleeding, so the cuts couldn't have been very deep. I breathed a sigh and shook my head, looking out at the snow-dusted world beyond the aircraft. A buzzing roar came rumbling through the wall, and the ground fell away swiftly below us, revealing snow-covered fields and trees, and a vast length of wall stretching all the way to the Mississippi River. The river itself was clear of vehicles, but I could see that the second wall the Screechers were building spanned the river, too.

A jolt of sudden acceleration jerked us against our restraints, and Rachel cried out in pain. My gaze snapped to her, and I slowly shook my head, blinking tears, and wishing I could reach her.

Akron raised his voice, arguing loudly with the Screecher busy interrogating him. I couldn't understand what they were saying, but Akron's tone was defiant.

The Screecher stepped back and raised its arms. Weapons deployed with clicking sounds and bright green lasers converged on his chest.

He spat at the robot. "*Púdrete!*"

The lasers grew brighter and his sweater began to smoke. Akron's eyes widened, and then an agonized scream burst from his lips. His sweater burst into flames and the lasers vanished. He was on fire, and still screaming.

The Screecher interrogating him said

— 479 —

something else, and I picked out the word *Haven* once more. Akron gave no reply besides his screaming. The rotten stench of charred fibers and skin filled the air, and I cringed, nauseated by the smell.

"Esta bien!" Akron roared. *"Te diré!"* The second Screecher stepped forward and put out the fire by patting it with its hands.

A flicker of movement caught my eyes. OneZero's arms were up, weapons deployed and tracking. A staccato burst tore out, and the robot standing in front of Akron froze. Its eyes lit up from within and a muffled explosion sounded. It collapsed at my feet with a heavy *clunk*. In the same instant the dog-like Screecher sagged against its restraints.

OneZero's head turned to me, and our eyes met. "Friend," she said.

Shock rippled through me, followed by a profound sense of relief. I slumped against my restraints, watching as OneZero turned to Akron and said something to him in Spanish.

"What did she say?" Harry asked.

"She also wants to know where Haven is," Akron replied.

That gave me pause. Was this some elaborate version of *good cop, bad cop?* "Is that a good thing?"

Akron nodded slowly. "I think so. She says she wants to help us get there."

CHAPTER 60

OneZero left us where we were, hurrying around the circumference of the disc on some unknown errand. Maybe she was off to pilot the aircraft.

"It was all a ruse?" Kate asked.

I nodded slowly. "She didn't betray us. She saved us from both the army and her people, and now she's going to take us to Haven."

"What if *that's* the ruse?" Harry asked. "What if they're just trying to trick us into giving away its location?"

I frowned, wondering at that. My gaze landed on the disabled Screecher at my feet, and I shook my head.

"No," Akron added in a strained voice. "I was about to tell them where it was when OneZero shot the other two. I think that might be why she chose that moment to intervene. She wanted us to know that we could trust her."

"So why doesn't she let us go?" Deborah

asked.

Before anyone could venture a guess, the disc tipped forward, giving us a view of the sky, and accelerated suddenly. The buzzing roar of the rotors rose to the shrill whine of a jet engine. I felt my stomach drop and the blood rushing away from my head. Rachel cried out in alarm, and I saw dark spots dancing before my eyes.

"It's okay, Rach!" I said, yelling to be heard over the sound of the aircraft's engine. "It'll be over soon!"

The acceleration eased and OneZero came striding back around the ring. I noticed that the floor had somehow slanted, allowing OneZero to walk straight despite the aircraft's forward tilt.

OneZero dropped to her haunches in front of Rachel and opened her restraints first. To my surprise, Rachel leapt into OneZero's lap and wrapped her arms around the robot's neck.

"I knew you weren't bad!"

I smiled tightly at that. Rachel let go after just a moment, and OneZero went about releasing the rest of us. Akron was last in line to be released. When it was his turn, he and OneZero had a brief conversation, and then they hurried off together.

"Where are you going?" I called after them.

"To show her how to get to Haven!" Akron

called back.

* * *

April 28th, 4:30 PM
1 HOUR BEFORE THE ROGUE'S ARRIVAL

OneZero sat at the pilot's station, strapped in like a fighter pilot rather than with metal clamps. OneZero's seat was the only one on board, and we weren't in a hurry to clamp ourselves to the wall again, so we stood and sat behind her, bracing ourselves for any sudden changes in direction.

We'd been flying for an hour already, and so far no Screechers had come after us. I hoped that would hold true until we could get to Haven.

A vast, rippled expanse of water appeared in the distance.

"That's Lake Pontchartrain," Akron said.

I nodded as if I knew where that was.

"New Orleans is on the other side," Akron added.

"Then we're almost there!" Deborah put in.

"Almost," Akron agreed.

We streaked out over the lake. The far side was hidden by smoke or mist, but before long, New Orleans came swirling out of the haze. I spotted the Mississippi River snaking through the city, and the rippled blue expanse of the Gulf of Mexico in the background. The city didn't look like it was flooded yet. I checked my watch. It was just after midday.

"We've got less than an hour before that rogue star arrives," I said, remembering the news headline I'd read back at the Peabody.

"You think we'll see the tidal waves?" Alex asked.

"We'd better not," Akron said. "Anyway, we still have time. At the speed it's moving, the rogue should still be a few million miles away."

We'd probably see the tidal waves rolling through the Gulf of Mexico as we flew the rest of the way to Haven.

Akron pointed to what looked like a harbor on the far side of the lake and said something to OneZero.

I rocked forward onto the balls of my feet, and Kate stumbled, grabbing my arm for support. Our airspeed was dropping. The ripples on the lake below became more noticeable, and I realized that our altitude was dropping, too. OneZero was taking us down for a landing.

"What's going on?" I asked.

"I thought we were going to Haven?" Deborah added.

Akron glanced over his shoulder, his gaze flicking from me to her. "We are. But we have to take my submarine to get there."

"But what about the tidal waves?" Kate asked.

"We still have time." Akron pointed to the ripples on the lake below. "The waves are only a couple feet high right now."

My brow furrowed. "I thought the captain took your submarine back to Haven?"

"I lied. There is no captain. It's self-skippering. The coordinates are stored in the computer. I didn't want to tell you about it, because then you'd be able to use it to get to Haven."

"But you told us how to find Haven, anyway— an oil rig 300 miles south of the Mississippi Delta."

"More like southwest, and more like a hundred and fifty miles," Akron explained.

I snorted and shook my head. Of course that had been another lie.

The harbor grew steadily larger, and I scanned the docks looking for something lurking beneath the water. To my surprise, I didn't even see any regular ships, let alone submarines.

"Where are all the boats?" Kate asked.

"People used them to get away when the Screechers arrived," Akron said.

"I wonder if anyone managed to escape,"

Harry said.

Akron shook his head. "Most of them will run out of fuel before they can leave the gulf and start heading North, and the whole of the Gulf of Mexico is in Screecher territory."

"So is Haven," I said, wondering for the first time if it would actually be a safe place for us. "How do you know the Screechers won't find it?"

"I don't, but I do know that it will be hard to find. As long as Haven doesn't transmit any signals, and as long as the Screechers don't spot our solar farm or start building ships, we should be able to stay hidden. Assuming, of course, that they don't capture us before we can get there."

I shook my head. "They don't know our language. They couldn't interrogate us if they tried."

"Then why is my chest barbecued?" Akron nodded to OneZero. "She knows Spanish, and she's already proven that she can share that knowledge. It's just a matter of time before they learn all of our other languages, too."

I grimaced. He was probably right. I wondered what they'd have to say to us once they did. Where did they come from? What did they want? We still didn't know. I stared at the back of OneZero's head, wondering what secrets she had to tell us.

I was just about to suggest to Akron that he ask some of those questions when OneZero adjusted our speed again and hovered us down to an empty parking lot behind the docks. We were out of time for chitchat now, but maybe we'd have a chance to talk while Akron's submarine took us to Haven.

As we came in for a landing, I noticed no snow dusting the ground, and that the trees here had yet to lose any of their leaves. I wondered if New Orleans was farther south than San Antonio, but even if it was, I doubted it could be that much farther south. It was probably because New Orleans was a coastal city and the water helped regulate the air temperature.

OneZero unstrapped from the pilot's seat and stood up. We followed her around the ring of the disc to the landing ramp. It was already open. OneZero led the way down, metal feet clomping as she went.

Before we'd even reached the bottom, a distant buzzing sound reached my ears. I looked up and saw two glinting discs screaming across the lake toward us.

OneZero said something to Akron and then charged back up the ramp. I hesitated, about to usher my family up after her.

"We have to run for it!" Akron said. "She's

going to try to hold them off!"

CHAPTER 61

As we ran across the parking lot to the docks, OneZero's disc shot into the air and tipped up, zipping out over the water. Stuttering lines of fire streaked out from the two pursuing discs and ricocheted off its armor. OneZero fired back as she led them away.

I stopped at the water's edge and gaped at the dogfight, watching those discs dwindle to glinting specks against the hazy line of the horizon.

"They're coming! Into the water!" Akron shouted, and raced by us, pounding down the wooden docks. He dove off into the choppy gray water with a splash.

Everyone ran after him. I hesitated, looking for whatever Akron had seen. Why jump in the water? A soft buzzing noise broke through my daze, and I remembered that the Screechers are heat-seeking. I tore off down the docks, catching up to the others. Alex and Celine jumped in with a tandem splash, followed by Deborah. Kate lingered, trying to convince Rachel to go next.

"No!" she said. "I don't want to!"

I scooped her up in my arms. "We're going to jump together, okay?" Waves knocked against the wooden planks of the docks, sloshing over the sides and wetting our feet.

Rachel writhed in my grip, trying to break free. "No!" she screamed.

I glanced back the way I'd come. The buzzing sounds were getting closer, but I still couldn't see the source. That was good. It meant we still had time to hide.

"Hold your breath!"

"I don't want—"

I jumped, and the water swallowed Rachel's objections. It was dark below the surface, but blissfully warm. My jacket, boots, and clothes weighed us down as they soaked up water. Rachel's arms locked around me, pinning one of my arms in place and making things even worse, but I was a good swimmer. I kicked hard and used my free hand to help. I broke the surface beside the docks a moment later. Waves tossed us around, smacking us into the wooden pillars and threatening to sweep us under the walkway.

Akron was already there, watching us from the shadows. "Get under here!" he hissed. Just because

Screechers were heat-seeking didn't mean they couldn't see in the visible spectrum, too.

I grabbed the nearest pillar and helped Rachel swim under the docks before following myself. I almost smashed my head on the beams as a wave picked me up, but I pushed off the beams and drifted through in the trough behind the next wave.

Everyone else was already there. We trod water as quietly as we could, holding onto the pillars for support and struggling against the push and pull of the choppy water. Waves slapped the pillars and splashed up against the bottom of the docks with a *clug-clugging* sound that made me think of waves lapping the sides of Richard's boat when we went fishing on Calaveras lake. Back then there'd been a dark cloud of impending doom hovering over my head, but now those seemed like happy memories.

A wave grabbed Rachel and ripped her away from her pillar. She cried out in alarm. I managed to grab her and pull her back. Akron shushed her with a dark look.

If it was this wavy inside a harbor on the *lake,* what was it like on the open ocean? I hoped Akron's submarine wouldn't be affected by the tidal waves, but I was getting ahead of myself. At this rate we might not even make it there before those waves arrived and drowned us like bugs in a toilet.

Explosions *boomed* in the distance, cutting off my thoughts in mid-stream.

"What was that?" Kate whispered.

I hoped that hadn't been the sound of OneZero getting blasted out of the sky.

The buzzing sounds grew close enough that we could hear them through the slapping and clugging of waves against the docks.

Everyone watched the sky warily through the boards over our heads, but I watched the parallel lines of light shining between those boards as they danced across the water. A shadow flickered through those bars of light—followed by another, and then a third. The buzzing sounds stopped directly above us.

So much for hiding our heat signatures in the water. I cringed, and braced myself for a hail of bullets to come splintering through the docks.

CHAPTER 62

Something came roaring toward us with a sound like a jet fighter. The staccato roar of cannon fire tore through the air, followed by clattering debris *thumping* on the docks and splashing into the water around us. The next thing I heard was a streaking roar, followed by a titanic *boom.* A bright flash of light illuminated the underside of the docks, and I poked my head out to see one of the disc-shaped aircraft gushing fire as it tumbled into the harbor. A massive splash followed, and the flaming debris lay floating on the surface.

I deduced what must have happened. OneZero had seen that we were in trouble, and she'd come back to help. She'd shot down the smaller Screechers hovering above us only to get shot down herself.

The distant roaring of Screecher aircraft faded into the distance, and silence fell. Was it possible that the ones OneZero had shot down above our heads hadn't communicated our location to any of the others?

We stayed where we were for a few more minutes, none of us daring to talk or come out of hiding. Water struck the docks, and flames crackled amidst the flotsam of OneZero's aircraft.

How much longer did we have before real tidal waves came and swept us away?

I checked my watch, but the hands were frozen at 12:34. It wasn't waterproof. For all we knew we only had a few minutes left. Maybe that was the real reason the Screechers had left. They knew we were goners anyway.

"They're gone. We have to go!" I said to Akron. "Where's your submarine?"

He nodded over my shoulder. "Down at the end of the docks. We should swim there to avoid detection."

"I can't!" Rachel said.

"I don't think I can either," Deborah said. "I'm too heavy with all of these clothes."

"We'll have to risk running down the docks," I said.

Akron made an irritated noise in the back of his throat. "We'd better be fast!"

I helped Rachel duck out from under the docks, but I could see that she was struggling. "Get on my back," I said. She wrapped her arms around my neck, and I pushed off from the pillar, swimming harder than I ever had in my life. I began to sink almost immediately, but thankfully we weren't far from the edge of the harbor. The water was high. I waited for a wave to buoy us up, and then grabbed the bottom rung of a steel railing, but I was too tired and too heavy with Rachel on my back to pull us out.

"Grab on!" I said. My arms were shaking, and my water-logged gloves were slipping on the railing. Rachel grabbed it and pulled herself up easily. Alex and Harry reached the railings and pulled themselves out next. Akron and I followed. Kate and Deborah were still struggling to get out when Harry and I reached over to help them up.

We took a moment to catch our breath, shivering and dripping all over the sidewalk beside the railings.

Akron pulled his sweater off and dropped it at his feet with a wet *slap*. Then he clapped his hands together to get our attention. "Let's go!" Not waiting for us to reply, he took off at a run, heading back to the docks.

I scooped Rachel up into my arms and ran after him with the others. Harry lagged behind, trying to help Deborah take off her water-logged jacket. The zipper was stuck.

Our feet sounded like thunder on the wooden boards, but we had to slow down, because waves were washing clear over the dock now. If one of us fell into the churning cauldron below, I had a bad feeling we wouldn't make it out. I tightened my grip on Rachel, and she hugged my neck painfully tight.

A faint buzzing noise reached my ears through the splashing roar of the waves.

"They're coming!" Rachel said.

My heart leapt and a surge of adrenaline stabbed through me. I glanced back to see three glinting discs racing after us. They were the smaller ones, but it didn't matter. Even one of them would have been enough to take us all out.

"Run!" I screamed to Harry.

He turned to look over his shoulder. He and Deborah were still bringing up the rear.

Bullets whistled through the air, followed by the sound of faint explosions. Rachel whimpered, and I cringed, half expecting the dock to collapse under my feet as I ran. It shuddered violently with heavy footfalls. There was no way they belonged to Harry or Deborah. A silvery blur went racing by me, catching up with Akron in seconds. I heard the familiar babble of Spanish as the two of them spoke in rushed voices.

A grin curved my lips, and I pushed on, running faster to catch up. Somehow OneZero had made it out of that wreckage alive. That's what those explosions had been. She'd taken care of the Screechers behind us.

I pulled alongside Kate, gasping for air. She glanced at me and flashed a tight smile. The end of the dock was just ahead of us. We were going to make it.

Just as I thought that, a dark shadow fell over us and cast everything in a dim, bloody red hue. The rogue had arrived.

CHAPTER 63

A dark circle rimmed with orange fire blotted out the sun. Akron and OneZero waved us over from a gangway at the end of the docks. It led to the top of what might have been a submarine, but it was hard to tell with the waves washing over the gangway. Kate and I were the first to arrive. I turned to see Alex and Celine lagging behind, waiting for her parents to catch up.

"Come on!" I waved to them, and then hurried down the gangway to Akron's sub. He had the hatch open by the time we arrived. Waves sloshed over the sides and poured into the sub.

"Faster! We're taking on water!" Akron said. OneZero was already inside. Kate climbed down first, then I passed Rachel to her and Akron, and hurried down the ladder myself.

"Is Alex there yet?" Kate called up to me.

I stopped with my head just above the hatch, scanning the docks. Alex and Celine were leaning over the side, and I couldn't see either Harry or

Deborah. I deduced that one or both of them must have fallen in. As I watched, a cresting wave took Alex and Celine over next. My heart leapt into my throat, and I started back up the ladder. Just as I did so, the hatch swung down over my head, forcing me to duck. It slammed shut with a resounding *boom.*

I rounded on Akron, expecting to find him sharing the ladder with me, but he wasn't there. Trying to open the hatch, I found it locked. I banged on it and yelled down to him. "Open the fucking hatch, Akron!"

"Where is he?" Kate screamed.

"He got swept off the docks! We have to go back for him!"

The submarine's engine thrummed to life. Water sloshed around below us, and the submarine rocked violently in the waves.

"Akron!" Kate screamed. I jumped down the ladder and landed with a splash beside her. Rachel stared at us with huge eyes.

Kate and I ran to the front of the submarine, racing past row upon row of seats. We emerged inside a bubble-shaped glass canopy. Akron stood there with OneZero, looking out into the murky depths of the harbor. Flat-screens with readouts and gauges cluttered the walls along with a scattering of analog gauges below them.

"They didn't make it!" I said.

Akron turned to me, his expression grave. OneZero just looked at us, her dark eyes boring holes into my head.

"You have to go back!" Kate said.

Akron shook his head. "If we go back now, we're all dead."

Horror and anger warred inside of me. They'd been right there, just a dozen yards behind us! "We can't leave them!"

Akron gave no reply. Instead, he walked silently over to one of the flat-screens on the wall, and spent a moment tapping options on the display.

"Are you listening?" Kate said, and began pounding on his back with her fists.

OneZero pulled her away, and Akron turned aside so that we could see the display. It showed the mouth of the harbor, dead ahead of us, and a wall of water rising swiftly beyond that, obscuring the horizon.

"That's the view from the periscope," Akron said.

The wave couldn't have been more than a minute away.

"Turn the periscope around," I demanded.

"Show me the docks!"

Akron did so, and I saw that the dock was gone, completely submerged by the rising tide. I also saw a big Screecher disc hovering over the roiling harbor, trailing arms like tentacles. As I watched, the gloomy red hues of the rogue eclipse brightened to gold, and I saw the Screecher aircraft pulling small, dark human shapes out of the water. I counted four in all.

Akron breathed a sigh. "At least they're safe."

"They're prisoners!" I snapped; then I noticed that two of them were sagging, rag-doll limp in the Screecher's grasp. "And we don't even know if they're alive!" Would Screechers even be able to perform CPR? I wondered.

Akron tapped his screen again, and the wave appeared, curling as it reached the harbor. "They stand a better chance than we do," he said. "Find something to hold onto!"

"Can't this thing go any deeper?" I asked. "Rachel!" I spun around to look for her, and found her standing right behind me. The 'something' she found to hold onto was my legs.

"If we go too deep, the wave could slam us into the bottom and crack us open!"

Kate came over and made it a group hug. I spied handholds beside the door leading to the control room where we stood. Just as I reached for one of them, OneZero ran into us from behind and sent us sprawling through the door. She landed on top of us and held us down in the sloshing water on the deck. I heard the door slam shut behind us, and then the wave hit, and my stomach lurched into my throat. The sub tumbled dizzyingly and the water inside the sub pooled over our heads every couple of seconds, water-boarding us. In between the external roar of the crashing wave and the sound of water stuffing my ears like cotton, I heard loud *thunking* noises ringing against the hull. Debris pelted us. The door to the control room *thumped* with a particularly heavy impact. I hoped it wasn't Akron being tossed around in there. Remembering the bubble-shaped glass canopy, I winced, thinking that it wouldn't take much to break it open. Our submarine could end up stranded, bobbing like a cork in the middle of New Orleans.

Another *thunk* sounded against the hull, followed by the sound of water hissing in from somewhere nearby. We wouldn't be bobbing like a cork for much longer.

CHAPTER 64

OneZero let us up. We sat coughing on the deck to get the water out of our lungs. I slapped Rachel on the back in an effort to help. She was sobbing between coughs. So was Kate, but I suspected they were crying for very different reasons. My thoughts went to Alex and the Hartfords, to the sight of their limp bodies being pulled from the harbor, and I fought back tears of my own.

Akron stumbled over from the row of seats behind us. Relief washed over me. At least he hadn't been in the control room.

"Is it over?" I asked between coughs.

Akron shook his head. "The tide is going to keep coming in for at least another hour. He stepped over us, following the hissing sound to its source. A fine spray of mist was creeping in around one of the portholes.

"It should hold," Akron said. "I set the algorithms to keep us near the surface."

I pushed off the floor. Kate and Rachel joined me in standing and flopped down into water-logged seats to one side of the aisle. Kate cradled Rachel in her lap, and stared vacantly out of the porthole beside her.

OneZero stood in the aisle with Akron and I. She said something to Akron in Spanish, and he replied, shaking his head.

"What?" I asked, my eyes flicking between them.

Rather than answer me, Akron walked by us to the control room door. He tried the handle, then body-checked the door, but it didn't budge. "It's flooded," he said.

"So we're stranded."

Akron held up a hand and placed a finger to his lips. "Listen."

I heard the thrumming of the submarine's engines, and felt their vibrations rippling through the deck.

"We're still moving," Akron said. He went to sit in one of the rows of seating.

"You're not going to do anything?" I demanded.

"I don't have to," he replied. "If we're moving, it means everything is still working. It's self-skippering, remember? The sub knows where to go and how to get there with or without someone in the control room."

"And what if it doesn't?"

"If there were any major system failures, the engines would have shut off."

OneZero sat across the aisle from Akron, and I did the same opposite my wife. I reached for her hand and gave it a reassuring squeeze. As the shock wore off, our wet clothes took their toll, and we began to shiver. I moved to Kate and Rachel's side of the sub and the three of us held each other for warmth.

"We're lucky the water is still warm," Akron said. "We're surrounded by it, so we should be okay."

"How long before we reach Haven?" I asked.

"Five or six hours," Akron said.

I blinked in shock. "That long?"

"Submarines are not fast. This one can't make more than thirty knots, and that was before the control room was flooded. Haven is over a hundred and fifty miles away."

"We just left him," Kate said slowly.

I glanced at her, and hugged her shoulders a little harder. "We'll find him."

"No, you won't," Akron said.

My gaze snapped to him. "What?"

"You got your wish. You're on your way to Haven, but for the safety of everyone there, none of you can leave—especially not on some fool crusade to rescue prisoners from the Screechers."

I scowled and jerked my chin at him. "What about you? You left."

"That was during the Exodus. Now that the Screechers have established their border and mostly evacuated the South, there's no chaos for us to get lost in. We can't just blend in with the crowds. You saw what happened back at the harbor. They were all over us. As soon as OneZero took out one group, another one came. You'd be captured in seconds if you went back."

"What does it matter? Alex and the Hartfords have already been captured."

"Yes, but they've never been to Haven. And they can't lead the Screechers to this submarine to show them how to use it to reach the colony. But if we're lucky, the Screechers that picked the others up won't know about Haven and won't even bother to question them. They'll probably just deport them. If you mysteriously appear days or weeks later in the middle of New Orleans, the same thing won't be true. They'll wonder how you got there."

"We're not leaving our son behind," Kate said.

"You can't make us do that."

"Why not?" Akron asked. "You made me leave *my* sons behind. And unlike your son, I don't have the hope of maybe bumping into them ten years from now when we emerge from Haven. My kids will be on Mars, and I'll have no way to reach them."

Neither Kate nor I had anything to say to that. Silence fell but for the sound of water sloshing on the floor and hissing in around the porthole.

OneZero said something in a quiet voice, and Akron replied. They spoke at length for the next half an hour, and I listened with interest, watching Akron's expression become increasingly awed.

"What is it?" I asked as something that OneZero said left Akron speechless.

He turned to us, slowly shaking his head. "I know why they drove us North."

CHAPTER 65

"They're not robots," Akron explained.

I glanced at OneZero's gleaming body and shook my head.

"Well, they are," he amended. "But they weren't always. Their world was also dragged away from its sun by the rogue, but theirs was captured, and they had to adapt. One of the ways they did that was to transfer their consciousness to machines. Now that they've found Earth, they're going to transfer back."

"So what are they?" I asked, looking at OneZero's humanoid body.

"They're made up of several different species, all of them sentient. And this one—" Akron pointed to OneZero and slowly shook his head. "I don't know whether to believe her or not, but she says that she was human."

I gaped at Akron and studied OneZero with new eyes. That would certainly explain why she looked so much like us, but how was that possible?

"And the other ones like her...?"

"Also human."

"They're the same as us?" Rachel asked in a soft voice.

I squinted at OneZero, and she stared back at me. "That's impossible."

"That's what I said," Akron replied. "She explained that her ancestors were abducted from Earth a long time ago."

"Abducted by aliens..."

"About fifteen thousand years ago," Akron added.

"That's... what were we doing fifteen thousand years ago?"

"Rubbing sticks together to make fire."

"And the other Screechers? What about the four-legged ones, and the discs?"

"According to OneZero, each of the different models represent distinct intelligent races."

"Even the bug-sized assemblers?"

"Even them," Akron confirmed.

"And all of them were somehow living in harmony with each other? That's hard to believe."

Akron shrugged. "I don't know how much harmony there was—" He turned to OneZero and asked something in Spanish. She replied at length, and he translated. "She says a social hierarchy and peace was established after many bloody conflicts. The flying discs are in charge, followed by humans, and then the bug-sized assemblers. Last of all are the four-legged ones."

"This is absurd," I said. "If they had the ability to abduct people from Earth, and to invade us now, then they sure as hell had a way to escape their planet. Why would they just go along for the ride until they reached us?"

"Maybe Earth was the closest habitable world besides their own," Akron suggested.

"Then why not take off in their spaceships and come here faster?"

Akron turned to OneZero and asked her something. They spoke for a few minutes.

"Well?" I prompted as soon as their conversation lapsed.

"She says that they *did* leave, but there weren't enough spacecraft to evacuate everyone. They're the ones who got left behind. Rather than go looking for a new home, they turned themselves into machines and built their civilization under the surface of their world. And the ones who came to Earth are just a fraction of their total population— they're the ones who want to return to their organic bodies."

I shook my head. "Still. Wouldn't it have just

been easier to build more spaceships?"

Akron spoke with OneZero again. A moment later, he nodded to me. "They did. There was constant migration to other planets the whole way here. She says they colonized dozens of star systems along the way. Earth was an after thought because they knew that it was already inhabited, and they thought that by now we would be more technologically advanced than them."

"Why would they think that if they abducted us on spaceships when we were still rubbing sticks together to make fire?"

"That's a good question," Akron replied. He translated it for OneZero, and she explained.

I waited for him to translate for me.

"Apparently *they* didn't abduct us. A species she calls *los Primordiales*—the Primordials—did that, but then they disappeared. Apparently, all of the other races they abducted were just as primitive as we were."

"And they expected us to advance at the same rate as they did," I said.

"Faster," Akron said. "They wasted a lot of time with in-fighting."

I snorted. "So did we... Then the reason they didn't come sooner is because they were scared of invading us?"

Akron nodded. "The signals they sent were a test to see how we would react. When we didn't send any spaceships to investigate, they realized that we must be less advanced, not more."

The implications of all that sunk in belatedly, and I whistled softly. "If that's all true, this is incredible. It means we're not just making *first* contact. We're making first, second, third..."

"Who cares?" Kate said, throwing up her hands. "Alex is out there, and all you can talk about is the kind of aliens that took him?"

I looked at Kate. "You don't get it."

"No! I don't!"

"If there are humans among them, then they're not all aliens, and like OneZero, some of them might be sympathetic. What's more, humans are pretty high in their pecking order, which means that Alex and the Hartfords probably won't be tortured or executed."

"Probably?" Kate echoed.

I winced, realizing how bad that sounded. Turning to Akron, I added, "Ask her what she thinks the others will do with them."

He did, and then translated. "She thinks they'll be taken back to the border. The Screechers don't want to hurt us. That's why they evacuated everyone from the South rather than killing them."

"Then they'll freeze to death!" Kate said.

"Not if someone helps them," I said.

She gave me a dubious look, as if to say that humans helping humans in the middle of this crisis was more than we could hope for.

"If they don't want to hurt us, why did they want to know about Haven?" I asked.

Akron and OneZero spoke once more, and the billionaire explained: "That's how she got us across the border—by telling them about Haven. She described it as a hidden city. The Screechers wanted to know where it was because they're worried about pockets of resistance in their territory."

When I heard Akron call them *Screechers* another thought struck me. "Why haven't they tried talking to us in whatever language their ancestors used on Earth?"

After asking OneZero, Akron's gaze swept back to me, and he shook his head. "She says too much time has passed. The Screechers developed a more efficient, universal language after they all turned themselves into machines. That screeching you hear is an acoustic form of binary. That's why it sounds so high-pitched. The frequency has to be high in order to pack in more data."

I remembered the sounds made by old dial-up

modems and supposed that made some sense. Silence fell inside the submarine as we sat processing all of the information.

"I'm cold, Mommy."

I glanced at Rachel as Kate rubbed her arms in an attempt to warm her up. For my part, I was actually pretty warm now that my body heat had been transferred to my wet clothes. Akron was right, the water outside was keeping the inside of the sub warm. Rachel was probably cold because she was hungry. We all were. There'd likely be plenty of food for us in Haven once we arrived. That thought made my mouth water, and then I remembered Alex and my chest began to ache. Guilt, grief, and despair churned around inside of me. Where would the Screechers leave Alex and the Hartfords? Would their clothes still be wet by the time they were kicked out into the snow? I imagined Alex collapsed somewhere on the side of the highway, his skin as pale and cold as the snow around him.

A shiver tore through me, and I glared at the back of Akron's head. He couldn't force us to stay in Haven. He'd let down his guard eventually, and then I'd find a way to sneak out and rescue my son.

CHAPTER 66

By the time we finally arrived at Haven, the hazy blue water had turned black, and the water in the bottom of the sub was up over our ankles. The only way we knew we had arrived was by the sensation of the sub slowing down, and by the subsequent *clunk* of something metallic touching the top hatch.

"Let's go," Akron said.

Everyone got up and followed him back to the ladder we'd climbed down hours earlier. He went up the ladder first, and opened the hatch with a manual lever and crank wheel. Whatever electronic locking system the hatch might have had was non-functional now from all the water that had poured in when we'd boarded the submarine.

Akron opened the hatch and we climbed up into an airlock. He shut the hatch behind us. Once it was sealed, he opened a panel inside the airlock to reveal what looked like an intercom. He touched a button and spoke into it, confirming my suspicions.

"This is Akron Massey in airlock two fourteen requesting ingress."

He released the button and waited for a reply with his ear to the speaker grille. "Massey?" an astounded voice replied. "Is that really you?"

"It is. Open the hatch, would you?"

"You have a Screecher with you. *Please* tell me you didn't lead them all here."

"I didn't," Akron replied. "Don't worry, she's on our side."

"She?"

"Yes, she. I'll explain everything once we're in."

"Okay..." the voice replied.

I heard locking bolts *thunking* and then the hatch swung wide, revealing four men with harpoon guns already waiting for us on the other side. Their eyes found OneZero, and all four of them shifted their aim to her.

"Don't shoot!" Akron said. "She's friendly."

* * *

Our armed escort led us down a short corridor and around a curving walkway lined with broad windows to a large, circular chamber with a domed glass ceiling.

The floor was an illuminated aquarium just a

few feet deep, with colorful coral, rippled sand and darting fish. The center of the room sported a bar, and I assumed, a kitchen. Concentric circles of coral-crusted booths and tables ran around that, each of them beneath their own glowing jellyfish light fixtures, attached by invisible strings to the metal frame supporting the glass dome above our heads.

I marveled at all of that. Akron had obviously spared no expense in building Haven. He led us over to one of the booths, and we caught horrified stares from late-night diners as we approached. I knew they were looking at OneZero. I smiled and nodded to them, but none of them acknowledged my greeting.

Once we were all seated—except for OneZero, who didn't fit at the table—Akron told one of the four men with harpoon guns to go find Richard Greenhouse and someone named Wesley Parker. He told a second man to go get us some towels and dry clothes.

The other two remained standing beside our table, their eyes and weapons never leaving OneZero.

"So?" Akron said, his gaze finding us across the table. "What would you like to eat?"

"Pizza!" Rachel said, before any of us could

reply.

Akron laughed and smiled. "One pizza coming right up."

I looked around for a waitress, but there weren't any in sight. Akron spoke to the table. "Computer, we're ready to order."

"Of course. What would you like?" a pleasant female voice asked from a familiar black cylinder in the center of the table. I remembered the ones like that in Akron's Bel Air mansion, and I realized that this was the same technology, or some subsequent evolution of it.

"Two large pizzas," Akron said. "One with..." he trailed off and he looked to Rachel with eyebrows raised.

"Pepperoni!"

He nodded and his eyes flicked to me. "And?"

"Whatever you like," I added.

"One with pepperoni and one with Italian sausage."

"Yes, sir. And to drink?"

"Four hot cocoas and lots of water, please."

"Coming right up. To whom should I charge the account?"

"Akron Massey."

"Very well. Your order will be ready in thirty minutes. Please retrieve it from the bar when your name is called."

I marveled at the degree of automation Akron had achieved here. "You could have changed the world with technology like that," I said.

Akron snorted. "Yeah, it's a pity the Screechers beat me to it."

The conversation lapsed into an uneasy silence, and we sat staring out into the black depths beyond the dome. It felt wrong to be sitting here without Alex, waiting for food, as if the world hadn't just ended and our son was actually someplace safe and warm like us. I felt like I should be trying to swim to shore or beating up the guards on my way to hijack the nearest submarine.

Instead, I just sat there, paralyzed with exhaustion and aching with hunger. It wasn't right. It felt like I was giving up. How could I relax and enjoy this, knowing that my son was out there somewhere, hungry and cold?

"You made it!" a familiar voice said.

"Uncle Richard!" Rachel said, and bounced out of our laps. Kate and I watched as she collided with him and hugged his legs. He leaned down to kiss the top of her head, his eyes never leaving OneZero.

"What's that thing doing here?" he asked quietly.

"That's OneZero," I said.

Richard frowned, and Akron waved him over. "Sit down and I'll explain."

He took a seat beside Akron. Rachel crawled back into our side of the booth, laying her head in my lap and making a pillow out of her arms.

"Where's Alex?" Richard asked.

"They took him," Kate replied in a cracking voice.

Richard's expression became troubled. "I see." He turned to Akron next. "And your family?"

"On their way to Mars."

Someone else came striding across the illuminated floor, flanked by half a dozen harpoon-gun-carrying guards.

Akron looked up and waited for the man to arrive.

"This *thing* can't be here," the man declared, jabbing a finger at OneZero. I took him in at a glance—tall, bald, with glasses and a face that could have been chiseled out of stone. He had an air of authority about him, which Akron confirmed with his next breath.

"Wesley Parker, this is the Willis family," he said by way of introduction. "Kate here is Richard's sister." His gaze turned back to Kate and me, and he added, "Wesley is the elected mayor of

Haven. He took over after I left."

I nodded to Wesley. "OneZero is on our side. We would never have made it this far if it weren't for her."

"OneZero?" Wesley asked, his brow furrowing and his glasses lifting. "You mean the robot?"

I nodded, and he scowled. "Will it come willingly to the brig, or do we need to start shooting?"

That sounded like an empty threat to me. Shooting in an underwater chamber surrounded by glass? They wouldn't dare.

Akron said something to OneZero in Spanish. She replied, and then held out her hands to the men, as if waiting to be hand-cuffed. I frowned at that.

Wesley looked on incredulously. "It speaks Spanish?"

"It's a long story," Akron replied. "She'll go willingly."

"Good. Deputy Cole—" Wesley gestured to one of the men flanking him. "Cuff it."

The man moved haltingly toward the robot, producing a set of handcuffs from his belt, which he then clasped awkwardly around OneZero's wrists.

I smirked at that, remembering how one of the

humanoid models had rolled a car off a bridge. Those handcuffs couldn't restrain her.

"It's okay," I said to her. "We'll sort this out."

OneZero's eyes bored into mine for a moment, but her head dipped in a shallow nod.

The mayor nodded to us with a tight smile. "Welcome to Haven. Enjoy your meal." To Akron, he said, "We'll talk in the morning."

"Of course," Akron replied.

"Where are you taking her?" Rachel asked, lifting her head suddenly from my lap.

"Shhh," Kate replied. "Go back to sleep, honey. They're just going to show her to her room."

"Oh. Okay. Can we go see her later?"

"In the morning."

Rachel nodded and laid her head back down in my lap. I watched OneZero go. She glanced over her shoulder, and our eyes met. I couldn't help feeling like she was accusing me, as if to say, *this is the thanks I get?* I smiled reassuringly at her, and she turned around.

"Well?" Richard prompted. "Is someone going to explain what the hell happened out there?"

Akron spent the next half an hour doing exactly that; then Massey's name was called from the black cylinder on the table, and he and Richard went to pick up our food. Silence reigned as we ate and drank our hot cocoa. Someone had obviously forgotten about our dry clothes, but it didn't matter anymore. After six hours in that leaky submarine and another hour here, we were mostly dry already anyway.

When there were only a few slices of pizza left, Rachel went back to sleep in my lap. Kate leaned her head on my shoulder, and I laid mine back against the booth, listening as Akron and Richard discussed the implications of alien robots that had once been humans, and might be again soon. They seemed to think that was a good thing, like maybe the human-aliens would be nicer to us once they got settled on Earth. They had obviously forgotten how well us humans had treated each other throughout history. This was like what happened when European settlers came to North America and met the Native Americans, except that this time we were the natives.

When they finally finished talking, Richard looked to us, his eyes bright with sympathy. "I'm really sorry about Alex. I know this is hard to accept, Kate, but you're going to have to forget about him."

Kate's eyes blazed, but she said nothing.

Richard looked to Akron for support, and the billionaire shook his head. "I already explained that they can't leave."

"You can't hold us prisoner," Kate replied.

"Actually, that's exactly what I *should* do," Akron replied. "Just be thankful I didn't insist that you join OneZero in the brig."

"What if it was *your* son?" Kate demanded.

Akron slammed his palms on the table and our plates rattled. Rachel jumped and woke up with a whimper. "It *is* my son! Both of my sons! I'm never going to see them again, and instead of whining about it, or trying to punish the people responsible, I'm treating them to a hot dinner and offering them sanctuary in my refuge. Just you think about that." Akron's face was flushed. He looked to Richard. "If you'll excuse me, I'm going to go change and get some sleep. When they're finished, please show them to my quarters."

"Of course..." Richard replied, and slid out of the booth with a half-finished slice of pizza draped over one hand.

"Your quarters?" I echoed, watching Akron as he slid out next.

"Where else did you think you were going to sleep? We're already at maximum capacity. Your family was supposed to take my family's place, remember? Four for four." Akron smirked and shook his head. "You can thank me later."

With that, he stormed off, and I watched him go, feeling guilty and angry at the same time. Kate's hand clutched my leg, her eyes wild with fear. "We can't leave him out there," she whispered to me.

I caught Richard watching us as he slid back into the booth, so I leaned over and kissed Kate on the cheek. "We won't," I whispered back. As I withdrew, I added for Richard's benefit, "We don't have a choice. He'll be fine. He has the Hartfords to look after him."

Richard's eyes found mine, and he nodded stiffly to me as we each grabbed another slice of pizza. "He's a tough kid. He'll be okay," Richard added.

"Yes, he will," I agreed. *Because I'm going to find him and bring him here.* I switched topics to avoid raising his suspicions. "Rick, there's one thing I forgot to ask."

"What's that?"

"Did you ever manage to decode anything from the Screechers' signals?"

A slow smile spread across Richard's lips, and he nodded. "We decoded them, all right. They were in an obfuscated form of binary."

"And? What did they say?"

"They didn't say anything. It was pixel data for

a black and white image."

An image. That made sense. "What was it?"

"It was a scale diagram of all the planets in our solar system, listed in order of their distance from the sun. They also added the rogue star, and another planet—a gas giant with three moons. I managed to gain remote access to the James Webb Space Telescope and use it to find them. We believe the Screechers came from one or more of those moons. They still have atmospheres, and two of them are as big as Earth."

I nodded along with that. It corroborated what OneZero had told Akron while we were traveling here in his submarine.

"But that's not all," Richard said, shaking his head.

I arched an eyebrow at him, and waited for him to go on.

"When we put that planet and its moons into our simulations, we discovered that our Sun is going to capture them."

"What does that mean?" Kate asked.

"It means we're going to be sharing our solar system with an advanced alien race—or several of them, if what that robot told you is true. And it means that the invasion we experienced was just the first wave. There's probably billions more

Screechers out there just waiting to come to Earth."

GET THE SEQUEL FOR FREE

THE STORY CONTINUES IN

Rogue Star: New Worlds
(Coming October 10th, 2018)

Pre-Order the e-book for $2.99
(reg. $3.99)
http://smarturl.it/roguestar2

OR get a FREE e-book if you post an honest review of this book on Amazon and send it to me at http://files.jaspertscott.com/roguestarnw.htm

Thank you in advance for your feedback!

I read every review and use your comments to improve my work.

THE SCIENCE AND A CHANCE TO WIN $20

1. How do You Hide a Star?

When I began writing this book, I knew I wanted it to be as realistic as possible. I imagined a rogue star surprising us with a close flyby of Earth, and I wondered what might happen as a result. For reference sake, a "rogue star" is a star which has escaped the gravitational pull of its galaxy and is headed for intergalactic space. Rogue stars do not orbit the galactic center.

The first thing I had to do was figure out how a rogue star that's already relatively close by (ETA 10.921 years) could have hidden under our noses for so long. As it turns out, there's a few problems with that. The first problem is that we've scanned the entire sky with all kinds of different telescopes and instruments. We've found all of the nearest stars, and we know that the very closest one is Proxima Centauri at 4.25 light years away. Even if Proxima were a rogue, there's no way that it could reach us in any kind of time-frame that would take us by surprise or pose an imminent threat. We'd see it coming for thousands of years. As for the discovery of a new, never before seen star, it's just not possible for one to be hiding from us within any useful proximity of Earth.

While I was researching this book, someone suggested that it could be hiding behind our sun. But the problem with that, is that the Sun is moving, and Earth moves around the Sun, so nothing can hide behind it for long. With that in mind, I went another route. The only real way that a star could hide from us is if it is extremely dim. The dimmest class of stars in existence are Y brown dwarfs. The coldest brown dwarf that we've discovered so far is *WISE 1828+2650*, with a surface temperature of 25 degrees Celsius, or 80 degrees Fahrenheit.[1]

Thanks to NASA's WISE space telescope, we've found six Y brown dwarfs within 40 light years of Earth.[1] Again, to have missed one that's somehow already made it to within less than a light year of us is inconceivable.

The closest known Y brown dwarf is WISE 1541-2250 at 9 light-years away. That's still way too far to make sense for the events in this book.

At this point you might think I had to give up

on coming up with a realistic scenario. But then I thought, what about a dead star, a so-called *black dwarf*? Stars that have run out of fuel to drive the fusion in their cores will eventually grow dark and cold, and they'd be extremely hard to spot. When I looked into this, however, I learned that the universe hasn't been around long enough to generate any black dwarfs.[2] Failed stars, however, are all over the place. What is a failed star? A brown dwarf that never ignited, or one that did, but quickly ran out fuel. *Bingo.*

"Most brown dwarfs race through their deuterium in about 100 million years - a flash, in cosmic time. (By comparison, our sun will be stable for about 8 billion years.) Once the star has burned all the deuterium it can reach, it's burning days are over. The heat it built up through burning deuterium will slowly fade away, and the dwarf will truly be a 'failed star.'"[3]

I decided that a failed, rogue star should be colder than Neptune if it were to escape detection. Such a cold body lurking beyond the outer planets would be incredibly difficult to detect with current instruments. We are planning to launch a new telescope, however, which will be uniquely well-suited to discovering these cold stars via its infrared scanning capabilities. This telescope is the James Webb Space Telescope, whose launch has coincidentally been delayed until 2020.[4] So, let's suppose that with the launch of this new telescope we finally discover the incoming Rogue.

2. ETA 10.921 Years

Okay, so now that I could explain how we missed seeing the inbound rogue star, I had to come up with some real numbers to explain where it is, how fast it's moving, and how long it'll take to reach us. These details ultimately determined the time frame of my story.

So I arbitrarily set the ETA for this inbound star to be about 10 years 11 months and 2 days (10.921 years). After that, I did some research into the velocity of known Rogue stars. The fastest one we've ever detected is moving at an eye-popping 1200 km/s.[5] That sounded too fast to me. What about a more modest speed of 904 km/s? With the speed set, and the ETA of 10.921 years, I calculated the distance from Earth at the time of discovery: 904 km/s * 344,404,656 s (number of seconds in 10.921 years) = 311,341,809,024 km—three hundred and eleven billion kilometers away. That sounded like a long way off. To find out just how far, I needed to put that in some perspective. For example, where is the edge of our solar system?

The edge of our solar system is not strictly defined, but one definition is the extent of the Sun's solar wind and magnetic field.[6] This boundary is called the heliosphere. At its leading (closest) edge, the heliosphere is 90 AU (astronomical units) away.[7] Note: one AU is approximately 150 million kilometers.

Converting the distance of my rogue star to astronomical units using google's search engine gives me 2081 AU. That means the rogue star is located well beyond our solar system.

On a related, but somewhat tangential topic, the Sun itself is moving around the galactic core at a whopping 240 kilometers per second.[8] With that in mind, please note that for the purposes of this book, the pre-determined 904 km/s of the rogue star is a relative velocity (relative to that of the Sun), and not the Rogue's actual outbound velocity from the Milky Way.

3. Frozen Earth

So, in 10.921 years the world will end, Nibiru style. What might happen if this rogue star makes a near pass with Earth on its way through our solar system? I realized I had no way to mathematically calculate a realistic scenario for that. If I was going to base subsequent events on anything close to actual science, I was going to need some help.

That was when I discovered Universe Sandbox 2. Using this program I was able to simulate exactly what would happen to Earth's orbit (and it's climate!) based on actual data and physics.

I discovered that after a near miss with an extremely dim rogue star of 70 Jovian masses that's moving at 904 km/s, the Earth's orbit will shift significantly. Depending on where the Rogue passes us, that could make Earth either much warmer or much colder. I wanted to go with colder because Frank Herbert already wrote Dune, so I adjusted my simulation until I saw Earth get dragged into a more distant orbit. The Earth's orbit becomes more eccentric / elliptical as a result of the rogue's passing, and the effect is a gradual slide into sub-zero temperatures that plunges Earth into an ice age. Now you know why this book is called Rogue Star: *Frozen Earth.*

So when you read about people talking about how cold it's going to get, and how fast the Earth is going to turn into a snowball, remember that I based those details on an actual simulation. I'm sure that simulation is still far from accurate, but at least I didn't pull those numbers out of my hat!

Note: I did make one concession where I sacrificed realism for the sake of story elements and drama. The eclipse depicted in the book never should have happened. See if you can figure out why, and send me your answers here: http://files.jaspertscott.com/roguestarcontest.htm The first person to figure it out will get a $20 gift certificate from me for Amazon.com. Subsequent winners will get the consolation prize of a free e-book.

4. Tidal Waves

The Moon's gravitational pull causes the tides on Earth. So if a small, failed star passed us, what kind of tidal forces could we expect? The answer depends largely on three factors: how close does the rogue get, how massive is it, and how long does it spend tugging on our oceans as it flies toward and away from us.

I already had to input some of that data for my Universe Sandbox simulation. The rogue is 70.0 times the mass of Jupiter, and at its closest approach, it passes Earth at 0.104 AU—that's 40.5 times the distance from Earth to the Moon at perigee (the closest point in the Moon's orbit).

Given that info, I used an online calculator for the Moon's gravitational force to calculate an answer for the passing rogue.[9] For reference sake, the Moon's gravitational force is $7.79*10^{18}$ Newtons at perigee. Inputting the mass of the Rogue ($1.3286*10^{29}$ kg), and it's nearest distance from Earth gives a gravitational force of $2.1*10^{20}$ Newtons for the passing rogue.

That's 26.9 times stronger than the Moon's tidal force!

Next, I looked for the average high tide from the Moon, but I couldn't find this data. What I did find was tidal data for specific locations. E.g. New York, New York has a high tide of about 5 feet.[10] If we assume a linear relationship between gravitational force and tidal swell, then 5 feet x 26.9 = 134.5 feet. That's a massive tidal wave. Although, technically, the tide would rise to that level in a series of increasingly-larger waves over a period of several hours as the rogue approaches. How many hours?

Considering that the rogue's speed is 904 km/s we can calculate how far it would travel in an hour: 904 km * 60 (seconds per minute) * 60 (minutes per hour) = 3,254,400 km / hour. The closest approach is $1.56*10^{7}$ km = 15,600,000 km. Divide that by the speed of the rogue per hour and you'll find that it will take 4.79 hours to travel from double the closest approach distance to the actual closest approach where the tide will surge by 134.5 feet.

According to the calculator I used before, at 3.12*10^7 km (double the closest approach) the gravitational force would be: 2.63*10^19 Newtons (N). That is only 3.37 times the force of the Moon's gravity at perigee. Again, assuming a linear relationship, that means a tidal swell of 5 * 3.37 = 16.85 feet. Not small, but not massive either.

At 6 hours out from closest approach, the rogue is 3,254,400 km/hour * 6 hours = 19,526,400 km + 15,600,000 km (closest approach distance) = 35,126,400 km away. Putting that distance into the calculator results in a gravitational force of 1.84*10^19 Newtons. That's only 2.36 times the Moon's gravitational force, which results in a high tide of 5 * 2.36 = 11.8 feet.

The Moon's own tides may very well add or subtract from that along the way, but it's safe to say that tides will begin surging noticeably when the rogue is still six to seven hours away. There will also be a delay in the arrival of those tides, which corresponds to the speed of the Earth's rotation (this is what determines the arrival of high and low tides from the Moon as well).

For some perspective on the eventual 134.5-foot tidal surge, Hurricane Katrina produced one of the highest storm surges ever recorded of between 25 and 28 feet.[11] At almost five times that height, the Rogue's passing would cause unimaginable flooding of coastal regions all around the world.

5. Conclusion

Between rising tides and falling temperatures, there's a lot to worry about in Rogue Star: Frozen Earth. The scary part is, this is all something that could actually happen. Of course, the odds of it happening are extremely small, so you can relax—unless you believe the prophecies about Nibiru, that is.

SOURCES

1. Choi, Charles Q. "How Cold Is a Y Dwarf Star? Even You Are Warmer." Space.com. Accessed June 04, 2018. https://www.space.com/12714-coldest-failed-stars-brown-dwarfs-wise.html.

2. "Black Dwarf." Wikipedia. July 14, 2018. Accessed July 20, 2018. https://en.wikipedia.org/wiki/Black_dwarf.

3. "How Hot Are Brown Dwarf Stars When They Are Burning Deuterium?" Astroquizzical. Accessed July 20, 2018. https://astroquizzical.com/astroquizzical/how-hot-are-brown-dwarf-stars-when-they-are.

4. Lewin, Sarah. "NASA Delays Launch of James Webb Space Telescope Until 2020." Space.com. March 27, 2018. Accessed June 04, 2018. https://www.space.com/40102-james-webb-space-telescope-launch-delay-2020.html.

5. Cofield, Calla. "Fastest Star in the Galaxy Has a

Strange Origin." Space.com. May 19, 2015. Accessed June 04, 2018. https://www.space.com/28737-fastest-star-galaxy-strange-origin.html.

6. "How Big Is the Solar System?" Universe Today. March 16, 2017. Accessed June 04, 2018. https://www.universetoday.com/104486/how-big-is-our-solar-system/.

7. Dunbar, Brian. "Did You Know..." NASA. June 07, 2013. Accessed June 04, 2018. https://www.nasa.gov/mission_pages/ibex/IBEXDidYouKnow.html.

8. "Distance & Speed Of Sun's Orbit Around Galactic Centre Measured." Universe Today. February 20, 2017. Accessed June 04, 2018. https://www.universetoday.com/133414/distance-speed-suns-orbit-around-galactic-centre-measured/.

9. "Tidal Force Calculator." High Accuracy Calculation for Life or Science. Accessed June 04, 2018.
https://keisan.casio.com/exec/system/1360312100.

10. "Tide Times for New York." Tide times and Tide Charts. Accessed June 04, 2018. https://www.tide-forecast.com/locations/New-York-New-York/tides/latest.

11. "Storm Surge Overview." Glossary of NHC Terms. Accessed June 04, 2018. https://www.nhc.noaa.gov/surge/.

KEEP IN TOUCH

SUBSCRIBE to my Mailing List
and get two FREE Books!
http://files.jaspertscott.com/mailinglist.html

Follow me on Twitter:
@JasperTscott

Look me up on Facebook:
Jasper T. Scott

Check out my website:
www.JasperTscott.com

Or send me an e-mail:
JasperTscott@gmail.com

OTHER BOOKS BY JASPER SCOTT

Suggested reading order

Dark Space 2: The Invisible War

Dark Space 3: Origin
Dark Space 4: Revenge
Dark Space 5: Avilon
Dark Space 6: Armageddon

Dark Space Universe Series (Standalone Follow-up Trilogy to Dark Space)

Dark Space Universe (Book 1)
Dark Space Universe: The Enemy Within (Book 2)
Dark Space Universe: The Last Stand (Book 3)

Early Work
Escape
Mrythdom

ABOUT THE AUTHOR

Jasper Scott is a USA TODAY bestselling science fiction author, known for writing intricate plots with unexpected twists.

His books have been translated into Japanese and German and adapted for audio, with collectively over 500,000 copies purchased.

Jasper was born and raised in Canada by South African parents, with a British cultural heritage on his mother's side and German on his father's, to which he has now added Latin culture with his wonderful wife.

After spending years living as a starving artist, he finally quit his various jobs to become a full-time writer. In his spare time he enjoys reading, traveling, going to the gym, and spending time with his family.

Made in the USA
Lexington, KY
12 August 2018